THE PILGRIM SONG

★ GILBERT MORRIS

BOOKS BY GILBERT MORRIS

Through a Glass Darkly

THE HOUSE OF WINSLOW SERIES

1. *The Honorable Imposter*
2. *The Captive Bride*
3. *The Indentured Heart*
4. *The Gentle Rebel*
5. *The Saintly Buccaneer*
6. *The Holy Warrior*
7. *The Reluctant Bridegroom*
8. *The Last Confederate*
9. *The Dixie Widow*
10. *The Wounded Yankee*
11. *The Union Belle*
12. *The Final Adversary*
13. *The Crossed Sabres*
14. *The Valiant Gunman*
15. *The Gallant Outlaw*
16. *The Jeweled Spur*
17. *The Yukon Queen*
18. *The Rough Rider*
19. *The Iron Lady*
20. *The Silver Star*
21. *The Shadow Portrait*
22. *The White Hunter*
23. *The Flying Cavalier*
24. *The Glorious Prodigal*
25. *The Amazon Quest*
26. *The Golden Angel*
27. *The Heavenly Fugitive*
28. *The Fiery Ring*
29. *The Pilgrim Song*

THE LIBERTY BELL

1. *Sound the Trumpet*
2. *Song in a Strange Land*
3. *Tread Upon the Lion*
4. *Arrow of the Almighty*
5. *Wind From the Wilderness*
6. *The Right Hand of God*
7. *Command the Sun*

CHENEY DUVALL, M.D.[1]

1. *The Stars for a Light*
2. *Shadow of the Mountains*
3. *A City Not Forsaken*
4. *Toward the Sunrising*
5. *Secret Place of Thunder*
6. *In the Twilight, in the Evening*
7. *Island of the Innocent*
8. *Driven With the Wind*

CHENEY AND SHILOH: THE INHERITANCE[1]

1. *Where Two Seas Met*

THE SPIRIT OF APPALACHIA[2]

1. *Over the Misty Mountains*
2. *Beyond the Quiet Hills*
3. *Among the King's Soldiers*
4. *Beneath the Mockingbird's Wings*
5. *Around the River's Bend*

LIONS OF JUDAH

1. *Heart of a Lion*

[1]with Lynn Morris   [2]with Aaron McCarver

THE
PILGRIM SONG
★ GILBERT MORRIS

BETHANYHOUSE
PUBLISHERS
MINNEAPOLIS, MINNESOTA

The Pilgrim Song
Copyright © 2003
Gilbert Morris

Cover illustration by Bill Graf
Cover production by Becky Noyes

Published by Bethany House Publishers
11400 Hampshire Avenue South
Bloomington, Minnesota 55438
www.bethanyhouse.com

Bethany House Publishers is a Division of
Baker Book House Company, Grand Rapids, Michigan.

Printed in the United States of America by
Bethany Press International, Bloomington, Minnesota 55438

Library of Congress Cataloging-in-Publication Data

Morris, Gilbert.
    The pilgrim song / by Gilbert Morris.
        p.   cm. — (The House of Winslow ; bk. 29)
    ISBN 0-7642-2638-X
    1. Winslow family (Fictitious characters)—Fiction. 2. Parent and adult child—Fiction. 3. Depressions—Fiction. 4. Widowers—Fiction. I. Title. II. Series: Morris, Gilbert. House of Winslow ; bk. 29.
PS3563.O8742 P55   2003
813'.54—dc21   2002152601

TO GINGER CONLON

You will alway be a miracle to me, my dear Ginger.
Words could never express how proud I am to have such
a woman in my family.

GILBERT MORRIS spent ten years as a pastor before becoming Professor of English at Ouachita Baptist University in Arkansas and earning a Ph.D. at the University of Arkansas. During the summers of 1984 and 1985, he did postgraduate work at the University of London. A prolific writer, he has had over 25 scholarly articles and 200 poems published in various periodicals, and over the past years he has had more than 175 novels published. His family includes three grown children, and he and his wife live in Gulf Shores, Alabama.

CONTENTS

PART FOUR
October 1930 – January 1931

THE HOUSE OF WINSLOW

★ ★ ★ ★

THE HOUSE OF WINSLOW

★ ★ ★ ★

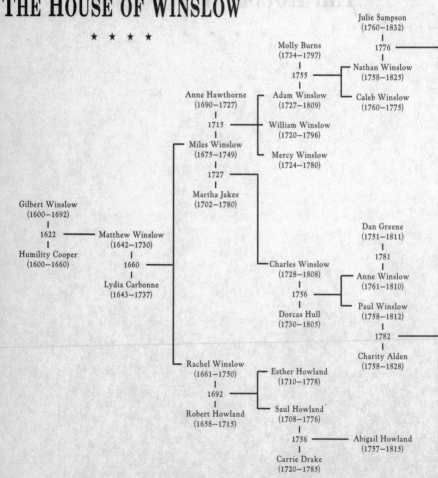

Julie Sampson
(1760–1832)
|
1776

Molly Burns
(1734–1797)
|
1755
|
Nathan Winslow
(1758–1825)

Anne Hawthorne
(1690–1727)
|
1715
|
Miles Winslow
(1675–1749)

Adam Winslow
(1727–1809)

Caleb Winslow
(1760–1775)

William Winslow
(1720–1796)

Mercy Winslow
(1724–1780)

1727
|
Martha Jakes
(1702–1780)

Gilbert Winslow
(1600–1692)
|
1622
|
Humility Cooper
(1600–1660)

Matthew Winslow
(1642–1730)
|
1660
|
Lydia Carbonne
(1643–1737)

Dan Greene
(1751–1811)
|
1781
|
Anne Winslow
(1761–1810)

Charles Winslow
(1728–1808)
|
1756
|
Dorcas Hull
(1730–1805)

Paul Winslow
(1758–1812)
|
1782
|
Charity Alden
(1758–1828)

Rachel Winslow
(1661–1750)
|
1692
|
Robert Howland
(1658–1715)

Esther Howland
(1710–1778)

Saul Howland
(1708–1776)

1756
|
Carrie Drake
(1720–1785)

Abigail Howland
(1757–1815)

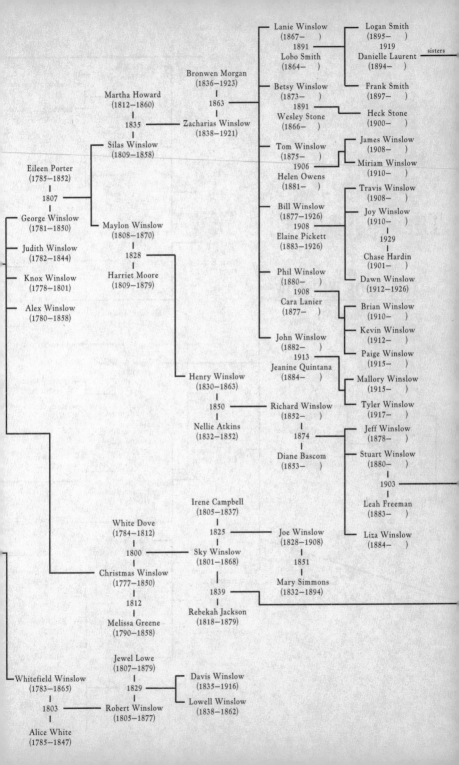

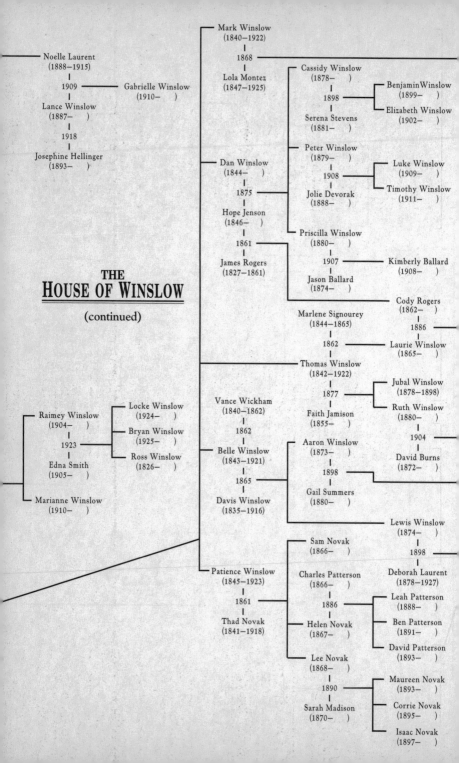

THE
HOUSE OF WINSLOW

(continued)

Noelle Laurent
(1888–1915)

1909 — Gabrielle Winslow
(1910–   )

Lance Winslow
(1887–   )

1918

Josephine Hellinger
(1893–   )

Mark Winslow
(1840–1922)

1868

Lola Montez
(1847–1925)

Dan Winslow
(1844–   )

1875

Hope Jenson
(1846–   )

1861

James Rogers
(1827–1861)

Cassidy Winslow
(1878–   )

1898

Serena Stevens
(1881–   )

Benjamin Winslow
(1899–   )

Elizabeth Winslow
(1902–   )

Peter Winslow
(1879–   )

1908

Jolie Devorak
(1888–   )

Luke Winslow
(1909–   )

Timothy Winslow
(1911–   )

Priscilla Winslow
(1880–   )

1907 — Kimberly Ballard
(1908–   )

Jason Ballard
(1874–   )

Cody Rogers
(1862–   )

Marlene Signourey
(1844–1865)

1886

1862 — Laurie Winslow
(1865–   )

Thomas Winslow
(1842–1922)

1877

Faith Jamison
(1855–   )

Jubal Winslow
(1878–1898)

Ruth Winslow
(1880–   )

1904

David Burns
(1872–   )

Raimey Winslow
(1904–   )

1923

Edna Smith
(1905–   )

Marianne Winslow
(1910–   )

Locke Winslow
(1924–   )

Bryan Winslow
(1925–   )

Ross Winslow
(1826–   )

Vance Wickham
(1840–1862)

1862

Belle Winslow
(1843–1921)

1865

Davis Winslow
(1835–1916)

Aaron Winslow
(1873–   )

1898

Gail Summers
(1880–   )

Lewis Winslow
(1874–   )

1898

Deborah Laurent
(1878–1927)

Patience Winslow
(1845–1923)

1861

Thad Novak
(1841–1918)

Sam Novak
(1866–   )

Charles Patterson
(1866–   )

1886

Helen Novak
(1867–   )

Lee Novak
(1868–   )

1890

Sarah Madison
(1870–   )

Leah Patterson
(1888–   )

Ben Patterson
(1891–   )

David Patterson
(1893–   )

Maureen Novak
(1893–   )

Corrie Novak
(1895–   )

Isaac Novak
(1897–   )

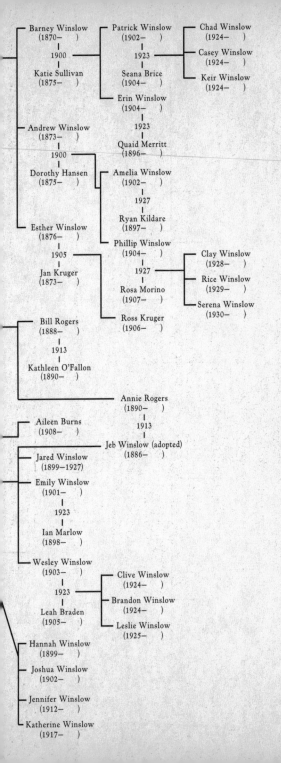

PART ONE

New York City

September–November 1929

★ ★ ★

CHAPTER ONE

A Birthday to Remember

★ ★ ★ ★

Kat Winslow sailed through the back door so fast it slammed with a bang, but she did not pause for an instant. She threaded her way through the servants who crowded the kitchen, and Susan Mason—never called anything but Cook—turned from the stove, a harried look on her face. "Why aren't you dressed, Katherine? You look awful!"

The twelve-year-old simply grabbed a cookie from the counter, laughed, and sped out of the kitchen. The sound of the musicians warming up for the dance caught her attention for a moment, but then she ignored it. Turning up an ornate curving staircase, she raced to the top and then to the door at the far end of the long hallway. She opened the door and stepped inside but was halted when a cry met her.

"Kat, shut that door! I'm not dressed!"

"What kind of underwear is that?" Kat asked, ignoring her sister's protests. She advanced and walked around her sister, her head cocked to one side.

Jenny Winslow was wearing a peach-colored satin bra, embroidered at the edges with white flowers, and a girdle attached to fine silk stockings. Jenny was a striking young woman of seventeen with red hair and unusually dark green eyes. Her face was heart shaped, and her lips were broad and expressive. Right now they were expressing distaste. "Don't you ever bother to knock?"

"Not for family I don't."

"What are you wearing those overalls for? It's almost time for my party to begin. And you're filthy! What have you been doing?"

"I've been in the garden digging up worms. I'm going fishing in the morning." Kat went over and plumped herself down in a chair and examined her older sister curiously.

Kat had gray-green eyes and tawny hair, and she cared nothing for what she called "girlie" stuff, including clothes and makeup and parties. A summer's tan coated her skin, and a few light freckles were scattered across her nose.

Marie DuPree, the dark-haired French ladies' maid at the Winslow house, made a face. "I never see a girl like you," she snorted. "You care nothing for clothes, and you go around looking like a hobo. Hurry now—you need to take a bath and get into your party dress."

Ignoring Marie, Kat stared at her sister and demanded, "Jenny, when will I have bosoms?"

Jenny blinked with shock and gasped slightly. "Kat, do you *have* to say everything that comes into your mind?"

"How am I going to say it if it doesn't come into my mind? When will I?"

Jenny laughed shortly and shook her head in disbelief. "You ought to be more careful what you say. It's not polite to talk about such things."

"Why not?"

"It's not genteel."

"But when will I?"

"Very soon, I suppose. Maybe next year. Now go get dressed, and Marie will come and help you do your hair."

"I can fix it myself."

"I know how you'll fix it! You mind what I say." She smiled and ran her hand over Kat's hair. "It's my birthday, remember. I get to have my own way."

Kat grinned broadly. "You always get your own way."

"Out of here—go!"

As the door closed behind Kat, Marie said, "Do you theenk she will ever outgrow—whatever eet eez she has become?"

"She's just a tomboy, Marie. She'll grow out of it."

"Were you zat way when you were her age?"

"No, I was certainly never that way, but I'm not worried about her. She'll change."

Marie crossed the room to pick up Jenny's dress, holding it for a moment and running her hand over it fondly. A thought struck her, and she motioned with her head. "And Miss Hannah, will she be at zee party?"

"You know she won't, Marie."

"I thought, maybe, since eet was your birthday—"

"She used to come to parties when it was just the family, but you know how she hates to be around parties and things like that with outsiders."

Marie cocked her head to one side. She was an attractive young woman of twenty with intense black eyes. "Was she always so . . . so strange?"

"No, I don't think so."

"Why she eez so afraid of people?"

"I can't say."

"And she eez thirty now—never married? That eez not normal."

A troubled light touched Jenny's eyes. She took the dress from Marie and held it up in front of her. Her eyes were on the large full-length mirror, but her mind was on her sister. "I don't understand Hannah," she sighed. "All she wants to do is read sermons and go to church. Here, help me put the dress on."

Marie took the dress and helped Jenny slip it on, then fastened it. "It eez a beautiful dress!" She sighed. The sleeveless dress was made out of cream silk chiffon and had a low cowl neckline. The bodice fit snugly to the waist, and the smooth silk skirt flowed gently out until it touched the ground in soft drapes around her legs.

Jenny turned around, looking at the back, then said, "Go up and see if you can talk Hannah into coming. I know she probably won't come, but I bought her a new dress, so ask her."

"I will go, but you are right, Miss Jennifer. She probably will not come." Marie shook her head and looked back over her shoulder before leaving the room. "She eez not *natural*, that one!"

★ ★ ★ ★

Kat rushed into her own bedroom, slammed the door behind her, then gave the room a quick glance. How different it was from Jenny's ornate room. Instead of feminine accouterments, hers was filled with specimens she had caught—butterflies pinned to the wall, insects in jars, and a dried snakeskin hanging from a peg. Books were scattered everywhere, all of them having to do with bugs or snakes or animals. A clipper ship model, half finished, filled a table, and clothes littered the room. Pictures cut from magazines and newspapers were pinned carelessly to the walls. The room was a despair to the maid, but nothing anyone said changed Kat's habits. Remembering her sister's admonition, she peeled off her overalls, snatched up a blue robe, then dashed down the hallway to the bathroom, where she took a quick bath, splashing water all over the floor. She left a dirty bathtub ring, for she had indeed gotten grubby digging for worms, but she knew the maids would take care of that.

When she returned to her room, she slipped into the pretty new dress Jenny had bought for her. It was a shiny green cotton with shoes to match. She put on the shoes, then gave her hair a few swipes with a brush. She liked keeping it short and would have cut it even shorter—like a boy's—but both her sisters and their father drew the line at that.

Leaving her room, Kat heard the orchestra again, and when she reached the foot of the stairs, she saw people coming in the front door being greeted by her father. Standing beside him was Lucy Daimen, and Kat involuntarily made a face. *I don't see why he has to marry that old Lucy!* she thought. She wove her way back to the kitchen and picked up some diamond-cut canapés, one in each hand, and went outside through a side door. She stopped abruptly when she saw a man and a woman standing in the shadows of the side garden. The chauffeur had his arms around the new maid. Mabel Bateman was only seventeen, and in the faint light from the kitchen window, Kat could tell that her face was red.

Kat said very loudly, "What are you doing, Earl?"

Earl Crane, a burly man with tow-colored hair and hazel eyes, whirled quickly, anger twisting his face. "Nothing!" he said. "Go on back to the party!"

"I'll bet Daddy wouldn't like it if he knew you were kissing Mabel."

Mabel took this opportunity to pull away and dash past Kat into the house.

"You're a pretty nosy kid," Earl complained.

"I won't tell Dad if you'll do me a favor."

"What kind of a favor?"

"Teach me how to drive the car."

"I can't do that! Your dad would fire me!"

"He won't have to know. You teach me to drive when nobody's around, and I won't tell Dad you're kissing the maids."

Crane laughed conspiratorially. "Okay, kid, we'll do it."

Kat was pleased with this arrangement. She had often asked her father to let her drive, but he had always refused. Now she thought about what fun it would be to drive, and she skipped back into the house. For the next ten minutes she wandered around tasting the canapés and petit fours. She was finally interrupted by her father, who appeared with Lucy Daimen at his side.

"Are you ready for the party, Kat?" he asked.

Lewis Winslow carried his fifty-five years well. He had always been slim and had gained little weight over the years. His light brown hair had minute flecks of gray, and his dark brown eyes peered at her from his squarish face. For some reason, he did not seem particularly happy at this moment, though he smiled warmly at his youngest daughter.

Lewis's fiancée clung to his arm. Kat did not like Lucy, who at thirty-four was in her opinion much too young for her father. Lucy was sharp-featured but not unattractive, with auburn hair and brown eyes. Now Lucy murmured sweetly, "Your hair's not combed, dear. Do you want me to help you with it? Why didn't you get Marie to help you with it?"

" 'Cause I did it myself," Kat said, turning quickly and darting away.

Lucy shook her head. "We've got to do something with that child."

Lewis watched Kat disappear, a fond look in his eyes. "She'll be all right." He looked at the gathered crowd and shook his head. "This is some party, Lucy. You've worked so hard on it, you must be exhausted."

"No, I love it! You know how I love to do things like this." Her mind was still on Kat, and she squeezed Lewis's arm possessively. "After we're married, I'll teach Katherine how to be a lady. I'll bring her out of her tomboy ways."

Lewis smiled and shook his head. "I hope so."

He had known Lucy for five years. She was the only child of Leo Daimen, a wealthy railroad man. She had a quickness about her that pleased him, and she had brought Lewis out of his solitary ways. He had surprised himself by proposing marriage and was even more surprised by her acceptance. Deep down, Lewis knew he was doing it for his children more than for himself.

"And I can help Hannah too. She'd be quite pretty if she'd dress more suitably."

"I hope you can help her. I worry about Hannah a lot. She's become nothing but a recluse."

"We can fix that. Trust me." Lucy smiled brightly.

For a moment Lewis stood silently, thinking about his wedding. He had lost his first wife, Deborah, two years earlier, to the flu. During the last decade, he had made a bundle of money in the stock market, which had come as a great surprise to him. It had been fun while Deborah was alive, but after her death he had sunk into a deep depression, throwing himself into his business and making even more money to fill the emptiness. In a way, he could understand Hannah's reluctance to be here, for he himself did not usually care for large parties.

"I'm too old for you," he said abruptly.

"Nonsense!" Lucy retorted. "It's going to be a wonderful marriage. We're going to do tremendous things. You'll see."

"I hope so." He shook his head sadly. "I'm worried about Hannah—and about Joshua."

"He can change too. I'll take him in hand. Come along, now. We've got to be better hosts than this!"

★　★　★　★

Joshua Winslow handled the big Packard with reckless ease, his wrist drooped over the wheel. It was obvious he'd had a few drinks. He turned and grinned at his friend Arlen Banks, who sat beside him. "Nervous, Arlen? Afraid I'll pile us up?"

"You drive like a maniac, Josh! You'd scare anyone." Arlen Banks was a tall, lanky man with dark hair, deep blue eyes, and aristocratic features. The two men were the same age and best friends. "It's going to be a huge party, I understand. Jenny said Lucy invited half the people in New York."

"Yes, she did. Even the Roosevelts are going to be here and maybe some of the Astors. You know Lucy."

Arlen turned quickly. "You don't sound too enthusiastic about your future stepmother."

"She's all right." Josh shrugged. "She'll shake Dad up a bit. I've been worried about him ever since Mom died. He hasn't been himself." He took a curve too fast and laughed as Arlen grabbed the seat to steady himself. "What about your brother Preston? What's he doing now?"

"He's in Europe on an extended honeymoon. Been there nearly a year," Arlen said.

Josh swerved to avoid a chuckhole and did not answer at once. At the age of twenty-seven, he still possessed a boyish look. He was lean, and his alert gray eyes and tawny hair made him the cynosure of women's attention. "You know, we all thought he'd marry Hannah. Does he ever talk about her?"

"Never mentions her." Arlen hesitated before saying, "Is she any better?"

"No, she's not. Can't get her out of her room except to go to church. I think she's getting worse."

"Did she ever tell you why she broke off her engagement with Pres?"

"No, she never would discuss it, but it broke Mom's heart. You know, up until that happened, Hannah was a lot like Jenny is now—lively and lots of fun, always doing things."

"Yes, I remember. Has she ever been to see a doctor?"

"Dad made her go about a year after it happened, but it didn't do any good. Of course people think she's crazy."

"Oh, I never hear that."

"Well, they do, believe me. They think she's a mental case, but she's not. She's as smart a woman as I ever saw."

Josh pulled the car up in front of the Winslow house, an enormous brownstone mansion set far back off Fifth Avenue, bordering other properties of the rich and famous, right across from Central Park. Numerous cars lined the circular driveway, with chauffeurs waiting in each one while their employers enjoyed the party. Arlen studied the house as he got out. Lewis Winslow had bought it only a year earlier. The Romanesque house with a corner tower and a rounded-arch entrance was surrounded by short, thick colonnades. Arlen did not particularly like it, thinking it looked like a prison. "Do you like this house, Josh?"

"No, as a matter of fact, I don't. It's like living in a museum. Lucy talked Dad into buying it."

"It'll be a little strange having a stepmother only a few years older than you are, won't it?"

Josh did not answer, and Arlen knew he'd touched a nerve. His friend had enough intelligence to do anything in life he wanted. Josh had studied archeology in college but had dropped out before his senior year. Arlen had always vaguely connected his change of attitude with the enormous amounts of money Lewis Winslow had made. Sudden wealth had somehow taken the drive out of Joshua, and he had become the proverbial playboy, enjoying fast cars, too much drink, and parties almost every night. Since he had quit school he had done nothing but waste his time. Arlen had once asked him if he would ever go back to college, but the answer had been curt. *"Nope. What's the use?"*

Earl Crane approached Joshua at the front entrance, saying, "I'll park it, Mr. Winslow."

"Thanks, Earl. Come on, Arlen."

The two entered the massive front foyer under a glittering chandelier and were greeted at once by Lewis Winslow and Lucy. Lewis caught the scent of liquor on Joshua, and his lips tightened, but he merely said, "Hello, son. Hello, Arlen. It's good to see you."

"Good to see you too, Mr. Winslow, and you, Miss Daimen. You're lovely—as always." He brought her extended gloved hand to his lips and gave an elegant bow, then turned and spotted Jenny dancing in the expansive drawing room turned ballroom for the occasion. He grinned saucily. "I'm going to cut in on Fred. He can't dance anyway."

As Arlen headed for the dance floor, Lewis said darkly, "I don't see why you had to drink tonight, son."

"I just had a couple, Dad. Don't start preaching."

Lewis shrugged his shoulders. "Why don't you go up and talk to Hannah. See if you can get her to come down. It is Jenny's birthday, after all."

"All right. I'll see what I can do."

Josh took the steps up the curving front stairway two at a time as Arlen threaded his way across the dance floor. He tapped Fred on the shoulder, and when the young man turned, he said, "Cutting in, Fred."

Fred Simpkins said sourly, "I thought you would. Thanks for the dance, Jenny."

"You're welcome, Fred. Ask me again."

Arlen took Jenny in his arms and swept her around the floor. "I like this better than the Charleston."

"Nobody does the Charleston anymore," Jenny said.

"I'm glad to hear that." He spun her around, then said, "You're looking very beautiful."

"I knew you'd say that."

"How did you know?"

"You always say that."

"Well, you're always beautiful."

Jenny laughed. She couldn't help liking Arlen Banks. She had begun seeing him only six months earlier, and he was fun to be with. He had plenty of money, as his father owned a number of factories that manufactured farm equipment. But Arlen was ten years older than Jenny—far too old to take as a serious suitor.

As they danced Arlen asked, "You know what I'm wondering?"

"What?"

"I was just wondering, if you were a little older, what kind of a married couple we'd make."

"Arlen, that is the most unromantic thing a man has ever said to a woman!"

"What do you want me to do?" Arlen grinned. "After all, you're only seventeen. I'll have to wait at least another three or four years before you're old enough to get married."

"Well, it won't be to you!"

"Why not?"

"Because you'll be too old then."

Arlen laughed. "I suppose you're right, but I can always dream. What's your father going to get you for your birthday?"

"He's already gotten it. A new mare. She's gorgeous!"

"You're going to break your neck one of these days riding those spirited horses."

Without warning, Arlen leaned forward and kissed her square on the lips without missing a step, then laughed. "There. Happy birthday."

Caught off guard, Jenny smiled and giggled as she shook her head. "You are the most unromantic man I have ever known! I would never marry you in a hundred years!"

"What if I learned to write poetry and play the guitar? How would that be?" He continued to tease her, and as they danced, she thought about how much she liked him and wished he were five years younger.

★   ★   ★   ★

As soon as Joshua tapped on Hannah's door, he heard her say, "Come in." He went inside and glanced around, thinking how different the room was from Jenny's. Stern, utilitarian, with few decorations. A massive rolltop desk dominated one wall, and across the room a set of enormous bookcases packed full rose to the ceiling. It was almost like an office, except for the mahogany bed with the lace canopy and the cherrywood antique wash-stand. The few pictures on the wall were original oils by well-known painters in the city—very expensive, Joshua knew. Even her choices in artwork were rather severe, he thought—tradi-tional gardens and architecture, nothing splashy or modern. Hannah rose from the desk.

"You're not dressed," he said.

"Yes I am."

Hannah Winslow, at the age of thirty, was attractive, with large brown eyes and shiny, thick auburn hair, though she insisted on pulling it back into a bun as a much older woman would wear it. She was not as beautiful as Jenny, but her features were stronger. Her eyes were expressive and her mouth firm. But there was a vulnerability about her that Josh had never been able to pin down. She'd had a happy childhood but then had disap-pointed her family. They had all expected her to marry well and have children. Instead, she'd broken her engagement to Preston Banks and had confined herself to the house, refusing most social invitations. She read constantly and helped to manage the large house and servants but was little more than a recluse. She cared nothing for stylish clothes. Instead of the maroon evening gown Jenny had bought her for the party, she was wearing a plain light blue day dress that did not suit her.

"I thought you might come down for Jenny's party."

"No, I don't think I will."

"But Jenny said she bought you a new gown for the occasion."

Hannah shook her head, and Joshua saw that gentle persuasion was not going to work. He stood there uncertainly and said, "You used to come to the birthday parties."

"Just when it was the family." Something changed in Hannah's face. "I remember how wonderful it was when Mother was alive. We didn't have a lot of money. Remember the house we grew up in?"

"Yes, of course I do."

"It was a home, Joshua. At times I wish Father hadn't made so much money."

"I don't wish that."

"Josh, why did you give up on college?" Hannah's voice was quiet, and there was a soft pleading in her eyes. She put out her hand and touched his arm. "You could have done anything you wanted to, but you just quit."

Josh cringed at the stinging words. "It didn't seem to matter anymore. We had plenty of money. I didn't see any sense in working myself to death." Then he made a remark he would not have made if he had been completely sober. "Why did *you* give up? I may be a drunk, but you're a hermit. Neither of us can face life." As soon as the words were out, Josh was repentant. "I'm sorry, sis," he said. "It's the liquor talking."

Hannah whispered, "It's all right, Josh, but you go on. There's nothing down there for me."

★　★　★　★

Leo Daimen was a tall, heavyset man of sixty. He had all the marks of the wealth he'd accumulated in railroads. He was very opposed to his only daughter's marriage to the much older Lewis Winslow and had done all he could to talk Lucy out of it but without success.

"It's a nice party, isn't it, Father?" Lucy asked him.

"I suppose," Leo replied gruffly. "But a bit ornate for a seventeen-year-old, I'd say."

"Just between you and me, this party is as much for Lewis as it is for Jennifer. I want Lewis to come out of himself more, and I believe he will once we're married."

"I worry about this family, Lucy. They're not stable. Why, just think of that older sister. She's nothing but a hermit—something's not normal there. And Joshua is becoming a fall-down drunk."

"I'll get them all straightened out once we're married. They just need the influence of a sophisticated woman in this house, that's all."

At that moment Kat came along, and Lucy said brightly, "Oh, Katherine! Are you having fun?"

"Yes, actually I am."

Lucy's face fell as she spotted Kat's shoes. "Why, you've got dirt all over your shoes."

"I went outside for a bit."

Lucy shook her head. "You should go to the kitchen and clean them off." She looked at the paper bag in the girl's hand. "What's that?"

"Nothing."

"Come on, now. We have no secrets. Let me see it."

"Do you really want to, Miss Lucy?"

"Of course I do."

"Are you *sure*?"

Lucy laughed. "Yes, I'm sure."

"Well, all right." Kat handed the woman the sack, and Lucy opened it. She froze as a small green snake stuck his head up out of the sack. She screamed and dropped the bag, and Kat whisked it up, grinning. "Don't you like snakes?"

"Get it out of here! Take it away!" Lucy cried as she ran to the other side of the large room.

Lewis had just entered the room, and he came over and asked his daughter what happened.

"She wanted to see what was in my sack," Kat said innocently.

"And you gave it to her?"

Kat shrugged. "She insisted. I don't think she liked it much."

Lewis tried to conceal a grin. "Most ladies don't like snakes."

Kat looked up at him and said seriously, "I like snakes better than I like some people."

Lewis laughed and hugged her. "I'd have to agree with you, but don't tell anybody."

He went to find Lucy to make his apologies, but she was highly upset and would not be consoled. He listened to her patiently, then shook his head. "She's a little bit like her mother."

"Well, she'll have to change."

"I suppose so," Lewis said, and for the moment he tried to look ahead, thinking what changes would come when he and Lucy were married. Marrying Lucy had seemed like a good idea, but lately he'd been having some doubts. *Maybe we'll be all right*, he tried to assure himself. *I certainly need help from somebody. . . .*

CHAPTER TWO

Jailbird Gardener

★ ★ ★ ★

Lewis Winslow spread the paper out on his desk, glanced at the date, September 20, 1929, then ran his eyes over the stock market report. He shook his head and muttered sourly, "This is *insane*! It can't go on. . . ."

He checked the Dow Jones Industrial Average, wondering if the whole country had lost its mind. Buying stocks had become a national mania. Even the poorest of working people were pooling their funds and buying five shares of some stock, without the least idea of what they were buying. He read an article that said more than a million Americans had bought stock and that three hundred million shares of stock were being carried on margin, meaning on credit. The papers were replete with stories of people who'd made fortunes. Lewis himself knew of a broker's valet who had made nearly a quarter of a million in the market. He'd also heard of a nurse who had made thirty thousand dollars by following tips given her by grateful patients. With a gesture of disgust, Lewis shuffled through the paper, catching up on the other news of the day.

He read with interest about the travels of Charles and Anne Lindbergh, who had married in the spring and were now flying to many foreign lands together. He also read of the explorer Richard Byrd, who was waiting in the Antarctic darkness at his base named Little America for his chance to fly to the South Pole.

In sports, the colorful American tennis player Bill Tilden had won his seventh amateur tennis championship, Bobby Jones ruled the world of golf, and Babe Ruth was still hammering out home runs.

The door opened quietly, and Lewis's secretary, Miss Handley, stuck her head inside. "There's a gentleman here to see you, sir."

"What's his name?"

"Mr. Fred Davenport."

"Fred Davenport? Well, show him in." Lewis got up from his chair and moved across the room. When a diminutive man wearing an outdated light brown suit entered the room, Lewis said, "Fred, it's good to see you!" He took the man's hand, noticing that it was hard and calloused. "Where in the world have you been?"

"It's good to see you too, Mr. Winslow." Davenport's apprehensive expression was replaced with a relaxed smile at Lewis's greeting. "I hated to bust in without an appointment—"

"Never mind all that. Come in and have a seat." Lewis waved at the chair, and as his guest sat down carefully, holding a worn derby in his lap, he went to the door and said, "Could we have some coffee please, Ellen?" He shut the door and said, "This is fine! I haven't seen you in—oh, I don't know how many years."

"It's been a long time, Mr. Winslow."

"Oh, never mind the 'mister,' Fred. Lewis was good enough for us in Cuba."

"Well, yes it was, but things have changed."

Lewis pulled his chair closer to Davenport's and began questioning him. Davenport had been in his squad in the Spanish-American War. They had been under fire together, and Davenport had once saved Lewis from getting hit by pulling him back just as a fusillade of shots rang out. Lewis had later distinguished himself in that war by winning the Congressional Medal of Honor.

The coffee arrived, and for twenty minutes the two men exchanged their stories. Finally Davenport said, "Well, I've come asking a favor. That's the way it is with old acquaintances, isn't it? You don't see 'em for years, then suddenly there they are with their hands out, wanting something."

"Why, don't worry about that, Fred. What is it?" Lewis knew

that Davenport was a workingman, though he did not know what kind of manual labor he had worked at recently.

"Well, it's not for myself, Lewis. You see, I have one sister. We grew up together on a farm in Tennessee. She married a man named Longstreet and had a family, but he died several years ago, and the farm played out. One of her boys, Clinton, has given her a little trouble. He's a restless sort. He worked the farm until a few years ago, when his mother married again. Evidently the boy didn't get along with his new stepfather, so he hit the road and has been just about everywhere in the country. He went to sea about a year ago shovelin' coal, but he didn't like it. He came back about a month ago to stay with me and hasn't been able to get work."

"I take it he's in some kind of trouble?"

"He got in a fight over a girl down on Water Street. It was a fair fight, but Clint got the best of it. Handy with his fists, he is."

"Did he get arrested?"

"That's the problem, Lewis. He beat up the wrong fella. You know James Garvey?"

"You mean the attorney general?"

"That's him. It was his boy Clint beat up, and Garvey's gonna press charges. He's got the judge on his side, of course."

"Which judge?"

"Name is Ramsey. I been to talk to him, and he says he's gonna give Clint some time in jail."

"I see," Lewis said. "Why don't you let me work on this. Garvey's a friend of mine—and I supported Ramsey in the last election."

Relief washed over Davenport's face. "That would be great if you could get him off, Lewis, but Judge Ramsey says Clint has to have a job."

"Well, I'll find him something." He stood up and when the other man rose with him, he clapped him on the shoulder. "I think we can work this out. Don't worry about it, Fred."

"That's like you, Lewis. You haven't changed a bit."

"We old soldiers have to stick together."

Lewis waited until Davenport left, then checked a number in his address book and picked up the phone. "Operator, give me 6617. . . ."

★　★　★　★

Kat swung her mallet sharply and struck the wooden ball. It made a straight path through the wicket, and she threw her mallet into the air, shouting, "I win—I win!"

Jenny laughed as the mallet cartwheeled and came down in the grass nearby. "Yes, you do. You're too good for me."

"Let's play one more game, Jenny. Bet I beat you again."

"Well, maybe just one more. . . ." She paused and turned to look at the vehicle that had pulled into the driveway. "That's a police car," she murmured.

"A police car? Have they come to arrest us?" Kat's eyes were big.

"I doubt that." Jenny smiled. "They're probably lost and looking for an address." She watched as the door opened and a bulky officer got out and opened the back of the paddy wagon. A tall lean man wearing rough-looking clothes and a worn fedora stepped down. She heard the officer say, "Come on, this is where you get off."

Jenny waited until the policeman and the other man approached, then asked, "Are you lost, Officer?"

"I don't think so, miss. This is Mr. Lewis Winslow's place, isn't it?"

"Yes, it is. I'm his daughter."

"Well, Miss Winslow, I'm turning this fellow over to you."

"You're doing what?" Jenny stared at the muscular man. His sandy hair crept out from beneath the fedora, and he had steady gray-green eyes. His nose appeared to have been broken at one time, and he had a scar on the right side of his chin along the jawline. He had a heavy lower lip, high cheekbones, and very large hands with oversized knuckles. "What do you mean? Who is he?"

"His name's Longstreet. Your father asked us to deliver him here. Is Mr. Winslow home?"

"No, but you can't leave a prisoner here."

"He's safe enough." The man grinned. "Would you sign right here, miss?"

Jenny protested furiously, but in the end she gave in at the officer's insistence that this was her father's instruction. He took the clipboard back, obviously finding something amusing in the situation. "You two enjoy yourselves," he said as he returned to the car. He waved out the window as he pulled away.

Kat had hardly taken her eyes off of the tall man. "Are you a criminal?" she demanded.

"I guess I am."

"Are you a murderer?"

A smile turned up the corners of Longstreet's mouth. "Maybe I am. You'd better run."

Kat stared at him calmly and shook her head. "I'm not afraid of you. What's your name?"

"Clint Longstreet. What's yours?"

"Kat Winslow. I'm twelve."

"You come with me, Mr. Longstreet," Jenny said brusquely. She turned and marched away, leading Longstreet around the side of the house. Kat fell back and twisted her head up, studying the stranger as he strolled along. He had very long legs and adjusted his pace to stay behind Jenny. Kat looked down at his right hand and noted that the tip of his little finger was missing.

"What happened to your finger, Clint?"

"Bear bit it off."

Kat laughed. "That's a story!"

"Yes, it is. Got caught in some machinery." He held it out for her to examine, and she continued to put questions to him.

"Stop asking questions, Kat," her sister demanded. "I don't want you talking to him."

Kat glanced at Jenny, then back at her companion. "She's not usually that impolite."

"I don't expect Yankees to have fine manners."

Jenny flushed, turned, and glared at Longstreet. She marched on, then stopped in front of the chauffeur, who was washing the big Packard, and said, "Earl, will you keep an eye on this man until Dad gets home?"

"I saw him get out of the police car. Who is he?"

"Some kind of a criminal," Jenny said stiffly.

"I'll take care of it, Miss Jenny."

"I'll wait here," Kat said. "I want to talk to Clint some more."

"You come in the house with me, Kat," Jenny ordered.

"No, I won't!" Kat complained. "And you can't make me."

Furious, Jenny stalked away. Earl watched her go, then said

to Longstreet, "You'd better watch yourself, fella. I don't want no trouble out of you."

"I don't expect you'll get any."

"You sit over there," Earl said as he pointed to a garden bench.

Kat accompanied Longstreet to the bench and plopped herself down beside him. "What happened to your nose?" she asked.

"It got broken. . . ."

★   ★   ★   ★

Jenny went straight to her father's study and called his office, but his secretary informed her that he had already left for the day. As she came out into the hall she encountered Hannah and demanded, "Do you know what our father has done? He sent some kind of a . . . a *criminal* here."

Hannah smiled. "Oh, Father told me what he was going to do. Don't be upset. The man is the nephew of a good friend of Father's, someone he was in the army with during the war in Cuba."

"Well, we can't have a convict here."

"I think it will be all right. He's not a serious criminal."

"What is he, then?" Jenny demanded.

"He just got into some sort of minor trouble. Father's going to give him a job."

"Doing what?"

"He's going to help the gardener. Poor Jamie's got arthritis so bad he can hardly get around. It's painful to watch him work. Hopefully this man can do the hard work."

"Well, I'm going out to talk to him," Jenny said. "I'll take him over to Jamie's cottage."

Jenny left the house and returned to where Kat was still peppering Clint Longstreet with questions. "You come with me," she said sternly to the man.

"Maybe I'd better go along and keep an eye on him, Miss Jenny," Crane spoke up.

"That won't be necessary, Earl. You just wash the car."

"All right, but let me know if he gives you any trouble."

Jenny turned and said, "Kat, you go in the house."

"I'm not through talking to Clint yet."

"Stop calling him Clint!"

"Well, that's his name—Clint Longstreet!"

Jenny knew the stubborn streak that lay in her younger sister and gave up for the moment. "Well, you can come, but be quiet."

Jenny walked stiffly away and led Longstreet down a cobblestone path to a small cottage nestled between two big trees next to the garden. When she knocked on the door, there was a considerable pause, but it finally opened and a small gray-haired man stepped out. "Why, Miss Jenny!" Jamie's eyes went over toward the tall form of Longstreet; then he turned back to Jenny and said, "Won't you come in?" He had the burr of old Scotland in his voice, and his eyes were sharp and alert, though his body was bent.

"No, I just came by to bring this man," Jenny replied. "His name's Clint Longstreet. Dad got him out of jail and hired him to work with you, but you'll have to watch him."

Jamie MacDougal was not easily flustered. He was sixty-four years old and had been a gardener all of his life—first in Scotland and then in this country. Now with his arthritis getting so bad, it was difficult to continue his lifelong work. As he studied the strong-looking man with the tanned features, he nodded. "I can use a wee bit of help."

"You'd better keep a close eye on him, Jamie," Jenny warned again, then lifted her chin in a challenging way and stared up at Clint. "We don't know anything about him—except he's been in jail."

"I'll talk to him, Miss Jenny."

"You come on, Kat."

Kat protested as her sister dragged her away.

MacDougal waited until they were out of sight, then said to the man, "Come in." He stepped aside and noted that Longstreet took his hat off as he entered. "So your name is Clint Longstreet, eh? What were you in jail for?"

"I got into a fight."

"That's not a jailin' matter."

"It is when you beat up the son of the attorney general for the state of New York."

"Och, man, you tell me you did that?"

"I didn't know who he was. It was just a fight over a girl, but I found out pretty quick that he was the wrong man to pick a fight with in this state."

"Do you know anythin' aboot gardenin'?"

"Not much. I know something about farming, though." Clint grinned. "I followed a mule long enough to know how to go about that."

"Weel, you look strong enough, but I'm the gardener here, and ye'll do what I say, mind you."

"It beats going to jail."

"I'll have no loafers, mind!"

"I don't think you'll have to worry. That Miss Winslow would be sure to have her father throw me out if I didn't work."

"Weel, she might do it." Jamie nodded and smiled. "She can bend her father around her little finger, but in case you do stay on, I got a room here. Where are your things?"

"A friend of mine is holding them."

"Come along. There's still time to get some work done today. See if you got anythin' in you."

★ ★ ★ ★

As soon as Lewis entered the front door of his house, Jenny appeared before him. "Dad, we can't have a criminal working for us!"

"Oh, he came, did he?" Lewis took off his coat and hat and handed them to Gerald Mason, the butler. He turned back to Jenny and said, "I promised his uncle we'd give him a try. He may not work out, of course."

"But he's a *criminal*, Dad! Think about Kat. What if he assaults her—or me?"

Lewis stopped and turned to face Jenny. "Did he seem like a criminal type to you?"

"He looked like a tough. He's been in a fight. I can tell that."

"That was the trouble. He beat up the wrong man." Lewis explained the situation to his daughter and said, "I'll have to give him a try, Jenny. He's the nephew of a very dear friend of mine. As a matter of fact, if it hadn't been for Fred Davenport, I might not even be here now."

"What do you mean?"

"He pulled me to safety when I was in a place where I shouldn't have been—a place full of bullets. They for sure would have picked me off if Fred hadn't pulled me out of the way. So, you see, his nephew has to stay." He smiled and patted Jenny's shoulder. "Don't worry. If he doesn't work out here, I'll find another place for him. What did you do with him?"

"I took him out to Jamie's cottage. Hannah said you wanted him to help the gardener."

"I'll just go out and have a word with him."

Lewis left the house and went to the gardener's cottage. He knocked on the door and it opened after a moment's hesitation. "Hello, Jamie."

"Ah, Mr. Lewis, I suppose you've come to see the new gardener."

"Yes." Lewis stepped inside and looked at the man who had risen from a chair. "Clinton Longstreet, I believe?"

"Yes, sir."

Lewis put out his hand, and it was almost swallowed by Longstreet's massive hand. "I'm glad to meet you," Lewis said pleasantly. "Your uncle saved my life back in the war."

"He thinks a lot of you, Mr. Winslow."

"And I think a lot of him as well." Lewis shot a grin at Jamie and said, "If you get in another fight, just be sure you don't choose the son of the attorney general."

Longstreet had been stiff, not knowing what sort of a man he might be facing, but now he smiled. "Yes, sir, I'll be sure of that." He had a soft voice with a distinct southern accent. There was an alert look about him, and his skin was bronzed deeply by the sun.

"I understand you've been at sea, Mr. Longstreet."

"Yes, but I'll never go back."

"Didn't like it, eh?"

"I guess I thought it would be like in the old days of the clipper ships, where you hauled the sails up. Instead I was below-decks shoveling coal ten hours a day. No future in that." Then he added, "I appreciate what you've done for me, sir."

"Oh, it was little enough to do for an old friend. Why don't you work things out with Jamie? I'll pay you ten dollars a week until we see what you can do."

40

"That'll be fine, sir."

Lewis nodded and left, and as soon as he was gone, Jamie said, "Weel, I reckon Miss Jenny wasn't able to get her father to run you off."

"I was expecting it."

"I was too, to tell the truth. Weel, man, are ye hungry?"

"Yes, I guess I am."

"Come along and we'll have a bite. We always eat in the kitchen. You'll like the food. Cook is as good as you'll find."

★ ★ ★ ★

Clint said little as he ate with the other servants at the big table in the kitchen, listening in on their conversations and learning their names. Seated around the table were the butler, Gerald, a tall man with thin features, and his wife, whom everyone called Cook. They both appeared to be in their midforties. Alice Cookson was a maid with dark brown hair and snapping eyes that she put often on Clint. He learned that the attractive maid with dark hair and dark eyes, Marie DuPree, was from France. The other maid present was Mabel, a very young woman with blond hair and shy blue eyes who hardly said a word. Finally there were Jamie and Earl.

Earl made it a point to announce that the newest member of the staff had been delivered by the police. He dared Clint with his eyes and made several disparaging remarks about jailbirds. Clint studied the burly man, knowing that Crane would never be happy until he had demonstrated his strength, but it was too early for that.

Alice asked, "Where are you from, Mr. Longstreet?"

"You don't have to call a jailbird 'mister,'" Crane said, grinning.

"That's right, ma'am. Clint's good enough," he said. "I grew up in Tennessee."

"A real farm boy, I bet, are you?" Crane laughed as though he had said something witty. "Well, clean your boots off before you come in the house."

Jamie watched Clint carefully. He took note when his new

helper had finished his meal, then took his dishes over to the kitchen sink.

As Clint left the kitchen, Cook put her eyes on Crane and said loudly, "Well, he's got better manners than some I could name."

"Yeah, but you'll have to watch him. He'll probably try to steal the silverware." Crane reached over and squeezed Mabel's shoulder. The girl drew away from him, and he laughed. "Someday you're going to like me just fine, Mabel."

When all the servants had finished their meal and gone back to their duties or their quarters, Cook and her husband finished cleaning up. "What do you think of that new man, Gerald?"

"He looks able enough. Poor Jamie needs all the help he can get."

"I'm surprised that Mr. Lewis would get somebody out of jail."

"There's more to it than that." Gerald shook his head and said, "You know, I'm not so worried about the new man as I am about Crane. He can't keep his hands to himself."

"I agree he doesn't fit in here."

"Frankly, I'm uneasy about both him and Longstreet here together. They're bound to come to blows."

★　★　★　★

After breakfast the following morning, Jamie led Clint out to a section of the formal garden and said, "This all has to be dug up and wheelbarrowed over into that bed over there."

"All right," Clint said. He noticed how painfully MacDougal seemed to get around, and the younger man began to work diligently.

MacDougal watched closely for two hours and saw that Clint was a good worker, handling the shovel like a toy and tossing the dirt as if it were made of air. He filled the wheelbarrow quickly, wheeled it over, dumped it, then came back and immediately began again. Finally Jamie said, "You're good with a shovel, Clint."

"I had a lot of experience on that steamer."

" 'Twas not a good job, now, was it? I don't see how a man

stands it doon underneath, cut off from the sun and all that God has made."

"It's not for me," Longstreet agreed, resting for a moment on his shovel and wiping his brow with his sleeve.

At ten o'clock Alice came out with a pitcher of iced tea and two glasses. "I thought you might be thirsty," she said, batting her eyelashes at Longstreet.

Jamie grinned. "Well, you've never worried aboot me before. Must be some other attraction."

"You leave me alone, Jamie." She smiled and poured the glasses full. She watched as Clint drank his tea and said, "You'll like it here."

"I think I will. Nothing like easy work and pretty girls to bring you iced tea."

"Oh, you've kissed the Blarney Stone!" Alice giggled. They chatted for a few moments before she returned to the kitchen.

Jamie laughed shortly. "You made a conquest there. Pretty lassie too."

"I doubt if I'll be doing much partying around here."

The two men sat down under one of the trees, and Clint asked, "Have you been here long, Jamie?"

"Not long. Two years. Before that I worked for Mr. Vanderbilt."

"Fast company."

"Yes, not a good man to work for, but Mr. Winslow, now, he's fine."

"Do you have a family?"

Clint saw that the question disturbed Jamie.

"I have a son and a daughter," the gardener said slowly. "My boy's a veterinarian in Pennsylvania. He's got a fine wife there."

"Where does your daughter live?"

The question brought a bleak look into MacDougal's eyes. "New Jersey."

"Is she married?"

"Why are you asking?"

"Just curious."

Jamie did not answer for a time, but finally the words came out reluctantly. "I have nothing to do with my daughter. She has shamed the MacDougal name."

Clint took a big swallow of the cold tea and studied the older man. "What'd she do?"

"She ran away with a man—an actor."

"That must have been hard for you, MacDougal."

"Weel, they did marry finally just a year and a half ago." Then he added, as if it hurt him to speak the words, "They have a child now, a wee boy."

Clint drained the glass and crunched the ice between his white teeth. "What's the boy's name?"

"Same as mine."

"She named the boy after you?"

"I suppose so."

Clint put the glass down and turned to face MacDougal. "How long are you going to hold your daughter's mistake against her, Jamie?"

"It's none of your business!"

"I guess it's not, but I have to say it seems that your reaction is a little harsh."

"You would understand if you were a father."

"I hope I wouldn't hold a grudge, especially against one of my own children."

MacDougal stood to his feet, gave Clint a furious look, and said, "Finish your work!" and stalked off, his back rigid with anger.

★　★　★　★

"How's Longstreet working out, Jamie?" Lewis asked the next day as he approached the old gardener.

Jamie had been trimming the rosebushes, one of the jobs he was still able to do. The gardener scratched his chin thoughtfully and looked up at Lewis. "Weel now, I'll have to say the man's a fool for work."

"Is that right?"

"I never seen a harder-workin' man in all my life, and tough as boot leather, 'e is."

"I'm glad to hear that. How have the servants taken to him?"

"Very weel—except for Earl. He's all the time pokin' at him for bein' a jailbird."

"Maybe I'd better have a word with Earl."

"It would go amiss, Mr. Lewis."

"Well, I need to deal with that, then. Earl always seems to have a chip on his shoulder. But you say we should keep Long-street on?"

"Aye, sir, I think so," Jamie replied. "I know I'm not much good to you," he said quietly, "but I've got the knowledge, and this young man's got the strength."

"You'll stay with me as long as you want to, Jamie." Lewis smiled. "Don't you worry about it."

"Thankee, sir."

As his employer left, Jamie stood for a long time thoughtfully staring at the ground. He had not been able to forget his conversation with Longstreet concerning his daughter. In all truth Jamie MacDougal was a good man and a Christian as well. He had long known that he was entirely in the wrong. His daughter had written him several times begging for forgiveness, but he had stubbornly refused. Clint's words had been like a sharp needle, and he had slept poorly.

Finally he threw the shears down and stalked back to his cottage. He sat down at the table, pulled out a sheet of paper, and picked up a pen. He sat very quietly for a time and then said, "Good Lord, please forgive me. I have wronged my daughter and wronged you." He began to write slowly and painfully:

Dear Matilda,

You may not want to hear from me after all the hard things I have said to you, but I've been thinking much about what happened. If you can find it in your heart to forgive me . . .

CHAPTER THREE

A MATTER OF PRIDE

★　★　★　★

October swept into New York, bringing cold, crisp air in the early mornings. Thin streaks of white clouds raced across the sky, and the pale sun threw out little heat. Veteran New Yorkers, recognizing the signs, began to dig out heavy winter clothes and stock up on coal and wood. Soon winter would come and bring with it paralyzing cold that the poor could not easily escape but from which the affluent could take refuge in their elaborate, well-warmed homes.

Clint had taken an interest in the small vegetable garden Jamie had planted outside the kitchen door in the spring and had gone out to dig the sweet potatoes. Kat, who had become an almost constant companion, had joined him. When she was not at her studies, she would often put on her worn overalls and ragged straw hat to follow him while he worked. Clint had discovered that the girl had a feel for growing things, and since he had the same gift, he enjoyed her company. Now he drove the turning fork into the ground and pulled up a forkful of loamy earth. When he turned it upside down, the potatoes spilled to one side, and Kat snatched them and put them into a large basket.

"I love sweet potatoes," she announced. "I'm going to have Cook make a sweet-potato pie." And then without any change of inflection, she asked, "Do you have a wife, Clint?"

Accustomed to her abrupt changes of subject and also her pointed questions, Clint straightened up and met her gaze. "Nope, no wife."

"Why not?"

Clint laughed. He had become very fond of Kat during his brief stay at the Winslow estate. "I just never met the right girl."

"How old are you, Clint?"

"Twenty-seven."

"That's pretty old not to be married," Kat observed. She picked up another potato, brushed the dirt off of it, and tossed it in the basket. "Have you ever had a sweetheart?"

"One or two, but nothing ever came of it."

"What were their names?"

"Don't you ever get tired of asking questions?"

"How am I going to learn if I don't ask questions?"

Clint reached over and gently pinched the girl's arm. "If asking questions makes somebody wise, you ought to be the wisest girl in the world."

"I don't know about wise—I'm just curious! Did I tell you that Earl is going to teach me how to drive?"

"Aren't you a little young for that?"

"I might be a little young, but I think I'll be a good driver. But he hasn't started teaching me yet. Every time I ask him he says he's too busy right now."

"That's what we adults say when we don't want to do something."

"I know. Tell me what you did when you were my age."

Clint chewed thoughtfully on his lower lip. He made a lean, powerful shape in the pale sunlight. He wore no coat despite the coolness of the day, and the muscles of his upper body were delineated through his thin work shirt. His muscles were long rather than bulky, and his chest was deep rather than wide. There was a durable look about him, and he bore scars evidencing the run-ins he'd had at times. Now he rubbed the scar along his jawline and asked, "Have you ever had a boyfriend?"

"No, I don't care anything about that. Jenny's had a lot of boyfriends, though. She likes to make men jealous. She went around with Charlie Jacobs for a long time. She didn't like him, but she did it to make Arlen Banks jealous."

"She wouldn't appreciate your telling on her."

"I don't tell everybody," Kat said. She snatched her straw hat off, spilling her tawny hair, and lifted her head to the sky. As the breeze ruffled her hair, she observed, "Hannah's afraid of people."

Clint had never seen Hannah Winslow, but he had picked up enough information to become interested. He asked casually, "Why do you suppose that is?"

Jamming her hat back down, Kat shook her head. "I don't know. I think she's had a 'tragic past.' That's what they call it in the romance novels Jenny reads sometimes. I'm real sad for her. We don't have a mother, you know." She suddenly changed the subject. "Will you take me fishing over at the lake in Central Park?"

"I couldn't do that, Kat."

"Why not?"

"Well, it's not part of my job."

"But when you get off, could you take me?"

Clint grinned at her. "I'd have to have your father ask me to do it."

"Oh, he will. I'll ask him tonight, Clint. It'll be fun. I've been fishing there three times, and I've caught fish every time."

★　★　★　★

At dinner Lewis was silent, and Hannah, who was sitting beside him, asked quietly, "Is something wrong, Father?"

He shook his head and pushed a bit of beef around with his fork. "I'm worried about the stock market. Such crazy things are happening! I don't know what to do."

Joshua looked up and said, "I heard that a lot of investors are selling out. Some of the foreign investors are taking their money back to Germany."

Lewis shook his head. "If stocks fall as quickly as I think they could, a lot of us are going to be in trouble."

Kat interrupted what to her was a dull conversation. "Daddy, I want to go fishing over at Central Park. Will you take me?"

"I'm sorry, honey, I just don't have time right now. There's so much work at the office, and I've been ignoring Lucy lately. I promised her I'd go over wedding plans with her this week."

Kat frowned at the mention of Lucy. "Well, Clint said he'd take me if you say it's all right."

Jenny lifted her head and snapped, "You're not going anywhere with that man!"

"Why not?" Kat challenged. "Nobody else will take me anywhere."

"I think Jenny's right, Dad," Joshua said. "We don't know much about the fellow."

"Please, Daddy, I want to go!"

"Maybe later when things calm down at the office."

"You never take me anywhere," Kat said angrily, throwing down her napkin and running out of the room.

Lewis shook his head. "I ought to take her myself."

"Yes, you should, Father," Hannah agreed. "She loves for you to do things with her."

Lewis nodded firmly. "You're right. I'll take her the first chance I get."

"Just don't let her go with Longstreet," Jenny pleaded. "We don't know anything about him except that he's been in jail."

"He's not a criminal," Lewis said with exasperation. "He just got in a fistfight with the wrong man. There's no crime in that."

But Jenny was adamant. "He may not be a criminal, but I still say he's going to cause trouble."

★   ★   ★   ★

Clint got up from his place at the kitchen table with the other servants and took his plate and tableware to the sink, as he always did. He smiled at Susan Mason. "That was a fine breakfast, Cook."

"You always say something nice, Clint," she replied. "Some people just fill their bellies and act like the food cooked itself."

"Not me. I always want to stay on the good side of the cook." Clint turned and left the kitchen. As soon as he stepped outside he saw Earl holding Mabel's arm. She was trying to pull away, and Earl was laughing at her.

"Come on, sweetheart," he said, "gimme a kiss."

"Turn me loose!"

Earl merely laughed at her struggles and pulled her close, trying to kiss her.

"Let her go, Earl!"

The bulky chauffeur whirled about at the threatening voice but did not release Mabel's arm. He stared at Clint, anger flaring in his eyes. "Butt out of this, jailbird!"

Clint approached until he was only an arm's length away from the big man.

Crane weighed fifty pounds more than Longstreet and had experience as a brawler. "I said clear out!" he growled.

"Earl," Clint remarked in a summer-soft tone, "if you don't turn loose of her arm, I'm going to clean your clock."

Earl Crane was a tough man, but something in Longstreet's expression held him back. Clint stood before him in an almost leisurely fashion. There was no threat, no uplifted fist, but his eyes held Crane's steadily. Earl was confident of his own capability, but he had seen Longstreet's lean strength, and this confrontation with the tall, lanky man gave him pause. Finally he shook his head, released the girl, and turned away.

"Thank you, Clint," Mabel said, her eyes soft. "I wish he'd leave me alone."

Clint smiled briefly. "If he doesn't, I'll have more than a word with him. I'll see you later, Mabel." He made his way to the garage and the big old 1918 model truck he had discovered on his second day at the estate. When he had asked Jamie what it was used for, the old man had said, "It's nothing but a heap of junk the former owner left here. Mr. Lewis intends to get it hauled off."

Clint had begun to spend his free time working on the truck. The body was sound, and after dismantling the engine, he soon discovered it was not past repairing. It would cost a few dollars, but a plan was forming in his mind, and as he worked, he amused himself by fleshing it out. He whistled softly, stopping a moment to stare at the wall of the garage as an old memory came to him. It was simply of a song he had heard a woman singing months ago inside a house he was passing by. He had never seen her, but the song was plaintive, and the voice was beautiful. He had wondered about her many times, who she was and why she sang such a sad song.

A sound caught Clint's ear, and he turned to see Jamie walk

in, holding a letter in his hand and with an odd look on his face. "Hello, Jamie," Clint said, "what's going on?"

The old man came over to where Clint was leaning into the truck engine tightening a bolt. "I just got a letter from my daughter," he said. "The one I told you about that I had the trouble with."

"I remember. How is she?"

"She's very weel. And thanks to you, she wants me to spend the weekend with her."

"What do you mean, thanks to me?"

"Do you remember that conversation we had last week about how I hadn't forgiven her?" Clint nodded. "Well, I finally let go of my pride and wrote her a letter, asking her forgiveness."

"You did? That's wonderful."

Jamie nodded and gnawed his lip thoughtfully. He tried to speak but seemed to be choked up. "I didn't treat my girl right," he whispered, "but I'll make it up to her and her husband."

Clint laid the wrench down and straightened up. He put his hand on the old man's shoulder and squeezed it. He was surprised at how thin and frail the flesh was beneath his touch. Quietly he said, "I know you will, Jamie. And now you'll get to see that grandchild of yours."

★   ★   ★   ★

The next day in the garden, a gust of pleasure touched Clint as he broke up the ground under the rosebushes with a hoe. It was an odd thing to be pleased about. He realized that while he was growing up on the farm he had never enjoyed this sort of thing. Perhaps the hard work he had endured had worn him down, but now the sun shone, and a summery warmth had returned at least for a brief time. He moved steadily down the garden beds, breaking up the earth and pulling out the weeds. When he reached the end of one row, he turned and started back down the next one.

He paused occasionally to lift his head and smell the loamy scent of the earth and the sweet fragrance of the flowers. From the neighboring properties he could hear the barking of dogs, and over the tall garden wall the muted rumble of the city traffic along Fifth Avenue. Looking up toward the sky, he was pleased to see a hawk circling. He loved being outdoors and thought for a moment of the long miserable months he'd spent shoveling coal deep in the steel bowels of the steamship. It had been worse than being a prisoner, and he suddenly felt a wash of gratitude at being set free.

He worked steadily as he methodically cleared and tended the flower beds. It gave him a sense of accomplishment, small though it was, and he was so engrossed in his work he was startled when a voice called his name.

"You—Longstreet!"

Clint turned, holding the hoe in his right hand as he watched Jenny Winslow lead her mare carefully down the garden path up to him and dismount by his side. She held the reins in her left hand and a riding crop in the right. The mare fidgeted behind her and seemed skittish.

Clint removed his straw hat and noticed how she didn't look up at him. *I reckon she'd like to be six feet tall so she wouldn't have to look up to any man,* he thought. "Yes, miss?" he said aloud. "Something you need?"

Jenny had not intended to talk to Longstreet. She was just returning her new mare to the stable after her daily ride in Central Park and had seen the tall man working in the garden. She had remembered what Kat had said about going fishing with him and decided to talk to him. Annoyed that she was forced to look up at him, she said more loudly than necessary, "Kat tells me you offered to take her fishing."

"She asked me to take her fishing."

"Well, you'll do no such thing. I forbid it."

Clint did not answer for a moment. He studied her, how the light ran over the curve of her shoulders and how her riding trousers shaped her into a slim but womanly fashion. Her shirt fell away from her throat, revealing smooth ivory skin, and her red hair gave off rich gleams as the sun touched it.

"I told Kat I couldn't take her anywhere unless her father gave permission."

"Well, he's not going to give permission," Jenny snapped, "and I'd appreciate it if you would not spend so much time with her."

Clint shook his head. "I don't seek her out, Miss Winslow. She just loves working outdoors in the garden."

Jenny didn't want to accept this, even though she knew it was true. "Mind what I say. I want you to stay away from my sister. Don't let me have to speak to you again."

Clint had no time to reply, for she whirled about to remount her horse. He had nothing to say in any case, for he was well aware that Jenny Winslow did not like him. He started to turn back to his work, but then as Jenny lifted her foot to put it in the stirrup, the mare snorted and suddenly wrenched toward her. Clint spotted a long snake on the path that had startled the horse. Clint leaped forward, catching the girl as she was driven backward by the weight of the mare. With one motion he lifted her clear off the ground, putting himself between her and the horse. She screamed at him to put her down, which he did at once, but before he could move out of the way, she had lifted her riding crop and slashed him across the left side of his face. It burned like fire, and he blinked and stepped back, making a grab for the horse's reins. He caught them and then stared at her coldly. Her face was pale as she said, "Don't you ever put your hands on me again!"

"You'd better not take another step backward, Miss Winslow." He pointed and Jenny turned around. She froze when she saw the large black snake coiled on the walkway. Turning blindly, she ran right into her horse. Clint grabbed her arm, seeing that she was mindless with fear.

"See here, it's not a poisonous snake. It can't hurt anything. It probably came out from under a rosebush to sun itself on the warm cobblestones."

Jenny could not catch her breath. She had always been terrified of snakes, and this one was enormous. She leaned against the flank of the mare, which had quieted down, and took a deep breath. She turned to watch the snake as it slid back under the rosebushes. She gave a sigh of relief, then noticed that Longstreet was watching her. Blood trickled down his cheek where her whip had broken the skin, and she felt a keen pang of remorse. She almost apologized but could not find her voice as he picked up the whip she had dropped and handed it to her.

"Here's your whip," he said. "I've got one more cheek left. I think that's what the Bible says, isn't it? Something about turning the other cheek."

His tone caused Jenny to shudder, and without a word, she snatched the whip and, in one fluid motion, mounted her horse. She tapped the mare with the whip and expertly led the animal back down the garden path toward the stable. Clint touched his face as he watched her disappear. He'd had worse injuries, but the cut was bleeding, and he knew it would leave a mark, possibly even a permanent scar.

Slowly he picked up the hoe and, grasping it in both hands, struck a hard blow to the ground in frustration. As he continued down the row, bitterness rose up in him, and he felt a strong surge of dislike for Miss Jennifer Winslow.

★   ★   ★   ★

Jenny went through the rest of her day upset, saying little and keeping to herself. The incident had frightened her. She did not care that the snake was harmless; she was terrified of all snakes. She was also miserable over the way she had struck Longstreet and, no matter how hard she tried, could not put the scene out of her mind. She had a quick temper, and she had honestly thought he was being forward when he grabbed her. She had been wrong, of course, she realized now as she played the incident over and over in her mind. *Why did I do it? I should have known better than to hit him!*

At three that afternoon she went into her father's study, where he was talking with Hannah. The two spent much time together, for Hannah handled the books for the household, a considerable task.

"Dad, Maria Steinmark invited me to spend the weekend with her," Jenny said. "Is that okay?"

Hannah and Lewis both looked up, and Lewis said, "Sure, that's fine, daughter."

Jenny was about to turn and leave when her father said, "I passed by that new man on the way in. He has a bad-looking cut on his face. Do you know what happened?"

Jenny shrugged. "I haven't heard."

No sooner was the lie out of her mouth than she knew she could not hide what she had done. She swallowed hard, then said, "No, Dad, that's not true. It . . . it was my fault."

Lewis looked at her, surprised. "What was your fault?"

"That mark on Longstreet's face. I . . . I hit him with my riding crop." She saw the two staring at her strangely, and being honest at heart, she spilled out the whole story, ending with, "I thought he was grabbing me, that he was being fresh—but he was just trying to keep me from falling on that snake."

"And you hit him with your whip?"

"I did it before I could think."

"Well, perhaps it was understandable if you thought he was forcing himself on you," Lewis said. "But when you learned the truth, I assume you apologized."

Jenny swallowed hard and shook her head. "No, I didn't."

"You didn't! Why not?"

"I don't know. I just couldn't."

"You couldn't apologize!" Lewis rarely got angry with his children, but he was very upset now. "You'll have to apologize to him, Jenny."

"I can't do it. I won't!"

"Why not?" Hannah asked.

"It's a matter of pride."

"A matter of pride!" Lewis lifted his voice. "Well, that's the wrong kind of pride, Jennifer, and if you won't apologize, then I'll do it for you! You're spoiled to the bone, and I'm downright ashamed of you!"

He left the room abruptly, and Jenny looked at Hannah. She had been hurt by her father's words, and she swallowed hard. "I guess you think he's right."

"I think he is this time," Hannah said. "You'll really have to say something to the man. I don't know him, but it sounds like you did him a wrong."

★　★　★　★

Lewis found Clint in the garage working on the ancient truck. When Longstreet saw his employer, he stood up and greeted him. "Hello, Mr. Winslow."

"Hello, Clint." He cleared his throat, ran his hands through his hair, then began, "I've heard about the misunderstanding between you and Jenny." He waited for Longstreet to comment, but when the tall man said nothing, he went on, "I'm sorry for all of it, Clint. She's a spoiled young woman, and I've told her how ashamed I am."

"Don't worry about it." Clint lightly touched the raw wound, then shook his head. "I've gotten hurt worse than this lots of times."

"That doesn't make it right. I don't know what's wrong with Jenny. She's got a good heart, but she's as proud as Lucifer, as much as I hate to say it."

"Don't worry about it, Mr. Winslow. It was a misunderstanding. I've already forgotten it." This was not exactly true, and Clint knew that everyone who saw the wound would ask about it, so it could not be forgotten that easily. But he had something else on his mind. "About this old truck, Mr. Winslow. Jamie tells me you're going to get rid of it for scrap."

"That's right. The motor's no good."

"I wouldn't say that. I'd like to make a deal with you."

"A deal about the truck?"

"I think I could make it run. If I buy the parts and get it going, would you sell it to me?"

"Sell it to you! Why, you can have it. I was just going to have it hauled off to the junkyard. Do you really think you can make it run?" Lewis looked at the parts that were scattered out on a table and shook his head. "I was told it was beyond fixing. It's pretty old."

"It's a good truck," Clint said. "I'll be leaving here someday, Mr. Winslow. I'd like to fix it up and have something to drive."

"Why, of course, Clint. It's all yours."

"Thanks a lot. I appreciate it."

"Try not to be too angry at Jenny," Lewis said, then turned and left the barn.

★　★　★　★

Clint had worked on the truck all evening. Finally, just after ten o'clock, he turned out the lights in the garage, closed the door, and started toward Jamie's cottage. When he was almost to the door, he halted abruptly, for he vaguely saw a shape. The moonlight was bright, but he could not make out who it was walking along the garden walkway. He spoke up. "Who are you?" He heard a woman's stifled gasp, and he said quickly, "Didn't mean to scare you."

"Who are *you*?"

"Clinton Longstreet, the gardener's helper."

The figure came closer, and the moonlight fell on her face. He realized that this was the other Winslow daughter, and she identified herself as such.

"We haven't met. I'm Hannah Winslow."

"Yes, ma'am. It's nice to meet you."

"You're out late tonight. I've been wanting to tell you how much I appreciate what you've done with the garden and grounds. They look so much better in the short time you've been here. You've done a wonderful job, and Jamie can't say enough good things about you."

"Thank you, Miss Winslow."

He was able to see her features dimly in the pale moonlight. The hint of a smile played at the corners of her mouth. The faint smell of lilac came to him, and he was impressed at her serenity. From hearing others talk about her, he had formed in his mind a picture of a skinny woman with sharp features, but as he studied her, he saw a repose in her face that stirred his curiosity. He found himself trying to find a name for it.

The silence ran on, and he thought with pleasure, *She's not afraid to endure a little silence,* and at that moment she spoke.

"Jamie told me how you had helped him over his problem with his daughter. I think that's so wonderful. I've been trying to get him to forgive her for a long time." She smiled then, and it changed her whole face, making her look much younger. "Yet you did it in just a few days."

Clint shook his head modestly. "I think he wanted to do it all the time. He just needed a little push. I'm glad for him."

She hesitated and then said, "If you'd like to come to church with us, it's not far from here. We'd love to have you come."

"Well, I don't have any churchgoing clothes." He expected her to argue and to say the usual thing—that clothes aren't the most important thing in a church—but she studied him in a curious fashion and did not argue. Finally she said, "Good night, Clint."

"Good night, Miss Winslow." As she moved back toward the

house, he thought of all the things he'd heard about her. She seemed completely normal to him, but others had told him she was a hermit, afraid of people. Even Kat had said so. She disappeared into the house, and he filed the meeting in his mind, knowing he would ponder it later.

I don't

CHAPTER FOUR

New Face in Church

★ ★ ★ ★

Hannah was sitting in her room reading, so totally engrossed in her book that she started at a loud knock on her door. She leaped up, still carrying the book, and threw open the door to see her father standing there, obviously agitated. "What is it, Father? You look terrible."

"It's Josh," Lewis said with his lips drawn into a white line. Stress marked his pale face, and Hannah, concerned, took his arm.

"What is it?" she asked. "Has he been hurt?"

"I don't know . . . I don't think so."

"But what happened?"

"I just got a call from the police station. He's under arrest."

Hannah's eyes opened wide, and she took a sharp breath. "Under arrest for what?"

"He was involved in an accident. I couldn't get many of the particulars. He was allowed only one call, so he called me."

"But what did he say?"

"He just said that there'd been an accident and that he'd been arrested for reckless endangerment and driving while intoxicated." Lewis's face twisted with disgust. "I've got to get a lawyer down there. We'll have to make bail—at least I hope they'll let him out."

Hannah was so distressed she could not speak for a moment,

and then she put her hand on her father's arm. "I know this is hard for you."

Lewis had been disturbed about Hannah's behavior for years. Her refusal to go out into society had grieved him deeply. He had always looked forward to her marrying and having children and a happy home, but none of that had come to pass. Who would want a wife that refused to leave the house except to go to church? He had tried to talk to her, to get her to see doctors, but nothing seemed to work.

Yet in times of stress Lewis always came to Hannah to seek solace. Before his wife, Deborah, had died, the two of them had each other, but when she was taken away, he had no one. His fiancée, Lucy, was not much comfort to him. She would just tell him to stop being so negative and look on the bright side. He couldn't talk to Josh about problems, of course. Josh was too deeply mired in his own egotism and was not sober half the time. Jenny was still a hope in his life, but she was young and immature and couldn't be of much help when problems such as this one arose.

But Hannah had something of her mother in her. Despite her eccentricities, she had a quiet, mild spirit that made her a good listener. She had a way of listening intently as Lewis talked his problems out. Most of the time she did not have a solution, but her presence and quiet spirit were a help to him. Now he looked at her with pain etched in his eyes. "What's the matter with us, Hannah? The whole family is out of step! Josh could have been an archeologist by now and had a fine future, but he just quit. And Jenny is so selfish she'll never be able to help anyone, not even herself, unless she changes. And—"

When her father broke off, Hannah nodded. "And there's your oldest daughter, who's nothing but a hermit, afraid to get out of the house."

"I wasn't going to say that, Hannah. You know how I've worried about you for years. I wish you'd talk to me about it—whatever it is that frightens you."

Once or twice, Lewis remembered, Hannah had almost unburdened herself. He remembered clearly those times when he had hoped she would at least try to tell him what was troubling her so deeply. Now he saw it in her again, and he waited expectantly. Her lips parted, and her gaze had something in it he could not quite identify. Perhaps it was fear. He knew she was afraid of something, although she never spoke of it. She did have terrible nightmares at times. She had not had them as a child, but they began shortly after she broke off her engagement to Preston. He and Deborah had expected they would pass away, and for a time, it seemed, they had, but now there were times when she still had them. She would sometimes come to the breakfast table pale with fatigue. Lewis waited for her to speak, and she finally gave a short gasp and said, "I . . . I don't know what's wrong with me, Father. I just don't know."

Lewis, as disturbed as he was about Joshua, felt a keen pang of disappointment. "I wish you could talk to somebody, Hannah. Whatever it is that's troubling you, it needs to come out." He took her hands and looked down at them. "I don't know what's going to happen to our family." Pain crossed his face again, and he said, almost as if to himself, "We've left God out somewhere along the line, and He's going to demand an accounting."

He turned and left the room, and as soon as he did so, Hannah whirled and crossed the room, falling upon her bed. Sobs welled up in her throat, and she wept, "I want to tell somebody! I do, but it just won't come out!"

★　★　★　★

"You're gonna get your nose pinched off if you don't move back, Kat." Clint pulled on Kat's pigtails until her head arched backward. He had been putting the finishing touches on the truck, and she stayed right in his way constantly. Rather than be annoyed, however, he had developed a real affection for the girl.

Kat straightened up and said, "Joshua got drunk and was in a wreck. A man and a woman got hurt, and Daddy had to pay a lot of money to make it right."

Clint, of course, knew this already, but he shook his head and said, "You shouldn't tell family things to strangers, Kat."

"You're not a stranger."

"Well, I mean, to people who aren't members of the family."

"You're not going to tell anybody."

"How do you know that?"

"I just do." She was wearing a dress for a change instead of the grubby overalls she loved so dearly, and a smudge of grease had found its way onto the front of it. She watched him work for a few moments and then said, "Clint, do you hate Jenny?"

Surprised, Clint turned around and saw the girl's big eyes intent upon him. "Why would you ask a thing like that?"

"Because she was mean to you." She reached up and touched his cheek. "She hit you with a whip."

"It was just a misunderstanding."

"But do you hate her?"

"Well"—Clint managed to smile—"I don't like her as much as I like you."

"I'm glad! You know she had a big fuss with Hannah about you. Hannah said she was awful and that she should ask your pardon, and Jenny said she never would."

Clint found no answer for that but straightened up and wiped his hands on a rag. "Stand back. We're gonna put this hood down, and then we'll start this crate up—if it *will* start, that is."

"Clint, I'm sorry for what she did, even if she isn't."

"Okay, that's fine then. As long as you and I are pals, it doesn't matter what Jenny does. Now, let's see if this piece of junk will run."

Kat climbed up into the front seat of the truck. Clint set the spark, went to the front, and gave the crank several turns. Finally the engine coughed and broke into a roar. Swiftly Clint raced around and threw himself into the seat and adjusted the controls. "Well, the engine runs. You want to give it a trial?"

"Yeah, let's go!" Kat cried.

"All right, hang on." He cautiously put the truck in gear and pressed the accelerator. It crept out of the garage, and he let it roll to a stop. "Well, how's that?"

"Oh, Clint, let's go fast!"

Clint was pleased with the sound of the engine. He got out and said, "We'll go in just a minute. I want to check something."

Kat got out on the other side and joined him as he looked under the hood, explaining what he was doing.

"Come on, Clint, let's ride!" she cried impatiently.

Clint laughed. "All right, get in." He closed the hood and got back in behind the wheel. "Here we go," he said. He carefully stepped on the gas and eased the ancient truck down the drive and out into the city traffic.

"Go faster, Clint!" Kat yelled.

From her window Hannah Winslow was looking down on the pair. She was somewhat envious of the attachment that Kat had formed with the new gardener, but she had smiled when she saw the two working on the truck. Now as she watched the truck disappear into the New York traffic, a longing tugged at her heart. *I'm glad at least she has a good friend.* She could not admit even to herself that she too longed for a friend.

★ ★ ★ ★

"What's the matter with you, Lewis? You look absolutely glum."

Lewis was pushing his salad around with a fork. He had eaten very little. He had brought Lucy to a restaurant but only after they had done a great deal of shopping. Their wedding date was only a month away, and Lucy was busy looking at furniture and décor for the house she intended to change.

"I guess I'm just bothered about Josh, Lucy."

"Oh, I know it's bothering you, dear, but you mustn't let it. It's going to work itself out. Was it very expensive paying off that couple who got hurt in the wreck?"

"Yes, it was. I didn't want it to go to court, so we let the lawyers settle it."

"But at least Joshua didn't have to go to jail."

"No, that was part of the deal. They dropped the charges, and the police let him go. But it'll happen again. He's drinking almost all the time now. I tell you, Lucy, you're marrying into a family that's got more problems than any family needs."

"Now, Lewis, we've talked about this so often. Jenny's just spirited, and Joshua is going through a bad time. But Hannah's going to come out of whatever it is that's bothering her, and Kat's having some growing pains. The first thing I'm going to do is burn those awful overalls of hers! She'll learn to behave like a lady if she dresses like one."

"I think it goes a little deeper than that, Lucy."

Lucy, however, waved this aside. "I've been thinking about

Hannah a lot. I think she's just gone overboard on religion, but after we're married I'll help her to get her life back on track."

Lewis had heard this often, but he never, for one moment, believed that it would be that easy. Looking back, he could not remember exactly what had caused him to propose to Lucy. She was from a wealthy family, of course, but that didn't matter to him. He concluded that it must have been that he needed someone to talk to more than anything else, and Lucy had at first been eager to listen to him. But as time went on she had gradually become the one to dominate their conversations. Now as he contemplated their future together, a dark depression settled on him, and he found he could not get into the spirit of Lucy's shopping and wedding plans.

★　★　★　★

October was coming to a close, and Clint had spent a great deal of time working on the truck. He had spent most of his wages on parts, but he wanted it in near perfect condition. He had bought four new tires and was just putting on the last one when Hannah came into the garage. It was Saturday morning, and he was surprised to see her. He got up at once and said, "Good morning, Miss Hannah."

"Good morning, Clint." She looked at the truck and smiled. "You've spent a lot of time on this truck."

"I've always liked to work on machinery."

"Maybe you should be a mechanic."

"No, I don't like to be inside too long."

"You grew up on a farm, didn't you?" She had learned this much from him. "Do you miss the life?"

"Not the way it was." He picked up a rag and wiped his hands. "I can remember so many years of getting up before daylight with nothing but a piece of cold corn bread for breakfast. We'd go out and put in a sixteen-hour day of hard work and come home to not a lot to eat, then do the same thing the next day."

"It must have been a very hard life."

Clint shrugged his shoulders and shook his head as if to drive the memories away. "Well, that's over now. I don't care if I never see a plow again."

"Clint, I came to ask you something, but I don't want to be impertinent."

"You couldn't be impertinent if you tried, Miss Hannah."

"Yes, I'm afraid I could, and you'll probably think so too."

"Well, what is it? Just come right out with it. Set it right on the front porch."

"I've been wondering, Clint, if—" she hesitated and then blurted out—"if you're a Christian."

Clint was not offended. "No, ma'am, I'm not. My father was. He took me to church until I was grown, and then I went a lot just to please him, but . . ." Something crossed his face, sorrow perhaps, and Hannah did not miss it. "Of course, I haven't been back since the day he died."

"Do you believe in God?"

The question was put softly, and Clint nodded. "Sure I do. I'm the one that's out of step, not God."

"Then I've come to ask you a favor. Would you go to church with us in the morning?"

"I don't have any clothes. I've told you that."

Hannah reached into her pocket and came out with some bills folded together. She laughed, which surprised him. "I knew you'd say that. That's what you said the last time. God's not interested in your clothes, but others might be. Would you go with us if you had some clothes?"

Clint looked at the money and for some reason was amused. "You're offering to buy me clothes so I'll go to church with you?"

"Yes."

"Why, I can't take your money for nothing."

"Clint, please do this thing for me. Money doesn't mean anything to me. Father's always urging me to spend more, but there's nothing I really want. I spend a little money on clothes once in a while, but I give most of the rest of it to the church. So I'm not giving you something that means anything to me really, but it would mean something if you would go to church."

"What'll your family say?"

"They can say anything they please. Kat would like it, and I would like it."

Amused by the little drama that had unfolded before him,

Clint smiled. His teeth were very white against his tanned skin, and he reached out and took the money. "All right, I'll do it. Makes me feel odd taking money from you, though."

"Money is the cheapest thing in the world. The streets of heaven are paved with gold." She was happy, Clint saw, and he was glad to find some way to bring a little lightness into her life. The few times he had seen her, she had seemed to be under a tremendous weight, but now he saw a lightness and a sweetness about her he had not seen before.

"You go to Johnson and Taylor's Men's Store on Fifth Avenue and Fifty-seventh. I've written a note here. They'll fix you up fine and give you a discount. Ask for Mr. Johnson. He goes to our church."

"I'll do that. I hope the ceiling doesn't fall in when I go to church. It's been a long time."

"It won't." Hannah suddenly dropped her head. "I know this may be wrong of me, but it's something I want to do." She turned then and left, and as soon as she was out of sight, Clint stuffed the money into his shirt pocket. He finished putting on the tire, then stood and wiped his hands off. "Well, I wish everybody could be made happy as easily as Miss Hannah Winslow." He shook his head, somewhat surprised at his own willingness to please her, then headed toward the house.

★ ★ ★ ★

Hannah waited until Sunday morning breakfast was over before mentioning her secret. She was apprehensive, but taking a deep breath, she announced, "I asked Clint to go to church with us."

Her family's reaction was approximately what Hannah had expected. Josh had given up on church but gave her a look of startled disbelief. Jenny choked back a remark, but from her expression it was obvious she was displeased. Kat, of course, exclaimed, "Goody! I get to sit by him, don't I, Hannah?"

Lewis had been surprised but not overly so. Hannah believed in sharing her faith with those few she came in contact with. "That's fine, Hannah."

"He'll be conspicuous in his working clothes," Jenny said stiffly.

"Oh, he'll have some new clothes," Hannah said. Now that the worst was over, she felt happy. "I expect we'd better hurry. We're a little late."

The family put on their coats, for it was snappy outside. October was drawing to a close, and the wind was chilly.

The big Packard was outside the front door, with Earl Crane waiting in it, wearing his uniform. As they approached, he got out and held the door for Lewis. "Good morning, Mr. Winslow."

"Good morning, Earl. There'll be one more with us this morning."

"Yes, sir, who's that?"

Lewis could not help smiling, as he knew something of the antagonism that Crane had for Longstreet. "Clint will be going with us." It delighted him to see the big man's face register his shock.

"There he is!" Kat yelled. She ran to meet Clint, who was coming from the direction of MacDougal's cottage. She ran right up to him before stopping. "You've got all new clothes on, Clint."

"How do I look?"

"You look great!" She grabbed his arm and urged him forward. "Look at Clint! He's all dressed up in new clothes!"

He was wearing a smart double-breasted, reefer-type jacket, which fitted his lean, strong body like a glove. It was a light blue, and the trousers were a darker blue. A handkerchief showed at his breast pocket, and he wore two-toned shoes of black and white. A crimson necktie was knotted at his throat, and he had also gotten a haircut, Hannah noted. The left side of his face still bore the mark of the whip, but he was close shaven and looked handsome indeed.

"Well, we're glad to have you, Clint," Lewis said. He did not mention the new clothes, but he thought, *They say clothes make the man, and I guess they're right*. "I guess we'd better go," he said aloud. "Suppose you and I sit up front with Earl, and you ladies crowd in the back. It'll be a little tight."

On the way Kat carried on a conversation with Clint as if no one else were there. When they arrived at church, Earl stopped the car at the front door to let them all out, and Lewis waited for everyone to emerge.

"Come along, Clint," Lewis said, "we'll get some good seats."

"I get to sit beside Clint," Kat announced. She grabbed for his hand and held it as they went inside.

Bethany Church was a beautiful building. Its high-arched ceiling was alabaster white, and the graceful stained-glass windows were ablaze with the morning light. Clint had never seen a church like it. He was glad to have Kat by his side, for she kept a tight hold on his hand. When they finally chose a pew, he found Hannah on his left and Kat on his right. Hannah had to lean over and tell Kat to be quiet twice, but Clint said nothing. He was aware of Jenny's displeasure, but he had expected no less.

The service was a revelation to him. He knew a few of the songs and joined in, which brought a warm glance from Hannah, who whispered, "You remember them."

"I heard that one every Sunday until I was eighteen years old," he whispered back.

The pastor, a small man with curly brown hair and a pair of smart gray eyes, preached a sermon on following Christ. Clint heard little of it. It was all too strange to him. All he was concerned about was pleasing Hannah, and he knew that he had done that.

After the service was over, they filed out but were stopped when Lucy Daimen and her father, Leo, intercepted them.

"We saw you come in, but we couldn't get to you in time." She turned and looked expectantly at Clint, waiting for an introduction.

There was an awkward silence, and then Lewis said quickly, "Clint, may I introduce my fiancée, Miss Lucy Daimen, and her father, Mr. Daimen. May I introduce Clint Longstreet."

Clint shook hands with Mr. Daimen while they exchanged hellos. The two were intensely curious but did not ask any questions. As they filed out of the church, however, Lucy held Lewis back so that she could whisper without being overheard. "What a fine-looking man. Is he one of Jenny's young men? I've never met him."

"No, he's not."

"What does he do?"

Lewis could not find any answer to give except the truth.

"He's our gardener," he remarked and then waited for the shock to register.

As he expected, Lucy gasped and said faintly, "Your . . . your gardener?"

"Yes—a good one too. And as you say, he is a fine-looking man, isn't he?" He knew he would hear more about this later, but for some reason her obvious displeasure pleased him. He left feeling much better and wondering whether he ought to inform Leo Daimen that he had gone to church with their gardener.

The trip home was, once again, mostly punctuated by Kat's remarks, but when they got out of the car and Clint started to walk away, Hannah followed him and called his name. He paused and she said quietly, "Thank you for coming with us, Clint. I know it may have been a little uncomfortable."

"I was glad to do it, Miss Hannah." He looked into her eyes and said, "I'll go again if you ask me."

"Oh yes, please do!" She turned and left, and Clint watched her, thinking, *She's sure an easy woman to please.*

CHAPTER FIVE

OCTOBER 24, 1929—
BLACK THURSDAY

★ ★ ★ ★

Clint stood in the shaft of pale sunlight that rose in the east and found its way to the Winslow garden through the tall city buildings. For the space of half an hour the garden stood bathed in the morning freshness, and he loved its coolness and the peaceful quiet of the autumn morning. Over the wall to the west he could see the sunlight filtering through the trees along Fifth Avenue and those of Central Park, their fall colors intense in the light. It was a clear and brilliant time that soon passed away and brought with it the activities of the day.

His thoughts went back to the many fall seasons he had endured on the small mountain farm in Tennessee. The land had been half dirt and half rocks, and the struggle to wring a living from it had made women and men prematurely old, disillusioning their bright childhood hopes. Still, he remembered the pleasant things—the vegetables layered between straw and earth and the garden corner, the corn dried and milled, the flour sacked in the pantry, the apples packed away in the barn. And always during harvest season there had been something that had been fulfilling and satisfying, a fatness and a comfort that gave the illusion of security. Now he remembered the smells of the earth that he enjoyed with the keen pleasure of a man whose feet had to know the touch of earth—the odor of the dead grasses from the past year, the acrid sharp smell of burning leaves, the smell of freshly turned loamy dirt.

He lifted his head to see an arrow-shaped flock of geese and wondered for the thousandth time how they knew when to leave their summer home and how they knew where they were going and what power it was that put this instinct in them. He envied their clear purpose in life as they pierced the blue morning skies, flying so definitely toward a goal. He wondered who decided which one would be at the point of the arrowhead and which ones would fall back into lesser positions.

The peacefulness of the morning was an illusion. He knew life was not like that but could be caught only in fleeting fragments, and he remembered a woman who had once told him, *"You have to kiss joy as it flies."* He had pondered that for years. She had also told him, *"You're so innocent, Clint. You're like a wild beast prowling around, and you know there are a lot of beasts out there, but you think nobody's ever going to get killed in the fight. I guess you think everybody's a gentleman."*

Her name was Drucilla, and he had thought for a time that perhaps she would be a permanent part of his life. But she had gone, faded away, and now he had only a memory of her. *One day she'll be old with silver hair,* he thought, *perhaps without any teeth, but I'll still think of her as a young girl—starry-eyed and anxious for love.*

Taking the spade, he turned over another shovelful of earth where he was planning a new flower bed and savored the odor of it. He moved steadily, enjoying the work. He was glad that there were rare times like this when the purposes of living were clear and uncomplicated and sweet. He thought suddenly of Kat. "She's like that," he murmured. "I wish she could always stay the way she is now." He knew she could not, but he still longed for it. He hated to think that she would change and become less than she was now in the dewy time of life between childhood and womanhood.

He straightened up when he heard someone approaching. He turned to see Jenny Winslow, dressed in a gold wool dress under a snow-white coat that came down to her fingertips. Her red hair caught the rays of the sun. He saw that her face was drawn into a tense expression. Her lips were tight and her eyes half shut as if she were about to leap off of a high place into the unknown. He did not speak, but as she drew up in front of him, he nodded and removed his hat.

"I've been wanting to talk to you," she said breathlessly. The bony structures of her face made definite and pleasing contours. Her eyes glanced at what was left of the wound on his face, and she swallowed hard, then threw back her head. "I was wrong to hit you, and I . . . I apologize."

Clint was touched with the difficulty she had getting the words out. He had disliked her intensely, but he knew what it had cost her to finally make this apology. He smiled slightly and shrugged his shoulders. "Not necessary."

"Maybe not for you . . . but it is for me. I . . . I hate to be wrong, and I hate to apologize." She started to turn as if to move away but then wheeled to face him again. "It's taken me all this time to work up to this."

Clint's voice was soft. "I guess everybody hates to say they're wrong."

"Kat doesn't."

"No, I suppose not."

"Hannah doesn't either. I'm the black sheep in this family." Suddenly she put her hand out, and he took it, feeling its warmth and strength. He returned the pressure of her hand, and suddenly she blurted out, "I'm sorry." She turned and ran back toward the house.

"That was pretty hard for her to do," Clint murmured. "I don't think she's had much practice at such things."

He continued to work for another thirty minutes before Jamie came to tell him it was time for breakfast.

"Sounds good," Clint said, laying down his spade.

The two men started toward the house. The old man had been more talkative since he had made his peace with his daughter. As they rounded the house heading toward the back door, they saw Mabel Bateman, the young maid, struggling to get away from Earl. Clint's anger flared, and he rushed to them, grabbed Earl by the arm, and forcibly wheeled him around. Without pause he smashed the big man in the face, throwing his weight into the blow.

Jamie was shocked at the sight of Earl flying through the air and landing on his back. Blood spurted out of his nose and down his chin, and as he struggled to get up, it dripped onto his white shirt. His eyes were glazed, and he put his hands up in a defensive gesture and began to mumble, "What are you—"

"Shut your mouth, Crane! You say one more word, and I'll put you in the hospital!"

Silence fell across the small group. Mabel's eyes were wide with shock, Jamie saw, and he himself felt a brassy taste in his mouth.

Earl Crane was a tough man, but it looked like the blow had broken his nose. He glared at Clint Longstreet and then whirled away without another word.

Clint turned to Mabel and said, "He won't bother you anymore, Mabel."

The maid backed away at the look in Longstreet's eyes and swallowed hard. "Thank you, Clint."

Clint turned to the gardener and said, "Let's eat, Jamie."

Jamie saw that the mood had passed. It had been like a mindless flash of lightning striking Earl Crane down with force and violence. He nodded and said in a subdued voice, "All right, Clint."

Clint seemed perfectly normal during breakfast, even joking with Cook, but Jamie had been shocked by what he had seen. He left before the others were finished and started back to his cottage, encountering Hannah on his way out. He did not know the woman well, but she stopped him to ask about planting some bulbs for the spring. As he struggled to answer her, she said, "Is something wrong, Jamie? You look disturbed."

Jamie hesitated, then told her what had happened. She listened carefully, and he finished by saying, "The violence just seemed to leap out. I never would have guessed it was in him."

Hannah studied the face of the gardener, then said, "I think we'll have to let Earl go. He's been causing such trouble with the maids."

"It might be best, Miss Hannah."

"I'll discuss the situation with Father. He may need to reprimand Clint as well."

Hannah turned away and tried to picture the scene in her mind. She had received complaints about Earl before, but she had not seen this side of Clint Longstreet, and it troubled her.

★ ★ ★ ★

Hannah had been listening to the New York Philharmonic on the radio, but at two o'clock a program of popular music came on. She was writing a letter and listening only halfheartedly as they played the new record "Happy Days Are Here Again" and then "Wedding Bells Are Breaking Up That Old Gang of Mine." She listened as a singer named Hoagy Carmichael, who couldn't sing very well, introduced one of his songs called "Stardust," which she didn't care for.

"They ought to slow that down," she said, getting up and turning the radio dial to a newscast.

The announcer seemed disturbed as he said, ". . . and although stock prices opened steady, the unexplainable has happened. Everyone seems to be selling, and prices are plummeting. United States Steel opened at $205 but dropped to $200 and is now at $193. Other stocks are plummeting faster than anyone has ever seen in the history of the stock market. A spirit of fear appears to be ruling the day, and no one is buying. Everyone is trying to sell. Exactly where this will stop no one knows, but one thing is certain. We are witnessing an event in America that has never happened before. The big bull market, for all intents and purposes, is over." The announcer hesitated and then said, "If you have stocks, you'd better sell them, folks, while they're still worth something."

Hannah turned off the radio with a frown on her face and went downstairs. She was aware of her father's recent anxiety over the stock market. For months now he had been troubled. Just two days ago he had said, "Hannah, America's been on a wild spending spree, and they're buying almost everything— including pianos, records, and radios—on the credit installment, and people are doing the same thing with stocks—margin buying. That simply means they're buying shares on credit. It wouldn't take much to tip the whole structure over."

Hannah found Joshua in the kitchen fixing a sandwich. He had come home sometime after three, obviously inebriated, and now there were deep circles under his eyes. She did not rebuke him, for that did no good, but she asked, "Have you heard the news on the radio?"

"No, what is it?"

"Something's happened to the stock market. All the stocks are going down. I'm worried about it."

Joshua took a bite of the sandwich and shook his head. "It's gone down before. Dad will know what to do."

★ ★ ★ ★

Hannah had stayed close to the radio all day. She cared as little about money as Kat did, but she knew that her father would be worried.

At suppertime all the children sat down for the evening meal.

"Where's Dad?" Kat piped up.

"There's a problem at the office," Hannah said quietly.

Jenny looked up. "What kind of problem?"

"Haven't you been listening to the radio?" Hannah asked.

"No, what is it?"

"The stock market has gone crazy. The bottom is dropping out of it."

Jenny knew nothing about the stock market and shrugged her shoulders. "I hate for Daddy to work this hard. He's got enough to do thinking about making wedding plans."

"I think this is more serious than usual," Hannah said anxiously.

Josh stubbornly shook his head. "That stock market goes up and down all the time. It'll come back."

They had almost finished their meal when they heard the front door close.

"There's Dad now," Jenny said.

They all turned to look at the door, and as soon as Lewis entered, they could see that he was shaken. He stood behind his chair, his hands resting on the back, pale and holding himself up with great effort.

"Is it bad?" Hannah said. "I've been listening to the news on the radio."

"Yes, it's bad," Lewis said, his face stiff and his voice hoarse.

"What's bad?" Kat piped up.

Josh studied his father's face and asked, "What's happening, Dad?"

"I think the crazy way this country's been living lately has caught up with us, son. Everybody's buying everything on credit and it has turned the economy upside down."

"But it'll be all right, won't it, Dad?" Jenny asked, looking to her father for reassurance. It frightened her to see him so troubled. He could barely keep his hands from trembling as he clung to the back of the chair.

Lewis dropped his head for a moment, then looked up and said, "You'll have to know about this. It's worse than anything I could imagine." He struggled to get the words out, and he looked at each one of them, misery written on his face. "You'll find out sooner or later, but the truth is—I've lost everything!"

The children all stared at him, shocked into silence. Josh was the first to speak. "Well, I know it's bad, but surely there must be something left."

"No. I've been as big a fool as the other fools out there. This white elephant of a house—I had to borrow up to the hilt to get into it, and we spent a fortune on it. All that we had was in stocks, and now they're not worth the paper they're written on."

"But they'll go up again . . . won't they?" Jenny asked nervously. The thought of a moneyless future terrified her. It was something she had never considered, and now her voice was unsteady. "Surely they'll come up."

"I don't think so." Lewis's voice sounded hopeless. "I blame myself for all this. We'll lose this house and everything else."

Kat had been listening but only understood a little of the conversation. "You mean we're going to be poor, Daddy?"

Lewis Winslow looked at his youngest daughter. He swallowed hard, then cleared his throat. Finally he nodded and whispered, "That's the way it's going to be, Kat. We're going to be poor!"

★　★　★　★

Things were strangely quiet around the Winslow house after the bleak day that was already being called Black Thursday. It was not just a local phenomenon. The whole country had been shaken to its core. The big money men rallied to try to do something, but nothing worked permanently. From time to time there would be a slight rise in the market, but then that would be wiped out the next day.

Each of the Winslows took this in his or her own way. Josh faced the problem by drinking. Jenny went out and bought new clothes. Kat spent her days as she always had, and Hannah grieved for her father. She knew he blamed himself for losing everything and tried to comfort him. She herself had difficulty coming to grips with the loss of money and property and spent a great deal of time in her room praying, mostly for her father.

The servants, of course, were all shaken too, and they spent a lot of time discussing their future. Gerald Mason, the butler, summed it all up when he said bitterly, "We might as well get used to the idea of leaving this place."

Lewis was gone all day every day. Hannah understood that he was trying desperately to salvage something, but she saw him come in night after night pale and speechless. The news reports spoke of Black Monday, and then Black Tuesday—October 29—when the bottom fell out of the market completely.

It was on November second that the final blow fell to the Winslow family. Lewis came in earlier than usual and called them all into the drawing room. When they were there, he paused and looked around at the expensive pictures, the ornate and lavishly decorated room. An expression of panic and fear crossed his face. "I've got to tell you the worst," he said. "We're going to have to leave this house."

"But where will we go?" Jenny said in bewilderment.

"I . . . I don't know."

Joshua's eyes were bloodshot, his speech slurred. "There's got to be *something* left, Dad. It can't *all* be gone."

"I'm afraid it is, Josh. I've been a fool. We've lived on credit, and now everything's gone." He swept his arm around and cried desperately, "Even the furniture and the pictures—they were all bought on credit. We'll have nothing left but the clothes on our backs."

Jenny shivered in horror. "But, Dad," she cried out, "we've got to do something. Lucy's father will help."

Lewis looked at her with an expression Jenny would never forget. "No, he won't. I got a letter today from Lucy." He tried to go on but could not.

"What did she say?" Hannah asked quietly.

"She ... she said good-bye. What she didn't say was her father would never let her marry a pauper."

Suddenly Lewis began to cry. None of his children had ever seen him weep. "It's all my fault," he choked. "I've ruined us all."

Kat jumped and ran to her father, throwing her arms around him and declaring defiantly, "God will take care of us. He'll send an angel. He's got lots of them!"

CHAPTER SIX

GOD PROVIDES AN ANGEL

★　★　★　★

For a moment Hannah paused outside her father's bedroom. She lifted her hand to knock, then pulled it back. Her pliant features suddenly grew sober and dark from the things she was remembering. Finally she squared her shoulders, raised her hand again, and knocked firmly on the door. No sound rewarded this, and after a moment she knocked again louder and called out, "Father—I have to see you."

From inside the room came a muffled noise she could not make out, but she waited and finally the door swung open. Her father stood there, his clothes rumpled as if he had slept in them. Shadows darkened his eyes, and his face was branded with loneliness. His eyes especially frightened Hannah, for they were like empty windows staring out at nothing.

"Father, the servants are leaving."

"I can't come down, Hannah."

"You really must. They need to be thanked, and they have to be paid."

Lewis shook his head and did not answer. Then, as if gathering courage, he took a deep, raspy breath and said huskily, "There's no money, Hannah—and I can't face them."

"I have the money to pay them. I kept a little saved, but please come and say just a few words."

For a moment Hannah thought he intended to refuse, but then he nodded.

"Let me change clothes, and I'll be right there."

"I'll wait outside."

Hannah stepped out and leaned back against the wall. She was very tired, and the problems of the week had quickened her breath and tightened her mouth. Her father had been so drained by the disaster that he could barely speak, and he was not eating properly. She tried to encourage him, but there was little she could do. Josh had been worse than useless, keeping himself in a state of perpetual drunkenness. Jenny was not much better. She was badly frightened, and her self-confidence had withered away to nothing. Now with her father almost unable to function, she clung to Hannah for strength.

As for Hannah, she had forced herself to be strong as the rest of the family declined. She had quickly discovered that Lewis's worst fears were accurate. The house, of course, would have to go. Bankruptcy proceedings had already been started, and all of the assets had been frozen. This even included most of the jewelry, all that had been bought in the past two years. Hannah had little of that, since she did not wear much jewelry. She only had a pearl necklace that had been her mother's. The bulk of the jewelry had belonged to Jenny, and she had wept when Hannah had insisted on confiscating it all.

As she stood in the hallway waiting, Hannah felt desperation creeping up on her. She had prayed almost night and day and struggled with the bills, but there was no relief in sight. She tried to put this out of her mind for now and think more hopeful thoughts, when finally the door opened and her father stepped out. He had combed his hair and put on a fresh suit of clothes. "All right," he said in a dull voice, "might as well get this over with."

The two went downstairs to the kitchen, where most of the servants were gathered. Earl Crane was already gone, having been dismissed earlier. Clint had offered to stay and work for the family at no charge in gratitude for taking him in when he needed help. He'd said he would help with packing or with any other jobs that needed to be done with the other servants gone.

Lewis looked around at the waiting servants, seeing the fear in their eyes, and took a deep breath before launching into his speech. "I suppose this comes as no surprise to any of you. You know what's happened to the stock market, and we've been hit hard by it. I've written good references for all of you; you'll find them in the envelope with your final payment. I've written to several family friends who I hope have weathered this situation and asked if they would consider hiring you. I wish I could afford to give you all bonuses, but I can't. Hannah will see that you're all paid up to today. Thank you all for being so faithful, and God bless all of you. I trust that you will find other employment soon."

Lewis shook hands with each of them and then practically fled. He could not bear to linger with these people who had depended on him. *Another failure,* was his only thought as he retreated to his private quarters.

Hannah had taken from her store of emergency cash the wages of each servant and put them in envelopes. She passed them out and received their thanks, and finally, they all turned to leave—all except Gerald and Susan Mason.

"What's the family going to do, Miss Hannah?" Cook asked gently.

"We'll make out somehow. God will provide for us."

"We wish you well, Miss Hannah," Gerald said, bowing in his well-trained butler manner as he took her hands. "Good-bye."

"Good-bye, Mason. Good-bye, Cook." Hannah watched them go, then turned around, listening to the eerie quiet of the empty house. She shook off the feeling of doom that threatened to envelop her and busied herself as quickly as possible.

★   ★   ★   ★

Lewis sat in his study staring at the wall. The desk was littered with papers and bills. He and Hannah had shuffled them about, trying to juggle the figures, but it was hopeless. He looked up when Jenny entered and handed him an envelope. "We got a letter from Uncle Aaron, Dad."

Lewis opened it, read it quickly, and said, "He's invited us to come live with them."

Jenny's eyes lit up with a ray of hope. "Could we do it, do you think?"

"No, they're hard hit too, and there are too many of us."

He handed his brother's letter to Hannah, who read it and said gently, "That was kind of Uncle Aaron, but of course we can't do it."

"No, it's quite impossible."

"But what are we going to do?" Jenny said, her voice unsteady. "We've got to do something, Dad. We've got to be out of here next week."

"I don't know. I just don't know." Lewis stared at the papers on the desk and then looked up. "Where's Joshua?"

"He's drunk—as usual," Jenny said bitterly, flopping down in a leather armchair and laying her head back in defeat.

"God is going to have to help us with this," Hannah said calmly.

Lewis struck the desk angrily, causing papers to slide off on both sides. "I've ignored God for years! Why should He help us now?"

Hannah stood her ground and faced her father squarely. "The Scripture says, 'If thou, Lord, shouldest mark iniquities, O Lord, who shall stand?' The Lord is going to do something. I just know it. In the meantime we'll just have to wait."

★   ★   ★   ★

Unable to sleep, Hannah put on her heavy coat and went outside to the dark garden, where a cold wind roughed up the leaves that had drifted down from the oaks. A thin moon lay low to the south, and from one of their neighbors' homes she heard a dog howling plaintively.

As she walked back and forth on the cobblestone walk that bordered the rose garden, she prayed, trying to comprehend what was happening. As was her custom, she prayed aloud, though softly. She had discovered long ago that if she voiced her prayers, she seemed to find the presence of God much more quickly. "Oh, God, I've read so much about how you delivered your people time and again, but now I need more than a story—I need *you*! What are we going to do? We have no money and no one to take us in. I feel so alone, but I know that you haven't forgotten us. I know you are watching us."

As she prayed, verses of Scripture leaped into her mind. She took this as a message from God to her heart. One Scripture came from the book of Genesis. She recalled the story of how Abraham had a child by a servant maid named Hagar. Sarah, Abraham's wife, could not bear this and forced Abraham to turn the young woman out. Taking her child with her, Hagar wandered in the desert, hungry and thirsty, and finally sat down, prepared to die. But then God appeared to her and promised her that she would live and the child would prosper. That God had seen Hagar in her distress and made this promise to her burned into Hannah's heart amid the darkness and fear that struggled to gain a hold of her spirit. She looked up at the stars overhead and whispered, "Like you saw Hagar in the wilderness, I know you see me too, God. You can see that my family is helpless. Dad is sick with worry, Joshua is drunk, and Jenny is beside herself with fear. Show me what to do!"

She grew very still then and finally went back to her room. She looked up the passage that she had been thinking about in the Bible and read it several times, then began to pray again. "I know you see us, Lord, and I know you care." She looked around the room and thought about how she had hidden here for years. Her eyes took in the bookcases filled with volumes of sermons and theological studies, and she wondered how all of her reading could help her now. She knew that whatever future lay before the family, it would not be something she might read about in a book, but it would be lived, worked out in flesh and blood and perhaps amid tears and hardship. Up until now this room had been a haven for her, but she could no longer use it as a place to hide.

★ ★ ★ ★

As soon as dawn broke, Hannah washed her face and went downstairs. She started cooking breakfast and was surprised to look out the window and see Kat and Clint. No one else was stirring yet. She watched the pair for a while. They seemed engrossed in some deep conversation. The tall man leaned against one of the oak trees and Kat moved about him, waving her arms expressively, words pouring forth like a fountain.

Moving to the door, Hannah called out, "Kat, you and Clint come in."

She waited until they came into the kitchen and then turned to say, "What are you two discussing with such passion so early in the morning?"

"I've been telling Clint that I've been praying for God to send an angel to help us," Kat said briskly.

Despite the problems that faced her, Hannah could not help smiling. "That's a good prayer," she said. "I'll agree with you on that one."

"Do you believe in angels, Clint?" Kat demanded.

"I guess so . . . but I've never seen one."

"You may have seen one," Hannah said with a smile. "The Bible says that sometimes we entertain angels unawares."

Clint nodded. "I remember hearing that. Maybe I have seen an angel or two, but they've never identified themselves. Can I help you with the cooking?"

"Can you cook?"

"Just simple stuff. I can scramble eggs."

"Good, you do the eggs, then. Kat, you make the toast, and I'll fry up the bacon."

The three started cooking breakfast, and Hannah sent Kat to get the rest of the family down to eat. As soon as the girl disappeared, Hannah turned to Clint and said, "You two have become good friends, haven't you?"

"She's a sweet girl. As open as anybody I ever saw."

"Yes, she is. Some people say she's too blunt, but she just says what she thinks."

"If everybody would do that, it'd be a better world, wouldn't it? On the other hand, maybe it wouldn't. We might not want to hear everything that people think."

Hannah wondered what Clint meant by this, but she did not ask. Instead she said, "I'm worried sick about Father. He's not eating at all. He's lost weight, and he's not sleeping either."

"It's hit him pretty hard. Miss Jenny too."

"Yes, she's never experienced anything like this."

"I don't expect you have either, have you?"

"No, but it's different with me."

"Why would it be different with you?" Clint asked in a puzzled tone.

"Because Jenny wants more than I do."

Clint came over and stood beside her, studying her face. "What do you want, Hannah?"

Hannah was flustered. She had grown to admire Clint Longstreet. She had so few friends and usually did not make them easily, but for some reason she felt comfortable with him. She had been disturbed when she had heard of his violent treatment of Earl Crane, but at least she had been glad it was for a good cause. "Oh, I don't know. I just want the family to be all right."

"That's a good thing."

"Do you have a family, Clint?"

"Not much anymore. My dad died, and my mom remarried. He's done pretty well. I've got two sisters and a brother. They're all married and kind of scattered about the country."

"What are you going to do now that your job here is over?"

"Oh, I'll find something."

"Aren't you worried about it?"

"No, not really."

Hannah felt relieved. Here was at least one person who was not worried sick about the troubled times. "I'll miss you," she said suddenly.

Clint grinned at her. "I'll miss you too, and Kat most of all."

Somehow Hannah was embarrassed at speaking so personally to a man she had known such a short time. Clint noticed her discomfiture and did not press her but began to speak of other things.

Finally the family gathered, and Hannah insisted that Clint sit down and join them. Lewis looked at the food and then at Hannah. "The others are all gone, the servants?"

"Yes, they are, Father."

"Then I guess you cooked this."

"Clint and Kat helped. Could I ask the blessing, Father?"

Lewis shot her a quick glance. They used to pray before every meal, but somewhere along the line they had gotten out of the habit. He bowed his head, and Hannah prayed, "God, we thank you for this food and for all you've given us. Help us to be grateful for everything. In Jesus' name, amen."

As they ate, the others were silent as Kat carried on a long conversation with Clint about hunting coons back in the South. Finally Lewis, who had eaten little, put his fork down and said,

"What in God's name are we going to *do*?" Panic tinged his voice, and his mouth moved as if he were in pain.

"I think you said it right, Father," Hannah said quietly. "In God's name we'll find a way."

"That's right. God's going to send somebody," Kat piped up. "Maybe an angel."

Joshua rolled his eyes at her and shook his head but said nothing. Jenny's face was pale, and she finally asked, "When will we have to leave?"

"In less than a week," Hannah said when Lewis did not respond. "We need to start packing those things that we're able to take with us."

"What difference does it make?" Lewis muttered. "We don't have any place to take it to."

"We will have," Kat insisted. "He's going to send an angel, isn't He, Clint?"

"If you say so," Clint murmured. He felt out of place as the family discussed their difficult situation, but his eyes met Hannah's, and she reassured him with a smile.

★ ★ ★ ★

"Why don't you come stay with my family, Jenny? We've got plenty of room."

Arlen Banks had offered to store anything that the Winslows wanted stored, and Hannah had seized on the opportunity at once. She was now busily directing the men who were carrying the boxes to the truck. They had packed all of their personal effects that were not covered by the Bankruptcy Act.

Arlen moved closer to Jenny. The two were standing beside the window as the men moved the boxes outside.

Jenny turned to stare at Arlen, and her face seemed almost paralyzed. "How is it going to be all right? I can't come and live with you."

"Why not?"

"It wouldn't be proper. Besides, I can't leave my family."

Arlen shifted his feet. "You know, Jenny, you're too young for me now, but I always thought we might make a match of it."

"Not anymore, Arlen. Your family survived and mine didn't."

"Don't talk like that!" Arlen said sharply. "It's been hard on you, I know, but it'll come out all right. You'll see."

Clint was helping load the truck, and then when it moved off, he saw Arlen get into his car. He had watched him speaking earnestly to Jenny and wondered what that was all about. He watched as Jenny turned, then spotted him and came over. "Thanks for staying around to help, Clint. You may as well leave. I guess it's all over now."

Clint studied her, thinking how the spirit had been drained out of her. She had always been one of the liveliest young women he had ever known. Now she looked beaten down and so forlorn. She hadn't even been able to keep the horse that she had so recently received for her birthday, since it was purchased on credit. "Hannah's praying for a miracle," he offered. "She says God's going to do something. Kat says God's going to send an angel. I thought I'd stick around. Always wanted to see a miracle."

"Well, that's exactly what it's going to take!" Jenny's words were bitter, and she pressed her hands to her temples as if she could drive the thoughts away. She dropped her hands abruptly. "I'm afraid of being poor."

"Sure you are. You've never been poor, and we're always afraid of things we don't know or have never done. It's no fun, but it won't kill you." She did not speak, so he continued. "Don't you believe in God like Hannah does?"

Jenny looked at him as if he had said something particularly stupid. "No!" she said sharply, her mouth a white line, then turned and walked away, her back stiff.

★ ★ ★ ★

Two days after Arlen Banks had come to store the Winslows' personal effects, Hannah burst in on her father in his study. "Father," she exclaimed breathlessly, "look what I've found!"

Lewis looked up to see Hannah holding some papers in her hand. Even though her eyes were bright with excitement, he could not rouse himself. "What is it, Hannah?" he asked wearily.

"I was cleaning out those papers in the filing cabinet, and I found this document. It's a deed. I had forgotten all about it."

Lewis took the paper and ran his eyes over it. He straightened up. "Why, it's the deed to your mother's old place in Georgia. I'd forgotten about it."

"Yes, Mom talked so much about it, but I thought it was sold."

"No, she wanted to keep it, so we did." A light flickered in Lewis Winslow's eyes as he read over the deed. "She didn't want to sell the place, Hannah. She grew up there, you know. We leased it out for a while, but the renters moved out a couple years ago. I never did anything about rerenting it. It slipped my mind."

"Does it still belong to us?"

Lewis stood up, a flicker of hope in his eyes. "I think it does. The bankruptcy wouldn't touch this. It's in your mother's name. It would be easy enough to have it transferred to mine. Maybe we can sell it and get enough money out of it to rent at least an apartment."

"What's it like, Father?"

"I'm not sure; I've never been there. I know it's a farm, about a hundred twenty acres, I think, and the house looked rather nice in the pictures your mother had."

"Father, we've got to go there!"

"Go there! What are you talking about, Hannah?"

"This must be from God! We can't sell it. Nobody would buy it with this depression on. The papers all say that. They can't even sell mansions for a hundredth of what they're worth, so you can imagine that nothing is selling down in rural Georgia. We don't know what shape the house is in, but we can go there. At least we'll have a place to stay. We'll find some way to make ends meet."

"Hmm. This certainly puts a new twist on things. Go get the others. We'll have to talk about this."

★　★　★　★

Clint was sitting on the front stoop of Jamie's empty cottage, wondering if the old man was all right. He had grown to like the gardener a great deal in the short time they had worked together. *It's a good thing Jamie made up with his daughter when he did, or he wouldn't have had anywhere to go.* His thoughts were interrupted when Kat came flying down the walk. Her eyes were big with excitement, and she talked loudly as always.

"Clint, guess what's happened!"

"I don't know. Tell me."

"We've got a place to go!" Kat said, dancing around Clint with excitement. "It's in Georgia, and it's a farm! Hannah wants to go there. Josh and Jenny don't, but I think we're going to have to. We've got nowhere else to go."

"Why, that's great. You'll like it on a farm, Kat."

"I will, won't I? But Daddy says there's no way for us to get there," Kat said, growing sober. "We have enough money to go on the train, but if we used all the money for the train, we wouldn't have any money for food once we got there."

Kat kicked at stones as she paced in front of Clint, deep in thought. Suddenly her eyes started to glow, and he knew that she had one of her ideas.

"I know, Clint—you can take us in your truck!"

Clint grinned. "That'd be something to see. The Winslows heading south in a beat-up old truck."

"We don't have any other way to get there, Clint. Can't you see what a great idea this is?"

Clint tried to reason with Kat, but she was carried away with her idea. She took his hand and pulled at him, urging him to agree. "Please, Clint, you've got to help us! There's nobody else."

"I would really like to help you out; you know I would. But that truck has never been farther than around this neighborhood. I don't even know if she could make it to the state line. And besides, there's not enough room for your whole family and their belongings."

Suddenly Clint saw tears in Kat's eyes. He had never seen her cry, and it went right to his heart. She was such a happy child, and he hated to see her sad. "Don't cry, Kat," he said quietly. He held her small hands in both of his large ones and said, "You know I would help you if I could."

"There's nobody else, Clint. I've prayed for an angel, and he hasn't come. Maybe God sent you here to help us."

Kat's simple reasoning amused Clint. "Well . . . I'm no angel."

"Please, Clint, you've got to do it. We can't get to our farm any other way."

"It just wouldn't work. I'm sorry, Kat."

Kat pulled her hand back and gave Clint a reproachful look. She wiped the tears from her face, and the sadness that showed there was as deep as the joy she had shown when she had received her inspiration. She said in a small voice, "All right, Clint, I just thought . . ."

Clint watched as she left and shook his head. "Poor kid," he muttered, "it's too much for her." He grew angry that such things could happen. He had seen bad things happen to people before, but for Kat to be trapped in this mess was upsetting, and he wanted to strike out at something.

★　★　★　★

"Come on in, Clint," Lewis said. "We'll eat up the food that's left before we get thrown out."

Clint entered and saw that Hannah and Jenny had fixed soup and sandwiches. The table in the kitchen where the servants usually ate was set, and he took his seat. He bowed his head while Hannah asked the blessing, and they began to eat. He was aware that Joshua had been drinking, although that had become the norm. As they ate Hannah was trying to encourage them, saying how God would help them.

Josh looked up, his handsome face in a sneer. "Don't tell me about God!" he snapped.

"The world's not over, Josh," Clint encouraged.

"It is for us."

"Somebody took your toys away and now you're mad," Clint returned. "You're gonna have to live like a man now, and you can't take it. Is that it?"

"Shut up, Clint!" Josh said bitterly.

"Listen, I know you've never had to fight your way in life, but I have. I don't claim to be a Christian myself, but Hannah's right. God's real."

"Will you help us, Clint?" Kat pleaded.

Jenny passed a confused look to Kat. "Be still, Kat. How could he help us?"

"He could take us to Georgia—to our new home." Everyone stared at Kat, and she blurted out, "He could take us in his truck, couldn't you, Clint?"

Clint felt trapped. "Well, I'm not so sure—"

"Could you really do that, Clint?" Hannah said with hope glimmering in her eyes. "We have such little money, barely enough for railroad fare. Could you really get us there in that truck?"

"I just don't know if the truck is all that reliable! I've never taken it farther than the other side of Central Park."

"Have you had any problems with it when you've taken it around the neighborhood?"

"I guess not, but—"

"Don't even think about it!" Jenny fired. "It's out of the question!"

"Why?" Kat demanded. "We need to get there, and Clint can take us."

Joshua laughed roughly. "That's all we need—to go like a bunch of hobos in a beat-up old truck."

"Be quiet, Joshua!" Lewis said, and he sat up straighter in his chair. His face was wan, the lines of strain obvious. He did not speak for a moment, but then he turned to Clint. "What do you think, Clint, would you be willing to give it a try?"

Clint was shocked with the turn things had taken. He saw that Hannah and Lewis were deadly earnest about this, and of course, Kat was dying to make the trip. Jenny and Joshua were not so happy, but he was not concerned about them. "I guess it wouldn't hurt to try. If the truck breaks down, I'll just have to figure something out on the road."

Lewis turned to Hannah. "What do you think, Hannah?"

"I think God may have brought Clint into this household for this very reason. This is the answer to our prayers."

"We couldn't all fit into that truck, not with all of our things," Jenny protested.

"There's an old trailer and hitch in the garage," Clint said. "I could put them on the truck, and we could put all the gear you have into the trailer, and we could make beds in the truck to sleep on the way. Wouldn't have to pay any lodging bills that way."

This idea intrigued Kat. "We could camp out on the way," she said excitedly, "and cook outdoors. It would be fun!"

"There wouldn't be room for much," Clint put in. "Just maybe a suitcase apiece."

"Why, I couldn't get by with that! What would I do with the rest of my clothes?" Jenny wailed.

"Sell 'em to a used clothing store," Clint said almost harshly. "Take the money with you. You'll need it when you get there. It was rough enough in the South before this thing broke. It's going to be even harder now."

"Why, I couldn't go sell my clothes at a store!" Jenny said and lifted her chin. "I just couldn't."

Clint laughed. "*I* could. You'd go with me, wouldn't you, Kat?"

"Yes, and we'd make 'em pay good for us too!"

Clint pushed his chair away from the table and said, "I'm going to go outside and let you folks talk about this. This is family business. I don't think you realize just how difficult it would be to live on a farm in Georgia. You don't know what shape that house is in, you don't have much money, and things are going to be tight. But if you want me to, I'll take you back to Georgia even if it snows ink!" He got up and left, and as soon as he stepped outside, he took a deep breath. *I sure hope I'm not going to get this family into a bigger mess than they're already in.*

★　★　★　★

Clint pulled the truck up the circular driveway to the front door of the Winslow estate. He got out on the driver's side, and Kat got out on the other side. The girl ran to meet Hannah, waving a bunch of bills. "We sold them all, Hannah! Look at all the money we got."

Clint walked over and saw Hannah counting the bills. "Didn't get too much, Miss Hannah, but it's better than throwing those nice clothes away."

Hannah hugged Kat and then smiled warmly at Clint. "You did fine, Clint, you and Kat. Do you have any ideas about what we ought to take?"

"You'll have to have blankets—all you've got. We'll be sleeping outside, and when we get there, there probably won't be any blankets at the house. We'll have to have pots and pans and dishes too, both for when we get there and for on the road. I'm going to take all the tools I can lay my hands on around here. You'll need tools to make that farm work."

"What would we do without you, Clint?" Hannah said sweetly.

He smiled at her. "You may like it now, but by the time we get to Georgia, you'll want to shoot me for dragging you into this."

"You're not dragging us," Kat protested. "God sent you."

Clint laughed and tugged her pigtail. "You just keep on thinking like that, sweetheart. I'll need all the supporters I can get before we even get to Georgia!"

★ ★ ★ ★

After a final breakfast at the big table in the kitchen, the family had worked together to pack the trailer until it was dangerously overloaded. Clint had included as many tools as he could, and Hannah had seen to it that they brought all the remaining food. Clint said with a grin, "At least we won't starve to death on the road."

Now that the moment had actually come, Jenny felt weak and fearful. She stood on the front step for the last time and looked at the truck suspiciously. It was so old she couldn't imagine getting very far in it. The trailer hitched to the back was piled high and covered with a tarpaulin. She wanted to run away, but there was no place to run, so she walked over to the truck.

Hannah gave her a motherly hug and said, "You and Kat and I will squeeze in the front seat with Clint."

"Maybe I could let you drive, Kat." Clint grinned and winked at her. He saw the look on Jenny's face and knew better than to prolong the moment. "All right, everybody in. We've got a full tank of gas and a long way to go."

Lewis and Josh crawled up in the back of the truck and tried to get comfortable on the blankets that would serve as bedding. Clint had already informed the women that he had brought a tent for the three of them.

Josh said not a word, but Lewis managed to smile. "Take us to Georgia, Clint."

"Yes, sir." He started the engine and then got in behind the wheel and said, "It's a long way."

"We'll make it," Hannah said with a confident smile. Jenny, however, was in tears.

Kat was squeezed in between Hannah and Clint, almost sitting on his lap. "I think you are our guardian angel, Clint."

Clint laughed and put the truck in gear. He pulled out of the driveway, saying, "Lots of things I don't know, but I'm positive about one thing—I'm no angel."

The truck moved slowly away from the brownstone mansion, mingling with the busy New York City traffic. Lewis Winslow, sitting in the back, caught one final glimpse of the estate and knew that life would never again be the same for his family. He closed his eyes, remembering some of the happier times he and the children had had in the short time they'd lived there. He put his head down as the truck rumbled through the streets of Manhattan. Georgia seemed like another world to him, and in his heart he said good-bye to all he had ever known.

PART TWO

Georgia
November – December 1929

★ ★ ★

CHAPTER SEVEN

A Long, Tiring Journey

★ ★ ★ ★

A solid gust of frigid air struck the old Studebaker, nearly wrenching the wheel from Clint's hands. *We picked a bad time to be on the road,* he thought as he brought the truck back to the right side of the highway. *But then, I guess we didn't have much choice.*

The weather had roughed up the land, and the late-afternoon November sun was nothing but a pale disk, giving meager light and no heat. Glancing to his right, Clint noted the weariness etched on the faces of both Hannah and Jenny. Recent events had been hard on them.

They had just crossed into Maryland, and he kept close watch for a place to camp. Twenty minutes later he crossed a small bridge and, putting on the brakes, eased the truck down onto a dirt road that paralleled the stream. He brought the truck to a halt and turned to say, "We'd better stop for the night while we've got light enough to see by."

Jenny said nothing, but Hannah, who was sitting next to Clint, found a smile, weary though she was. "It's been a long trip. How far do you think we've come?"

"We're almost to Baltimore. I guess we've made close to two hundred miles." Getting out of the car, Clint stamped his feet to restore circulation, then moved to the back and opened the gate. "Everybody out," he said cheerfully.

Kat, bundled in the warmest clothes she owned, had transferred to the back an hour earlier and fallen asleep. She came awake at once and jumped down to the ground. She stamped her feet and said, "Where are we?"

"Almost to Baltimore. You fellas all right?"

Lewis was wedged in, his back against some boxes, a mound of blankets pulled up over him. Slowly he stirred and got out stiffly. His face was pale in the late afternoon light, and he looked around for a moment without speaking. The trip had been hard on him. He was unaccustomed to roughing it, and now the cold wind nipped at his face. He stuck his hands in the pockets of his overcoat and said, "We staying here tonight?"

"It's not fancy, but it's free," Clint said. He glanced at the mound of blankets in the back of the truck and realized that Joshua had not moved. Clint called again but got no response. "See if you can get him out of there, Mr. Winslow. We're gonna have to work quick before it gets dark."

"All right." Lewis crawled back into the truck and began pulling at the still form, calling Josh's name.

Clint leaped up in the back and grabbed the tent and tossed it on the ground, then jumped down. "We'll set this up against those trees. They'll be a breaker for that north wind."

When they got the tent opened up, Joshua finally descended from the truck, but the odor of alcohol was on him, and his replies were short. Clint showed the two men and Kat how to put up the tent. It was a fine wall tent, large enough for the women to get in out of the cold, and as soon as it was ready, Clint jumped back in the truck. He came out bearing three folding cots under his arms and bent to set them up inside the tent. "Better get all the cover you can, Hannah," he said.

She smiled faintly. "You're so good to think of all these things, Clint. We would have been sleeping on the ground, I suppose, if you hadn't brought these cots."

Clint said, "This'll be better for you ladies, and the men can sleep in the truck. Well, we'd better get a fire going. Think you could break out some grub and the cooking gear while I build a fire?"

"Of course," Hannah replied. She was wearing a wool dress that reached well below her knees. At Clint's advice she was wearing thick stockings and her heaviest pair of shoes, which were not designed for outdoor weather. "Come on, Jenny, let's cook up a good meal. I think we all need it."

Clint had brought a box of kindling and stashed some firewood against the side of the truck bed. He had planned ahead for cooking and knew that most of the burden would fall on his shoulders. Quickly he built a small fire, beginning with the kindling and then adding some sticks. He doused it all with a little kerosene and touched it off with a match. He stood back, feeding it until a fire blazed, making a cheerful crackling that filled the air as the darkness deepened.

The supper was simple. Hannah had brought along some steaks from the remaining food in the kitchen, and now she put the skillets on the grill that Clint had set over the fire. Soon the smell of cooking meat was sharp in the air. Jenny had opened several cans of beans and poured them into a large saucepan, heating them until they bubbled.

"Smells good," Clint said cheerfully as he drew near. "Kat, get the dishes and some knives and forks."

Kat willingly found the dishes, and soon all of them were eating. They ate standing up, for the ground was cold. Clint relished the steak and said, "You're a good cook, Hannah."

"Anyone can cook steaks."

"Not me," Clint said. "And I've had some pretty bad ones in restaurants once in a while."

Lewis ate slowly. He enjoyed the coffee that Hannah and Jenny had made in the large pot, but the day's travel had been physically hard on him. Even more trying were all the thoughts that troubled his mind; the uncertainty of what lay ahead was wearing him down. As soon as he finished his meal, he murmured, "I think I'll turn in."

"Good night, Father," Hannah said. Seeing his despondency, she hugged him warmly, saying, "We're on our way. We'll be in our new home soon."

Lewis tried to take comfort, but his face was taut as he moved stiffly away from the fire. After Lewis left, Joshua finished his meal slowly, not eating very much. He had been drinking heavily, and finally, without even a good-night, he moved off to join his father in the shelter of the truck.

Clint called after him, "Let that canvas down over the back. It'll keep some of the heat in, Josh."

"I'm not ready to go to bed yet," Kat said. "Why, it's only eight o'clock."

"You almost went to sleep while you were eating." Clint grinned.

"I know, but I want to sit up for a while."

"You can help us clean up," Hannah said. They all pitched in until finally Clint threw a blanket on the ground and sat down close to the fire. Kat came over and sat close to him, staring into the fire. "I bet you've camped out a lot, haven't you, Clint?"

"Quite a bit. Used to go out and stay all night chasing foxes. I had me a fine coon hound."

"What did you do when you caught one? You didn't eat it, did you?" Kat looked up into his face.

"No, we didn't even try to catch them. We just liked to hear the dogs chasing them. Every man could tell his own dog's baying, and we could figure out exactly what they were doing."

Hannah was tired but was reluctant to go to bed. She got a blanket and sat down by the fire, looking up at Jenny. "Come on and let's soak up some of this warmth. That tent's going to be cold."

Jenny sat down beside her, and for a while a silence played over the small group. Kat shivered, and Clint put his arm around her and pulled her close. "You wrap up good when you go to bed, and keep your socks on. Maybe put on a couple of pairs." He looked up at the sky and said, "It's not going to snow, but it'll be pretty nippy."

"I've never slept outside," Hannah murmured. She looked across the fire at Clint, and she was thankful for his presence there. He made a strong shape as he sat on the blanket holding Kat loosely within the circle of his arm. The fire threw flickering shadows over his face, and he seemed preoccupied staring into the blaze. *What would we have done if he hadn't come along? I can't imagine it. . . .*

For the next hour the four sat there, Clint doing most of the talking. He had traveled a great deal, and Hannah listened intently as he spoke of his adventures. Finally he said, "I guess we'd better get to bed. I want to get an early start tomorrow. We'll go through Washington in the morning, and then we'll see how far we can get into Virginia before we make camp."

Reluctantly Hannah rose, and Jenny followed her. "Good night," they said in unison.

Kat rose and said, "There are no bears around or anything like that, are there?"

"Nope. Plumb civilized around here."

Suddenly the girl threw her arms around Clint and hugged him. "Good night, Clint."

Clint Longstreet was touched by Kat's affection for him. He could not remember the last time he'd received so much attention from a child, which he considered Kat to be. He hugged her tightly, then said, "All right, you sleep tight, punkin."

Kat accompanied the two women to the tent, where they all stepped inside. But Kat suddenly stopped. "What about a bathroom?"

Hannah smiled. She was unaccustomed to having to think of such things. Bathing and sanitary facilities had always been something she had taken for granted, but now, however, she knew it would be different. "Just step outside and find a bush to hide behind, Kat."

Kat gave her a startled look, then grinned. "All right."

As soon as Kat left, Hannah glanced at Jenny. "It's a little different from the life we've known, isn't it?"

"Yes, it is. I'll never get used to it!"

"Oh yes, you will. It'll be fine." She began to arrange the blankets on her cot, then sat down and put on another pair of socks. When Kat came back, Hannah got up and saw to it that the girl was under her blanket, then said, "Well, excuse me."

When she stepped outside in the darkness and moved around toward the back of the tent, she saw Clint still sitting in front of the fire. He was staring into it motionless, and once again a warm rush of gratitude came to her. *We all depend on him. What would we do if he got sick? We'd be helpless.* She took one more look at him, then turned into the darkness.

★　★　★　★

Breakfast the next morning was a strain for all of them. Apparently only Kat had slept soundly. The faces of the others were drawn and pale as they emerged from their sleeping places in the scant light of dawn. Clint had awaked before anyone else to build up the fire and start breakfast. Now he said, "Come and get it. We've got a lot of miles to cover today."

As soon as they had finished their bacon, eggs, and coffee, Clint helped the men break down the tent and pack it. The women washed the dishes and repacked them, and soon they all piled into the truck. "I'm already getting sick of this blasted truck!" Joshua complained as he crawled into the back. Hannah wanted to chide Josh about his drinking but knew it would be useless.

They passed through Washington, D.C., in the morning, and Kat wanted to go see the Capitol building, but Hannah shook her head. "We don't have time. We've got to get home."

Clint looked at her and smiled slightly. *Well*, he thought, *she's talking about their new place as home, and I reckon that's good.*

They traveled all day, stopping several times to stretch their legs while Clint added water to the radiator. The Studebaker had a slow leak in the cooling system, and Clint had brought along a five-gallon jug to keep it filled. He also checked the oil and tinkered with the engine constantly. He knew the engine was their salvation. If it stopped running, they would be in poor shape indeed.

When they made camp that night in central Virginia, Hannah was pleased to discover that she could manage the cooking, such as it was. Jenny took no interest in the chore, but Kat had her nose in everything. As soon as the meal was finished, everyone except Hannah and Clint made for their beds.

Hannah and Clint cleaned up, then sat down on blankets as close to the fire as they could get. "We can make it all right, Hannah," Clint said. Hannah was weary, but for a time the warmth and cheer of the fire encouraged her. She asked Clint many questions about his early life, and he answered sparingly.

From time to time, Hannah would pick up a stick and poke at the logs and watch the golden sparks fly upward. "Look at that, Clint. It looks like the sparks are mingling with the stars up there."

"Mighty pretty. I've always liked to be out sitting in front of a fire in the woods."

"Did you hunt a lot when you were a boy?"

"All the time. For us, it was like going to the store. People with money would go buy their meat at the grocer. We had to bring ours down. I must have killed a hundred deer, and no telling how many quail."

"What do you think you'll do with yourself—I mean, for the rest of your life?"

Clint laughed. "Guess I'm not making plans that far ahead."

Hannah was fascinated by Clint Longstreet, for she'd never known anyone like him. "I can't imagine where I'm going."

"I don't even try to imagine," Clint said. He turned and put his glance on her, his eyes narrowing. She had wrapped a heavy scarf around her neck over her wool cloak, and her eyes looked enormous in the night. He had always thought she had beautiful eyes, large and expressive, and now he saw that she looked lonely—and probably had felt lonely for a long time. "Sometimes," he said, "life just drifts on for years, and nothing unusual seems to happen, and then something comes along that changes you—changes everything. That's kind of a frightening thing," he added thoughtfully. "That's what has happened to you and your family. But you're taking it very well, Hannah."

Hannah was pleased with his compliment. She drew her cloak closer about her and held her hands out to the fire, conscious of the uncertainties of their life. It touched her nerves, and she felt the cold brush of doubt. "I get afraid, sometimes, of what's going to happen."

"I suppose everybody does, but we'll make it."

"Clint, you really think we will?"

"Sure we will. I don't know why people are always talking about how hard things are now. It's always been hard. Life's no more dangerous now than it was a hundred years ago. Back then a man might have died from fighting Indians. Now he can get hit by a truck. We're all going to die somehow."

As he said this, he reflected on his own life. Mostly he remembered small things—the brief flash of a woman's shining eyes and the time he had drawn down on a magnificent ten-point buck and had refused to shoot because the animal was so beautiful. His life was a series of unrelated pictures that faded out behind him, and now he was headed forward but did not know his destination. He knew there was a melody in the world, for he had heard it, and he knew there was meaning for people, for he had seen that too. But for him the future was a lamp glow of hope far away that flickered dangerously low at times.

Reaching into his pocket, Clint pulled out a harmonica. Placing it to his lips, he began to play a tune. Hannah listened, then when he stopped, she asked, "What song was that?"

"Just an old one I learned a long time ago."

"Do you know the words?"

Clint put down the harmonica and sang:

"I am a pilgrim and a stranger,
Traveling through this world below;
There is no sickness, toil nor danger,
In that bright world to which I go.

"I got a mother, sister, brother
Who have been this way before.
I am bound to go and see them,
Over on that distant shore."

"It's a sad song, I guess, but I've always liked it," Clint said. "Somehow I've always felt like a pilgrim in this old world. Never stopping long at any one place."

Hannah dropped her head and murmured, "I'm a pilgrim too, Clint. My whole family, we've all got no place now."

Clint nodded thoughtfully. "I guess all of us are pilgrims in one way or another. Better get to bed. Another long day tomorrow." He watched as she rose and said good-night. When she was gone, he poured another cup of black coffee and sat there holding it, wondering what the end of all this would be.

★ ★ ★ ★

They traveled through Virginia all day, and Clint finally pulled off the road just before they crossed the border into North Carolina. "We'll cook up something good tonight, Hannah," he said as he opened the door and climbed out.

Hannah smiled back at him, then she and Jenny got out, followed by Lewis and Joshua. They were all stretching and shaking their legs. Lewis looked around the pasture and asked, "Where are we?"

"Almost to North Carolina, Mr. Winslow. If we can get across

North Carolina tomorrow, then we'll be in northwest Georgia the next day—assuming the truck holds up," Clint said. "Do you think you two could set up the tent by yourselves?"

"Do you think we're helpless?" Joshua snapped. His face was flushed, and Clint wondered how much liquor he had left. Even during Prohibition Josh apparently had no difficulty finding alcohol, but with the family's wealth gone, sooner or later the whiskey that Josh had brought would run out. He did not answer Josh but pulled the ax out of the truck and went to chop firewood. He found a dead tree and soon had chopped enough of the limbs off to make fires for supper and breakfast. Grabbing a load under his arms, he started back.

As he approached the truck he grew wary, for a man was facing Lewis and Josh, his voice loud and strident.

"I want you off of my land, you hear me?"

Lewis tried to speak peaceably. "I'm sorry, sir. We didn't know it was private property."

"Who'd you think it belonged to? Can't you see them fences?" The big farmer's face was florid, and underneath his bulging worn overcoat he looked enormous. As Clint approached the man turned quickly and shouted, "You're another one of 'em! Get off this here property!" A string of profanity followed to emphasize his point.

Josh stepped forward and growled, "We'll leave, but you watch your filthy mouth."

All of them were taken off guard by what happened next. The farmer swung, moving swiftly for such a large man. His blow caught Josh in the chest with a crushing force, driving him backward. Jenny cried out, and Lewis stared at the man with incredulity. It had happened so fast he could not think of what to say.

Josh struggled to his feet and tried to throw himself forward, but Jenny and Hannah hung on to him, crying, "Please, Joshua, don't make any trouble."

Clint dropped the firewood. "Everybody get in the truck."

He moved to stand between the big man and the others. His voice was quiet as he said, "Sorry, we didn't intend any harm."

The big man was tense, as if ready to spring into action again. "If you want some of what I gave him, you can have it."

Clint shook his head. "We'll be moving along as quick as we

can." He glanced over his shoulder and saw that they were all getting in the truck. He turned to the farmer and said, "Thanks for the hospitality."

Turning, he got into the truck and pulled away. Jenny stared at him for a moment, then said, "I thought you were going to fight him."

"It's his land."

Jenny found Clint's behavior difficult to understand. "But you fought Earl."

"This is different. This is his land, not ours. He's a pretty rough customer, but the land is his."

Something about the way he pronounced the words struck Hannah. "The land. That means a lot to you, doesn't it?"

"I guess so." Clint was not overly disturbed, for he had met with rough situations before. He kept his eyes open for another place to stop, and ten minutes later he said, "We can camp down right over there. No houses anywhere close, and we'll be off the road."

They made camp quickly, and Clint was wary enough to keep watch. No one came to disturb them, and after supper, they all sat around the fire under blankets enjoying the warmth. It wasn't as chilly as it had been the first two nights on the road, and they were all grateful.

"How much farther is it?" Josh asked during a lull in the conversation.

"Not too far. Like I said, we should be able to cross most of North Carolina tomorrow, and then we'll get to Summerdale the day after that."

Josh was sullen and said no more. He finally got up and headed toward the truck. As soon as he was gone, Hannah said quietly, "It bothered him getting cursed by that farmer. He's not used to taking abuse like that."

"Well, Josh will have to eat his peck of dirt just like the rest of us."

"What does that mean?" Jenny asked.

"It means all of us are going to have trouble. You're having yours right now, Jenny, and it won't be the last."

"I don't see how it could get any worse," Jenny said bitterly. The trip had exhausted her, and now she sat hugging her knees to her chest and shaking her head. "We don't know where we're going or what we'll do."

"Yes we do," Kat said. She was sitting beside Jenny and reached over and punched her playfully. "We're going to our farm, that's what, and I'm going to have my own horse someday, aren't I, Clint?"

"I hope so, punkin." He smiled at the girl and winked at her. "You're going to be a farmer. You'll have to learn a whole new way of life."

"I don't care. I'm glad we're going."

Hannah was weary to the bone, but she found Kat's attitude encouraging. "I wish we were all as tough as Kat," she said.

"You will be, Hannah," Clint encouraged. "You will be."

★ ★ ★ ★

The next day they passed through the most beautiful country any of them had ever seen. The mountains were softly rounded, and there was a strange beauty about the land.

Finally they arrived at Waynesville, North Carolina, and found a place to set up camp for the night.

"These aren't very high, are they, Clint?" Hannah said as they walked down the road. After sitting in the crowded truck all day it felt good to stretch the legs.

"They're not like the Rockies."

"You've been there?"

"Oh sure. Went through Jackrabbit Pass, but I didn't like the Rockies. They're like the bones of the earth sticking up bare. Not like these hills. These are friendly. I think it'll be like this around Summerdale. Beautiful country." He glanced at her and said, "You're pretty tired, Hannah."

"I'm soft and spoiled."

Clint shook his head. "You're doing fine."

The two of them were usually the last ones to bed. Kat stayed up as long as she could keep her eyes open, but she had stumbled off, and now the two of them were alone.

Hannah, always a light sleeper, dreaded going to bed and said so. Clint said, "You're not afraid, are you?"

"No, I'm just afraid I'll miss something." She smiled wanly at

Clint. They had returned from their walk and were sitting in front of the fire.

Clint laughed low in his chest. "You're not gonna miss much out here." He leaned forward and put another chunk of wood on the fire. When he leaned back, the two were silent for a long time. It was as if silence covered the earth, and he enjoyed it—it was something he was used to.

As for Hannah, the silence troubled her. After all the years she spent hiding from the world in her room, being thrown out into uncertainty like this shocked her more than she had allowed anyone to see. They had stopped at different times on the trip, going into stores to buy bread and milk and other necessary things while Clint tinkered with the truck, and even this had disturbed her.

Clint became aware that Hannah was very quiet. He had almost forgotten her, and now he turned to see a strange expression on her face. She was staring unseeingly into the fire. "Something wrong, Hannah?"

Hannah turned to him, and without warning, tears came into her eyes. She could not speak for a moment.

"I think the trip has worn you down. You're not used to roughing it like this."

"I . . . I guess not."

"It'll be all right. It looks bad now, but things like this have a way of working themselves out. You'll have a house, and somehow we'll make out."

It was his use of the word *we* that was the final straw. She felt so helpless and alone, and now as he sat beside her, he was like a tower of strength. She had felt herself leaning more and more on his strength, and the weakness that had come over her suddenly seemed to fill her. "Clint, I'm afraid."

Without thinking, Clint put his arm around her and hugged her. "No need to be afraid."

Hannah looked up at him. His face was only inches away, and she felt the strength of his body as he held her. His arm was comforting, and she whispered, "Clint, thank you."

Clint had no intention of doing so, but he lowered his head and kissed her full on the lips. If he had thought about it, he never would have done it, but her face had been so close to his and she had seemed so helpless and vulnerable. He did not linger with his kiss, but he was aware that she did not pull away. When he lifted his head, her eyes were wide with astonishment.

Hannah did not know what had possessed her, except that she was weak and exhausted. It was the first time a man had kissed her in years, and she was shocked at her desire to respond, which she thought had been long dead. She drew back and got to her feet. "Good night, Clint."

"Good night, Hannah."

Hannah stumbled to the tent blindly and quickly lay down on her cot, pulling the blankets over her.

Why did I do that? she cried out inside her spirit. She was confused, for she had long ago written all relationships out of her life, and now she was troubled by her own feelings. He had been merely meaning to comfort her, but even so she knew she would think about the kiss for days to come.

CHAPTER EIGHT

Fair Oaks

★ ★ ★ ★

"Well, there it is—our new home, Summerdale, Georgia."

Clint announced the name of the town with satisfaction. He had not revealed to anyone how worried he was about the ancient truck making the distance, but the farther south they got, the more uncertain he had become that they would ever reach their destination. The trip through the Carolinas and northern Georgia had been touch and go the whole way, but finally, after threatening to conk out completely several times, the old truck had delivered them to their destination. Clint slowed to a halt in front of the Huntington General Store.

Hannah looked eagerly out the window and scanned the main street of the small town. On the far side of the street she saw a movie theater called the Majestic, and next to it was a pool hall. The rest of the buildings comprised a furniture store, a restaurant, the Elite Café, and a bank on the corner. Down past the general store she could see Farley's Drug Store and a barbershop. Looking still farther, she saw the sign of a blacksmith's shop and a garage, and at the very end was a square with a church and what she supposed was the city hall.

"Not very big, is it?" Kat said, wide-eyed and twitching with anxiety. "Let's get out and go look the town over."

"We need to find out where your place is first," Clint said. He got out of the truck and opened the door for Jenny. Next Kat scrambled out, and then Hannah stepped to the sidewalk. Joshua stumbled around the corner of the truck, followed by Lewis, both of them rumpled from the long days of being cramped together in the back with all the gear.

"Is this it?" Joshua demanded. He shook his head. "We came all the way from New York for *this*?"

A man was standing with his back against the general store. Lewis approached him and said, "Good day, sir."

"Howdy." The man was not overly tall but thickset with a deep chest and a massive neck, which made his head look small. He had on a black fedora pulled down over his eyes, and when he moved, a star pinned to his shirt caught Lewis's attention. "I'm Noel Beauchamp."

"I'm glad to meet you, Sheriff," Lewis said. "I wonder if you could give me some directions."

"Depends on where y'all wanna go. Are you just passing through?"

"No, we've come here to stay."

"You're from up north," Sheriff Beauchamp said, his eyes narrowing. "Where are y'all planning on settling?"

"At my wife's old home. Her name was Deborah Laurent."

"Oh!" Interest quickened the sheriff's eyes, and he put his gaze fully on Lewis. "You've never been here?"

"No, I never have, Sheriff."

Sheriff Beauchamp studied Lewis for a moment, then shrugged his bulky shoulders. "You take that road out of town, and you'll come to a fork. Take the left one—that's the old military road. Keep going until you pass a white church on your right, and just past it there's a road that turns off. Go a mile down that road, and you come to the place. People call it Fair Oaks."

Lewis nodded. "Thank you, Sheriff." He would have turned away, but the sheriff's voice stopped him.

"You may have some difficulty, Mr. Winslow."

"Difficulty? How's that, Sheriff?"

"Well, in the first place, the taxes ain't been paid on the old place."

Lewis chewed his lip nervously. "I guess I'd better take care of that, then."

The sheriff turned and nodded. "Down that way, at the end

of the street, is the city hall. Gerald Thackery will take care of you."

"Thanks, Sheriff."

"One more thing. Somebody's been living in the old place."

"It was rented out, but I've lost track of it."

Sheriff Beauchamp started to speak, then shrugged his shoulders. "Folks that are in there are a little troublesome. Their name's Cundiff. You pay your taxes, Mr. Winslow, and get that cleared. Then if Cundiff gives you any trouble, tell him I said for him to move on. Far as I know they're just squattin' there. You say they ain't paid no rent?"

"No, I didn't even know who was living there."

"They're a little touchy, so watch 'em."

"Thanks, Sheriff."

Lewis turned and said, "Hannah, we've got to go pay the taxes down there at the city hall."

"All right, Father."

"We'll wait in the store," Clint said. "I need to get some oil for the truck—and I'd better have the blacksmith over there cut me a piece of rod to repair the truck. We'd better get a few groceries too if we're settin' up housekeeping."

Lewis and Hannah walked along the sidewalk, conscious of the stares they received from the few citizens they passed.

"I guess they're not used to many strangers," Lewis said. "It's a pretty quiet town."

"It'll be different from New York."

They reached the city hall, and Lewis paused beside a tall, lanky fellow who was leaning against one of the white pillars and said, "Could you tell me where the tax collector's office is?"

The man looked at him with suspicion. He leaned over and spat a stream of tobacco juice, then turned around and walked away without even answering.

"I guess Yankees aren't too well received here, Hannah."

"Come on, we'll find it."

They did, indeed, find Gerald Thackery's office. He was a short man of some fifty years with a round face and an inquisitive nature. After Lewis introduced himself, Thackery began tossing questions out until finally Lewis said, "We need to pay the back taxes on Fair Oaks."

"Fair Oaks? You mean the old Laurent place?"

"That's right. It belonged to my wife's family."

"Why, sure, I remember Deborah. I went to school with her. Now, ain't that a coincidence?"

It took some doing to get Thackery down to business, and finally, after going through the books, he announced, "The taxes are a hundred and twenty-one dollars. You nearly missed out on it, Mr. Winslow. If somebody else had wanted it they could have paid that and took up the place—likely the banker, Mr. Wheeler."

The sum troubled Lewis, and he looked at Hannah, who was digging in her purse. She was carrying the cash and turned slightly away so that Thackery could not see how thin the roll was. She counted the money out, then turned back and smiled. "Here it is, Mr. Thackery."

Thackery grunted, took the money, and made out a receipt. "All paid up for another year," he said. "You intend to farm the place?"

"Our plans aren't fully made yet."

"Watch out for them Cundiffs. They won't take lightly to being shoved out. They come from up at Dog Town, you know. That's a bad bunch up there. You watch yourself. By the way, be glad to have you come to church Sunday. First Baptist right across the street there."

"Thank you," Hannah said. "I'm sure we'll be seeing you."

★   ★   ★   ★

Josh had separated himself from Clint and noted that Jenny and Kat were across the room. The general store was packed with a wide assortment of items, including farming supplies, bolts of cloth, and a plentiful supply of home remedies. A tall man wearing an apron approached him and nodded. "My name's Huntington. You're new in town, I take it."

"Yes, I'm Joshua Winslow. My father's name is Lewis. We've come back to live in the old home place."

"And which would that be?"

"It was my mother's. Her maiden name was Laurent."

"Oh yes, the old Laurent place." He studied the young man for a moment before asking, "Can I get you something, Mr. Winslow?"

Josh shifted uncomfortably. "Well, to tell the truth, I'm looking for something to drink."

"None of that here. It's against the law, you know."

"Well, of course I know that, but usually there's a way."

"Not in my store." Huntington's manner had turned cold, and he offered nothing else.

Joshua turned and walked stiffly out of the store, and as he did, Clint caught sight of him. He walked over to the man Josh had been talking to. "Howdy, my name's Longstreet. This your place?"

"Yes, my name's H. G. Huntington. You with these people?"

"Yes, I drove them down from New York."

"You'd better tell that young man to be careful. Sheriff Beauchamp is rough on moonshiners and anybody that buys the stuff."

"I'll tell him. I wonder if you have any motor oil."

"Sure. How much do you need?"

"A couple gallons, I guess. The truck's got a leak in it."

Huntington produced the motor oil, draining it out from a drum into two containers. Lewis and Hannah entered the store, and Clint introduced them. Huntington seemed friendly enough, but there was a wary look in his eyes. "Glad to have y'all in the community, Mr. Winslow. I remember your wife's people."

"Well, we're new at this. We all grew up in the city except for Mr. Longstreet here. We're pretty green."

The confession seemed to warm Huntington. "You'll make out fine," he said. "Any way I can help you, you let me know."

"Thanks, I'll do that."

Huntington hesitated, then said, "You might have some problems with the folks that are living in your house."

"Yes, Mr. Thackery told me that."

Huntington nodded but said no more. When they were outside, Lewis said, "Sounds like a pretty rough bunch has taken up in our house."

"They'll have to leave," Hannah said, "but I hope we don't have trouble over it."

They loaded into the truck, which Clint had filled up with gasoline, and left town. They reached the old military road, and Clint nodded. "We turn just past a small white church."

He drove carefully, and when they passed the church, he

said, "There's a road. I suppose that's it." He made the turn, and they passed a wagon driven by a black man, who lifted his hand in a salute. Clint waved back and kept his eye on the road. The road was not well kept, and the fields on either side looked untended. "Things are run down pretty much," he observed to Hannah.

Hannah suddenly said, "Look, that must be it." She pointed down a side road, and there sitting back from the road, outlined against a line of oak trees, was a house.

"Look," Kat said, "it's got oak trees. That must be why they call it Fair Oaks."

Clint slowed down, and they drove between the line of huge, towering oaks. "These trees must be over a hundred years old," he observed. "Right pretty."

Hannah was crowded against Clint, although she had tried not to be. She had not forgotten the kiss that he had given her, although he had not spoken of it, and his manner toward her had been no different. She decided it had meant little to him, but she had been considerably shaken by it. Now she put her attention on the house and saw that it was larger than she had anticipated.

"That's an old-timer," Clint observed. "Looks like it's at least seventy or eighty years old."

The house had two stories, with four columns in the front. The white paint was peeling, and the bare siding showed. A chimney rose from each end, rising up past the second story, and from one of them a thin curl of smoke showed against the iron gray sky. A large porch went along the front of the house, and several of the windows were broken. A picket fence surrounding the yard had fallen in on the left side and was leaning crazily on the right. A large pig wandered by, rooting in the ground, and as they pulled up in front of the house, they saw that the front yard was littered with cans and bottles.

"It looks terrible!" Jenny whispered. "Could anybody live in this?"

"It's not as bad as it seems, Jenny," Clint said. "It just hasn't been cared for. They built houses pretty well in those days. I'll bet the beams are hand-hewn." Clint tried to be as encouraging as he could. He shut the engine off and got out. The others piled out and started toward the house. They had gotten as far as the porch when three men suddenly appeared. They were obviously all from the same family. They wore faded overalls and heavy boots, and their thin faces bore the family likeness. The oldest of the men, who looked like he was fifty-five or sixty, spoke in a rusty voice. "Whad'ya want?"

Lewis stepped forward and said, "My name's Lewis Winslow. Is your name Cundiff?"

"Whad'ya wanna know fer?"

Lewis took a deep breath. He hated unpleasantness, and he saw something rising here. He was disappointed to find that Clint had gone back to the truck; Lewis didn't want to face these men alone. He cleared his throat before declaring firmly, "This is my place."

Cundiff did not speak for a moment; then he spat a stream of amber tobacco juice and laughed. "You come to collect the rent?"

"No," Lewis said as calmly as he could manage, "We've come to live here."

One of the two younger men laughed, revealing more than one broken tooth. He held a rifle loosely in his right hand. "Whad'ya think of that, Perry? They think they's gonna move us out."

The third man was somewhat older, in his thirties. He was a thickset, hulking brute with the same brown hair as the other two. "They'll play hard doin' that," he grunted. The man looked as if he enjoyed trouble.

Lewis saw a thin woman with gray stringy hair come to the doorway. She stared at them suspiciously. Another woman, younger and with a baby in her arms, appeared beside her. The two women didn't speak.

"I guess we can pay maybe twenty dollars a month rent," Cundiff said. He started to fumble in his overalls pocket, but Lewis interrupted him.

"I don't want any rent. I brought my family here to stay. You've got to move on."

"Can't help you. We done settled in. I'm offerin' to pay rent. That's fair."

The big hulking one named Perry said, "Look at 'em, Ace. They're Yankees, ain't they?"

"I 'spect they are," Ace said with a smile. "You might as well move on, Yankees. We ain't leavin'."

Lewis had never encountered a situation like this, and he said tensely, "Sheriff Beauchamp said to tell you—"

"I don't care what the law says. We're stayin' here. He ain't got no authority outside Summerdale, so now you git!"

Jenny was standing behind her father and feeling her fear rise. These were obviously the lowest class people, and she had no doubt they were violent. She had heard that of southerners, and now the one with the rifle spat on the ground and moved closer to her. "You ain't a bad-lookin' heifer. Me and you might go two-steppin' some night."

"You'll have to go," Lewis said desperately. The situation was beyond him, and his voice was not steady.

Bart Cundiff merely laughed. "Ace, see that these Yankees don't take nothin' when they leave."

Jenny suddenly saw Clint, who had stepped behind the truck for a moment and now came out from behind it. He held the shotgun that belonged to her father, and the way he handled it showed practiced use.

"Watch out!" The younger man called Ace started to lift the rifle, and suddenly the air was tense. It all happened in a moment. Jenny saw Clint raise the shotgun and look down the barrel. The sound of the hammer being drawn back made a sharp, pronounced clicking sound that seemed to strike against her like a warning.

Ace Cundiff had his own rifle half lifted, but suddenly he was looking into the muzzle of the shotgun, and the eyes that stared at him caused him to cry out, "I ain't shootin'!"

"Just lay that rifle down, and you'll be all right. Do it now!"

Ace laid the rifle on the ground, and Clint lowered his own but kept it handy. "You can take your stuff out, but you're leavin'."

Perry started toward him, but when Clint swung the shotgun, he stopped as abruptly as if he had run into a wall.

"We'll have the law out if we have to, but I think you'd best be gettin' your stuff and clearin' out," Clint said evenly.

★　★　★　★

It took two hours for the Cundiffs to hitch up a wagon and load their possessions in it. Clint and Lewis watched them carefully, having appropriated their rifle and ejected the shells. While Clint and Lewis kept an eye on the packing operation, Joshua climbed back under the blankets in the truck, and the girls took a look around the property. They found a barn out back as well as a smokehouse that looked to be in pretty good shape. They noticed that there were a number of tools in the barn, and they hoped the squatters planned to leave them.

They returned to Clint and Lewis and described the things they had found. Clint was encouraged that they would have many of the necessary tools and equipment for survival.

Now the women came out and climbed into the wagon, and the younger one turned and gave them a baleful look. She was no more than sixteen or seventeen but looked as hard as any of the men.

"I'm sorry about this," Hannah said but received only a curse from the young woman.

Bart Cundiff said, "We got crops in the ground."

"I'll figure that's some rent for the time you were here," Clint said coolly. "Now, move out."

Ace said, "What about my rifle?"

Clint picked up the rifle, which had been leaning against the pillar, and grasping it by the barrel, extended it.

Ace Cundiff snatched it and glared at Longstreet. "This ain't over yet!" he said with a threat in his voice.

"It'd better be." Clint nodded. "You go on now."

He watched as the wagon rumbled off, and then he turned and said, "Welcome home, Mr. Winslow."

"It's a good thing you were here, Clint," Lewis said. "I wouldn't have known how to handle it."

"Well, don't count on having this much fun every day." Clint smiled slightly and said, "Let's go take a tour of your new house."

They all went inside eagerly, and they were all equally shocked at the condition of the house. They stepped into a large foyer and saw a dining area to the left. The kitchen was behind it. They returned to the foyer and checked out the living area and discovered that the doorway on the far side led to a bedroom. "It'll take a lot of wood to keep this house warm," Clint said as the group paused in front of the fireplace in the living room.

"Everything is so filthy," Jenny said. "They lived like pigs."

The house was indeed a wreck. The wallpaper was peeling off the walls, and the remnants of carpet looked as if they had never been cleaned. The ceilings were black with the smoke of years' accumulation. They climbed the stairs and found the bedrooms upstairs in equally poor condition. As Jenny peered in one of the doors, she shuddered. "We can't sleep in these filthy things."

"No, I expect we ought to burn these mattresses. But the bed frames appear to be sound," Hannah said. "We can sleep on our cots until we fix something."

They continued the tour downstairs in the kitchen. "At least there's a cookstove here," Hannah was happy to report. "We won't have to cook in the fireplace."

"I'd better check the wood supply," Clint said. He looked at their faces and said quietly, "It looks pretty bad, but with some soap and water and hard work, it'll be all right." He turned and left, and Lewis looked after him.

"I guess you were right about him, Kat."

"What's that, Daddy?"

"He just might be our guardian angel."

The little group wandered around the house, overwhelmed with the task ahead and not knowing exactly where to start. Lewis finally directed them to bring all their belongings in and try to get ready for the night.

Clint came back in and said, "There's some chickens out there. Anyone for fresh fried chicken?"

"Oh, that sounds good, Clint." Hannah smiled.

Clint looked over and winked at Kat. "About time you learned to be a country girl, Kat. Come along, and we'll go get those chickens ready for supper. Mr. Winslow, maybe you and Josh can start a fire and get some water boiling."

Kat followed Clint out and said, "I'm so glad you're here, Clint. I was afraid of those men."

"They won't be back. Don't worry about them." He found that the chickens were tame enough and reached down and picked one up. "Well, this is the hard part of life, Kat." He stroked the chicken, which clucked at him, and then he took it by the neck. With one swift movement, he tossed the chicken up, made a wide swing, and popped the neck loose. The headless chicken rolled over, got up, and began running around wildly. Kat stared with shock until the chicken finally moved slower and then finally fell over, pumping bright arterial blood.

"I bet you never thought about having to do that when you were eating chicken, did you, punkin?"

"No, I never did."

Clint reached over and picked up another chicken. "You want to try this one?"

"No, I don't think so."

"Okay, you can help me pull the feathers off, then."

★　★　★　★

"It's nice to sit down at a table and eat," Lewis said. They had used their own dishes and cooking utensils, and the chicken had been cooked on the stove, which seemed to work very well.

Lewis paused in between bites of food and looked around at the house, saying, "This was a fine place once. Deborah told me how beautiful it was."

"It will be again, Father," Hannah said. "Mother would be so happy to know we're here and are going to fix it up."

"But we don't have any money to fix it up."

"Well, we've got hands and backs, and we can work."

Josh had said little. His hands were shaking, and Clint knew that he was going to have a hard time being cut off from his liquor. His eyes met Hannah's, and he knew that she was thinking the same thing, that she was worried about her brother.

Kat said, "Did you see the woods over on the other side of the field? I saw a river down there. Maybe we can fish there."

Jenny dropped her head and began to cry. "This is awful. We'll starve to death here."

Hannah went to her sister and bent over to put her arms around her. "It looks pretty bad now, Jenny, but God's given us this place. We've got a roof over our heads and chickens to eat. It'll be all right."

Jenny shook her head and refused to be comforted. "Why did this have to happen to us? Why?"

Clint quickly finished his meal and left the room. He did not want to witness Jenny's fit of grief. He stood out in the darkness of the backyard listening to the chickens clucking and watching the clouds pass by the moon. Even though they weren't related, he felt that he was somehow tied to these people. He was a man of very little faith in God, but he knew Hannah and Kat believed that God had sent him into their lives. He pondered the strangeness of it all.

★　★　★　★

The hours had flown by as everyone worked hard—even Joshua. Exhausted and ready for a good night's sleep, they had picked out their bedrooms. Lewis took the one downstairs, and upstairs, Hannah and Kat slept in one and Jenny in the other. Josh had taken the one in the northeast corner, and Clint had the room adjacent to that. There was a fireplace in his room, but he built no fire there.

Instead he went downstairs, where he found Hannah sitting in front of the fire in the living room. "Everyone's bedded down," he told her.

"Yes, everyone's exhausted. Aren't you tired?"

"I could use a little sleep. It was a hard trip for all of us."

Hannah motioned to the rocker, and Clint sat down in it carefully. "It looks like the furniture can be used, most of it. It was good stuff before it got abused."

"I'm so glad we're here," Hannah said. She closed her eyes and absorbed the radiant heat that came from the flickering fire. "I feel like we've crossed over the last river or something."

"Lots to do," he observed.

Hannah did not answer, and the two sat there for a long time. Finally she asked Clint what he thought could be done to the house, and he spoke about the needed repairs and even of planting an early garden. He suddenly shook himself, for he was growing drowsy. "We're just sitting here like a man and wife talkin' over the problems of the family," he said.

Hannah did not speak for a moment; then she looked over at Clint and saw that he was watching her in a peculiar manner. "Didn't mean to offend you."

Hannah looked into the fire and said quietly, "I guess you're wondering why I never married and why I haven't had much to do with people—at least until all this happened."

"Yes, I've wondered. Is it something you can tell me? But I don't want to pry."

Hannah lifted her eyes, and he saw despair in them. She was exhausted from the trip, and now he thought for a moment she was going to let her barrier down. The words came slowly, and she shook her head for emphasis. "Something happened to me, Clint. I'll never marry now."

Clint Longstreet knew she was trying to tell him something but couldn't put it into words. He sat there silently for a while before finally rising to his feet. "Never say never, Hannah." He turned and said, "Good night. I'll see you in the morning."

CHAPTER NINE

SURVIVAL

★　★　★　★

Jenny awoke to find herself curled into the smallest possible ball, with a rough blanket against her cheek. As consciousness swam back to her, she allowed herself to daydream about her soft sheets back home in New York. The thin blanket provided little warmth, and a shiver overtook her. She hunched herself closer together, her legs drawn up, dreading to throw back the covers.

I wish I were home again, she moaned to herself. But even as the thought passed through her head, she recognized that she *was* home. The memory of loss gripped her, and she pressed her fist against her eyes as if to shut out the world. The trip had drained her of all strength. She wanted to scream, cry out, simply run somewhere—but there was no place to hide.

She heard a tiny noise, so slight she thought she might have imagined it, but then it came again. Cautiously Jenny lifted her head. The cold air struck her shoulders, and she saw that the windowpanes were frosted, emitting only pale light from the sun. There was no warmth in the meager light, and her shoulders shook with the cold. The noise continued, clearer now. Her feet were numb with cold. Several times during the night she had almost gotten up to find heavy stockings, but she had lacked the courage to face the cold floor. Now, taking a deep breath, she flung back the covers and with a gasp, almost like a swimmer entering a cold plunge into icy water, she swung her legs over, and her feet touched the bare pine floor. She leaped out of bed and skittered to the bureau, where she had stored her few items of clothing. She yanked open the drawer and reached down to pluck out a pair of stockings, when at her feet she saw a mouse.

She screamed, "Get away—get away!" and almost fell down as she leaped backward. She wheeled around and threw herself into the bed, pulling the covers over her head again, trembling from cold and fright.

Almost at once she heard the door open, then Kat's voice.

"What's the matter, Jenny?"

Throwing the covers back again, Jenny stared at her younger sister, then pointed with a trembling finger. "There's a rat over by the bureau!"

Kat glanced over and then giggled. "It's nothing but a mouse."

"Get him out of here! I can't stand him!"

Kat shooed the mouse into a tiny hole at the base of the wall and said, "It's all right. He's gone now."

With a shudder of relief, Jenny sat up but still hugged the blanket around her. She saw that Kat was already dressed in a pair of overalls and a brown wool sweater buttoned up tightly. "It's so cold," Jenny moaned.

"Not as cold as it would be back home! It's warmer downstairs. Clint's got a fire going. You'd better get cleaned up."

"I can't clean up in cold water." Jenny looked over at the walnut washstand. She had brought up a porcelain pitcher and a cracked enamel basin, but now she could not face the thought of the cold water.

"I bet you need to go to the bathroom too." Kat grinned.

Suddenly Jenny was aware of the pressure and said, "Yes."

"Why don't you go on and take care of that, and I'll heat you some water. You can wash up downstairs where it's warm."

Jenny stared at Kat, mumbling, "All right. I'll be right down."

Kat turned and left, and Jenny stepped over to the pegs on the wall that served for a closet. She picked the heaviest, warmest outfit she had—a long green dress of fine wool. Quickly she skimmed out of her nightgown and into her clothes, including two pairs of stockings. She slipped into her lightweight shoes—more appropriate for dancing than for life on the farm—

and she knew they would not last long here. Quickly she jerked a coat off another peg, put it on, and stepped out into the hallway. She went downstairs, unable to ignore the filth that surrounded her, and for the first time in her life, Jenny thought of how valuable servants were. As she slipped down the stairs, she thought, *I wish we had just one servant here to clean up this filthy house!*

She realized with a sharp pang that she might never have servants again, and the thought depressed her. She cut through the kitchen and tried to hurry past Clint, who was putting a piece of firewood in the stove. She was embarrassed when he turned and said good morning.

She mumbled good morning before dashing outside. She was mortified that he knew her mission. Such things had always been private, but how could one go to an outside bathroom in private?

There were two privies, as she had discovered yesterday— one for men and one for women. Jenny turned toward the one toward the east side of the house and quickly ducked inside. It was dark, and the thought of snakes sent chills up her spine. She shivered and reminded herself, *There are no snakes in November. Now, don't be foolish!*

When she emerged, the sun had risen enough to send pale gleams soaking into the earth. She hurried toward the porch, noticing that the outside of the house was as filthy as the inside. Tin cans, papers, and other refuse of all kinds were strewn everywhere. As she stepped into the kitchen Kat said cheerfully, "I heated some water, Jenny. You can wash your face and hands."

Kat poured the water into a basin from the teakettle, then set the kettle back on the stove. Jenny saw a bar of soap, rather mushy from previous use, and almost rebelled against using it. Still, she was so dirty she could not turn it down. "There's a washcloth hanging up right over there," Kat said.

Jenny quickly washed her face and hands and dried off on a towel made from a flour sack.

Turning from the washbasin, Jenny saw that Clint was bringing a pan from the wood stove. He was wearing the same clothes he had worn on the journey, his plaid wool shirt open at the throat, and seemed impervious to the cold. He said cheerfully, "Did you ladies sleep well last night?"

Jenny responded with a noncommittal, "Mmm . . ."

"Sit down, Jenny," Kat said. "Clint and I have fixed breakfast—eggs and biscuits."

Before Jenny could speak, Hannah entered, her face drawn and her whole countenance downcast. "Good morning," she said wanly, then moved over to the fire. "Ooh, this feels good!"

"Come sit down and eat," Kat said. "I cooked the eggs, and Clint did the biscuits." She seemed happy, her eyes sparkling. She nodded toward the plates. "They don't match very well, but they'll do. I found the eggs myself, Hannah. The hens have just laid them everywhere. It's like Easter—only we eat these eggs."

They sat down, and Clint looked over at Hannah. "Reckon you'd like to say a blessing."

"Yes, I would." Hannah bowed her head, and the others followed suit. "Lord, we thank you for this food and for your provision. We thank you for bringing us home safely. Be with us and watch over us. In Jesus' name."

"Clint's going to teach me how to make biscuits," Kat announced, "and then I can make the whole breakfast."

"Better wait and taste these biscuits before you decide to use my recipe. I'm not much of a cook."

Hannah tasted the eggs and managed a smile. "You did so well, Kat. The eggs are good." She picked up a hot biscuit and juggled it.

"No butter, I'm afraid," Clint said.

Hannah bit into the biscuit cautiously, and as it cooled, she smiled and said, "This is *very* good, Clint! You'll have to teach me how to make them too. I'd better go get Dad and Josh up. They'll want to have a hot breakfast." She ran from the warmth of the kitchen, rubbing her arms in the cold hallway and dashing up the stairs to keep herself warm. She knocked on Josh's door, and when no answer came, she whispered softly, "Josh, are you awake?"

Still no answer, and she opened the door cautiously. The sunlight fell on the floor and on the half-covered sleeping man. Josh was fully dressed, his mouth open, snoring. Hannah moved closer and called more loudly, but he still did not move.

She glanced down and saw an empty whiskey bottle on the floor. She felt a wave of anxiety and pity for this brother of hers whom she loved so dearly. Knowing it was useless to try to wake him, she turned and closed the door silently. She made her way downstairs to her father's room, turning left at the foot of the stairs and crossing through the living room to the back of the house. She knocked on the door and called his name. After a moment of silence, she heard footsteps and waited until the door opened.

Lewis Winslow looked frightful. He was unshaven, and there were dark circles under his eyes. He passed his hand across his face and shook his head in confusion. "What is it, Hannah?"

"Breakfast is ready, Dad. Why don't you come and eat, then you can shave in the kitchen."

Lewis had passed a sleepless night. He had lain awake going over his life again and again, and more than once had moaned and whispered, *Why was I such a fool?* Now his weakness was evident in his appearance as he shook his head. "I'm not hungry."

"You've got to eat, Dad."

"Hannah, what in the world are we going to do?" The words rose from the very depths of his heart, for it was the question he had asked himself incessantly, but with no answers. His eyes seemed sunken far into his head, and as he raised his hand to run it over his hair, Hannah noted it was unsteady.

"You'll feel better after you get a good breakfast and get cleaned up. It'll be all right, Dad," Hannah said. Her heart went out to her father, and she realized that he was taking this harder than she was. This was strange, because she had always been the weak one, the recluse, the one who could not face the world. Now she saw fear and doubt in her father's wan features. She reached up to touch his cheek and said, "Bring your razor. After you eat, you can shave, and we'll discuss it."

★ ★ ★ ★

Breakfast was grim. The family ate in silence while Kat babbled on about finding the eggs and what fun it was and about her experimentation with cooking. Her eyes were bright, and her tawny hair tumbled about her head. She addressed much of her talk to Clint, asking him what it was like to grow up on a farm and what the land around here was like, about the river nearby and about the animals. The others were glad enough to let her dominate the conversation.

Lewis forced himself to eat, trying to ignore the rank odor of the kitchen, a legacy of the former occupants, who had obviously lived with no thought of cleanliness. The floor was black with grime, as were the mostly empty shelves. He broke off a bit of biscuit and ate the dry morsel.

"We'll have to get some butter and jelly or syrup of some kind," Hannah said.

"I saw some sorghum molasses in the store," Clint said. "That would be good."

"I've never had that. What does it taste like?" Hannah asked.

Clint grinned at her. "It takes sweet like syrup should. It's a little bit strong for some folks, but I've always liked it. As a matter of fact," he observed, "there's a sorghum mill out in the field. We could grow our own sorghum cane and make our own sweetening."

"Could we really do that?" Hannah wondered aloud. To her such a thing was as mysterious as magic. Food was something you bought at the store, not something you grew yourself. She had never even been aware of the small vegetable garden Jamie had planted at their home in New York. She realized at that moment that she was in a new world now.

"I don't see why not," Clint said. "We've got plenty of land. Sorghum is easy to grow. There's a little work involved in making the syrup but nothing we can't handle."

Lewis took all of this in but said nothing. When the meal was finished, he could no longer contain himself. With desperation etched on his features, he blurted out, "How are we going to live? We'll all starve to death!"

His outburst triggered Jenny's emotions, who with pale face and trembling lips uttered, "This place is awful! It's filthy, and it has rats and probably snakes in the summer. My clothes are filthy, and I am too. It's the worst place in the world!"

No one spoke for a moment, and then Clint took a sip of coffee from his chipped cup. When he lowered it, he shrugged and said, "It's a lot better than bein' in jail in El Paso, Texas."

Kat's eyes opened wide. "Were you in jail in Texas?"

"Sure was."

"What for?" she demanded. "Did you rob somebody?"

Clint laughed softly. "No, I was arrested for vagrancy."

"What's that? Is it like burglary?"

"No, it's not having a job."

"They can put you in jail for not having a job?"

"They can in El Paso."

Hannah was fascinated by the different life Clint had lived. It was almost as if he were an alien from another planet. She filed this bit of information away to ask him about later. But now she was more concerned about the despair in her father's face and voice, and she said to him, "We won't starve, Dad. We've got chickens, and we can plant a garden."

"I don't see how we're going to make it, daughter," Lewis whispered.

Hannah responded in a surprisingly strong voice, "We're Winslows, Father. Our people didn't always have it easy. You've read the journal of Gilbert Winslow. You know the terrible things he and some of our other ancestors have gone through. We've got the same blood in us. We'll make it."

"That's right," Kat piped up. "We'll ask Jesus for food, and Clint will show us how to farm, won't you, Clint?"

"Do my best."

Hannah was attempting to keep herself as outwardly cheerful as possible. Actually she was filled with fears, perhaps even more so than her father, but this was no time to give way to them. As she thought of Joshua dead drunk and of no use, and seeing the helpless expression on the faces of Jenny and her father, she knew she could never allow her fear to show. She glanced at Clint, who was sitting idly in his chair. He seemed so strong to her—and she realized that his strength had been forged in the crucible of trials and hard times. She noted again the broken nose and the scar on the side of his chin, the missing tip of his finger as his hands rested on the table.

"Tell us what to do, Clint," Hannah said quietly. "We don't know where to start."

Clint was startled. He had come to this family when they had everything and he had nothing, but now these people, so soft and gentle and so unused to manual labor, needed him. As his eyes met Hannah's, he saw a pleading and a cry for help there, and he knew he would do everything he could for this family. It was a strange turn of events. He had floated through the world, struggling and fighting his way, being hammered into shape, his mind and character toughened by adversity. But now someone else needed him. That touched a wellspring deep inside, and he felt a connection with them he had never felt with other people.

"Well," he said quietly, "you've got two problems. You've got to eat. That's number one, and then you've got to stay clean." He lifted his finger and rubbed his nose. "I guess you don't *have* to stay clean, but you do have to eat. And like Hannah says, nobody's going to starve. I took a little look around. I've seen signs of deer, and I'll bet those woods over to the north of the place have plenty of coons and squirrels and possums. The river over there's got fish and turtles. We're not going to starve."

Jenny lifted her chin defiantly. "I'm not eating a possum!"

"What do they taste like, Clint?" Kat inquired curiously.

"Well, they're not very good, but if you get hungry enough, you can make do."

"I'd like to get started in cleaning this place up," Hannah exclaimed. "It's filthy!"

Clint nodded. "I noticed a big washpot out back. I'll go get a fire started under it. Everybody go bring your dirty clothes, and we'll have a washday."

After everyone had gathered up the dirty laundry, Jenny chose to work with her father cleaning up the kitchen while Hannah and Kat went outside with Clint. Neither of them had the foggiest idea of how to wash clothes.

"What do you do first, Clint?" Kat asked.

"Well, the first thing is we'll have to make a battling bench."

"A battling bench? What's that?"

"Something to beat the clothes out on." Clint had moved over to the woodpile, saying, "It's a good thing they left some of this wood. It won't take long to put a battling bench together."

The two watched as Clint chose a large oak log that had been split in half lengthwise. It was about twelve inches wide and four feet long. Clint nodded with satisfaction. "This one's rough enough, you see."

"Why do you want it rough?" Hannah asked, moving closer.

"Well, when you're battling the clothes—that's what my ma always called it—you beat the dirt out in the cracks. If you have a log that's too smooth, you'll beat the dirt right back into your clothes."

Hannah and Kat watched as he took his ax and cut three pine poles, no more than five inches in diameter. He notched the ends of them and nailed them into place for the bench, two on one end and one on the other.

"I see there's a paddle already made here that'll do for a battling stick." The two looked curiously at the sticks, which were tapered and rounded.

Finally Clint said, "Good pot we've got here. I expect your mother's family left it here when they moved." He motioned to the large black pot that was sitting on a built-up platform of flat stone. "First thing we do is put a little water in it before we start the fire. That way the heat won't crack it."

"I'll do that," Kat said and immediately ran to the pump. She drew a bucket of water, came back, and poured it in the pot.

"That's good, Kat. Now, we'll just build a fire here, and we're on our way."

Using shavings and small sticks, Clint built a small pyramid under the pot, took out a match, and struck it on his thumbnail. It flamed up, and he cupped one hand around it to shield it from the wind as he laid it onto the kindling. The dry wood caught quickly. "Now, we keep adding wood until we get that water good and hot."

After the fire was blazing and the fire was hot, Hannah watched as Clint demonstrated how to wash the clothes. She learned that it was best to rinse them out in cold water first. Her hands were soon aching from the cold, but she did not complain. She followed Clint's instructions, putting the wet clothes on the battling bench, then pounding them with the short paddle, turning them over continuously. Then she rinsed each piece again.

Clint cut up a piece of yellow laundry soap and let it dissolve in the boiling water until it made a froth on the surface. "Just put the dress in there and stir it around," he instructed. "That's all there is to the washing."

Kat and Hannah went at it diligently. It was hard work, and even though the early morning coldness had passed away, the breeze was still sharp, and Hannah knew her lips and face, and especially her hands, were getting chapped.

Once Clint offered, "Why don't you two girls go inside? I can do this."

"No, we'll do it, Clint."

Clint glanced at Hannah and saw her determination to keep going. He thought of the timid woman who had hidden herself inside the mansion in New York, and he found himself marveling at how she was forcing herself to do this task that was so far from her upbringing.

"You're doing fine, Hannah," he smiled. "You'll make a pioneer yet."

As the three worked, Clint would pull out his harmonica from time to time and play a tune. Usually it was a cheerful one, and sometimes Kat would sing along with him. Once, however, he sang a mournful melody.

"I'm goin' down to River Jordan,
Just to bathe my weary soul,
If I could only touch His garment,
It would heal and make me whole."

"What's that song, Clint?" she asked.

"I guess it's called 'I Am a Pilgrim.' Kind of sad, isn't it?"

"No, I like it. Teach me the words."

Washing and rinsing the clothes again required a great deal of water, and Hannah was grateful for the pump. It wasn't like city water, but it was better than carrying it from a creek, which Clint had said he did as a boy.

When the washing was finished, they hung the clothes out to dry on a wire stretched from a chestnut tree to a huge walnut tree. Not having clothespins, Hannah simply draped them over the wire. By noon she was exhausted, although she did not complain.

Clint had been observing Hannah, and seeing her exhaustion, he said, "I guess we're close enough to a quittin' point. Let's go in and have a bait."

"What's a bait?" Kat demanded.

"It's a way of saying let's go have something to eat."

"Yes, let's go have a bait," Kat said, giggling.

The three went inside and found that the kitchen had been transformed. It was now at least presentable. The sink was clean, the floor swabbed, and the walls largely purged of the smoke that had darkened them.

"Why, this looks beautiful, Father!" Hannah exclaimed.

"You've done a good job," Clint said as he took it in.

Jenny was still at work scrubbing one of the walls. Her hair was damp and in disarray. "I never knew cleaning was such hard work!"

"Let's have something to eat. I want to have a bait!" Kat exclaimed.

The "bait" was not extensive. They had sandwiches of lunch meat, along with canned pork and beans. They all downed the meal quickly, and Hannah stopped once to smile at her father and squeeze his arm. "The kitchen looks so wonderful."

Lewis tried to smile. "Well, it's a start, but this big old house—it'll take a year to get it really clean and repaired."

At that moment Joshua came in. He was bleary-eyed and had not shaved in several days. His clothes were rumpled and had a rancid odor. He looked around at them and, without speaking, flung himself into a chair.

"Let me fix you something to eat," Hannah said. "Would you like some eggs?"

"I guess so," Josh mumbled.

Hannah got out a frying pan and began scrambling some eggs while Joshua sat there with a surly look on his face, not speaking to anyone. When she set down a plateful of steaming scrambled eggs before him, along with the biscuits Clint had baked, he began eating without a word of thanks.

"We divided up the work here," Lewis directed to Josh. "Kat and Hannah are washing clothes, and Jenny and I are cleaning the house. Maybe you could help us with that."

Joshua's hands were unsteady, and his head was pounding. Clint knew better than anyone in the room what a hangover felt like, and he could see the shadow of drunkenness on the young man. He was not surprised when Joshua grunted, "I'm not cleaning this pigsty of a house!"

Jenny's anger flashed out. "If I can clean house, you can too! You can't stay drunk all your life, Josh!"

Josh rose at once and started to leave, but Lewis's voice caught him. "Jenny's right. You're going to have to work, Joshua—along with the rest of us."

Clint felt out of place in the middle of a family argument. He rose hastily and said, "I think I'll go out and see if I can bag me some squirrels and maybe a couple rabbits for supper."

"Let me go with you," Kat begged.

"Next time, Kat. I'll be in a hurry today. There'll be plenty of time for hunting later."

Clint picked up the rifle propped against the wall on his way out the back door. As soon as he was gone, Hannah murmured, "I don't know what we would have done if it hadn't been for Clint."

"Can I go out and play awhile?" Kat said. "Maybe go exploring?"

"Sure, honey, you go ahead." Lewis smiled at her. "You worked hard this morning."

★ ★ ★ ★

Kat stayed outside exploring for nearly three hours. The country fascinated her. She went down to the river, where she threw rocks in and watched large fish swimming near the shore. She passed by a log that was the sunning spot for half a dozen odd-looking turtles. She tossed a pebble into the river next to them and laughed as they all slid off into the water and disappeared.

She saw squirrels and rabbits in abundance and decided she would learn to hunt. "Clint will teach me," she said aloud. "Then I can help put food on the table."

Kat had a good sense of direction and carefully kept track of her position so she would be sure to find her way home again. Finally, getting hungry and tired, she turned homeward, seeing the different kinds of trees along the way and wishing she knew the names of them.

She stepped out of the woods and started toward the house, noting that Hannah and Clint were busy doing something beside the house. She narrowed her eyes and saw that he was skinning a small animal and started to hurry forward. "I want to learn how to clean fresh game," she said to herself. She had not gone far, however, when she heard an odd noise, and stopping, she turned to see half a dozen young pigs emerge from the woods. They were very small and uttered shrill, squeaking cries.

"Oh, you're so cute! I wonder where your mama is." She walked slowly toward them, and the pigs at first retreated, but when she knelt down and cooed gently, they started edging toward her. She had nothing to give them to eat, but they still came closer. Finally one of them got within arm's length, and she put out her hand. He sniffed at her fingers and then nibbled at them, which delighted her. She reached out and picked him up, and he broke out into a shrill squeal that almost hurt her ears.

"I'm not going to hurt you!" she said, trying to keep the animal still as he struggled to escape. She finally decided that the pigs were not to be petted, and even as she put him down, she heard a rough coughing sound. Turning, she froze at the sight of an enormous pig charging out of the woods straight toward her. The sow's eyes were red with anger and fury, and Kat quickly regained her senses. She dropped the piglet and turned and ran, screaming, "Clint—!"

Her cries reached Clint as he was explaining what he was doing to Hannah. He whirled and took in the situation at one glance. Kat was running full speed, her face paralyzed with fright, with a monstrous sow charging a few yards behind.

In one rapid motion, Clint snatched up the rifle, glad that he had reloaded. Flinging the rifle up, he nestled his cheek against the stock, putting the bead right on the sow. It would be dangerous shooting around Kat, but he had no choice, for she was only a few seconds away from being thrown to the ground, and he knew what could happen when a sow that size had somebody down.

He squeezed the trigger and felt the recoil. He saw that the slug had struck the sow, but it had not stopped her. He fired again twice, and a gust of relief passed through him as he saw the huge animal collapse.

Hannah watched, petrified. Seeing the huge beast hit the ground, she began trembling uncontrollably.

"It's okay," Clint said. He kept the rifle in his hand and ran forward with Hannah following close behind. Kat ran straight into Hannah's arms and clung to her desperately.

"It's all right, Kat, the pig is dead."

The two stood holding each other, and then Kat turned and saw that Clint was standing over the dead sow. She released herself from Hannah's arms and walked over shakily. She reached out and took Clint's hand, her breath still coming in short gasps. "Thank you, Clint."

"You're welcome," Clint said, noting her pale face. He himself was shaken by the encounter. He knew the shots had been lucky, and he didn't even want to think about what might have happened had he not been nearby. Hannah joined the two, and he saw that her face too was pale as paper, and she was trembling. He wanted to reach out and put his arms around her but felt hesitant to do so. Instead, he simply laid his hand on her shoulder and said, "It's all right, Hannah. She's okay."

Hannah tried to speak, but her lips could not form the words. "You saved her life, Clint," she finally managed to say.

"Yes, you did," Kat echoed, looking up into his face.

Embarrassed by their admiring looks, Clint downplayed the event. "Well, I'm glad it turned out so well. And look at this, Kat. You were asking for food this morning at breakfast. Well, now we've got enough to last us all winter!"

Jenny and Lewis had emerged from the house at the sound of the gunfire, and after running across the field together, they now reached the trio standing by the dead pig. Even Joshua had come out of the house and joined them moments later. As Kat told them what had happened, Lewis gave Clint an odd look, but he could not express his feelings in words.

Clint again tried to escape from all the excess attention, saying, "Well, I was just saying we've got plenty here to keep us all winter."

"You mean to eat that thing!" Jenny exclaimed.

Clint Longstreet burst out laughing. He knew this young woman had never thought about how the meat she used to eat in her elegant dining room was once hairy and bloody like the pig before them on the ground. "Only if you like bacon, ham, pork chops, and ribs," he said.

At that moment Kat became aware of the crying piglets. "Oh, look, they don't have their mama! What'll we do with them?"

"You'll have to raise them, I reckon," Clint answered. "When God sends food, He sends a lot of it."

"I will. I'll raise them all!" Kat exclaimed.

Clint thought of all the work that lay ahead for this family. They had so much to learn, but he knew he had to take things one step at a time. "Okay," he said cheerfully, "any of you ever dress a hog?" He looked around at their panicked expressions and laughed. "Nobody here's too old to learn!"

CHAPTER TEN

A FAMILY PROBLEM

★ ★ ★

Clint Longstreet carefully concealed the smile that wanted to rise to his lips. He knew it was wrong, but he could not help being amused at what he knew would be the reaction of the Winslows to dressing a hog. If he had a mule or a tractor, he would have pulled the carcass to a more convenient spot. But having neither, he worked beneath a huge walnut tree near the spot the animal had fallen. The men had found a set of pulleys in the barn with which they had been able to hoist the carcass up in the air.

While Lewis and Hannah built a fire and put a large pan of water on to boil, Jenny and Kat gathered all the knives they could find. Clint taught Joshua how to sharpen them on a grindstone in the barn. "We're ready to go into business now." Clint dipped a ladle into the boiling water and flung it over the carcass to soften the hair. After repeating the process enough to thoroughly soak the hair, he said, "Let's get to work. Everybody got a knife?" They all looked at him painfully, except Kat, who was almost hopping up and down in excitement, and he grinned. "All you do is scrape the hair off." He reached out with his own knife and began to scrape at the carcass. "Come on, everybody join in."

Kat, who was using a small paring knife, found herself grinning. "I've never done anything like this before."

Jenny and Hannah had drawn their lips into a fine line at the noxious smell. The men did little better, but finally, after scraping for some time, the animal hung bald, slowly revolving, its white belly bulging obscenely. Then Clint said, "Get that tub under here, will you, Josh?" He waited until Josh had the empty washtub underneath and then, with one smooth motion, slit the carcass. The entrails went tumbling into the waiting tub, and Jenny and Hannah gagged and turned away, their hands over their faces.

"Ugh, how awful!" Jenny choked.

"What'll we do with that?" Lewis demanded, fighting to keep his own stomach from rebelling at the sight.

"Why, we can make chitlins out of them. You wash 'em, clean 'em out good, and stuff 'em."

"I'm not eating any of that!" Josh said stridently.

"I don't think I'd care for any either," Hannah murmured, her face still averted from the scene.

Clint grinned. "All right, it seems unanimous. No chitlins. Well, we'll get to the good stuff, then."

They reluctantly watched as he lowered the animal and began cutting it up, explaining all the while exactly what he was doing. The women especially were having a difficult time of it. He cut the head off and opened the skull with an ax and removed the brains from their nest of glistening bone.

"Put this in a pan. It's the best part of the hog."

"You mean you're going to *eat* that?" Jenny said, disgust wrinkling her nose.

"Why, sure. You scramble 'em with eggs and serve it up with grits and sausage. You'll love it."

Hannah smiled slightly. She was aware that Clint was making fun of them. "I think we'll all surrender that part of the hog to you, Clint."

"All right." Clint showed Josh how to slit the carcass down the backbone and then he taught Josh and Lewis how to butcher it into standard cuts, the hams and shoulders reserved for curing. He let Kat slip off the fat in great wads, saying, "We'll boil this down. It'll make some of the best white lard."

Then he cut the lean meat off and Hannah and Jenny diced it. "We'll grind this up. Put in some salt, red pepper, and sage. Make fine sausage."

Clint looked around. His hands were bloody, but he was

satisfied. *At least no one passed out,* he thought. Aloud he said, "It's a good thing there's a decent smokehouse here. I checked it out this morning. Why don't we all carry this meat to the smokehouse, then I'll get a fire going in there while the rest of you clean up."

"I'll help you, Clint," Hannah said.

"All right. It won't take long."

They all helped Clint carry the hams, shoulders, and jowls into the smokehouse, after which they went back to the pump to wash up. Hannah stayed with Clint, who told her, "We'll have to get a fire started with dry wood, but then we keep pilin' on green wood. We don't want flames, just smoke."

The smokehouse was built with logs and chinked with mud. All of the meat had to be salted, and fortunately their previous tenants had left two large sacks. Clint explained what he was doing as the fire was beginning to smoke. "You cover each of these with salt. I like to use eight pounds of salt for every hundred pounds of meat. I wish we had some molasses to mix with it. Maybe I'll get some tomorrow if we go to the store."

"You put molasses on meat?"

"Sure, mix a quart of it with two ounces of black pepper and three ounces of red pepper."

"All right. I'm learning, but I've got a long way to go."

Clint turned around and smiled at Hannah. "You're doing fine, Hannah. I'm proud of you. Most women who didn't grow up on a farm would have fainted at the sight of a gutted hog."

"I may do that yet." Hannah smiled, but she felt good at the compliment.

★ ★ ★ ★

Jenny stood in the middle of the kitchen floor and said, "I don't care what it takes, I've got to have a bath."

"It'll have to be in a washtub," Kat answered. "It's too cold to go to the river."

"Well, it's the washtub, then, and you need a bath too, Kat." Jenny set about making preparations. She dragged in the largest galvanized washtub and put it by the stove. She stoked the fire and filled every saucepan, kettle, and pot she could find with water. While the water was heating, she found a piece of rope, then went up to her room and removed some blankets from the beds. Coming back, she hung them over the rope to partition off the kitchen. "I'm taking a bath, Dad. You and Josh stay out of the kitchen."

When the water began to boil, she poured some of it into the tub, mixing it with cold water until the temperature seemed tolerable. She got one of the three bars of soap they had bought at the store and was glad to find that they had brought a few towels and washcloths with them from their home in New York. She got some fresh clothes from off the clothesline and put them next to the stove to warm.

Stripping off her filthy clothes, she threw them on the floor and stepped into the water. It was too hot at first, and she did a little dance, but then as she waited for her feet to adjust to the heat, she was able to slowly, inch by inch, submerse herself. Of course, the tub was too small for her to be completely submerged, but she soaked the washcloth and wrung out the warm water over her face. She stood up, worked up a lather over her whole body, and then sat down and luxuriated in the hot water. *I never thought a bath would feel so good!* She put all of their troubles out of her mind and thought of nothing but the pleasure of the hot water and the smell of soap. She washed her hair, rinsed it as well as she could, then stepped out and dried off. The feel of the clean clothing was almost sinful. She called out, "All right, Kat, let's empty this, and you can take your bath."

★　★　★　★

Night had fallen, and most of the family had gone to bed, exhausted from the busy day. Jenny was sleepy also, but she hated to leave the warmth of the fire in the living room and go to the cold bedroom. She had already planned to put on as many garments as she could, but for now she sat in one of the cane-bottom chairs, soaking up the heat. The fire crackled and snapped and sent the fiery embers up the chimney.

"Hard to leave the fire and go to bed, isn't it?"

Jenny turned and saw that Clint had entered. He had a load of firewood in his arms, and he dumped it in the woodbox. "I think I'll just sleep down here in front of this fire tonight," he remarked. "I need to go out every once in a while and be sure the smokehouse fire is doing all right."

"That's what I'd like to do too."

Jenny watched him covertly as he pulled up a chair and sat down. He leaned forward, putting his elbows on his knees, and cupped his chin. The firelight outlined his strong features as he sat there silently staring into the fire. Finally she said, "I never knew life could be so hard, Clint."

Turning to face her, he smiled. Even from where he sat he could smell the freshness of her clean hair. The fire highlighted its red tone, and he thought that she was a beautiful young woman indeed. "I guess it's all relative," he remarked. "A friend of mine spent some time in India. This seems hard to you, but they really have it tough there. People live on the streets and eat garbage. A place like this would be heaven to them."

"I suppose that's true. I never thought of it."

Longstreet stretched his muscles and blinked sleepily. He was tired, but he felt good about all that had been accomplished. He reflected back on his first encounter with this young woman and wondered if she still remembered it. He knew that he would never mention it again.

"You know," he said, "I read in the paper on the way down that several people have killed themselves because they lost money in the stock market. One of them, they said, was down to his last million, so he jumped off a twenty-story building. His last million," he whispered and shook his head with wonder. "Poor fellow."

"That was foolish, but I suppose he loved his fortune."

"I guess so."

Jenny had pulled her feet up in the chair like a small girl, wrapping her arms around her knees. She laid her head over to one side, relaxing in the warmth of the fire. "You've had a pretty hard time I guess, haven't you?"

"No harder than some others." Clint picked up a poker and jabbed at the logs. They shifted with a groaning sound, sending a myriad of golden flecks upward. He looked around the room and commented, "I wonder what's happened in this room?"

"What do you mean?"

"Why, you never know. This is an old house. Somebody may have been murdered in here."

"Murdered! What an awful thing to think!"

"People do get murdered. Could have been right here. Or maybe a man and woman fell in love here—right in front of this very fireplace."

"I suppose that could be true." She carried on his line of thinking. "Maybe right here in this room some girl found out that life isn't fair, or some boy made a mistake."

Clint turned to face her, surprised by the depth of her imagination. "There are a lot of echoes in an old house."

The two of them sat silently for a time, and finally, without meaning to do so, Jenny blurted out, "You must despise me."

"Despise you? Why, no, 'course I don't, Jenny. What makes you say that?"

"I haven't forgotten how I treated you the first time you came. I'm spoiled to the bone, Clint. I've always known it, but it didn't seem to mean much until now."

"Oh, don't be so hard on yourself."

She turned to him and lowered her feet to the floor. Leaning forward, she asked, "Are we going to make it, Clint?"

He knew exactly what she meant. "Yes, if you want to, you will."

"But we're all so weak, all except Kat." She wanted to be reassured. "I'm afraid," she whispered.

"These are the hardest times you've ever had, but you'll make it. You just have to dig in and do what needs to be done." He stood up and looked down on her. When she looked up at him, her eyes were glistening, and he knew she was depressed and frightened. "I worked with a blacksmith once," Clint said. "I wasn't very good at it, but I found out one thing. He had to heat the iron in the fire until it could be molded. I expect that's true of people. It seems that the hard things are what make us strong, not the easy things. Maybe that's what's happening to you."

"I heard something like that in a sermon once, Clint," Jenny said, nodding seriously. "Maybe God has brought these hard times on us to make us strong. Do you think He would do that?"

Clint shook his head. "I don't know, Jenny. You'll have to ask Hannah about that. I don't know much about God. Good night." He turned and walked out of the room abruptly.

Not wanting to stay by the fire alone, she went up to her room, put on another pair of socks and a sweater, and climbed under the covers. For a time she lay there thinking about the strange conversation she had had with Longstreet. She was frightened by their situation and anxious about the future, but she was determined not to cry.

"I won't let this beat me," she whispered to herself. "I won't!"

★   ★   ★   ★

By Saturday some sort of order had been imposed on the home place. The house was slowly being cleaned of the worst of the filth that the Cundiffs had left behind. Years of disuse had added a patina of grime, but by attacking one small area at a time, Hannah could see that this could be a beautiful house again. The floors, for example, were black with grime and stained, but when she struggled to thoroughly clean one section, she saw the beautiful golden color of the heart pine, as Clint had called it.

Joshua had gone to town to buy a few supplies while the rest of them continued to clean. The smokehouse had to be tended constantly, and Clint showed Kat how to lay the green wood on the fire so that it would not ignite but simply smolder. Clint had left after lunch to go hunting and had not yet returned when Hannah heard a vehicle approaching the house. She walked to the door and said, "Father, someone's coming."

Lewis came over to look out the window. "I wonder who that is?" he murmured.

Hannah watched as a tall, gangly man got out and then two children piled out of the ancient Ford. He reached out and grabbed their hands, and they pulled away, trying to make their escape. By the time he had stepped up on the front porch, Hannah had opened the door. "Hello," she said, smiling at the man.

"How do you do? My name is Crutchfield. I'm the pastor of the church in town."

"Well, Reverend Crutchfield," Hannah greeted him, smiling more broadly, "come in out of the cold. This is my father, Mr. Lewis Winslow, and I'm Hannah Winslow."

Crutchfield released the hands of his children but gave them each a warning look. He shook hands with Lewis and bowed slightly to Hannah, saying, "I'm glad to meet you both. I heard that someone had moved in, and I've been trying to come by for a visit."

"Do you have time for a cup of coffee?"

"I'm afraid not." Crutchfield was a tall, gangly man. He wore a black suit and removed a fedora, rather the worse for wear. He had warm brown eyes, very deep set, and his brows were as black as his unruly hair. He was a homely man, actually. Hannah thought he looked somewhat like a younger Abraham Lincoln with his cavernous, sunken jaw. He smiled and introduced the children. "This is Dorcas," he said as he indicated the taller girl, "and this is Jeff."

"How do you do, Dorcas and Jeff," Hannah said. Her father greeted them as well, and then Hannah said, "Is your church the one we saw on Main Street?"

"Yes. It's at the end of Main Street. I hope you'll feel free to come and worship with us."

"Indeed we will, Reverend Crutchfield."

Crutchfield shifted uncomfortably. "I'm afraid I've got a bit of unpleasant news."

Lewis blinked with surprise. "What could that be?"

"It's your son, Joshua. I'm afraid he's got himself into a little trouble."

Hannah felt a start of fear. "What sort of trouble, Reverend?"

"Well, the fact is he bought some illegal alcohol. Bootleg, as it's called, and he was arrested. I'm afraid he's in jail."

Hannah stared at the tall man, unable to speak. It was Lewis who said, "Will he be tried?"

"Not if you pay his fine. It's a rather common offense around here," Crutchfield assured him. "The fine will probably be around twenty or twenty-five dollars, depending on the mood of Judge Garrity."

"Dad, you've got to go, but the truck's in town."

"That's why I came," Crutchfield said. "I knew you wouldn't have any way to get to town. So I came to drive you in."

"That's very kind of you, Reverend," Lewis said. "Would you give me a few moments?"

"Of course," Crutchfield replied. "Come, children, we'll go outside and wait in the car." Before he left, he turned to Hannah.

"Miss Winslow, I'm sorry to be a bearer of ill tidings, but I felt it would be better if I did come."

"I'm sorry we had to meet under such conditions. Joshua's lost his way, and he needs your prayers—as do we all."

The smile that lit Crutchfield's face made him look much younger. It warmed his entire countenance. "I'll do that," he said, "and I'll look forward to seeing you at church tomorrow."

★ ★ ★ ★

Joshua looked up when his name was called. The jailer was unlocking the door. "Come on, Winslow, somebody's paid your fine. I think it's your old man."

Joshua got to his feet and put on his coat. He pulled his hat down square on his head, dreading what was to come. He followed the jailer out of the musty jail. As he stepped into the outer office, he saw his father standing there, displeasure in his eyes. "Come along, Joshua, your fine's paid."

The jailer, a huge man with a belly that overhung his belt, grinned. "You better watch out where you buy that bootleg liquor from, boy. It'll get you in trouble. That stuff you bought could have made you blind."

"Come along, Joshua."

Joshua followed his father out and saw that the truck was pulled up in front of the jail. Several people along the walks glanced their way. Some of them grinned, and one of them whispered loudly enough, "Well, the Yankee boy got himself out of jail. How about that."

The comment made Josh angry, but his father said sharply, "Get in the truck!"

Joshua climbed inside, and his father started the engine and drove away. "What were you thinking of?" he said as soon as they were clear of town. "Don't you have any sense at all, Joshua? You know that it's against the law to buy liquor."

Joshua Winslow wanted to lash out, but he felt completely stupid. He kept his jaw clenched tight, not answering. What could he say? He had come to town merely to buy supplies for the family, but the craving for whiskey had overtaken him, and he had stupidly approached a man on the street and asked where he could buy some whiskey. The man had sold it to him himself but then had immediately shown him a badge and arrested him. Joshua would not soon forget the broad humor that everyone had shown and the remarks about Yankees being pretty stupid to try to buy bootleg from a deputy.

As he sat there, the truck jolting over the roughness of the road, he tried to think of a way to escape. There was nowhere to go, no one he could turn to, and life seemed to close in about him. The craving for alcohol was still consuming him, and he knew that somehow he would find some, no matter what it cost. In jail he had overheard talk about the former occupants of their house—the Cundiffs—being bootleggers. He had heard they were living somewhere close by, and he had a little money. *They won't turn me in*, he thought. *I've got to have something to drink!*

CHAPTER ELEVEN

Sunday Service

★ ★ ★ ★

The next morning, Hannah set herself to the task of persuading the family to attend church. She was only partially successful. Joshua said flatly, "I'm not going, and I don't want to hear any more about it." He stalked out of the house after breakfast and disappeared into the woods, walking toward the river. Hannah stared after him, afraid that something terrible was happening to her brother. He had completely changed from the man he used to be, and it frightened her to think of what lay ahead for him.

Lewis protested the idea of going to church, but Hannah simply overrode his arguments, and when the time came to leave, he was dressed and ready. He wore a dark brown suit, wrinkled from being packed in a trunk, and his hair needed cutting, but there was no time for that.

Jenny knew it was better not to argue. She was wearing a dark blue wool dress and an expensive wool coat she had bought before the stock market crash in October. The fur-lined cap on her head was probably more than she needed on this pleasant day, and although she looked very nice, discontent marred her features.

Hannah glanced at Kat, relieved that she was not wearing her old tomboy clothes. The girl had on a maroon dress, a pair of sturdy boots, and a heavy wool coat with fur on the collar and around the wrists.

"All right, we're ready," Hannah announced. She herself was wearing a simple dress with an old-fashioned cut and the overcoat she had owned for three years. She picked up her Bible and started out of the house, and when she stepped out, she was surprised to see Clint leaning against the truck. He was freshly shaven and was wearing the suit she had bought him back in New York. A flush of pleasure rose to her cheeks, and her eyes brightened. "You're going with us, Clint?"

"Wouldn't miss it." He opened the door of the truck and said, "Why don't you drive, Mr. Winslow. I'll get in the back."

"I'll ride in back with Clint," Kat piped up, and before Hannah could protest, Kat scooted around and opened the back gate of the truck and leaped up in it. Clint followed her, and Jenny and Hannah got in the front. Lewis cranked the truck, then got inside. There was no heater in the truck, and rusty holes in the floorboards let in the cool air, so before they were halfway to Summerdale, Hannah's feet were like blocks of ice.

Lewis drove into the town center and noted that people were walking toward the Baptist church at the end of Main Street. He parked the truck, got out, and walked around to let the women out. Clint jumped out of the back and then turned around to help Kat out. He glanced at the church and smiled to himself. *First thing you know*, he thought, *I'll be getting religion. Wouldn't hurt me, I guess.*

The party made their way to the church, a tall, narrow white building with a high steeple and long stained-glass windows along the sides. As the family stepped inside, the warmth was welcome to Hannah. Two men were standing in the spacious foyer greeting those who came in. One of them, a big handsome man with black hair and black eyes, came over to the Winslow family and nodded. "Good morning. Good to see you."

"Thank you," Hannah said.

"Why don't you hang your coats on that rack right over there."

To Hannah's surprise, Clint spoke to him. "Hello, good to see you again."

"Why, it's Clint, ain't that right?"

"That's right, and you're Jude Tanner."

"I remember. I worked on the part for your truck."

Tanner was wearing a mauve suit that was pinched tight across his big shoulders. He had a pleasant smile and fine teeth. "Plenty of seats left this morning." He winked at Clint.

The group turned and went to the doors that led into the sanctuary. It was not as large as the church they were used to, but the ceiling was very high, giving it an illusion of spaciousness. The stained-glass windows turned the pale morning sunlight into shafts of green, crimson, and violet. The walnut pews were smooth, and a dark runner over the pine floor muffled the sound of their footsteps as they walked down to take their seats. The back pews were all occupied, so they had no choice but to go down to within five rows of the front. Hannah felt that everyone's gaze was directed at her and her family. She turned into one of the pews, and the family followed. She was seated next to Jenny with the rest of the family on their left.

Jenny sat next to a large woman who had watched them enter, and now the woman leaned over and whispered, "Good morning. It's so good to have you. My name is Ellen Flemming."

"I'm glad to know you. I'm Jennifer Winslow."

"That's my husband—Potter Flemming. He's the mayor." Ellen Flemming waited for some sort of reaction, but Jenny simply nodded, not overly impressed with Summerdale's bigwigs.

"You're new in town, are you?"

"Yes, we're living in my mother's old home place."

"Oh, indeed! Yes, I've heard about you. I believe it was your brother who was arrested for buying bootleg whiskey."

Jenny froze and turned away, but her silence and body language did not trouble Mrs. Flemming. The big woman just kept talking, chattering on now about various members of the church. "Have you met our pastor? Poor fellow. His wife died a little over a year ago. A sweet woman she was but too easy on those children. They're really a handful." She looked over toward a boy and girl across the aisle and shook her head. "A sad case. They need a touch of the stick is what they need." Without taking a breath, she went on, "Brother Crutchfield needs to marry again. He can't control those children. Lord knows I've tried to help him the best I can. They are several widows in our congregation. Right over there. You see that woman in the brown dress?"

Jenny looked over to see a thin woman wearing a plain brown dress. She was distinctly unattractive, and Jenny was surprised to hear that she was Ellen Flemming's choice for the pastor.

"She's a widow, and her poor husband got killed in a railroad accident three years ago. She's got two girls, and she'd make the pastor a fine wife." Mrs. Flemming nodded firmly, as though the idea was settled in her mind. "She's the president of the W.M.U."

"What's that?"

"You don't know? Why, it's the Women's Missionary Union!" She seemed scandalized that Jenny would not know this information. "But Pastor Crutchfield is a little too liberal for our part of the country. He's not from here, you know."

"Oh, indeed, where is he from?"

"Oh, someplace north. Ohio, I believe. In any case, he wants to start working among the black children of the county. That's not his place—" She broke off, for the pastor's children had gotten into a vociferous argument over who would hold the songbook.

Jenny watched them and shook her head. *At least the woman is right about one thing—those children do need discipline.*

As Mrs. Flemming continued to enlighten Jenny on the pastor's flaws, Hannah examined the building. The front was occupied by a raised platform with a massive walnut pulpit in the center. There were four chairs, two on each side of the pulpit, heavily carved of golden oak and upholstered with dark red fabric that matched the carpet. Behind these were a rail with a curtain and three rows of pews for the choir. They were empty right now, but even as Hannah watched, the door opened, and two men walked out. One was Devoe Crutchfield, the minister, and the other was a silver-haired man with a look of someone who knew his own importance. The choir piled in as the silver-haired man stood behind the pulpit and the pastor moved quietly to take a seat in one of the chairs. Mrs. Flemming leaned across Jenny to tell Hannah that the man was none other than Millington Wheeler, the president of the bank. He served as the congregation's song leader and choir director.

Hannah saw Crutchfield's eyes pick out her family, and interest quickened in his expression. He nodded slightly, and involuntarily she nodded back at him.

The song leader said, "Please stand for the singing of the doxology."

With a shuffling of feet, everyone stood. Hannah noted two children wedged in between two women in the third row. One of the women reached over and plumped the boy, who looked about six, on the head. He protested the blow at once. The blond girl next to him was wiggling impatiently, and Hannah wondered why they were so close to the front. They would have been better off at the rear, she thought.

After the congregation sang the doxology, the bank president led them in a short, businesslike prayer.

The choir anthem was next, followed by the offering, announcements, and a special song, a rendition of "The Ninety and Nine" by a man with a high tenor voice.

When Devoe Crutchfield rose to come to the pulpit, Hannah noticed that he was not a graceful man. He appeared almost disjointed. His homely face reminded her once again of a young Abraham Lincoln. His black hair fell down over his forehead, and she noticed that he needed a haircut.

The preacher read his text, which was taken from John, chapter fifteen. He read a longer passage, then read the ninth verse slowly and with emphasis. "As the Father hath loved me, so have I loved you." He bowed his head and prayed, then began to preach. Hannah sat quietly, her eyes fixed on the preacher, leaning forward slightly.

She was impressed by the sermon. It was very simple, the points clear: Jesus loved His people first without any change, second without any end, and third without any limitations.

"You need not fear death," he was saying, "for His love will not cease then. Christ will go with you even down to the grave. And He loves without any limitation—the same immeasurable love Jesus bestows upon His chosen ones. The whole heart of Christ is dedicated to His people, for He loved us and gave himself for us. . . ."

Crutchfield's homely face glowed as he spoke of the love of God, and when he came to the end of his sermon, Hannah felt warm and at peace. He smiled and looked much younger as he said, "We think that God loves people like *us* the most, but that's not so. He doesn't love us any better in America than He loves the Eskimo, or the cannibals in Africa, the Germans, or sinners like Mary Magdalene full of the devil." Hannah noticed this did not go over well with some of the congregation. There was a stirring, and she understood the reason. Most congregations wanted to think they were God's favorites, but Devoe Crutchfield did not believe this. He closed the Bible and said quietly, "A man or a woman can go wrong in a great many ways." He hesitated and looked over his congregation before adding, "But if you have love in your heart, God delights in it."

Hannah saw the banker, Mr. Wheeler, who had been sitting in the chair on the rostrum, shake his head, displeasure written across his face.

They sang the final hymn, followed by an invitation to anyone present who wanted to come forward and accept Christ, but no one came. Crutchfield called upon a man to pronounce the concluding prayer, and then the service was over. As they filed slowly down the aisle toward the foyer, Hannah waited for someone to greet her, but no one spoke. A few nodded slightly, but there was not a rush to greet the visitors. She was the first of her family to pass through the front doors, where Reverend Crutchfield was standing on the top step greeting his parishioners. He took Hannah's hand and smiled. "I'm glad to see you, Miss Hannah."

Pleased that he remembered her name, Hannah smiled. "That was a very fine sermon. Very biblical and most encouraging."

Crutchfield blinked as if he were unused to such compliments, and then he smiled. "I hope you'll come back often."

Hannah nodded, then moved on. Clint was at the end of the procession, and he too noted the coolness of the church members toward the newcomers. He knew little about churches but felt this one would not be his first choice.

Clint joined the family, and they made their way to the truck as Jenny complained about the choir. "Some of the women in the choir sang horribly off key. You'd think they'd hit the right note once in a while," she said with irritation.

"You're accustomed to the trained choir of a large church," Hannah responded. "In small towns like this they have to let anybody sing who wants to."

Jenny went on to tell about the gossiping Ellen Flemming, and she related the pastor's history. "Those two children misbehaved the whole time," she said.

"It's very hard on a man to raise young children alone," Hannah murmured.

As they headed home, Lewis was silent. He had enjoyed his church back in New York, but since his misfortune, he had given little thought to God. This morning, however, Reverend Crutchfield's sermon had spoken to him, clearly reminding him of his need for God. With the truck rattling and bouncing over the frozen ruts of the road, he thought, *If God loves me, why did He let all these terrible things happen?* Then he realized that others throughout history had asked the same question, including the patriarch Job, whom the pastor had referred to in his sermon.

★ ★ ★ ★

The next day Lewis was coming back from the barn. His old clothes were filthy from his work of patching the barn to prepare it for holding livestock. When he reached the back porch, he heard an approaching wagon and looked up. The Winslows' home was located near a fork in the road, with one branch leading into town and the other heading north. Lewis had noted that from time to time, people would come down from the north, usually in old wagons or battered automobiles. But this wagon coming down the road was new and the team of horses healthy. He was surprised when the wagon stopped and the elderly driver climbed out, then helped the woman beside him out. Lewis looked down at himself, embarrassed by his dirty condition, but nonetheless, he moved toward the wagon and greeted the pair. "Hello," he said. "How are you today?"

"Very well. My name's Jesse Cannon. This here's my wife, Dolly."

Lewis could see bits of Jesse's white hair sticking out from under his fedora. He seemed frail, but he had the brightest blue eyes Lewis had ever seen. His wife was a small woman, also with blue eyes and silver hair.

Lewis surmised that the two were expecting to be asked in. He could not imagine why, but he said quickly, "It's chilly out here. Won't you come in?"

"Thank you, sir," Mrs. Cannon replied. For an older woman she appeared to have a great deal of energy as she made her way vigorously up the steps. Then Lewis remembered that he had seen the couple in church on Sunday and told them so.

"Yes, we seen you there too," Cannon remarked. "Just came by to visit."

"Well, do come in."

Lewis moved up the steps behind them and opened the front door. When the couple entered, he was relieved to see Hannah approach. "Hannah, this is Mr. and Mrs. Cannon. My daughter, Hannah Winslow, and I'm Lewis Winslow."

In earlier days, Hannah would have fled to her room rather than meet strangers, but things had completely changed for her. She was glad to see the older couple, for she had been wondering if they would ever meet any of their neighbors. "Won't you come into the parlor?" she said. "We have a fire in there. It's so cold out."

Very soon the older couple was seated on the couch, which was rather the worse for wear, but the room was cleaned up, and Hannah gave a brief, hearty prayer of thanksgiving that they had not seen it as it was.

Cannon looked around with approval. "You shore got the place lookin' nice. The Cundiffs kept it like a hogpen."

"You know them, the Cundiffs?" Lewis asked.

"I know who they are," was the noncommittal answer. He leaned forward and said, "We were glad to see you in church Sunday."

"I enjoyed the sermon very much. The pastor's a fine preacher."

"I think so," Dolly Cannon said. "Such a tragedy, his losing his wife."

"Yes, we heard about that. It must be very hard for him."

"The poor man. He does the best he can. Those children are so . . . so lively."

"A pair of young devils is what they are," Cannon said, but he was smiling. "The women of the church want them to be angels, but they ain't that, and neither are any of the rest of the young'uns."

Hannah excused herself and went to the kitchen, where she found Jenny working on dinner. "We have company," she said. "An older couple from up the road. Is coffee made?"

Jenny nodded. "Yes, and there's the last of that cake left over."

"Well, this is a good time to use it. Come on, I want you to meet them."

Five minutes later Lewis and his two daughters were enjoying the coffee and cake with their guests. "This all your family?" Jesse Cannon asked.

"No, I have a third daughter and a son too."

"Was that your son with you in church, then?"

"No, that was Clint Longstreet. He's a friend. He helped us move down here."

"Longstreet? I wonder if he's any kin to General Longstreet?"

"You mean the Civil War general?" Lewis asked. "I'm sure I don't know."

"I served under General Longstreet."

Lewis and his daughters looked at one another and then back at the old man. Here was a relic indeed! "You actually fought in the Civil War?" Jenny asked.

"Went in when I was sixteen. Stacked my musket at Appomattox." The old man was proud of his accomplishment, and Lewis was fascinated. "I'd love to hear some of your stories."

"Well, it won't be hard to get that out of him," Dolly said, laughing pleasantly. "He loves to talk about General Longstreet."

"Best general in the whole war," Jesse declared, nodding firmly, then asking, "How is it that you folks have the old Laurent place?"

"It was my wife's home—Deborah Laurent—which she had kept even after we were married. She died two years ago, and then we had some misfortune last month and decided to move into it."

"The stock market thing. Is that it?"

"That's it."

Jesse looked at his wife, and they nodded. "I told you, Dolly." He turned back to Lewis. "We're shore sorry to hear of your loss. I knowed your wife."

"You knew Deborah?"

"Shore did! As a matter of fact, I guess we're kin."

"You're kin to us?" Lewis could see that his daughters were entranced as well.

"Ain't sure of the ins and outs of it," Jesse explained, "but it's like this. Wendell Laurent, Deborah's father, was my half brother. Carolyn, his wife, died when Deborah was born in 1878.

Wendell, he built up the plantation real good. Died in 1925. Never did remarry."

"Why, this is wonderful! I don't know much about my wife's people."

"Well, I'll have to say this. If you Winslows is as good o' folks as them Laurents was, then you'll all be in good shape come Judgment Day."

Lewis was more excited than he had been since the tragedy had struck them. "I'd really like to hear more. And if you're kinfolk, I guess we can use first names. I'm Lewis."

"Fine, and you can call us Dolly and Jesse. Folks around here are a mite suspicious of strangers, but lots of folks remember your wife's people. I will have to say, Wendell was a mite stuck up. A little snooty, if y'all knows what I mean, but I got on with him."

"Hush up, Jesse!" Dolly scolded.

"I ain't tellin' nothin' bad. Wendell was jist thataway. He was a good man, and Deborah was a good girl. I remember her at the brush arbor meetin's when Brother Wheeler come through preachin'. Had a sweet voice, she did, and her jist a young'un too."

Lewis dropped his head, remembering how Deborah had sung to him. "Yes, she had a sweet voice."

Dolly put her hand on her husband's knee. "We best be gittin' on."

"That's right. We jist dropped in to say howdy, and we gots a turkey for y'all out in the wagon. Always want to bring somethin' to newcomers. I bagged three plump ones yesterday while I was out huntin'."

Lewis found it wonderful that a veteran of the Civil War would have keen enough eyesight to hunt wild turkeys. "I'm so glad you came by, Jesse, and you, Miss Dolly."

He walked with them to the wagon, took the turkey, which was already dressed, and held it by its feet while Jesse and his wife drove away. When he went back inside, he looked down at the turkey and said, "Well, there are some good people here and our kinfolk too."

"Isn't that wonderful, Father?" Hannah's face was glowing. "Who would have thought such a thing?"

★   ★   ★   ★

That afternoon Kat had left the house at three o'clock to go to Seven Point River, the river near their house, which had fascinated her ever since they had arrived at the homestead in Georgia. Back in New York she hadn't been allowed to go anywhere by herself, but now that they lived on a farm, her dad gave her great freedom to explore. She had followed a deer through the woods, surprised that it did not flee at her approach. It was a female, apparently a very young one. She had followed it down a gully, then up the other side into an area of towering hardwood trees. She heard the chattering of squirrels and more than once had caught sight of them as they sailed from one high branch to another.

But now as she emerged into a clearing, she realized she had been exploring for more than an hour. Looking up at the sky, she muttered, "I'd better get back to the river. I've got to get home before dark."

She turned and walked the other direction, but a few minutes later she became aware that nothing looked familiar. She could not even find the gully she had crossed, and at that instant panic seized her. She was, after all, a city girl, and now the woods appeared ominous. Clint had told her just yesterday that he had seen panther and wolf tracks in the vicinity. With that thought, she began to run, spurred on by her growing fear.

She ran until she was almost out of breath and then realized she had no idea whether she was headed for the river or away from it. Her face and hands were scratched by the briars that grew throughout the woods, but this did not trouble her as much as the panic that rose in her. She stopped on the edge of a large grove of tall trees on her left. To her right was a group of smaller trees where the underbrush was very thick. She did not remember any of this territory.

Kat took a deep breath and tried to think which way to go. She did not know how long she stood there, but when she turned to look around her, a scream rose to her throat. Standing not ten feet away from her in the shadow of a grove of small evergreens was a boy. She guessed his age at somewhere between twelve and fifteen. He was much taller than she was, and he held a gun loosely in the crook of his arm.

Kat swallowed hard, and her breath came fast. "Hello," she said.

The boy did not answer but continued staring at her. His floppy hat was pulled down low, almost covering his eyes, and she saw that his features were lean. He was wearing a worn coat patched in several places, and a pair of rough-looking boots poked out from under a pair of oversized pants. She had time to note that they were tied with string instead of shoelaces.

"I'm afraid I'm lost," she said, her voice breaking slightly.

She expected him to speak, but he did not; he only turned and motioned with his free hand.

Kat did not know what to do, but actually there was no choice. "I'm looking for the river," she said, hurrying to keep up with him. "If you can take me there, I can find my way home. My name's Kat Winslow."

The boy glanced at her, and she saw that his complexion was dark and he had high cheekbones. He walked with a loose, jointed grace, making his way down a path.

Kat had to hurry to keep up with him, and since he did not speak, she assumed that for some reason he could not.

She was greatly relieved when ten minutes later they stepped into a clearing and she saw a wooden shack that was silver with age, with a chimney emitting smoke into the air. A roughly built barn sat over to one side, and in a corral, she saw two cows and a mule.

"Come on."

Well, he *could* talk! Kat followed him toward the shack, and when he opened the door, he stepped in first, and she followed him. She found herself face-to-face with a frightening-looking woman who had the same high cheekbones as the boy and eyes that glittered like chunks of coal. She was tall and thin and wore a floor-length dress with long sleeves. It looked like the boots that were poking out from under her dress were men's, and her black hair was pulled back and tied with a ribbon. "Who's this here girl, Dallas?"

"Found her." The entire end of the cabin was occupied by a massive fireplace built of river stone, and a fire crackled in it. Pots hung over it on large hooks.

"My name's Kat Winslow. I live at the old Laurent place. I got lost, and this boy found me."

"Bad to get lost," the woman said, making an abrupt movement toward Kat. Kat involuntarily stepped back, frightened at the woman's primitive quality.

"I'm Tennie. This here's Dallas."

"I'm pleased to meet you. Do you . . . do you think you could show me how to get home?"

"I reckon so. Dallas, you take this girl back to the Laurent place."

"Yes'm."

"You take Francis—it's too fer to walk." The woman hesitated, then said, "Here, better drink some of this. You look near 'bout frozen."

She dipped a tin cup down into a pot of boiling liquid hanging over the fire. She brought it back and said, "Drink all a'this. Hit'll keep you warm on the way home."

The cup emitted a sharp aromatic aroma as Kat lifted it to her lips. She couldn't identify the sharp taste. "What is it?"

"Sassafras tea," the woman named Tennie said. "You ain't never had no sassafras?"

"I don't think so."

"Hit's good fer you. Hit'll clear your blood out. I'll come by and give you some the next time I head thataway."

Kat drank the tea and then handed the cup back. "Thank you."

"You see, Dallas, this young'un's got manners," Tennie said. "Now, you take her on home, and you come right back. You hear?"

"Yes'm."

Feeling dismissed, Kat followed the boy out to the corral, where he picked up a bridle. They walked up to the mule, a tall, rawboned animal that lowered her head for the boy to put the rope halter on. He mounted with a swift leap, then turned to Kat and motioned. Kat went over and stood beside the mule. "I don't know how to get on."

The boy named Dallas gave her a surprised look, then he extended his hand. She took it, and with plenty of effort from both of them, she managed to get astride the mule.

"Git up!" Dallas called, and Francis the mule moved out

wearily but soon broke into a jolting trot. Kat felt her teeth jar, but she did not complain. She put her arms around the strange boy, for she was afraid of falling off, and when she touched him, she felt him stiffen.

The rough pace of the mule was not conducive to talk, but finally the boy slowed the animal down to a fast walk, and Kat said, "Was that your mother?"

"Granny."

"Oh, you two live there alone?"

"Yep."

Kat was finding it difficult to make conversation. Dallas would do no more than offer one-word answers. Kat soon saw the river, however, and relief washed through her. "We live over that way past that grove of trees."

A few minutes later the mule stopped in the back of the house. The door opened, and both Jenny and Hannah came running out. Kat slipped off the mule, and Hannah grabbed her and hugged her.

"Where have you been? We've been scared to death."

Jenny reached out and patted Kat, her face showing relief. "Dad and Clint are out searching for you."

"I got lost," Kat said. "This is Dallas. He found me and took me to his grandmother's house. She told him to bring me home."

Hannah summoned a smile for the boy, even though he had his face turned to the ground. She had been terribly worried, but now she said, "Thank you so much for bringing Kat home. Won't you come in and get warm?"

Dallas shook his head and, without a word, leaped on the mule and turned her away. Kicking her with his heels, he bounced away back toward the river.

"What a strange young man," Jenny marveled.

"He doesn't talk much, and his grandma looks like a witch," Kat said.

"What's her name?"

"She just told me it was Tennie. I don't know her last name."

"Well, we've got to go out and try to find the men. They're as worried as we were." Hannah reached out and shook her. "Don't you ever do that again. You'll never know how scared we were."

"I'm sorry," Kat said. "I just got turned around."

★　★　★　★

Later that night at a supper of sweet potatoes, pork chops, and biscuits, Clint commented on Kat's rescuers. "I've heard about that woman. She's an herb woman. Her name's Tennie Sharp."

"What's an herb woman?" Jenny asked.

"She collects herbs and makes medicine out of them. A lot of folks swear by it. They did back where I grew up too."

"What about her grandson, Dallas?"

"As far as I can make out, one of her daughters took off with a man and wound up in Dallas. Had this baby, and when he was six years old she died, and Tennie had to take him to raise. A lot of folks think the boy's retarded."

"He's not. He just doesn't want to talk," Kat put in.

Clint turned and said, "Kat, the next time you go exploring, don't go north along the river. Dog Town's up that way, and there are some pretty rough characters."

"That's right," Hannah said. "You go the other way—and don't you ever get lost again!"

CHAPTER TWELVE

JOSH'S TROUBLES

★ ★ ★ ★

The freezing wind whipped out of the north, swirled around Josh, and held him as if in a powerful fist. He had set out walking, and a sudden freezing rain had fallen, soaking him to the skin. Now as he stumbled along, he almost turned to go back, but gritting his teeth, he moved ahead. His feet were so numbed by the cold he could not feel them.

He had gone without a drink for four days now, and the craving was consuming him. He had not known how addicted he was to alcohol until now. Feeling the sleet stinging his face, he pulled his scarf up over his chin and mouth and his hat down. He had been sick for two days and had tried to ignore it, but his craving for whiskey had become so strong it drove him out of the house toward Dog Town.

Going back into Summerdale had been out of the question, for since his arrest there, he knew there was no way to get liquor. An old toothless man had stopped his wagon the last time Josh had set out on this road and talked with Josh. He had appeared ignorant and dirty and was headed north, so Josh had said, "You live up that way?"

"Shore, live in Dog Town. You know it?"

"No."

"Come up and see us sometime." He had made an odd clicking noise with his false teeth and then winked. "In weather like this a man needs somethin' to put some fire in his bones. We ain't got much up there, but we manage to keep warm."

The words had stayed with Josh and had drawn him out of the house, for he was as miserable as he had ever been in his life. He had six dollars in his pocket and knew he would give the last penny of it for a drink of whiskey. He remembered being in the Bowery in New York once on a Sunday morning with a friend. He had seen with disgust the bodies lying in doorways, men so drunk they couldn't roll over. They had watched as the paddy wagons loaded them like logs and hauled them off to jail.

I'm no better than they are, he thought, and he hated himself. Still, he kept walking until he finally turned the bend and saw a small scattering of buildings. It wasn't very much like a town— just a few stores with some shacks surrounding them in a disorderly array. As he moved down what passed for the main street, he saw a general store, a blacksmith shop, a saloon, a gas station, and several other nondescript buildings. He hesitated, then marched toward the saloon.

When he entered, he saw a wood stove glowing cherry red at one end of the room, and the heat from it almost hurt his frozen skin. Scanning the room, he saw four rough-looking men, all with their hats on, sitting around a table playing cards. Across the other end was a bar, and as he stepped over to it, one of the men at the table got up and went behind the bar. He obviously hadn't shaved or bathed in days, or even longer. "What'll it be, mister?"

Josh almost said, "Give me some whiskey," but then he remembered how he had wound up in jail the last time he had blurted this out. He did not know how to handle the situation, and he knew the other three men were all listening intently, their eyes fixed on him. Hesitantly, Josh said, "I guess . . . you got any coffee?"

"On the stove." The man picked a cup off the shelf and handed it to him. "That'll be five cents."

Josh fumbled in his pocket, came out with some change, and put down a nickel. Taking the cup, he went over and poured it full from the blackened coffeepot.

The coffee itself was black and rank, but at least it warmed him. It couldn't, however, dispel the chill he felt at the glares of the men who were all watching him. Overwhelmed by a sense of danger, he drained the cup and took it back to the bar, mumbled his thanks, then left as quickly as he dared. His craving for alcohol had been made worse by the coffee, and he shook his head in despair.

He trudged down the street, and a man came out of the blacksmith's shop wearing a ragged old coat. He muttered, "Can you spare a quarter, mister? I ain't had nothin' to eat all day."

Josh could not spare anything, but he reached into his pocket and separated a quarter and held it up. "Can a man get a drink of whiskey around here?"

The old man trembled as he reached out his hand. "Shore. You go right down that road a quarter of a mile. Back off on the left you'll see a house. That's the Skinners. They can fix you up, no questions asked."

Josh surrendered the coin, then frowned as the old man started off for the saloon. Josh knew that the quarter would not go for food but for whiskey. Angry with himself and his situation, he turned and briskly strode out of town. The wind had grown colder, and the precipitation was now half sleet and half snow. It bit at his face, and he shoved his hands far into the pockets of his overcoat.

He saw the house sitting back in the trees with a single dirt road leading to it, now glistening with white flakes. Desperately he marched toward it but had not gone halfway when a voice stopped him. "What do you want?"

Startled, Josh blinked and turned to find a man watching him. He had his hands in his pockets and his hat down over his eyes, but Josh could see he was a big rough fellow.

"I'm looking for a drink," he said. He did not care, at this point, whether he was arrested or not.

He could tell the big man was weighing him in the balances before finally saying, "Come on to the house."

As Josh followed him, the man asked gruffly, "What's your name?"

"Josh Winslow."

"You the fellow that run the Cundiffs outta their place?"

Josh shook his head. "Not their place. It belonged to my family. What's your name?"

"Jordan Skinner. How'd you know about us?"

"Some bum in town told me I could get a drink here."

Skinner said no more as he led the way to the house. It was unpainted and had a tin roof, but yellow light glowed out of the windows. Jordan removed one hand, kept the other in his pocket, and opened the door. "Go on in."

Josh stepped inside and found himself in a kitchen where a family had evidently gathered for dinner. A skinny man who appeared to be in his fifties sat at the end of a table. He had patchy gray hair on his head and stubble on his chin. His eyes were close together, sharp and penetrating. "Who's this, Jordan?"

"Name's Winslow. He's come to get a drink."

The good-looking young man sitting beside the older man said, "He's probably the law. What'd you bring him in here for, Jordan?"

"He ain't the law. He's about to fall down." Jordan pulled off his cap and pulled his hand out of his pocket, allowing Josh to see the pistol inside. "He looks like he's needin' a drink pretty bad."

Two other people were in the room. A thin woman with salt-and-pepper hair, her face worn with the rough life she had led, was cooking at the stove.

A young woman of no more than eighteen was seated at the table. He thought she would be pretty if she were fixed up, and she still was in a primitive sort of way. Her ragged dress clearly revealed the lines of her figure as she got up and moved closer. "What's your other name?"

"Josh."

"Hello, Josh Winslow. I'm Dora. You really come to get somethin' to drink?"

"Yes, I walked all the way here."

The older woman stomped over to him and stared in his face. "You look sick to me," she said in a sharp voice. "You don't need to come bringin' no fever in here."

Dora laughed. "He ain't sick. The man jist needs a drink." She turned and faced Josh squarely, challenge in her wide-spaced eyes. They were an odd color, hazel with bright green flecks. "Could you use a drink?"

Josh smiled uncertainly. "The last time I said yes to that, I wound up in jail."

"That was in Summerdale, warn't it? We heard about it." She walked over to the table and poured a glass half full from the heavy-looking jug that was sitting there. She handed it to Josh. "Here."

"He might be a revenuer." The speaker was the young handsome fellow who was now glowering at Josh.

"He ain't no revenuer, Billy Roy."

"No, I'm not. I just need a drink."

"Can you pay for it?" The old man spoke up harshly.

"Yes, I can pay for it. Will you sell me a jug?"

"It'll be five dollars."

"That's okay."

Dora watched the visitor carefully. There was something about him that spoke of quality, and she could not have put her finger on it, but she knew he was not rough like most of the men she knew. His hands, she saw, were finely formed, and his hair was neatly cut. He needed a shave, but even so she could tell he was fine looking, and he wore a fine coat.

"Take your coat off," she invited. "Sit down and have a bite to eat."

"You're mighty free with my groceries, daughter."

Dora simply laughed at him. "Don't be so miserly, Pa. Sit yourself down, Josh."

Josh hesitated but then sat. He threw down half of the contents of the glass and shuddered as the raw alcohol hit his stomach.

"Pretty strong stuff, ain't it?" Jordan grinned, showing his two missing front teeth. "They make it a little smoother than that where you come from, don't they?"

"Where do you come from?" the older man asked. "I'm Simon Skinner, by the way. This is my place."

"Came from New York," Josh mumbled.

"New York," Dora whispered. "Why'd you leave New York to come here?"

Josh drained the glass and braced himself against the force of the alcohol. It was warming his system now, and he felt better. "Our family lost everything in the crash."

"And what crash was that?" Jordan asked, a puzzled frown on his face.

"The stock market crash."

Jordan scratched his head in confusion.

"I read about that in the paper," Dora said. "Some fellas

jumped off a building when they lost all their money."

"Well, we didn't jump off buildings, but we lost everything."

"You run the Cundiffs outta their house," Simon said accusingly.

"It's my mother's old home place. They were just squatting there. We had to have a place to live."

"How many in your family?" Dora asked. She had sat down across from Josh, who couldn't take his eyes off her full lips. She listened as Josh named his family and then said, "Let's eat."

The whiskey had hit Josh hard. He noticed his hands were steady now, but his reactions were not. He took a plateful of food from Dora, and when he asked her what it was, she said, "Pigs' feet, grits, and taters."

Josh's stomach rolled at the mention of pigs' feet, but he found the concoction surprisingly tasty and realized how ravenous he was as he began to eat. After he had cleaned his plate, Dora said, "Maybe you need a drink on top of that." She refilled his glass. "Here," she said, "come on over and sit by the stove. You look like you're about half froze."

As Josh got up, he was conscious of a ringing in his ears and a numbness over his body. The whiskey was powerful, more potent than any he had ever had before. He slumped down in a cane-bottom rocking chair, took the glass, and sipped the drink. Dora pulled up another chair and said, "Tell me about New York. What's it like?"

★　★　★　★

"I don't know about this fella," Simon said, shaking his head. "We don't know him."

Dora looked over at the visitor, who was sleeping soundly. His head was back, his arms limp in his lap. She had poured drinks for him until he had passed out. "This fella might be useful."

Simon wasn't so sure. "I don't know. Useful for what? He ain't got no money. We took all he had."

"Pa, you know how bad things have been," Dora argued. "The law nearly got you the last time you tried to move some liquor. They're watchin' us all the time, you know."

"We'll just wait until they quit."

"I don't think they're gonna quit. That sheriff's determined to get us. He's got some Feds out here too."

Simon Skinner knew his daughter was right, yet his moonshine still was cleverly concealed so far back in the woods he didn't think any revenuer could find it. The Feds were afraid, he knew, for one of them had been shot while prowling around. The authorities had never been able to prove it was any of the Skinners, but the whole county knew they were the only likely candidates.

Simon leaned back and looked at his daughter. She and Billy Roy were the smart ones of the family. "What are you thinkin'?" he asked quietly.

"Josh here's a city fella. Nobody would suspect him of movin' bootleg. He says he's got a truck too. He could pick it up and drop it off to our dealers."

"He might at that, but we don't know if we can trust him."

"We know he's green," Dora said, "which is why nobody would ever suspect him. He's high class, Pa. You seen that, didn't ya?"

"Yeah, I seen it all right, but I don't know."

"We ain't got much choice, Pa. Besides," she said, grinning, "I can make him like me if I wanna."

Simon slapped his leg and laughed. "You shore can do thet, all right. You got half the men in this county runnin' around after you. You be careful, now, you hear? I don't want no grandbabies jist yet."

"I can handle him, Pa. Let him sleep for now. When he wakes up, we can talk to him."

★　★　★　★

Josh stared at the three men across from him and then glanced at the two women. Mrs. Skinner was back in the shadows, but Dora stood close to his side. Her eyes gleamed with excitement, and she urged him, "You should do it, Josh. It's a good deal."

Josh could not believe he was even considering such a thing. When he had awakened in a haze, Mr. Skinner had come right at him with his offer to move his bootleg whiskey. Josh hardly knew what he was agreeing to.

Now, his head a little clearer, he stood thinking, *I must be crazy! Why, I can't do this!* "It would never work, Skinner. I don't know anything about the country."

"There ain't nothin' to know. If you got a truck, you just come at the right time. The liquor won't even be here at our place. We'll stash it somewhere wheres you can pick it up, then we'll draw you a map. You won't have to make but a few deliveries. We wholesale it, don't you see. And you don't even need to start till January. We've got December covered."

"A man could go to jail for a long time," Josh said. "I've never done anything like this."

Billy Roy Skinner laughed. "But you ain't never wanted a drink and had no money to buy it either, ain't that right?"

Billy Roy had hit the nail on the head. *If I can do this just long enough to make some money and save it all, I can get back to New York. I should have stayed there in the first place. Arlen would help me get set up. I can go into business with him. His family still has plenty.*

Everyone's eyes were on him, and it was Dora who said, "You will do it, won't you, Josh?"

Josh nodded slowly and said, "All right, I'll do it."

"You understand this," Billy Roy said, pulling out a pistol from his pocket. He held it loosely in his hand, but Josh could not take his eyes off of it. "You say one word to anybody 'bout this, and I'll blow your puny head off. You got that?"

Josh nodded. He got it very well. He had no doubt that he was hearing the exact truth.

"I won't talk. After all, I'll be sent to jail as quick as anybody else."

"That's right," Simon said, grinning. "This will be a good thing for us, Winslow. Nobody would suspect you. You keep your mouth shut, and we'll make a lot of money together."

"Come on, I'll drive you home," Dora said.

★　★　★　★

Dora stopped the car a half mile from the Winslow home and said, "You'd better git out here. I don't want your folks seein' you ridin' with me."

"All right."

Dora had questioned him as she drove the Chevrolet along the rutted frozen road. As Josh grabbed the door handle, she reached over and pulled him back by the neck. She kissed him full on the lips, holding him there for a moment before releasing him. She was laughing, her eyes gleaming. "You and I could git to be real good friends, Josh."

Josh didn't know what to say. He picked up the jug and got out. Josh knew he was moving into dangerous territory, yet he felt there was no turning back. He had gone through a door and locked it behind him. The past seemed tarnished and dull, like a worthless trinket . . . but the future looked just as bad.

CHAPTER THIRTEEN

A DIFFERENT KIND OF CHRISTMAS

★ ★ ★ ★

As Hannah straightened up, her back gave a twinge. She had been down on her hands and knees scrubbing the upstairs hallway floor. She could not believe how the grime of years had ground itself into the wood. Beginning at one end, she had taken a square foot at a time and scrubbed fiercely with the strongest laundry soap available until the golden color of the heartwood pine came through. Now, as she stood up and looked down at the distance she still had to go, she sighed despondently.

The days of hard, grinding labor such as she had never before experienced had passed until it was now Christmas Eve. She could not differentiate between the days, for they were all alike, passing like the ticking of a clock with no face and no hands. A numbness filled her as she thought about what a grim Christmas it would be.

Slowly she picked up the bucket of filthy water and started downstairs to heat more. Moving down the stairs, a sudden thought flashed into her mind, even as tired as she was. She remembered a stone archway in the church she had attended in New York City. One of the ushers had once told her when he saw her looking at it, *"The keystone never sleeps. It holds the others in place."*

The words had stayed with her, and now they brought some sense to what she and her family were going through. Her weariness lately had been crowding out all other thoughts, but now she saw with great clarity that the keystone of their lives had crashed, the arch had fallen, leaving only a group of stones heaped together, where before there had been order and beauty. *How can our lives be put back together into something meaningful?*

When she reached the kitchen, she found Clint sitting alone at the table drinking coffee. He looked up at her, concern in his eyes. "You're worn out. Let me get that for you." He got up and took the bucket from her, opened the outside door, and threw the wash water onto the ground. When he came back in, she reached for it, saying, "I've got to go get more."

"It'll wait. Sit down and have some coffee."

Hannah willingly sat. He filled a mug with coffee and put it before her. "One of these days I'm going to have to learn how to harvest some honey. That'll taste good in our coffee."

She looked up, surprised. "Can you really do that?"

"I guess so. Jesse Cannon says he'll teach me."

"I'd like to come with you. I've never seen such a thing."

"All right."

The two sat quietly for a time, Hannah remaining even more silent than usual. She was not a woman given to light talk, and Clint had learned over the weeks to admire her stubbornness. He had seen her work when she was so tired she could hardly pick up one foot and put it ahead of the other. He glanced down at her hands now and noticed that they had changed. Once they had been well cared for and soft, but now they were roughened by the strong soap and calloused from the hard work. "The house looks good," he said. "It's a fine old place when you get through all the dirt and grime."

Hannah smiled faintly. "That upstairs hall is a horror. I've scrubbed half the morning and haven't gotten five square feet clean."

"I'll tell you what," he said. "Let me go over it with a blade of some kind. There's an old plane out in the barn. I can get the rust off of it, sharpen it, and plane off the grime right down to the wood. It'll look like new. I'll have to do a little sanding, but it'll beat all that scrubbing you're doing."

"Oh, but you've got enough to do, Clint."

He did not answer, but she knew him well enough now to know that he would do exactly what he said. He never seemed to tire, or if he did, he never mentioned it. She sipped her coffee and glanced at him. He appeared so solid and alert, the irregularity of his features so masculine. A small smile touched his lips, and she thought it signaled his inner character. It showed the world a serene indifference, yet there was also a sadness in him that she believed indicated he had lost contact with the world and could depend on nobody but himself. As they sat quietly together, she wondered about what truly guided his life. She knew he'd weathered some hard times, but he had survived those years and now used his experiences as a protective armor against the harsh demands of the world. She had ambiguous feelings about him, for she was aware she had fenced off men from her life. She had long ago put away all thoughts of marriage and children. Now she wanted to ask Clint if he had ever loved a woman, but she could not bring herself to do so.

"Stopped snowing," Clint observed, glancing out the window.

"That's too bad. I wasn't sure we'd see snow at all this year, so it's nice to have a little on Christmas Eve."

Clint did not miss the sorrow in her eyes. "You look sad," he said gently.

"I am, in a way. We always had such big celebrations at home, decorating and giving gifts and singing. I don't mind it so much for myself, but I hate it for Kat."

Clint stared into his coffee cup, turning it in his big hands. "It's not too late."

Hannah shrugged. "We don't have any money for gifts."

"Doesn't take much money." He smiled at her. "I've had quite a few moneyless Christmases. Tell you what. Let's do it up right."

"What do you mean, Clint?"

"I mean, there are plenty of trees out there. All we have to do is cut one down and bring it in. We don't have to have store-bought decorations, do we? We can make our own." He grew excited at the thought, and it struck her that it took little to make Clint content. This man could take an idea and run with it, and now the idea of having a Christmas celebration brightened his eyes. He straightened up and swept the air with his right hand. "It's Christmas Eve. Let's get started."

Hannah smiled. "All right. What do we do first?"

★   ★   ★   ★

Clint worked like a whirlwind all day, and his enthusiasm carried at least some of the family with him. Joshua had been strangely silent, almost sullen, for the past few weeks. He had disappeared from time to time, borrowing the truck, and Hannah had wondered what he was doing with himself but could not bring herself to ask him. In any case, on this particular day he actually made himself useful by going out with Clint and Kat to hunt for a tree. When they had found the right tree, Josh chopped it down, and he and Clint dragged it back to the house. Josh starting making a frame to hold it upright while Clint took his gun and went out again.

"A bunch of wild turkeys have been beggin' me to shoot 'em. The pesky varmints will probably disappear today," he said, grinning.

But he came back two hours later with a huge wild turkey. He tossed it down with a thump on the porch, saying, "I shot it. Someone else can clean it."

Lewis volunteered to do that messy job, and following Clint's instructions, Hannah and Jenny baked corn bread for the dressing.

As for Kat, her eyes glowed, she was so excited. She and Clint went out to gather red berries until they had a sackful of them. When they returned, he put her to work threading them on a string with a needle and thread. As for Clint, he directed the making of the corn-bread dressing as if it were a great project. Hannah crumbled the cooled corn bread and transferred it to a mixing bowl while Jenny chopped onions and diced an apple. She added a little oil to the mixture and then added it all to the crumbled corn bread. Hannah added a lightly beaten egg, some broth and salt and pepper, and mixed them all together.

"Now just cover it and set it on the porch till morning. Then we'll stuff it inside that big old bird I shot, and we'll have a fine meal tomorrow."

With preparations for the next day's festivities completed, the women worked together on the evening meal. By the time it was ready, everyone was hungry, so they ate generous helpings of eggs and ham. Since Clint had fenced in the chickens and built a hen house for them, the family's egg supply was plentiful. After eating, they popped popcorn and strung this on thread as well.

Lewis had built up a big fire in the living room hearth, and it threw its flickering shadows over the tree. The women sewed the berries and the men the popcorn, and as they finished each string, they draped it over the limbs of the tree.

Clint played the harmonica while they sewed, keeping them entertained with all the Christmas carols he knew. The family joined in singing, and from time to time, Clint would stop playing and would sing along too in his clear baritone voice. Curiously, Hannah asked him, "If you never went to church, how do you know so many Christmas songs?"

"Well, everybody sings them at Christmas. They just stuck in my mind, I guess."

"Did you have big Christmases when you were growing up, Clint?" Kat asked.

Clint hesitated and dropped his head. "No," he said softly, "I didn't."

Seeing the sadness on the big man's face, Hannah quickly intervened. "Give us another one, Clint. You play that harmonica so well."

After the tree was decorated, Clint said, "We ought to make some candy, but I don't know how to do that."

Lewis spoke up. "I know how to make taffy." They all turned to look at him in disbelief, and he shot back with some irritation, "Why is that such a surprise to you?"

"I don't know, Dad." Jenny grinned. "I just never knew you could cook anything. How do you make it?"

"First, we have to know if we have the ingredients." He looked over at Clint.

"We've got some molasses, a little sugar, and butter."

"Great!" Lewis said. "And how about vinegar and baking soda? Do we have either of those?"

Kat was wrinkling her nose in disgust. "Why would you put vinegar in candy?" she said. "I don't believe that'll be any good."

"You just wait," Lewis promised.

"We have a little, Father," answered Hannah. "Do you need much?"

"We only need a little of each. Okay then, I'll take care of the cooking, but then we'll all have to pull it."

The women went in to watch their father prepare the candy. He buttered the sides of a large saucepan, then dumped in two cups of sugar, a cup of molasses, and a quarter cup of water. Putting the pan on the stove, he brought the mixture to a boil, stirring it slowly.

After a time he lifted the pan, added two tablespoons of butter, a pinch of soda, and two teaspoons of vinegar, then poured the mixture into a buttered pan. He used a large butcher knife to turn the edges. "All right. Time to pull."

"What do we do, Daddy?" Kat demanded.

"Well, the first thing you do is put butter all over your hands," Lewis said as he demonstrated.

Kat laughed. "That'll be fun." She buttered her own hands and then ran to get Josh and Clint. The two men came in, and following the example of the others, they greased their hands.

"This is the way you do it," Lewis said. "You get the taffy up into a ball, and you pull it with your fingertips like this. You keep pulling at it until it's hard to pull, then you pull each piece into a long strand about an inch and a half thick. Then you cut if off with buttered scissors or a buttered knife. We need to get going. It gets hard quick."

The kitchen was soon filled with the sound of laughter, for as the taffy hardened, it became harder to pull. It was soon too hard for the women to handle, so the men finished the job, and Lewis said triumphantly, "Now, that's molasses taffy."

"That was such fun, Dad!" Jenny exclaimed.

As he looked at his daughter's glowing face, Lewis thought, *It's the first time she's looked happy since we left New York. We've got to do more things like this.*

Finally they went back into the living room and nibbled at the delicious taffy while Lewis said, "You know, I think it'd be a good thing if we read the Christmas story."

"That's a fine idea, Father. I'll go get my Bible." Hannah jumped up, ran upstairs, and was soon back with Bible in hand. "Here, Father, you read it."

"No, you read it, Hannah. You've got such a good reading voice."

Hannah hesitated and glanced around, but then settled down on a chair with the Bible on her knees. She began to read the story from the book of Luke, and they all listened attentively.

While Hannah read, Lewis let his eyes run around the room, feeling sad as he looked at his family. He glanced at Josh, who had drawn slightly away from the others, sitting in a shadowed corner, his head averted. A pang of grief caught at Lewis for the loss of his son. Josh was living in his own world, still drinking, though Lewis could not, for the life of him, imagine where Josh was getting the money to buy liquor.

His glance shifted to Jenny, and he was struck again with her beauty. Yet the hard times had changed her. She had lost the vivacity that was once hers. *It's all my fault. I should have had more sense somehow.*

His eyes moved to Kat, and here his heart warmed. *At least Kat's happier here than she was in New York,* he thought. *I'm glad of that.*

He observed Clint sitting back, his hands laced together, watching Hannah's face intently. *I don't know what we would have done without Clint. He's been our lifeline, and I don't know what we'd do if he left. We'd all sink. Thank you, God, for sending him to take care of us.*

Finally his eyes rested on Hannah, and as she continued to read the Christmas story, Lewis wondered, not for the first time, what was to become of his oldest daughter. She had been an enigma for years. *She should be married now with children, but she's never again talked about men since breaking up with Preston. I don't know what went wrong there, but it must have hurt her deeply.*

The soft sound of Hannah's voice filled the room, and the fire added soft poppings and groanings as the logs settled. Outside, the world was nearly frozen, but inside they felt warm and comfortable. Yet, as Hannah read, everyone in the room was wondering, *What will we do? How will we survive?*

When Hannah completed the reading, she closed the Bible and said, "That's a beautiful story, isn't it?"

Everyone just nodded, except for Kat, who said, "I bet this house is nicer than the stable Jesus was in."

She was sitting beside Lewis, and he reached over and put his arm around her, saying huskily, "Yes, it is, and I'm thankful that He made a place for us here."

His words warmed Hannah's heart, and she smiled. She was proud of her father. His emotions had been going downhill, but now, at least for this one moment, the Winslows were together and he seemed happier. Her eyes lifted, and she met Clint's gaze. He smiled at her and nodded, and then the wind outside rose into a keening whine.

"Tomorrow's Christmas," Clint said. "We'll have to hang those stockings on the mantel."

It had been Clint's idea to do this, and Hannah knew he had some scheme in mind. He had asked each person to provide a stocking, and as Clint fastened them with tacks to the mantel, she said, "You think Santa Claus will come?"

"Yes, I think he will."

★ ★ ★ ★

The next morning everyone's stocking was bulging with nuts, hard candy, an apple, and an orange. In Kat's stocking she was delighted to find a fine new pocketknife. Her eyes glowed. She knew that Santa Claus had not brought this, but she played the game. "Santa brought me exactly what I wanted."

Hannah was standing back with Clint. "Where did you get that?" she whispered.

"Picked it up at the store a week ago."

Hannah was filled with pleasure. "That was so kind of you."

Clint turned and looked down at Hannah, his smile lightening his whole countenance. "Children need Christmas," he said quietly.

Kat went over to Clint and reached up to plant a kiss on his cheek, her eyes sparkling. "It's a good knife, Clint. I'll keep it always."

"Always is a long time," he said, pleased that he'd brought some joy into her young life.

"I don't care," Kat said. "I'll give it to my little boy when he's my age, and I'll tell him about this first Christmas in Georgia."

"You're making pretty long-range plans," Hannah said with a smile. "The Bible says, 'Take therefore no thought for the morrow.'"

But Kat ignored her sister's admonishment. "Play that pilgrim song, Clint."

"Now? But it's not a Christmas song."

"It is in a way," Kat insisted. "We're all pilgrims, and one day we'll have a big Christmas in heaven—with Jesus there!"

Hannah felt tears rise to her eyes at this simple thought, and as Clint brought out his harmonica, she sang with Kat the words that had come to mean so much to her:

> *"I am a pilgrim and a stranger,*
> *Traveling through this world below;*
> *There is no sickness, toil nor danger,*
> *In that bright world to which I go. . . ."*

January—September 1930

★ ★ ★

CHAPTER FOURTEEN

TROUBLE AT SCHOOL

★ ★ ★ ★

"I don't want to go to school, Daddy."

Lewis had stopped the truck and was preparing to get out when he heard Kat's plaintive cry. He turned to look at her and saw that her face was tight with apprehension. He reached over and drew her close. "You've got to go to school, honey, you know that. And you'll make a lot of friends here."

"But I don't know anybody!"

"Well, you will before the day's out. Come on, now. We've already talked about this. You can make it either good or bad, so let's make it good."

Releasing the girl, Lewis got out of the truck and stood looking at the school. It was a relatively new two-story red-brick building. He had been told that this new school in town replaced several ancient one-room schoolhouses scattered throughout the county.

"Come along," he said.

Kat kept very close to her father, brushing against his arm. She glanced at the children playing in the yard, and when they stared back at her, she averted her face. Kat had always been good at her studies, but New York was a different world from Summerdale, Georgia.

The two entered the building, and Lewis asked the first

person they saw, a young man, if he could direct them to the principal's office.

"Right down there. Last door on the left."

Lewis followed his direction, and when they entered the office, a middle-aged woman sitting at a desk turned and said, "Yes, sir, may I help you?"

"My name is Lewis Winslow. This is my daughter Katherine. I need to enter her in the seventh grade."

"Come in, Mr. Winslow. You'll want to meet our principal."

Lewis and Kat waited until the woman had knocked on the door to her left, then opened it. "A new pupil, Mr. Latimer."

"Have them come in."

Lewis and Kat stepped into the principal's office, nodding to the woman, and saw that a smallish blond man was getting up from behind his desk, which was littered with papers. He wore gold wire-rimmed glasses and a dark brown suit. "I'm Gale Latimer."

"It's nice to meet you, Mr. Latimer. My name is Lewis Winslow. This is my daughter Katherine."

"You're new to the community, then."

"Yes, my wife's family used to live here. Her name was Laurent."

"Well, let's get this young lady settled. How are you today, Miss Katherine?"

"Fine," Kat said. The principal had a kind face and manner, and as he spoke with her, she felt somewhat more at ease.

The two filled out the necessary papers, and then Mr. Latimer said, "I'll have Miss Rogers take you to your classroom. Your teacher will be Miss Lane, Katherine."

"I'll just leave you here, Kat, but I'll be waiting outside when school is out."

"All right, Daddy."

Kat followed Miss Rogers down the hall to a room. The woman opened the door, and Kat followed her in. She shot a glance around the room and saw about two dozen students at their desks, all of them staring at her.

"This is Katherine Winslow, Miss Lane. A new student."

"Thank you, Miss Rogers."

Miss Lane was an older woman with gray hair and smallish eyes. She wore no makeup, and her hair was pulled back in a bun that seemed to stretch her eyes to a slant. She wore no jewelry, Kat noticed, and there was no smile on her face. "Well, Katherine, you'll be behind. You're late entering. Where did you go to school previously?"

"New York City."

The expression on Miss Lane's face changed, and Kat heard somebody mutter, "Why, she's a Yankee girl."

"That'll be enough from you, Johnny Satterfield! Katherine, take that desk in the third row," she said as she indicated the desk in front of the round boy who had just spoken. "We're going to start with geography today, but since you don't have your books yet, you can just listen."

"Yes, Miss Lane."

Kat had brought a small bag containing pencils, a small pencil sharpener, an eraser, a ruler, and her lunch. She put the bag down on the desk and sat down tensely. Miss Lane gave her a careful look and went on speaking. A map of the world was rolled down over the blackboard, and she began to call out the names of cities, asking different students which country they were in.

Kat was good at geography and was surprised that she knew them all. *Why, this is easy,* she thought. She was surprised when the other students had difficulty naming where Peking was located. Miss Lane grew impatient and said, "Well, come along. You must know where Peking is."

A voice directly behind her spoke out, "I guess it's in Japan."

"That's wrong, Johnny."

Miss Lane went around asking different students, and no one knew the answer. Finally she said with exasperation, "Doesn't anyone know where Peking is?"

Kat lifted her hand, and Miss Lane fastened her eyes on her. "Yes, Katherine?"

"It's in China."

"That's right. Now, the rest of you ought to have known that. Have you had World Geography, Katherine?"

"I studied it, Miss Lane."

"Well, I'll try you out." Miss Lane began to call off cities, and Kat knew where all of them were, except one in Russia.

"You children make me ashamed of you. Here's this girl from

the North who knows all the answers. You're going to have to work harder."

At that moment Kat's head was jerked back. "Ow!" she cried as the grip on her hair was released. She turned around to stare at a student named Johnny Satterfield, who was grinning at her.

"What's wrong with you, Katherine?" the teacher demanded.

"He pulled my hair," she said, pointing back at Johnny.

"Why, I didn't do no such a thing," Johnny said. "She just don't like me."

"How could she not like you?" Miss Lane snapped. "She doesn't even know you."

"Aw, you know how Yankees are. They don't like nobody from down South."

Miss Lane glared at Satterfield sternly. "The next trouble I have out of you, you're stayin' after school."

As soon as Miss Lane turned, Kat felt a pain, for Johnny Satterfield had pinched the back of her neck hard. She jerked away but kept her lips tightly closed.

★   ★   ★   ★

At lunchtime Kat took her paper sack and filed down to the cafeteria with the others. Most of them had brought their lunches, although lunch was also available in the cafeteria line. Her family had no money for this, so Kat moved away and took a seat at one of the empty tables. She opened her sack slowly, watching as the other students filled up the other tables. They were all talking and laughing, and some of them were even roughhousing.

She opened her sack and pulled out the sandwich and apple and began to eat. She had not taken more than three bites when a small girl about her age came over and said, "Hi, my name is Martha Logan."

"I'm Kat."

"I thought your name was Katherine," she said as she sat down and opened her lunch.

"That's my real name, but I like Kat better." She bit into her juicy apple and almost squirted her new friend in the eye.

"Well Kat, don't pay no mind to that Johnny Satterfield. He makes trouble for everybody."

"Why does he have to pick on me?"

"Because you're new. You live in the place with the big oak trees, don't ya?"

"Yes, I do."

"We live about two miles north of you. Maybe we could ride home together sometime. My dad picks me up every day."

Kat was worried about her father having to bring her every day. It took gasoline, and she was acutely conscious of how much it cost.

"I'll ask my dad. It would be nice to ride together."

While the girls ate their lunch together, Martha told Kat all about the other children in their class. She told her who the nicest girls were and which boys to avoid. By the time lunch was over, Kat was amazed at how much better she felt having found at least one friend.

"Come on, Kat, let's go outside and play."

"All right."

The two girls went out to the playground, and Martha said, "Look, they're playing Red Rover."

"I don't know how to play that."

"Oh, there's nothing to it." Martha shrugged. "There's two sides, and each side joins hands. Then the leader says, 'Red Rover, Red Rover, send somebody over.' And the other side sends somebody over. They try to break through the line. If they don't break through, they have to join that side. If they do break through, the one who did the breakin' gets to take somebody back to their side."

The game was relatively simple, and Kat grew to like it. No one called her to go over, but before long, the leader of her side said, "Red Rover, Red Rover, send Johnny Satterfield over."

Kat watched as Johnny Satterfield came running directly at her. She held Martha's hand tightly, but when Johnny smashed into them, he not only hit their hands, he threw himself against her. Kat's hand was torn away, and she fell down on the cold ground.

"You're not supposed to hit people like that!" Martha cried out, her faced flushed.

"Aw, if she cain't take it, let her go back to New York." Johnny grinned and grabbed one of the larger boys. "Come on, Ralph. You're on our side now."

Kat could no longer hold her tongue. "You're nothing but a big bully!" she hollered.

At which Johnny Satterfield called her a vile name. Kat had heard the word before, but she was shocked that anybody would say it out loud.

The game ended when the bell rang, but Kat kept her eyes glued to Johnny. She watched him approach two children, a boy and a girl much younger and smaller than Johnny. Kat recognized them as being the pastor's children, whom she saw every Sunday in church. He grabbed the two by the back of their necks and bumped their heads together.

Kat Winslow was usually even tempered, but this sent her into a fit of white-hot anger. She ran straight at Johnny in a rage and threw herself at his back, driving him to the ground. She was striking him with her fists, crying out, "You dirty old bully, you!"

Satterfield, of course, was taken completely off guard. He managed to roll over and tried to defend himself, but she struck him directly on the nose. He roared with anger and struck out at her, hitting her on the chest and throwing her to one side. He lunged at her, striking, and Kat did the best she could to defend herself.

Kat was getting the worst of it when suddenly a voice demanded, "All right, what's going on here?"

Kat was seized by the arm and lifted up, and a large man said, "Who started this?"

"I didn't do nothin'. She just hit me right in the back."

"He was picking on those little kids," Kat said, mortified with anger.

"Well, you two will have to talk to Mr. Latimer."

Johnny glared at her. "Now, you see what you've done! We'll both get a paddlin' for this. I hope he busts your behind."

★　★　★　★

"Where did you find the boat, Clint?"

Clint turned from scraping the bottom of the wooden boat.

"It was pulled up under some brush out behind the house."

"Isn't it all rotten?" Hannah asked.

"No. It's made out of cypress. Cypress lasts longer than most wood." He turned the boat over and admired it. "That's a nice johnboat."

"Why do they call it a johnboat?"

"I don't know why they call it that. It's just a boat with a flat bottom and a square end that's usually used on rivers. Maybe some guy named John invented it. Well, I could stand some fried catfish." The air was cold, and he wore no hat. The breeze blew his sandy hair, and he brushed it back with his hand.

"Do you fish with a pole?"

Clint smiled. "No, that's too slow. We'll run a trotline."

"What's a trotline?"

"Well, come on, and I'll show you. You can help me make it."

Clint led Hannah to a table out on the back porch. He reached down into a sack and began to pull out some items. "This is the line itself. See how stout it is? Even a hundred-pound catfish couldn't break that."

"Do they get that big?"

"No, not around here. Maybe in the Mississippi River some-times. You see, we tie this end of the line to a tree, and then we paddle across, let the line out, and tie the other end to a tree across the river. Then we put on the bait lines." Pulling a coil of smaller cord, he clipped off a two-foot length and then opened a box containing some large hooks. "Just tie it on like this." He demonstrated how to shove the cord through the eye of the hook and knot it securely. The loop made a circle. "Hold up your hand," he said. "Put your finger out."

When Hannah put out her finger, he showed her how to loop the line over the finger and shove the hook through. He tight-ened it and tugged at her finger, bobbing it up and down. "We put these about five to ten feet apart on the main line, put some bait on them, and bingo—we wait for the fish."

"Are you going to put it out today?"

"Right now."

"How are you going to get the boat down to the river?"

"I guess the only way I know is to haul it. You don't need to come. It's too cold."

"No, I want to. It'll be a break from housework."

"Let me get a rope to tow this thing with, then." He suddenly looked at her and smiled. "We'll be in harness together just like a pair of blue-nosed mules."

★　★　★　★

Hannah was out of breath by the time they reached the river, even though Clint had done most of the work. Now he showed her where he wanted her to sit in the boat and shoved it out into the water. Clint took his position in the middle of the boat and rowed across the river. "The first thing we'll do is put the main line across."

Hannah was uncomfortable in the cold wind, which was especially biting over the water. They put the line across, and then Clint said, "Okay, you put on the hooks just like I showed you, and I'll put on the weights and keep the boat steady."

They started back, and Hannah quickly learned to put the hooks on. It was simply a matter of slipping them over the main line and tightening them. She was careful, for the line jerked from time to time as the boat moved around. She watched as Clint fastened various weights at regular intervals. "What are those for?"

"To pull the line down to the bottom of the river. That's where the big cats feed."

When they reached the other side, Clint drove the johnboat up on the bank and said, "Okay, you can get out now, and we'll tie up." He waited until Hannah was out of the boat, and then he stepped out and pulled the boat up on the shore. "I'll come back a little before suppertime and bait up."

"Can I come with you?"

"You can if you'd like."

"I'd like to come."

Clint stared down at her. He knew she possessed vitality and a vivid imagination, but when he had first met her, she had kept these qualities tightly under control. The family's tragic losses had brought her out of her shell, and now as she stood in the cold wind facing him, he wondered what lay beneath her outer calmness and serenity. At times he had seen laughter and pride in her eyes, but often those same eyes revealed sadness, like a cloud passing over the sun. "Better get back," he said.

As the two made their way back to the house, he hummed a tune that she didn't recognize.

"What's that?"

"Oh, just an old song."

"Sing it for me."

Clint sang out the jaunty song in his clear baritone:

"Muskrat, muskrat, what makes your back so slick?
I've been livin' in the water all my life
There's no wonder I'm sick
I'm sick, I'm sick, I'm sick.

"Rooster, rooster, what makes your spurs so hard?
I've been scratchin' in the barnyard all my life,
There's no wonder I'm tired
I'm tired, I'm tired, I'm tired.

"Jaybird, jaybird, what makes you fly so high?
Been eatin' these acorns all my life
It's a wonder I don't die
I don't die, I don't die, I don't die."

"That's the gist of it anyway. I think there's another verse about a groundhog, but I forget the words."

"You know more songs than any man I ever heard of," Hannah said with admiration in her voice.

"Songs are cheap. Growing up poor, we had to entertain ourselves somehow."

"Was your childhood hard, Clint?"

"Well, not as hard as some, but it was tough enough. I guess," he said slowly, "a man just comes out of nothin', and he's headin' toward somethin'. Trouble is, I know what's behind me, but I'm not sure what lies ahead of me."

The two walked on, both filled with their own thoughts, and neither spoke until they came in sight of the house. As they climbed the porch steps, Hannah said, "Let's take Kat with us when we do the trotline later. She needs to have some fun. And she's so fond of you, Clint."

"Well," he said, grinning, "that's mutual."

★ ★ ★ ★

As soon as Kat came in with Lewis, both Hannah and Jenny knew something was wrong. "You're late," Jenny said. "Did the truck give you trouble?"

"No, not really," Lewis said wearily. He looked down at Kat and shook his head. "We had a little problem at school."

"It wasn't my fault!" Kat exclaimed. "It was that mean Johnny Satterfield!"

Jenny and Hannah listened as Kat poured out her story. She gave the details of the whole incident, her face flushed, and concluded with, "So we had to stay after school for an hour. I hate that old Johnny Satterfield."

Lewis said, "You'll just have to bite the bullet, sweetheart."

"Come on, Kat," Hannah said, "you can help me make supper. I'm going to make something new for dessert. Dolly Cannon gave me a recipe for something called sweet fried pies."

"Fried pies? I thought you baked pies."

"Not according to Miss Dolly. Now, come along. It'll be fun."

The two went to the kitchen, and soon Kat forgot her problems while working on Miss Dolly's sweet fried pies. They made a pie crust, but instead of putting it into a pie pan, they cut it into small circles. They put a dollop of canned peaches Miss Dolly had given them on each circle, folded the crust over, and pressed the edges together with a fork. Then they fried the pies in a pan of sizzling hot shortening.

"These are the best things I ever ate! I'm going to have them every night," Kat announced.

"Then you'll be as fat as one of your pigs."

"I don't care. They're so good!"

The sound of a car coming down the driveway interrupted their conversation.

"You go see who it is, Kat," Hannah said.

Kat started for the door, but she encountered Jenny, who was coming down the stairs. They went to the door together, and they were surprised to see the pastor and his two children. "Well, Reverend Crutchfield."

"I'm sorry to bother you, but do you have a minute?"

"Why, yes, come on in. Hello there," Jenny said, speaking to the children. They both muttered a sullen reply.

"Come into the kitchen. We're making fried pies," Kat said.

"Fried pies? I thought you baked pies," Devoe Crutchfield said.

"You'll have to have one, Reverend Crutchfield."

"I want a fried pie," six-year-old Jeff said. The boy had black hair like his father and dark eyes, while Dorcas, his sister, had blond hair and blue eyes.

"I get two. I'm bigger than you are," she said.

"Well, maybe there'll be enough for everyone. Come on," Jenny said, eyeing the children. She had seen them misbehave in church and had mentioned to Hannah they needed a good paddling.

When they entered the kitchen, Hannah turned around, surprised. "Why, Reverend Crutchfield!"

"Please, Miss Hannah, call me Brother Crutchfield. It's the custom here in the South. We don't care for titles too much."

"Then Brother Crutchfield it is. Why don't you sit down and we can have some fresh fried pies."

The pies went over great, and Devoe Crutchfield had a cup of coffee with his.

"I wish we had some milk," Hannah said, "but we don't have a cow."

Crutchfield grew thoughtful. "You know, I think I know where you might get a cow, and she's coming in fresh too."

"We can't afford to buy one right now," Hannah said regretfully.

"I think this one wouldn't cost you anything. There's a family called Logan. They live up north of you just a ways. They come to our church."

"I know Martha Logan," Kat said quickly. "She's in my class. She's nice."

"Well, they've got a tree they want taken down and cut up, and Mack told me that if somebody did the job, he's got a nice cow for them."

"I'll bet Clint could do it—him and Josh," Kat said quickly. "Then I'd get to learn to milk."

"I'll look into it," Hannah said. "It would be nice to have fresh milk."

Crutchfield moved his cup around and stared down into the depths of it as if it were a crystal ball. He seemed disturbed, and finally he said, "I want to thank you, Kat, for taking up for my children."

"Well, that old Johnny Satterfield is mean."

"Yes, I guess he is. He's a bully."

"If I was bigger, I would have whupped him."

"Well, don't do that again," Crutchfield said, smiling, "but I do want you to know how grateful I am." He looked over at the two women and said, "I'll tell you what. I need some exercise. I've got a saw and an ax. If Mr. Longstreet wants to take that tree down, I'll help him."

"Why, you don't have to do that, Brother Crutchfield," Hannah said.

"Be good for me."

Jenny turned to Kat. "Why don't you take the kids and play pick-up-sticks with them."

This turned out to be quite interesting, for both children, as Kat discovered, were spoiled to the bone. They argued about everything, and the game required a strong referee.

Crutchfield remained at the table and finally said, "I had another motive in coming here. I'm looking for someone to help me."

"Help you how?" Hannah asked.

"Well, I need a housekeeper, of sorts. Someone who'll come in the afternoon and clean up the house." He sighed and said, "I'm so busy it gets to be kind of a mess, I'm afraid."

Jenny said, "Why, I'd be glad to help you out, Brother Crutchfield." Actually Jenny was tired of the work around the farm and thought it would be nice to have a little ready cash.

"Do you think you might manage to come in the afternoon and do some cleaning and pick the kids up at school—and then maybe cook a meal?" He smiled sourly. "I've been eatin' my own cookin' so long I'm about to make us all sick. Of course, I couldn't pay much. You know Baptist preachers aren't rich."

Jenny made up her mind on the spot. "I'll be glad to do what I can, but I'm not the cook that Hannah is."

"You're better than I am, I'd guess." A look of relief washed across the minister's face. "Will tomorrow be too soon?"

"No, I'll be there at noon."

After the preacher and his children had left, Hannah said, "Are you sure you want to do that, Jenny?"

"It would be a nice change of pace. But you'll have to teach me how to cook some, Hannah."

"Well, I don't know much myself, but Miss Dolly can cook anything. Maybe she'll give you lessons." She thought about the minister and said, "He's lonely, isn't he?"

"Who isn't?"

"But we have each other. All he's got are those two children."

"And he's doing a sorry job with them. They're spoiled rotten."

Hannah shook her head. "Well, he clearly needs help."

"Yes, and we need the money," Jenny said. "Never thought I'd be taking a job, but things have changed for us, and we've all got to do what we can to pitch in."

CHAPTER FIFTEEN

JOSH AND DORA

★ ★ ★ ★

Josh sat quietly at the table eating the pancakes Jenny and Hannah had made, listening as the rest of the family talked. He had grown silent since his visit to the Skinners, and he slept little at nights. His conscience twisted in him like a sharp knife, but that did not stop him from sneaking off to the Skinners to buy his whiskey. He listened as Jenny spoke of going to the preacher's house, then asked, "What are you going to his house for?"

Jenny turned to him and shook her head, an odd look on her face. "I never thought it'd come to this, Josh, but I'm going to be a housekeeper for Brother Crutchfield." She laughed. "Quite a comedown in the world. I feel like a tragic character in a Shakespeare play."

"It isn't that bad," Hannah interjected. "The poor man needs help with those two kids, and I'll bet that house looks like a cyclone went through it."

"When do you start?" Josh asked, spearing a morsel of pancake and chewing it thoughtfully.

"Today at twelve o'clock."

"I'll take you in the truck," Lewis offered.

Josh's conscience might have been in poor shape, but his mind worked rapidly. "Dad, I forgot to tell you I had an offer to make a little money moving some hay for a man named Collins.

Let me take Jenny in, and then I'll move the hay and pick her up when she gets off."

Lewis was pleased. Josh had shown no interest whatsoever in helping with the family's finances. "That's fine, son. I'm glad to hear it."

His father's obvious pride disturbed Josh. *If he knew what I was really doing, he'd probably order me out of the house*, he thought bitterly. He continued to eat slowly, and after his last bite of pancake he got up and said, "I'm going to work on that fence. If we ever get any cattle, we'll have to have it."

Clint looked up with surprise. "Well, that's fine, Josh. You and me together can slap that fence together in no time."

Josh went out to the fields, and as if in penance, he worked harder that morning than he had since they had arrived at the farm. Clint spoke of some of his adventures on the road, and Josh was surprised to find himself liking the fellow. He had been resentful of Longstreet almost from the beginning because the tall man made him feel inadequate. Now he threw himself into the work and was surprised when Clint looked up and said, "It's almost eleven o'clock. I expect you'd better go in if you're going to get Jenny to that preacher's house on time."

"It has gotten late. You coming in?"

"I'll just go ahead and get the last of this section."

"I'll see you later, Clint."

As Josh made his way toward the house, he thought, *There's still time to get out of this. I haven't actually done anything yet, but if I get caught selling it, it'll be the penitentiary for me.*

He shoved this thought out of his mind because he had run out of whiskey the day before, and now, almost eagerly, he looked forward to making enough money to buy more—and to leaving this place if he could get enough money together.

★ ★ ★ ★

Josh pulled the truck up in front of Reverend Crutchfield's home and said, "All right, Jenny, I'll pick you up at six o'clock sharp."

"Don't be late, Josh. I don't want to have to walk home."

"I won't. Don't let those little devils get the best of you."

"They're only kids. Surely I'm tough enough to handle a six-year-old and an eight-year-old."

Josh nodded, waved, and drove away. As he left town he pulled the map Dora had given him from his overalls pocket. He spread it out on the seat beside him and glanced at it while he drove. Dora had written directions underneath it with surprisingly good penmanship.

He headed south for two miles, looking for a barn with Rock Island Salt painted on the side of it. As soon as he saw it, he slowed down and began looking to the left. Dora had told him it would be hard to see the road, for it was overgrown and barely wide enough to permit a vehicle. *"It's an old logging road,"* she had said, *"and it's all grown over, but you can get a truck in there."*

He almost missed the road, but he stopped, backed up, and then carefully nosed the ancient vehicle off the road between two towering stands of timber. He drove very slowly, hoping no one had seen him leave the highway. He had checked carefully, but you never could tell when a hunter might be around. The serpentine road snaked through the woods, and he muttered, "It's a good thing there aren't any other turnoffs. I would have gotten lost a long time ago."

Finally he reached an open spot where the timber had been cleared off.

"What next?" he said, picking up the map. Dora had written, *Look for a pine tree split into two at the edge of the old timber to your right.* He turned the truck to the right, driving over the seedlings that had sprung up since the trees had been harvested. He had not driven more than a hundred yards before he saw it. Without shutting off the engine, he leaped out and entered the shadow of the trees. It was just after noon, and the sun shone brightly in the clearing, but here the towering trees blotted out the light. Underneath the trees, the ground was soft with fallen needles. The last direction had said, *Go twenty steps, and you will see a tarpaulin. The whiskey is under it.*

He found the cache almost at once and quickly pulled the tarpaulin back. The whiskey was in jugs of various sizes, many of them two- or three-gallon containers. He tucked a smaller one under his arm and grabbed the crooked handles of two larger ones. He made his way back out to the clearing, looked around, and saw no one. Quickly he set the jugs down, opened the back gate of the truck, and pushed the whiskey in as far as he could reach. He ran back and got more, working feverishly for the next half hour. Finally the last jug was loaded on the truck, and he ran back to get the tarp. Returning with the heavy canvas, he leaped into the truck bed and pushed all the jugs toward the cab. The jugs being made of glass and stoneware, he wondered how he would keep from breaking them. "I should have thought to bring something to keep them from shifting," he muttered.

He packed them together as tightly as he could, then threw the tarp over them and tucked the edges firmly under the jugs. "I should have brought some hay or something to disguise this load. If they stop me, I'm a goner."

He shut the rear gate of the truck, got back into the cab, and turned very slowly. He drove even more slowly as he was leaving, not wanting to break any of the bottles.

When he got to the highway again, he paused at the edge of the woods and looked. No one was coming in either direction. Down the road he saw smoke from the chimney of a house but no cars. Inching the truck forward, he got back on the highway and then sped up. He found he was gripping the wheel so hard his hands were cramping, and he leaned back and forced himself to relax.

He picked up the paper and turned it over. He found the directions to the spot where the first delivery was to be made. He had studied it carefully, but now he was extremely nervous as he moved down the road. Several times he passed cars and trucks, and more than once he moved over to pass a wagon pulled by a team of mules. The delivery spot was thirty miles away, and he glanced down at the gas gauge, which was close to empty. His heart sank. "Should have gotten gas," he whispered desperately. He kept checking the gauge as he followed the directions, and finally he pulled off the highway down a narrow road to a farmhouse. He drove up to the front and got out.

A pleasant-looking man came out the front door and said, "Howdy, what can I do for you?"

"My name is Winslow." Josh was not sure if the man had been told his name, and he did not know how to ask if he was at the right place. Just the wrong word here, and he would wind up in jail for a long time.

"Why, shore, Simon told me you'd be comin'. Why don't you

pull around to the barn back behind the house."

Weak with relief, Josh nodded. He drove the truck around, and the farmer, who said his name was Foss, unloaded a third of the whiskey.

Foss pulled some bills from the back pocket of his overalls. "I got the money right here." Josh took the cash and nodded. He studied the man's face to see any signs of guilt, but Foss might have been buying watermelons for all that his face showed. He said cheerfully, "Tell Simon I'll need another batch in about a week, maybe two."

"I'll tell him," Josh said, then jumped in the truck and gunned the engine. Remembering the jugs remaining in the back, he slowed down and consulted his map again.

He did not relax until he had made two more deliveries. In each case the recipient of the whiskey paid him, and he felt the bulge of the bills against his thigh deep in his pocket. When he left the last location and headed for home, the pressure left him.

It was only four o'clock when he was within two miles of the Summerdale city limits, so he decided to go to the Skinners' first, give them the money, and buy a jug for himself. When he was turning off the highway toward the Skinner place, he saw a car pull out from where it had been hidden behind a clump of tall grass. His heart beat faster. "It looks like the law," he muttered. He pulled over to one side as they blew the horn, and the car nosed up behind him. Two men, wearing guns on their hips with their overcoats drawn back, approached him. One of them, a thickset man with a massive neck, said, "Howdy."

"Well, hello, Sheriff."

"Afraid we're gonna have to inspect your vehicle."

Josh forced himself to smile. "Sure, I'll open it for you." He got out of the truck and opened the back while the other man, a chunky, barrel-shaped individual with a hat pulled down to his eyebrows, glanced in.

"Empty except for that tarp, Ed."

"Okay, you can go on, mister," Ed said. "Sorry to detain you."

"It's all right, Sheriff." Josh shut the tailgate, aware that his knees were weak and his hands were trembling. He climbed back into the driver's seat, waved at the two revenuers, and headed on down the road. Shaken by the experience, he drove very slowly all the way to the Skinner place.

Seeing nobody in front of the house, he got out, and as he walked up the front steps, Dora came out. She was wearing the same dress she'd been wearing when he'd first met her—a flimsy affair that hung off one shoulder. The dress didn't seem warm enough for such a cold day. She didn't appear uncomfortable, however, even standing on the front porch barefoot. Her hand on one hip, she smiled at him with a lazy, bold insolence. "Why, come in, Josh. I've been expecting you."

Josh stepped tentatively inside and looked around. "Is your dad here?"

"No, him and the boys are out makin' up a new batch. Here, take your coat off. I got coffee on. Or maybe you'd rather have a drink."

"I really ought to be going, Dora." Josh started back out the door, but she grabbed him, pulling at his coat, and he had no choice but to slip out of it. Shivering from the cold, the idea of a drink pleased him. He reached into his pocket and came out with the roll of bills. "Here's the money."

She took it and began leafing through it. "You have any trouble?"

"Two lawmen stopped me, but it was after I'd gotten rid of the stuff. If they'd stopped me earlier, it would all be up."

"You're gonna have to disguise what you're carrying, Josh," she said, walking to the fireplace and grabbing a box from the mantel. She shoved the bills inside and said, "We should have thought of that."

"I thought about getting some hay. I could make a tunnel in it and put all the liquor in the back, and it'd look like a full load of hay."

"That's a good idea. We've got plenty of hay in the barn. We'll do that next time. Now, you sit down and make yourself comfortable."

Dora shooed two cats and a dog off the old, worn couch and indicated a seat for Joshua. She poured both of them a glass of whiskey from a jug in a corner cabinet, and as she did so, he could not help noticing again her skimpy dress and the way she filled it. As she turned with the drinks in hand, he averted his eyes before she could see him staring at her.

Dora had noticed, however, and she smiled knowingly.

"Drink up," she whispered, nestling close beside him on the couch.

He drank the fiery liquor too quickly, and it hit his stomach with a jolt. He gasped, his eyes watering.

"Don't be in such a hurry. We've got plenty of time."

"I . . . I have to pick my sister up at six," he muttered weakly. The whiskey began taking effect at once, and she watched him with a raw angular light in her eyes.

"Tell me about New York some more," she murmured. "What's it like?"

"It's big."

"Well, I know that! Did you go to the theaters a lot? Tell me about it. What about the women you went with there?"

He began to speak freely as the liquor loosened his tongue, and she urged him to tell her more of his exploits with women. He did not really have that many experiences to talk about, but she took great pleasure in the conversation, laughing heartily with him as she egged him on. Suddenly she said, "Oh, I'd better pay you." She pulled the box off the mantel and got out the roll of bills, peeling off several of them. Coming back to Josh, she handed him the money. "A little bonus in there and a jug to take with you."

"I'd better take more than one."

"No, I want you to come back soon. This way I know you will."

Josh tucked the money into his shirt pocket as she poured him another drink. He had been cold when he'd arrived, but now the room felt delightfully warm with the fire popping in the fireplace and the whiskey burning inside. Her face was growing hazy, and he shook himself. "I think I'd better go."

"My family won't be back until late tonight," she murmured, leaning hard against him.

Her meaning was unmistakable, and he tried to push her away, knowing that this road would lead to nowhere but trouble. But she got her arm around him and pulled his head down with surprising strength.

At that moment Josh Winslow could have turned and left, putting this woman behind him as one of many temptations. But the liquor had weakened his good sense, and all resistance left him. He returned her embrace and murmured her name as she pulled him to his feet.

"Come on, the bedroom's in here. . . ."

★　★　★　★

Jenny had worked hard since noon cleaning Reverend Crutchfield's house, and now at three-thirty she looked around with satisfaction. The house had indeed been a mess, and she knew that what she had learned since coming to live in the old farmhouse had toughened her. She put on her coat, went to the school, and waited until the children came running out, the noise of their cries filling the air. She spotted Dorcas and Jeff, and when they stopped before her, she asked, "Did you have a good day?"

Jeff nodded, but Dorcas merely shrugged her shoulders.

She doesn't like me, Jenny thought, *but I don't expect she likes many people*. "Come on, you can help me fix supper."

"I don't cook," Dorcas said stubbornly.

"Well, you can watch me, or maybe you can do your home-work."

★　★　★　★

While Jenny had the supper preparations under way, Devoe came home and looked around. The house was clean, the floor was swept, and he did not have to dodge his way between toys and garments. Besides that, the air was filled with the pleasing aroma of food.

"I'm home!" he called out from the front entryway.

Jenny stepped out of the kitchen, wearing an apron that had once belonged to his wife. When he saw her standing there, Devoe Crutchfield could not speak. He had loved his wife deeply and passionately, and now memories of her came flooding back.

Jenny saw something change in the tall, angular man's face, and she said, "What's wrong? Is something the matter?"

"No . . . not really," Devoe murmured. He forced himself to smile and waved his arm around expansively. "The house looks great. You've done a wonderful job."

"Well, I hope the supper turns out as well. I warned you, I'm not much of a cook."

They all sat down, and as Jenny expected, Devoe bowed his head and asked a blessing. As soon as it was finished, she said, "I'll bring the food in."

She had cooked pork chops, mashed potatoes, green beans, and biscuits. She had been worried about the biscuits, for she had only made them twice before, and neither time had been particularly successful. Fortunately, the Crutchfields had a better stove than the Winslows did at the farm, so they had turned out fine after all. The whole supper had turned out very well.

Devoe ate, praising almost every bite, but the children said nothing. Jenny noted a mulish look on Dorcas's face. The girl ate well enough, as did Jeff, but Jenny expected that she had been the object of talk between the two youngsters. *Maybe they resent me because they don't have a mother,* she thought, but that didn't seem likely. Her first opinion had been that they were spoiled, and nothing she had seen that afternoon had changed her mind. She had practically forced the two to clean up their rooms, and it had required stern threats.

"Now for dessert," she announced.

"You should have told me," Devoe moaned, holding his stomach. "I would have saved room."

Jenny smiled and went into the kitchen, returning with two pieces of coconut cake. She put one down in front of Devoe and the other one at her own place. Devoe apparently expected her to go back and get two more for the children, but she sat down and began eating.

"What about me?" Jeff cried. "I want some cake."

"So do I," Dorcas said.

"I had to tell the children several times to clean up their rooms, and when I told them they wouldn't get any dessert tonight if they didn't cooperate, they both said they didn't care. So they don't get any dessert." She took a bite calmly and then looked up to see Devoe staring at her in shock.

"Don't you think we might make an exception? After all, they did eventually clean their rooms."

"No, Brother Crutchfield, they have to learn to mind me without arguing."

Jeff cried, "You're mean!"

And almost at the same instant, Dorcas spat, "I hate you!"

Jenny did not change expressions but took another bite of cake and sat there feeling sorry for the minister. She could almost read his mind. *He loves those kids, and he wants them to have cake, but he knows they need discipline. I wonder who'll win, them or me?*

Finally Devoe took a deep breath and said, "Well, kids, that's it."

"You're not going to let me have any cake, Daddy?" Jeff whined.

"You had your choice, Jeff, and you too, Dorcas. I expect if you'll mind Miss Jenny promptly, there'll be plenty of cake tomorrow."

"That's right. It's a big cake," Jenny said. "It's good too, if I do say so myself."

Dorcas and Jeff stared at her; then Dorcas jumped up and left the room, crying, "I'll never do anything you say!"

Jeff, however, stopped and looked at the cake. "I'll do whatever you say tomorrow, Miss Jenny."

"Good, Jeff, then you shall have some cake. Maybe two pieces."

Jeff brightened immediately and left the room.

"Jeff's a little more easygoing than Dorcas. She's very strong-willed."

"They're beautiful children, but they are headstrong."

"I don't know where they get that from. Me, I suppose." Devoe shrugged sheepishly.

"I haven't seen it in you. Was your wife—" She sought for a word, not wanting to say *headstrong* or *stubborn*. "Was your wife strong-willed?" she finally asked.

He dropped his head and studied the piece of cake before him. "Very much so," he said, "but she was a wonderful woman. I miss her every day."

"I'm sorry I mentioned her, Brother Crutchfield."

He looked up and said, "It's all right. This is great cake, and by the way, I'll do the dishes."

"No, I've got another thirty minutes."

"Then I'll dry while you wash."

The two cleaned off the table together, and Crutchfield began telling her about his day. "It was wonderful not having to worry about the children today. I knew they were in good hands. And I can't believe how much work I got done. I'm very grateful to you, Miss Jenny."

"Well, you're paying me for a day's work, and that's what I meant to provide."

"By the way . . ." He reached into his pocket, came out with some bills, and handed her two. "That's not enough, but that's all I can afford."

Jenny took the two bills and stared at them for so long he was troubled.

"What's wrong?" he asked.

"This is the first money I've ever earned in my life," Jenny said. "Isn't that ridiculous at my age?"

"I wish it were more. Could you come tomorrow? I know it's Saturday, but I have more studying to do to prepare for my sermon. Could you come and keep the children and maybe fix another supper?"

"Yes, but don't let them have any cake tonight."

"I believe you're a little strong-willed yourself." Devoe smiled at her.

"So I've been told." At that moment the car horn blew, and she said, "There's Josh. I have to go."

★　★　★　★

When she climbed into the truck, she noticed that Josh was silent. She herself was proud of what she'd accomplished in one afternoon, and finally she said, "I made two dollars today. The first money I ever made."

Josh glanced at her, and she saw that his face was stiff. "I made a little money myself. Ten dollars."

"Why, that's great, Josh! You know, I'm feeling better all the time. If we all pull together, we can make it."

He did not answer, but she was very aware of the smell of alcohol on him and could not help blurting out, "Do you have to drink, Josh?"

Josh's face darkened at her rebuke and he stared ahead as the truck rumbled on over the road. After swerving to miss a chuckhole, he turned and glared at her. "I guess I do, sis."

CHAPTER SIXTEEN

A COMMUNITY CELEBRATION

★ ★ ★ ★

Spring had begun to touch the land, and Clint was on his way home from a visit with Jesse Cannon when the gorged clouds suddenly burst. The unexpected violence of the storm beat the winter's grass into pulpy brown masses, but Clint did not mind getting caught out in it. He stood in the mud, soaked to the skin, his face tipped toward the sun as it appeared from behind the fleeing storm clouds. There was something about spring that touched the deepest recesses of his soul. He loved watching the earliest spring birds returning, sweeping in graceful circles. He loved the rank smell of the wintry earth springing to life as the sun warmed the cold land.

He had had an enjoyable visit with Jesse Cannon, the elderly neighbor with whom he'd gone hunting twice during the winter. On their expeditions, Clint had been amazed at the old man's strength and endurance, and he hoped that when he got to be Jesse's age, he would still be that lively and alert.

He loved listening to Jesse's Civil War stories, of Gettysburg and that fateful day when Jesse had been among those who had moved upward across an open field, climbing into the very throats of the Yankee cannons. "A lot of us went up, but not many came back," Jesse had told him sadly. "I still think about those fellers almost every day."

One of the things that had come out of Clint's friendship with

Jesse Cannon was the offer of a team of mules. Jesse had mentioned it one night when they lay out on the hills listening to Jesse's foxhounds yapping and howling at their quarry. The stars had glittered overhead that night like diamonds, and the cold air had been as rich and invigorating as wine. "You gotta have somethin' to farm with, Clint," Jesse had said. "I got me a pair of mules I ain't used in two years. They're nigh on ten years old but big and strong. And they need workin'. You c'mon over when it's time for spring plantin' and fetch 'em."

Clint had taken the old man at his word and was now on his way home with the mules. He said nothing to the others, wanting it to be a surprise. The mules' names were Samson and Delilah, and the old man's bright eyes had glinted when he said, "Watch out for that Delilah. She's a mean, cantankerous, schemin' critter. Not like Samson there. Nice, steady mule. Never give no one no trouble. That's always the way of it, ain't it? The female's at the root of man's troubles." Clint laughed aloud as he thought of how Dolly had attacked the old man for that comment, beating him on the chest with her tiny fists. Of course, she didn't really mean anything by it. The two had been married for sixty years, and the affection between them was evident.

After the storm, Clint had mounted Samson and was riding him while leading Delilah by a rope around her neck. He had been thinking about the old couple when Delilah lowered her head and snapped at his leg. He reached back and struck her in the nose with his fist. "Settle down there, Delilah," he said firmly. "I'll make sausage out of you if you give me any trouble."

When he reached the yard, Kat came running out. It was a Tuesday in March, and she had just gotten home from school. "Can I ride, Clint?"

"Sure. Get up on this big one." He helped her get up behind him.

She hung on to his waist and said, "Why can't I ride the other one?"

" 'Cause she's downright mean and snaky. Tried to bite me just a ways back."

"What's her name?"

"Delilah, and this big fellow we're ridin' on is Samson."

"Samson and Delilah. What are you going to do with them, Clint, ride 'em?"

"No, we're going to make the biggest garden in the county."

As they pulled up in front of the house, the whole family emerged.

"Where'd you get them?" Lewis asked.

"From Jesse and Dolly. They said we needed them, which we do."

Clint slid off the mule and slapped the big animal on the shoulder. "They're fine mules. You could plant a crop of cotton with these."

"You think cotton would grow around here, Clint?" Hannah asked.

"I expect it would, but I don't think it'd pay to grow it. Nobody's going to have money to buy any."

"What'll we raise, then?" Jenny asked.

"We'll raise the biggest vegetable garden you ever saw. We'll get enough to eat for the next year and sell some of it too, if we're lucky."

Josh approached the mules cautiously. "I don't think I've ever seen a mule before. Are these good ones?"

"Mighty fine, Josh. I'll teach you how to plow. You'll probably be good at it."

★ ★ ★ ★

The deacons of the First Baptist Church formed a semicircle around the room. Brother Crutchfield had been surprised when the deacons had marched in one late afternoon. *Have I forgotten a meeting?* he asked himself. But as he looked around, he saw their uncomfortable expressions, especially on the face of Jude Tanner. The big blacksmith was usually a cheerful sort, but now there was a hangdog look about him, and he kept his lips pressed tight. *Must be trouble if Jude's bothered,* Devoe thought. "What can I do for you, brothers?"

Millington Wheeler spoke up at once. He was the chairman of the board of deacons and the most prominent member of the community, or at least the richest. He was only in his midforties, but people often thought he was older because of his fine head of silver hair. His fierce determination set him apart as a man who usually got his way. As was his habit, he cut to the heart of the matter at once. "Brother Crutchfield," he began, "you know the Bible tells us if we see our brother in a fault, we're to go to him."

"And what fault is it you've seen in me?" Devoe asked unnecessarily, having already guessed what bothered them.

Wheeler put it bluntly. "You're spending too much time with that Winslow woman."

"That's right," H. G. Huntington agreed, nodding. "It doesn't look right. She comes to your house at noon and stays until nearly dark."

"Are you accusing me, then," Crutchfield asked straight out, "of having an affair with the woman?"

"Of course not," Potter Flemming said. The mayor was a small man with a lawyer's big voice. "But the Bible says to avoid the very appearance of evil."

"We're all agreed on this thing," Huntington declared.

"No we're not!"

Everyone turned to face Jude Tanner, who towered over the others. "I don't agree, and I told them so. I think it's foolishness to even be here."

"You're not even a married man, Jude!" Wheeler snapped.

"You think unmarried men can't spot sin as quick as married ones?"

The ire of the deacons was directed momentarily toward Jude Tanner. Wheeler, however, quickly regained control. "That's all we're going to say. There are plenty of good women in our congregation you could get for a housekeeper."

"By good women you mean plain women?"

"Put it that way if you like." Wheeler flushed. He could not bear to be crossed, and now he jammed his hat down over his head. "This is our final word on the matter. It's not debatable."

"I quite agree," Crutchfield said evenly. "It's not debatable from my point of view either. Miss Winslow's family is in trouble financially. They need the work, and I have no intention of letting her go."

Wheeler's face flushed crimson. He opened his mouth to speak, then clamped his jaw shut before opening it again. "I would advise you to reconsider, Pastor." He turned and left the room, followed by all the others except Tanner.

"I'm sure sorry about this, Preacher," the big man said.

"Not your fault, Jude."

"Bunch of lunkheads! I'd like to knock their heads together! Anyway, it's not all about Miss Winslow. They're still mad at you for starting that Sunday school for the Negro kids."

"I know." Crutchfield stepped closer and laid his hand on Tanner's oak tree of an arm. Smiling, he said, "Thanks for trying to help."

"You'd better watch out," Tanner warned as he turned to go. "It's not over yet."

★   ★   ★   ★

It was a beautiful Saturday morning, and Clint took great pleasure in driving the mules down the long row. He had laid out a huge garden, having discovered that he could still handle a plow and a team skillfully. Kat ran behind him gathering up red worms in the furrows and placing them in a gallon bucket. "Can we go fishing after you finish plowing?"

"Maybe so, if we get through in time."

Kat ran to his side and trotted along, asking questions a mile a minute. "How do you plow such a straight line, Clint?"

"You don't look down at the ground in front of you. You keep your eye on the end of the row. Kinda like life, I guess. Always keep your head up and look to see where you're heading in the future, and you won't trip up or get off a straight path."

"I'm not good at thinking ahead, Clint. About all I can see is right now."

Clint laughed and looked down at her, the plowline around his neck and his two big hands gripping the plow. "I guess I feel about the same most days." His head snapped up at a man approaching. "Look, there's Jesse."

The two took the plow to the end of the row, and Clint stopped the mules, tying the lines around the plow. They walked over to greet Jesse, who was standing at the corner of the freshly plowed garden.

"Howdy, Clint . . . missy." Jesse doffed his hat and said, "Wanted to come by and tell you about the reenactment we're doing this afternoon. I meant to mention it to you earlier, but I guess I forgot."

"What do you reenact?" Clint asked.

"A bunch of us old-timers get together and try to reenact a local battle from the war."

"The Civil War?"

"That's right."

"I didn't know there was a battle fought around here."

"Well, it weren't no battle really," Cannon snorted. "No more than a little skirmish. Three Yankees got 'emselves killed, and one of our boys too, but everybody sure enjoys goin'. There's a heap o' dancin' and music and enough food for the whole Confederate Army."

"Who furnishes the food?"

"The politicians. They all chip in and buy a cow, and the women cook it up with all the fixin's. The beef's a lot easier to swaller than those speeches them fellers make. You be sure and come, now."

"All right. I think we all deserve a little break."

"You come too, missy. There's games for the kids and fireworks and all kinds of goin's-on."

"I sure will, Mr. Cannon."

As soon as Jesse left, Clint turned to Kat. "Well, I guess we can call it a day. We've worked pretty hard."

"I'm going to see if Dallas will go. He and Tennie never go anywhere."

"You go on ahead. You come right back, though."

Dallas was the boy Kat encountered in the woods the day she had gotten lost. Dallas knew the woods like no one else. He could name all the flowers and plants, and he had taken Kat squirrel hunting once, even letting her try her hand at shooting. She'd missed the squirrel but had had the time of her life.

Now she made the three-quarter-mile trip quickly and found the two out plowing their own garden behind a blue-nosed mule.

"Why, hello there, young 'un," Dallas's grandmother said, taking the black gum stick out of her mouth. It had to be black gum, Kat had been informed. Nothing else would do. "What are you up to today?"

"I came to be sure you and Dallas will be at the reenactment."

"Don't reckon so," Tennie grunted.

"Why not?" Kat demanded. "It sounds like fun. Jesse said

there'll be lots to eat and music and games too, and shootin' off muskets."

"We don't go to things too much in town," Tennie explained. "They don't keer for us there."

Kat shook her head with determination. "You've got to come. I want you both there with me. We'll do all the stuff together, and it's free." She was so persuasive that after ten minutes Tennie threw up her wrinkled old hands. "You'd talk a possum out of a tree, young 'un. All right, we'll come but don't reckon we'll stay long."

Dallas had said nothing this whole time. He was surprised that his grandmother had surrendered to Kat, but his eyes lit up when she did. When Kat came over to him and talked excitedly about the upcoming festivities, he finally uttered what for him was a long speech. "I reckon we'll come."

★　★　★　★

"Wouldja look at that!" Jesse Cannon snorted. He and Clint were standing together in gray battle dress, the others scattered around before an open field. Two lines of men in blue had approached, and one of them had stopped and let off a fusillade of shots. Clint hadn't wanted to participate, but at Jesse's insistence, he had put on one of the extra uniforms and was learning the routine as they went.

"Reckon if anybody ever shot for real at them boys, they'd run like skeered rabbits."

"I expect I would too." Clint grinned.

"No you wouldn't. You're like them boys in my old outfit. You'd go until you stacked your musket at Appomattox."

Lewis was standing close enough to hear this. "I'm surprised they found any men here willing to wear the Northern uniform."

"Oh, it ain't easy, but we all take turns now. One side gets to be Confederate one year and then the next year they gotta be Blue Bellies."

"Look, there's Tennie and Dallas!" Kat cried, running toward the pair with Jenny and the others close behind. Neither Tennie nor Dallas had bothered to dress up. They looked ragged and out of place.

Jenny felt a little ashamed at her thoughts about the pair. *Well, I suppose that's all the clothing they have, but they look like scarecrows.*

Tennie was looking apprehensive, not being used to crowds and knowing that the townspeople didn't think much of her.

Kat ran right up and pulled at her hand. "I'm so glad you came, Tennie."

"Well, I don't know if'n I am or not. Lotsa doin's."

"C'mon, you and Dallas, we were just going to go over and eat. You see those tables of food? It's all free!"

Kat led the pair to the refreshment tables filled with pitchers of lemonade and plates piled high with fresh-baked cookies. The others followed, and when the ladies that served them looked askance at the tattered pair, Kat said loudly, "There's going to be a tug-of-war. Will you be in it, Clint?"

"I doubt it. I believe Jude Tanner could outpull everybody in the village." He winked at Jenny and said, "I hear he's kinda sweet on you."

Jenny flushed but didn't answer.

Hannah was watching Tennie, feeling sorry for the old woman. There was nothing for her in life but hard work and hard times, nor had there ever been. Now as she watched the old woman's weathered features, she saw a gentleness in them and thought, *She's not used to people being nice to her.* Aloud Hannah said, "I've been meaning to come over and get you to show me the plants you find in the woods. I don't know anything about them."

Tennie smiled. "You just come any time you've a mind to, Miss Winslow. We'll get us some poke salad. Ain't nothin' like fresh pokeweed to set a body up."

★ ★ ★ ★

The Winslows wandered around during the speeches, which took up the greater part of the afternoon. They paused once beside a group of women, and one of them looked directly at Jenny and said in an audible whisper, "It's a shame the way some women take out after preachers, ain't it, Hazel?"

Hearing the remark, Jenny flushed but knew there was nothing she could say to make the woman understand that she was just doing her job.

Later on, when she encountered Jude, he said, "First dance tonight, Jenny, all right?"

"All right, Jude." She hesitated and then said, "You're a deacon, aren't you, at Brother Crutchfield's church?"

"Not a very good one, but yep, I am."

"Have you heard any talk about him and me?"

Jude looked uncomfortable at the direct question. "Well, a little maybe. The deacons are a bunch of knotheads. They confronted the preacher about the two of you."

"What did he say?"

"He put the run on 'em," Jude said with a laugh, then quickly sobered. "That ain't too good, though. In a Baptist church all it takes is a majority of the people to get rid of a preacher. Not like the Methodists or Episcopalians. They can stay on as long as their bishop says so."

Jenny walked around with Jude until the dancing started. She noticed that as she and Jude approached the dance platform, Clint was playing his harmonica with the musicians. Jude gathered her up in his arms and swept her around the floor, nearly lifting her off her feet. Enjoying the company of the good-natured young giant, Jenny tried to forget about the remarks concerning her and Brother Crutchfield.

Several young men cut in to dance with her, most often a blond man named Lee Foster. He was about twenty-five years old, she guessed, handsome and well dressed. He was witty, and she found herself liking him.

"I see where you caught the prize catch, Jenny." Jude grinned as he claimed another dance.

"Who's that, Jude?"

"Why, Lee Foster! Don't you know who he is?"

"No, who is he?"

"Only the son of the richest man in the county. If you catch him, you won't have to worry about nothin' in life. His old man's got enough money to burn a wet mule!"

Jenny laughed, saying she wasn't exactly sure how much money that was.

The next time Foster cut in, he leaned close and said, "Why don't you and I go over to Milton? They got a nice theater there and a cozy café. We could have a good time."

"You'll have to ask my father. I only go out with men he approves of."

Lee grinned at her. "I like old-fashioned girls. I'll do just that."

Hannah stood on the other side of the dance floor watching her sister dance with one partner after another.

"I reckon this is my dance, ain't it?"

She turned her head, startled by the voice, and stared up at a tall man with shoulders as wide as an ax handle. He was pushing his chest out and had obviously been drinking. "I'm sorry," she said quietly. "I don't dance."

Jordan Skinner was a prideful man, and even without any liquor in him, he had a short fuse. "You're gonna dance with me and make up your mind to it," he said, whistling the words through his missing front teeth. He grabbed Hannah's arm and yanked her onto the floor. She was helpless against his strength, although she tried hard to pull away.

"You're gonna dance, so you might jist as well—"

Suddenly Jordan's arm was seized, and he was swung around to face a lean, muscular man of his own height. "The lady doesn't want to dance."

"Who are you?"

"Clint Longstreet."

"Well, I'm Jordan Skinner." Skinner raised his chin high as if he expected the name to mean something. "We're gettin' along without your help here, Longstreet."

Clint was unimpressed. "I said the lady doesn't want to dance."

"And I say she does."

"Then why don't we go someplace private and settle it?"

Skinner scanned the crowd, seeing that the music had stopped and everybody was watching.

"Fine. You wait here, lady. As soon as I squash this bug, I'll be back." He turned and plunged through the crowd with Clint right behind.

In a moment Josh was at his side. "Don't fight him, Clint. He's busted up several men around here bad."

"Have to do it," Clint said steadily, then turned and eyed Josh with surprise. "You know him?"

Josh hesitated, not sure what to say, and Clint shook his head and left.

Jordan led Clint to an open area he thought was somewhat private, but when he turned to face Clint, he saw that all the men had followed to watch the fight. Not minding an audience, he smiled and looked around. "You watch, boys, I'm gonna bust his teeth till they ain't nothin' but snags. Then I'll bust his nose so he whistles when he breathes." His boast was meant to catch Clint off guard, but Clint was ready when the first blow was delivered. Had it connected, it might have ended the fight right there. Skinner was as strong as a bull, but he was also no faster. Clint simply moved his head back, and when the blow missed his face, Clint shot his right arm out and caught the big man full in the mouth. It had all of Clint's one hundred eighty-five pounds behind it and drove Jordan back on his heels.

Jordan touched his mouth, then looked at the blood on his fingers, enraged by the sight. "I'll kill you!" he yelled, throwing himself forward.

Longstreet wasn't worried. He believed he could beat most of the people he'd seen duking it out at the fights he'd watched. He did not try to put the man down, just moved around lightly, shooting lefts and rights and dodging the return blows. He soon had Skinner's face looking as if he had run into a meat grinder.

In his fury Jordan caught Clint with a surprise blow in the chest. The man's phenomenal strength drove him backward to the ground. Jordan ran forward and kicked him in the side, driving any remaining breath out of Longstreet. He rolled over quickly to avoid more, and several of the men rushed forward to hold Jordan off until Clint could regain his breath. He staggered to his feet, and the men backed off, allowing the fight to continue. Clint, even with his speed, could no longer avoid all the blows. He took a lot of punishment, but he still gave out even more. He saw that the more Jordan moved, the more out of breath he got, so Clint changed his strategy to try to wear him out. As he moved away, his opponent followed him every time, swinging wildly, and was soon snorting for lack of breath. He threw a punch at Clint, which missed; then Clint drove his fist deep into the man's stomach. Such a blow would have destroyed any other man, but it did not put Skinner down.

The two men were moving slower now, but Clint was still

fast enough to avoid most of Jordan's blows and deliver a few of his own. At one point Skinner's brother, Billy Roy, stepped forward intending to drive a blow into Clint's face from the side. But Billy Roy felt himself suddenly immobilized by a huge arm, and he squirmed to get loose. He turned around to see the face of Jude Tanner. Tanner simply squeezed harder, and Billy Roy gasped with pain. "You're crushin' my ribs!"

"You behave yourself, little man, or I'll break every rib you own."

The spectators stared in amazement. Many of them had seen Jordan Skinner demolish his opponents easily, and now they were watching him stagger around, his face bloody and his blows losing their power.

Clint drove another right into Skinner's face, and this time he felt the nose give. The man uttered a short cry and fell backward, wallowing on the ground. Clint stood over him and said, "Had enough?"

While Jordan struggled to his feet, Jude Tanner released Billy Roy and said, "You two get out of here."

Through bloody lips and eyes swollen almost shut, Jordan Skinner whispered huskily, "This ain't the end of it, Longstreet."

At that moment Sheriff Noel Beauchamp stepped forward. "I'd better not hear any more of this, Skinner. Now get on outta here."

He turned and said to Clint, "You'd better go on home too and soak in some water, as hot as you can stand it."

"I guess you're right, Sheriff." Clint smiled through a haze of pain.

Lewis Winslow, who had felt helpless at his inability to stop the fight, came forward and said to Josh, "Go get the others. We're going home."

Lewis turned to Beauchamp and said sternly, "Why didn't you stop it, Sheriff?"

"Because I wanted to see Jordan Skinner get what he deserved. I thought Longstreet looked like he might could do him in. I seen Skinner beat up a lot of decent men who did him no wrong. Good to see justice done once in a while."

"It was pretty hard on Clint too," Lewis said angrily.

"Yes, it was. Maybe I was wrong. Those Skinners don't forget things like this. You might keep that in mind, Clint."

*　*　*　*

Clint settled carefully into a big tub of hot water. Hannah had directed the operation, organizing the family to heat the water and bring the big tub into the kitchen, where she'd then hung up blankets around it for privacy.

Relaxing in the soothing water, Clint was feeling the blows now. He soaked until the water started feeling cool, then got out, dried off, and painfully put on his clothes. When he stepped outside the blanket curtain, he found Jenny waiting for him.

"I'm glad you did that, Clint," she said. "I hate fights, but he deserved it after what he did to Hannah." She reached up and gently pulled his head down, then very lightly kissed his cheek before turning and hurrying away.

Hannah had been standing in the doorway watching, although neither Jenny nor Clint had seen her. She now stepped back out of sight and leaned against the wall, feeling a strange tugging inside. No man had ever fought for her before, and she was very grateful to him. But seeing Jenny kiss him had made her lose her courage. Jenny was so beautiful and so winsome. . . . Hannah couldn't help her jealous thoughts as she turned away. *She can have any man she wants!*

CHAPTER SEVENTEEN

A TASTE OF HONEY

★ ★ ★ ★

The July heat of the Deep South was more oppressive than Lewis Winslow could have imagined. He moved down the rows of the garden with a hoe, chopping the weeds, trying to remember if summers in New York had ever been this hot. From time to time he paused to pull his bandanna from the hip pocket of his overalls and mop his forehead. "Don't think it was ever this hot," he muttered, "but then, I was usually inside, not out in the sun chopping weeds."

He moved steadily down the row, conscious that his hands were no longer blistered. He had worked up a set of callouses of which he was secretly proud. He still had not adjusted to a life of poverty and had lost several pounds. His skin had turned to tan under the hot Georgia skies, and he felt strong physically, but the shock of losing everything still felt like a fresh wound, and every day he had to wake up to his new life as a poor man.

A toad looked up at him with its jeweled eyes and lifted itself slightly, as if to hop away, then sat back down. Lewis tapped him with the blade of the hoe, but the toad merely uttered a raucous grunt, then settled down stubbornly in the shade of a pepper plant. Lewis smiled faintly, then moved on down the row, leaving the creature to its solitude.

The vegetables were coming in abundantly now, and the fresh produce was a welcome addition to the family's meals.

They had a plentiful supply of meat with the boar they had butchered and fish from the river, and Clint had been gathering edible plants in the woods. Tennie Sharp and her grandson had also given them some of the excess from their excursions into the woods to gather plants. The old woman seemed hungry for friendship, and her grandson had begun to speak more now. He had been silent as the sphinx at first, but Lewis smiled at how he and Kat now roamed the hills together looking for herbs and edible plants. "Strange pair," he muttered.

Getting to the end of the row, he cast his eyes back over the garden with a surge of pride. It was the one thing that gave his new life some order and meaning. Money was almost nonexistent, so the garden was a vital means of providing for his family now. True enough Jenny earned a little working for Brother Crutchfield, and Josh seemed to have found a source of ready cash in hauling things with the truck. But aside from that, the Winslows had to live on what they could grow or shoot in the woods. Lewis himself had become a better hunter of wild game than he would have thought possible, and now as he finished his gardening for the day, he was taken with an urge to go out and try his luck.

"Some squirrel and dumplings would go down pretty well," he told himself, and shouldering his hoe, he walked back to the house. When he went inside, he found Hannah alone patching a shirt. "I think I'll go out and see if I can bring in some squirrels, Hannah."

Hannah looked up and smiled. "That would be good, Father. We haven't had squirrel now in a couple of weeks."

"Where's Clint?"

"He went over to the Cannons' to see if they'd lend us a little sugar."

"I feel bad about having to borrow, don't you, Hannah?"

"We won't have to do it much longer. We'll have plenty of sorghum after that big field Clint planted comes in. We're lucky to have that old sorghum mill here. I'm looking forward to having our own sorghum for biscuits and pancakes."

"Still, you can't sweeten coffee with sorghum."

"It'll be all right, Father. Don't worry."

"All right. I won't be late. If I don't bag any squirrels, I'll just come home by suppertime."

"Which way will you hunt?"

"I believe I'll go south toward Tennie's place."

"Be careful."

"I will." Lewis picked up the twenty-two rifle and the box of shells. He carefully counted out the expensive shells, knowing he couldn't afford to waste them. He put twelve in his pocket and then left the house. When he reached the river, a whim took him to head the other direction. He turned and moved along the riverbank toward Dog Town instead. He had been there only once and had been shocked at how primitive the conditions were. *Don't guess I'll be visiting anyone there, but hopefully the squirrels will be plentiful.* The path along the river was well traveled, and from time to time he noted fishing lines tied out; some of them had been put there by Clint and Kat, he knew. Those two had become the fishermen of the family—running trotlines, putting out set hooks, and simply sitting on the bank waiting for a big one.

After some time he saw that the woods had grown thicker over to his right. The trees there were a mixture of pine and oak, probably first-growth timber, for they towered high in the sky. "Some logging operation will find this someday and clear it all out," he muttered. "That'll be a sad day." Leaving the river, he followed a path deep into the woods, moving quietly through the brush. He stopped several times, as he had discovered on past outings that sitting still was a better way to catch squirrels than moving around. He was rewarded by getting two plump gray squirrels and one smaller red squirrel by two o'clock. Jamming them into the canvas bag he wore at his side, suspended by a strap over his neck, he pondered whether to go back or to go a little deeper. Knowing he did not have enough to feed the whole family yet, he looked up at the sky and chewed his lower lip. "I'll go on another hour," he said. "If I don't get a bagful, we'll stretch these three by making a stew."

For the next hour he alternated between moving as silently as he could through the woods and pausing to allow the squirrels to show themselves. He saw no other game but spotted the signs of deer. "Next time I'll come back with the deer rifle. We could use a fat buck," he murmured.

Soon the woods had thinned out and he found himself on the edge of a deep gully, rimmed by scrub brush. Erosion had eaten away at the gully's steep walls—too steep to cross over, he figured, though the woods on the far side looked promising. He wondered if there would be a better place to cross farther down-river but then decided it was too late. He made a half turn, intending to go back home, but as he did, the ground gave way beneath his feet. He swung his arms wildly to regain his balance but to no avail. He made a complete somersault and then scrab-bled at the low bushes to try to stop himself from falling into the gully. He dropped his rifle and slid downward, hitting the rocky ground beneath him with a jolt. He cried out at the tearing pain in his right leg. He flipped over one more time, striking his head against the shale, and then, with a tremendous blow, landed on his shoulders. The force of the fall drove the breath out of him, and he lay gasping as the rubble bounced down the steep gully wall, splashing into the river several seconds later. As he regained his breath he tried to sit up, then cried out again, for his leg felt as if it were being cut off.

Gritting his teeth, Lewis slowly pulled himself up into a sit-ting position. He looked down at his right leg, dreading to see what was causing so much pain. "What'll I do if it's broken?"

He tried to move the leg, but the pain was too great. He searched the area frantically, starting at the river far below then moving up the steep gully walls, knowing there was little hope of climbing back up. His only hope was to crawl laterally until he found a grade he could manage. His rifle lay five feet away, half covered by the rocks that had fallen in the slide. Gritting his teeth, he pulled himself over with his hands, keeping his leg as straight as possible. By the time he got there, he felt weak with the pain that flooded through him. He picked up the rifle and then glanced up and down the river. He could not see any pos-sible avenue of escape, but he knew he had to do something. Slowly, grabbing the rifle by the end of the muzzle, he scooted back and pulled himself along. After traveling ten feet he tried to get up and use the rifle as a crutch, but the pain was unbear-able. With a gasp he lowered himself again and looked up at the sun. "It must be three o'clock or later by now," he muttered. "When I don't come home by sunset, they'll come looking for me."

Then it dawned on him that he had gone the opposite direc-tion he had planned. "I told Hannah I was going down toward

Tennie's place. They'll never think of coming north." Fighting off despair, Lewis tried to think rationally. "There's bound to be somebody who lives close to here."

The thought did not comfort him much, for the woods had been thick and deep, and the land he was in now was not fit for farming. He lifted his rifle, fired a shot into the air, and called out, "Help, somebody, help!"

Only silence rolled back after the echoes had faded. Lewis counted the shells. He had left home with a dozen, shot three squirrels, and had just fired one. He counted the eight shells again and wondered what would happen if nobody heard any of them.

Deciding to save the shells for now, he started crawling along the dirt, dragging the rifle beside him. The pain sickened him, and he could go no farther than thirty feet before he lay flat on his back, gasping under the full rays of the sun. Sweat ran down his neck, and he trembled all over from the brief exertion. *Got to do something, but I don't know what.* He rested for a time, then tried to move again, but finally had to give up. He pulled his hat over his face and lay still as the sun continued on its steady course across the sky.

★   ★   ★   ★

"Well, this is the last of the jam Tennie gave us."

Hannah set the almost empty pint jar of blackberry jam down on the kitchen table in front of Clint. He shoved it over toward Kat and said, "Here, you eat it. Young'uns need their strength."

Kat took the jar and fished out a small amount with her knife, spreading it on half of a biscuit. "That's all I want," she announced.

Hannah and Clint exchanged glances, certain that the girl was not telling the truth.

Clint shook his head vigorously. "I'll sure be glad when that sorghum gets ready to harvest. We won't run out of syrup then."

"Is it hard to make sorghum, Clint?" Kat asked.

"Well, there's some work in it," Clint admitted, "but it's worth it. I've been thinkin'. If we could round up some jars to put it in, we might go into town and sell some of it for a little cash."

Hannah smiled, but she knew that Clint's hope had little foundation. No one in Summerdale had any cash to spend on frivolous items like sorghum molasses. The depression had struck the area with a vengeance, and the farmers felt it most keenly. From time to time the Winslows got a newspaper from the Cannons, a few days old, and the stories all sang the same woes. The country had had to accept the breakdown of Coolidge-Hoover prosperity. It had been a bitter pill for the Republican Party to swallow, and Herbert Hoover, who had once delivered confident speeches about the abolition of poverty, felt it more keenly than anyone.

President Hoover had tried to fix the economic mess. He had promised to reduce taxes and he had bombarded the American people with promises that conditions were sound. "I'm convinced that we will reestablish confidence," he said in one fashion or another during the beginning of the new decade.

During the first three months of 1930, the stock market did seem to revive, but it quickly sickened and faded again. The country faltered and staggered, and one could hardly walk a block without seeing the changes that had come to America. Women's clothes reflected the depression as skirt lengths became lower along with the stock prices. Defenders of the knee-length skirt protested, but the new styles won out. Bobbed hair was losing favor too, and frills and ruffles and flounces were coming back in again. The minds and hearts of American women had changed since the depression began. No longer was it their ambition to simulate flat-chested, spindly-legged, carefree adolescents in children's frocks. Decorum and romance had begun to return to America.

One ritual that united most Americans occurred every evening at seven o'clock with the radio voices of Freeman Gosden and Charles Correll, better known as Amos and Andy. Andy's troubles became real to most American families, and phrases such as "I'se regusted!" became the currency of speech. But regardless of Amos and Andy's cheerful outlook, the country was in trouble, and the long lines of men waiting at the rescue shelters for a meal and a bed were a visible reminder that times were bad.

Clint stared at the remaining traces of blackberry jam and said with a vein of stubbornness, "Well, by gum, we're gonna have something to eat on biscuits and pancakes."

"What are you talking about, Clint?" Hannah said.

"Well, I'm not waiting for any sorghum. There's honey out there, and I'm gonna get us some."

"How do you propose to do that?"

"I've never robbed a hive, but Jesse has. He's been after me to go with him, and I think today's the day."

"Can I go too, Clint?" Kat asked excitedly.

"Sure, we'll all go. It'll be better than going to the grocery store. It'll all be free."

"But won't the bees sting us?" Kat demanded.

"Oh, we may get a sting or two, but what's that compared to having plenty of fresh honey?"

★　★　★　★

Jesse Cannon's bright blue eyes sparkled. "Don't nothin' please me better'n goin' out after honey. I need to find me a fresh batch—need it for my arthritis."

"Is eating honey good for arthritis?" Hannah asked. She was wearing a pair of overalls, as Clint had suggested, and a straw hat shaded her face.

"Eatin' honey is mighty fine, but that ain't what helps arthritis. I'll show you, missy."

"How do you find the bees?" Kat asked.

"Well, you just watch, honey, and I'll show you that too."

The amateurs watched as Jesse put the lid from a fruit jar down on a flat stump near the river. He had told them, "Always get close to water to find bee trees. The bees need water just like we do."

Now they watched as Jesse pulled a bottle out of his pocket and poured a dark fluid into the lid. "This here's the bait. Gotta be made just right, you understand. A little honey and some vinegar and warm water. You stir it all around, and you just watch what happens."

For a time nothing happened, and the four sat around waiting, Kat doing most of the talking. Suddenly Jesse interrupted her. "Look, there he is!"

"Hey, there's a bee drinking out of that lid!" Kat exclaimed.

"Pretty soon he'll make a beeline for the hive," Jesse said.

"What if we lose sight of him?" Kat said. "He's hard to see."

"We'll just wait right here. Before long he'll be back and bring a bunch of his relatives with him. They'll make a line we can see."

Jesse's prophecy proved true. Within thirty minutes a number of bees were gathered around the bait. They would fill up and then take off.

"C'mon," Jesse said. "Bring that ax and saw. We're gonna need 'em."

The party followed the bees with little trouble, and finally Jesse stopped and pointed up into a tall tree. "See that knothole up there? See them bees goin' in and out? That's what we're a-lookin' for. Chop that tree down, Clint. That's a job for a young feller."

"All right," Clint said. "You women better get out of the way, though. I wouldn't want you to get stung."

Clint was a good axman, and he made quick work of chopping a huge notch in the tree. When the tree began to totter he jumped back and hollered, "There she goes!" They all watched the tree as it fell with a crash, and Jesse rubbed his hands together. "Now we'll see about that honey."

Hannah was nervous about the bees swarming around the fallen tree. "You stay here, Kat."

"That's right," Jesse warned. "You womenfolk stay right where you are. Me and Clint'll get that honey."

Jesse slipped the straps of his overalls off his shoulders and unbuttoned and removed his shirt. He saw Hannah staring at him with big eyes. "Now I'm gonna get my arthritis treatment," he said. "You just watch."

Hannah watched with shock as Jesse walked right up to the section of the tree that contained the bees. She saw them lighting on the old man and whispered, "Clint, what's he *doing*?"

"Jesse claims there's somethin' in a beesting that's good for arthritis. I don't see how he stands it, though. I'd go crazy."

Jesse looked back and saw them staring at him and laughed. "Ain't nothin' to it. Once you been stung a few times you don't feel the rest of 'em. Give me that ax, Clint. We're gonna get us some honey."

Clint cautiously advanced, flinching as the bees attacked him.

"A feller's gonna get stung a bit," Jesse admonished Clint as he swatted at the insects. "If he wants honey, he might as well get used to that."

Clint moved back and brushed the bees away as best he could, watching while Jesse split the grain expertly with the ax.

"Ah, we got us a good 'un here. Go bring them buckets, Clint."

Clint ran back to where Hannah and Kat were waiting. He grabbed up the four buckets, and Kat said, "Your face is all swollen, Clint."

"Can't be helped. You stay back now, Kat."

Running back to where Jesse was clearing out a section of the tree, he put the buckets down. He watched as Jesse reached inside and began to bring out pieces of the broken comb. "You need help, Jesse?"

"No, you stay back, young feller. I'll take care of this."

Clint was willing enough to pay heed to that. He did not see how the old man could stand it, although he noticed that the bees were swarming less. He finally went forward and got two buckets and saw that they were filled with broken comb and splintered wood. He carried them back to Hannah, and Hannah and Kat stared down into them. "We'll have to clean it all out, but just taste a little of that." Clint reached down and broke off a piece of the comb and shared it with Kat and Hannah.

Kat squealed, "That's so good! I want some more!"

Finally the buckets were full, and Jesse came back, his face swollen and knots all over his body. He grinned crookedly. "That feels good. Amazin' how quick a little beesting or two will take away a feller's arthritis." He reached down, broke off a chunk of the comb, and stuck it into his mouth, ignoring the honey that ran over his chin. "This ain't as good as sourwood honey, but it's plenty good enough. C'mon, let's get along home."

As they started on their way, Jesse said, "I'll tell you what we'll do, Clint. We'll start our own hives. We've got to find a queen to get us a good hive goin', but it'd be a lot easier next year to have our own hives rather than goin' out in the woods and findin' one."

★ ★ ★ ★

"Stop here by the crick, Josh."

"What for?" Josh glanced over and saw the line of trees marking the creek that followed the road.

"It's hot. I want to get cooled off."

Josh pulled the truck over, and by the time he got out, Dora was already around the truck, her arm in his. "C'mon," she said, "follow me."

Josh allowed Dora to pull him along until they reached the stream. It was lined with trees that arched over it, forming a cathedral-like ceiling. The sun came through the green leaves in broken beams, and the clear water did look inviting.

"Let's go for a swim."

"Are you crazy, Dora? What if somebody comes by?"

"What if they do?" Dora laughed. She turned to him, her eyes challenging. "Don't tell me you've never been swimmin' in a crick before."

Josh returned Dora's challenging look. "I guess I'll just wade a little bit." He sat down and began taking his shoes off, and Dora stared at him for a moment, then laughed. "You must be a preacher's kid." To his surprise, she reached down and pulled her dress over her head, leaving on only her thin slip. She waded out into the creek, which was only waist deep, then threw herself into it, rolling over and kicking the water to pull herself along.

Josh sat on the bank, his feet in the water, and watched her. She made a tempting sight, and he knew exactly what was on her mind, for Dora never made any secret of her desires for him. But after that day in her cabin when he had first surrendered to her advances, he had tried to avoid being drawn in again by her charms. He thought of the trip they had just completed. It was the first time she had gone with him to deliver the bootleg whiskey, and now as he sat on the bank of the swift-flowing creek, he wondered what his family would think if they knew he had become a bootlegger. Josh was not proud of himself for this, but the money he'd made had come in handy, and besides, he was completely addicted to whiskey now. His family knew he drank, of course, but he had convinced them that he got the money for the whiskey by hauling hay and equipment for the farmers or from the merchants in town.

Josh had already imbibed freely of the liquor that day. After the delivery was made, he was relieved, as always, and Dora had encouraged him to drink up—indeed had joined him drink for drink.

The shade was cool, and the alcohol had dulled his senses. He sat there watching Dora until she finally came out of the river, her wet slip clinging to her, her eyes fastened on Josh with a determination he knew he couldn't resist. She sat down beside him and found his lips with her own. Her mouth was warm under his, and she began to murmur softly. She pulled him to the ground, and Josh Winslow succumbed once again, despairing that he had sunk so low that he could not control his impulses with this backwoods girl. But he had already shamed his family by becoming a drunk and a bootlegger. *So how could this be any worse?* he reasoned. As she clung to him, he threw away all restraints and seized her in a passionate embrace.

★ ★ ★ ★

Hannah chewed her lower lip and stared out of the window. The others were sitting at the table finishing supper, but the meal had been silent. Josh had returned home, quiet and sullen. He had eaten little, and now he sat at the table staring blankly at his plate.

Jenny had fixed pancakes for them all to enjoy with the honey they had gathered, but no one said much about it as they ate the sweet treat.

Finally Hannah said, "Something's wrong. Father should have been back by now."

Clint had been thinking exactly the same thing but had hesitated to speak up, not wanting to overreact. Now he got to his feet and reached for his hat. "I'll go look for him."

"I'll go with you," Josh volunteered.

"We'll all go," Jenny said.

Clint shook his head. "No, it won't do any good. You'll get lost in the woods."

"I can't wait here," Kat complained.

"You'll have to," Clint said firmly. "Somebody's got to wait in case he comes back. You women stay. Josh and I can do the looking."

* ★ ★ ★

When the men returned, it was obvious that their search had been fruitless. "Didn't find him?" Hannah asked.

"No, and now it's getting dark," Clint said. His lips were drawn tight, a wariness about him. "We'll have to wait until morning, and we'll have to have help. Josh, why don't you go into town and tell the sheriff. See if he can't get some men to be here in the morning. I'll go tell Jesse, and we'll round up all the neighbors we can."

"All right," Josh said. He whirled and left the room at once, and soon they heard the truck starting up.

"What could have happened to him?" Jenny asked Clint.

"I think he's probably just gotten lost. He's not that much of a woodsman." He put his hand on her shoulder. "We'll find him. Don't worry."

Hannah felt her legs go weak. She knew Clint was not saying all that he was thinking, and she herself did not want to put words to her fears. She saw Kat looking lost and noted that the youngster's lower lip was trembling. Hannah went to her sister and put her arms around her, saying, "It'll be all right, Kat. We'll find him. Don't worry." She wished she could take this advice herself, but she knew there would be no sleep for her that night.

CHAPTER EIGHTEEN

THE LONGEST NIGHT

★ ★ ★ ★

Lewis awoke when the sun touched his eyes. He had spent a horrible night in the gully. He knew now for certain that his leg was broken, and he also knew that it was useless to try to crawl to get help. He had made several attempts, and on the last one he had fainted from the terrible pain. He had dragged himself up close to the sheer wall that rose up from the river, but now the sun had spanned the ground, and he felt it touch his face with a heat that would only get worse.

His lips were dry and cracked, and his tongue felt swollen. He had not thought to bring water, for he knew the river was ordinarily close enough. Now, however, a raging thirst gripped him, but there was nothing he could do about that. After a time he pulled himself up and leaned back, gritting his teeth against the searing pain in his leg. He had pulled his pants leg up and was relieved to see that the bone had not punctured through the skin. He was, however, filled with a foreboding. He thought back to the time he had gone charging up San Juan Hill in Cuba with Teddy Roosevelt's Rough Riders. He had been afraid then, but it had been a clean fear, for he had known that death would either come quickly or, if he were wounded, there would be somebody to care for him. All through the night in the gully, long fingers of fear seemed to come down and touch him, chilling his heart. To die of thirst alone was a frightful thought, but he knew it could happen. More than once during the long night, he had berated himself for not sticking to his plan to go south. Now Clint and his family would not have the foggiest notion that he had turned in the other direction. He tried to guess the time, but without a watch, the best he could do was guess that it was midmorning.

He picked up the rifle, chambered a shell, then counted the ones that remained. "I'll shoot one off every two hours," he said to himself. "I can only hope that somebody will hear me." He fired the first shot, which made a puny popping sound to his ears. He then croaked out in a voice as loud as he could, "Help! Somebody please come and get me!"

The thin echo of his own voice came back to him, and Lewis was overwhelmed with the immensity of these Georgia woods. A man could walk for hours and see nothing. He sat there helpless, his hat pulled down to shade his face, and did the only thing a man could do in his place. He began to pray.

★ ★ ★ ★

By that evening Lewis had only two bullets left. In desperation he cradled one of them in his hand, having lost hope that anybody would come. He chambered the shell with numb fingers, lifted it upward, and put his hand on the trigger. Once the last shell was fired, there would be nothing else he could do. He could not possibly cry out loud enough for anyone to hear.

When he pulled the trigger and heard the sound of the shot echo, the last vestiges of hope drained out of him. He let the rifle drop, closed his eyes, and felt the tears running down his cheeks. "Take care of my children, God."

At that very moment he thought he heard a noise, and a faint hope returned. With trembling fingers, he awkwardly inserted the last shell and fired the gun. He cried out hoarsely, "Here! Come! I'm over here!" He waited . . . but heard nothing. He flung the rifle away from him with a sob.

★ ★ ★ ★

"Nobody knows the trouble I've seen;
Nobody knows but Jesus.
Nobody knows the trouble I've seen;
Glory, hallelujah.

"Sometimes I'm up, sometimes I'm down;
Oh, yes, Lord,
Sometimes I'm almost to the ground.
Oh, yes, Lord."

The song echoed through the evening air as the woman singing it sat on the seat of a two-wheel cart.

"Nobody knows the trouble I've seen;
Nobody knows but Jesus. . . ."

She glanced back into the bed of the cart and nodded with satisfaction. "You just mind your business there, turtles," she said, and a smile crossed her broad face, which was smooth and unlined. It was a strong face, as was the body outlined beneath the men's pants and khaki shirt. Her black hair showed beneath the floppy hat she wore, and as she looked at the turtles, she spoke, her voice breaking the silence. "Nothing I like better than good ol' turtle soup. When the cravin' comes on me, nothin' to do but go down to the river. So, you turtles, you're gonna be et, and that's what God made you for."

She had a warm voice, lower than most women's, and when she lifted her voice again to sing, the powerful sound filled the air. She took off her hat and let her hair fall down her back almost to her waist. "My, but that's a mournful song. I can do better than that, Lord." She began to sing "I Am Bound for the Promised Land," and as the cart bumped over the trail between the oaks and pines, she suddenly pulled the mule up. "Whoa, Mazie."

She sat very still . . . waiting, listening . . . and finally she called out, "Is anybody there?"

She waited and jumped when the sound of a distant shot came to her.

"What in the world could that be?" She leaped out of the wagon with an agile movement and said, "You stay right there, Mazie." Then she ran as quickly as her large size would allow. The sun was down behind the line of trees, creating long shadows, but when she emerged into the open, she stopped and looked around. "Is anybody there?" she called loudly. She paused and turned her head slightly, hearing a sound she could not identify. She ran over the broken ground until she came to the edge of the deep gully. She had hunted deer here from time to time and knew of this gully. Now she called again loudly, "Speak out! Make yourself heard!"

Again there was a faint sound, which seemed to come from beneath her feet. She looked down and saw nothing at first. Then as she turned to her left and looked again, she spotted a man lying flat on his back down in the gully.

"Lord, help him!" she whispered. She ran quickly to the point directly over him and called out, "Are you all right, mister?" She saw him twitch, but there was no answer. "Still alive," she muttered, making a quick decision to find a way down to him. She ran along the edge, and before she had gone a hundred yards, she found that the gully wall tapered and the ground was more solid. As she ran down, she was thinking, *I can get the cart down here to haul that feller out if he don't die on me.*

She hurried along the river until she was beside the man. She knelt and lifted his hat and saw that he was bright red with sunburn. She put her hand on his forehead and found that he was burning up, probably with the sunburn and possibly fever as well. "Can you hear me?" she asked. She put her ear by his mouth and was relieved to note his warm breath on her cheek. Then she turned and saw the leg. "Oh, my Lord! That's a bad one."

Resolutely she got to her feet. "I'm gonna have to get that cart down here. There ain't no other way to get this poor man up to the top." She turned and quickly made her way back along the gully wall and then back up to where she had left her cart, praying all the while in a loud voice, urgently and without restraint.

As she unhooked the mule from the cart, she spoke to the turtles. "Looks like you're gonna have some company back there."

★ ★ ★ ★

Lewis came out of unconsciousness when he felt hands on him, and when he opened his eyes, he saw that there was very little light filtering down into the gully. Someone was moving him, and he cried out as his leg sent a fiery pain through him.

"Sorry, I know your leg is bad, but we gotta get you out of here."

Lewis tried to speak, but his dry, swollen tongue would not allow it. Then he felt an arm around his shoulder and something cool touching his lips. It was a jug, and as he grasped at it he heard the voice saying, "Take it easy, now. Not too much."

Lewis was tortured by thirst, but he managed to gasp, "I fell."

"I see you did, and you broke your leg. I'm gonna have to pick you up and put you in this here cart. I can't carry you out."

Lewis could not answer, and the next few moments were bad. He cried out when he felt himself lifted up and then he lost consciousness momentarily as his leg seemed to be on fire.

He was not aware of the passage of time, but soon he knew that he was in a wagon being trundled through the woods. By twisting his head he could see the back of his rescuer. When he said, "Please, where am I?" the figure turned around, and he was surprised to see it was a woman. Her hair fell out from beneath her floppy hat, and it was a woman's voice that answered. "You be right still there. We're almost to home, but I can't go too fast with it almost dark. I'll have to get you inside, and that's gonna hurt. But it cain't be helped."

Lewis lay still, gritting his teeth against the pain. Finally the mule stopped and the wagon shifted as the woman got down.

"You wait right here while I get a bed ready."

Lewis lay still, his thinking fuzzy and confused. The woman was gone for a short time, and when she came back she said, "I know you cain't put no weight on that leg. I'm gonna have to carry you. Do you think you can straighten up and stand on your good leg—and then fall over my shoulder?"

"I'll . . . try."

Lewis felt her hands pulling at him. She was a big, strong woman, he could tell that. When he put his left foot on the ground, he summoned all his strength and stood up. He barely made it to a standing position before he doubled up, falling over her shoulder. "That's it. You be right still now."

Lewis gritted his teeth. He felt the strength of the woman as she moved. She had lit a lamp, but he could see nothing, for his sight was bleary in his exhaustion. When she lowered him into a bed, the pain was terrible.

She pulled him into a partially upright position and held a glass of a strong-smelling liquid to his lips. "Got to set that leg of yours," she said. "You drink this, and it won't hurt so bad."

Lewis drank the bitter-tasting liquid and groaned, "My family."

"I'll take care of that. First we gotta fix this leg. How long was you in that gully?"

"More than a day," Lewis whispered.

He lay there until the medicine, whatever it was, began to take effect, and he found himself unable to speak. The room was whirling around, and he thought he heard her say, "Now then, we'll see. . . ."

★ ★ ★ ★

Sunlight filtered in through the room and touched Lewis's face, but he knew he was no longer in the gully. He felt the bed underneath him, and his memory came flooding back. He opened his eyes and saw the woman sitting beside him in a chair. When he tried to speak, he found his voice was hoarse.

"Well, you're awake. Let me get you some water. I know you're dried out."

Lewis watched as she poured from a blue pitcher into a tumbler. He sat up, noting that his trousers were off and his right leg was in a splint. He gulped the water down thirstily until it was gone. "Could I have some more?"

"In a minute. Let that kinda soak into ya. What's your name?"

"Winslow . . . Lewis Winslow."

"I'm glad to make your acquaintance. My name's Missouri Ann Ramey."

Lewis was regaining his faculties quickly. He saw that she had jet black hair with a silver streak that began on the right side of her face. He couldn't keep from staring at it.

"I guess I'm right lucky my whole hair didn't turn silver. Don't know what done it," she said. She smiled at him and then put her big hand on his forehead. "Well, you ain't got no fever.

That's good. And your leg's okay too. Wasn't a bad break. I've set lots worse."

"My family . . . I've got to tell my family."

"You tell me where y'all live, and I'll send for 'em. I'm afraid to leave you right now." She gave him another half glass of water and said, "I'm gonna leave this by you, but don't you drink no more than a little bit. All right?"

"All right."

The woman left the room, and Lewis looked around, his mind still confused. A rush of gratitude came to him, for he knew that she had saved his life. "Thank you, Lord," he muttered. "I know it was your doing."

He was in a log cabin, he saw, a large room with a stone fireplace that took up one end. At the other end a set of stairs led upward to a loft, and a door at the back led to what was apparently a bedroom. The walls were filled with articles of clothing hanging from pegs, and the furniture, from what he could see, was sturdy and handmade. There was a small fire in the huge fireplace with a steaming black pot hanging over it. It gave forth a delicious smell, and he became acutely aware of his hunger.

Lewis drank the water sparingly and then dozed on and off until the woman returned.

"You hungry?"

"Starved."

"That's good. You need to keep up your strength." She went to the fireplace, picked up a bowl from the table beside it, and used a large spoon to fill it. She sat down beside him. "Here, you want me to feed you?"

"No, I can do it."

Lewis took the bowl and lifted a spoonful of the soup to his mouth. He swallowed and began eating eagerly. "This is good. What is it?"

"Turtle soup," Missouri said.

"Best soup I ever had."

"Eat all you can," Missouri encouraged him. She sat back and watched him, then went over and got a bowl for herself.

With a little food in his stomach, Lewis was starting to relax. "Do you have a family?"

"Did have. My husband, Ed, he died two years ago."

"Oh, I'm sorry."

"It was his time, and God took him. He was a good man. We had two children when we weren't much older than babies ourselves, but they both moved off. I live here all by myself now."

"How did you happen to find me?"

The woman reached up and stroked her hair. It was a feminine gesture, which almost struck Lewis as odd. She looked mannish in her clothes, although he could see she had a womanly figure. She was not fat, just large, and her large eyes and wide lips were attractive on her strong face.

"Well, I'll tell you, Lewis," she said. "It had to be of God."

"I believe that," Lewis said fervently.

"You a Christian man?"

"Yes, I am."

"That's good. Well, I don't go to the river much anymore, but I just took a notion to go. Thought I was goin' after turtles, and I got five big ones. But it was the Lord. If I hadn't gone, I don't reckon you would have made it."

"I believe you're right. I'm thanking God that you did go for those turtles."

"Oh, God's got everything under control." She smiled broadly, leaned forward, and took the bowl from him. "More soup?"

"Not right now, but perhaps in a little while."

She studied him for a time, and he could not understand the look that was in her eyes. "I'm sorry for all the trouble I'm causing you," he said.

"You're no trouble at all, Lewis. God brought you here, and He took me out to find you."

Puzzled, Lewis said hesitantly, "Well . . . I'm sure God must plan things."

"Plan things! Why, He plans it all!" Missouri exclaimed. Then she startled him by grabbing his hand. "I've been praying for a man, and you're the one God has sent."

Lewis stared at her blankly, thinking at first he had not heard her correctly. "What was that?"

"Why, I know you're a little bit surprised—or maybe more than a little bit!—but I've lost my man, and I asked God to send me another husband, so I'm thanking Him that He did."

There was no misunderstanding this. Lewis was very conscious of the woman's hand on his. He sat there unable to speak for a moment. Finally he squeezed out, "I guess I'm past such things as that, Mrs. Ramey."

"You can just call me Missouri. Everybody does. It was my mother's name." Starting again, she said, "What do you mean you're past such things? How old are you?"

"Fifty-five."

"Why, there's lots of men older than you that get married. You're able to love, aren't you?"

Her words brought a new flush to Lewis's already red face. He dropped his eyes. The question seemed innocent enough—it was as if she'd asked him if he liked to eat potatoes.

"I . . . I don't know how to answer that."

"Well, I do. God wouldn't send me a man that couldn't love. You see, I'm only thirty-eight years old, Lewis, and I love babies. So I asked God to send me a man who would give me some babies." She squeezed his hand and said, "I'll get you some more soup now."

Lewis watched the curious woman move across the floor to the fireplace. His mind was so confused he could not put his thoughts together. The closest he could come was to breathe a silent prayer, *Oh, Lord, what have I gotten into? What kind of woman is this?*

When Missouri Ann came back, she sat down and said, "I know it comes as a shock to you 'cause you've not been praying like I have. But the answer came to me right strong. I knew almost as soon as I seen you in that gully that you was God's gift. But I won't rush you none, Lewis. Won't rush you none at all. You just enjoy your soup."

★　★　★　★

Neither Hannah nor any of the other family members had spoken of their fears openly, but by the second morning after Lewis's disappearance almost all hope was gone. The neighbors had responded valiantly. Sheriff Beauchamp had rounded up at least thirty men from town, and they had combed the woods up and down the river. Clint had even taken a bunch across the river on the chance that Lewis might have crossed over.

But hope had almost faded, and now as Hannah stood beside

the stove pouring coffee, she glanced over at Kat, who had gone to sleep curled up in a tiny ball. *Poor thing*, Hannah thought. *She's taking it harder than any of us. It's so terrible.*

Jenny was asleep also, for they had all been up most of the night. Now Clint and the sheriff had taken the men out for another sweep. The sheriff had tried to be encouraging, and several of the women from town had stayed with Hannah and Jenny, consoling them and trying to be hopeful.

Devoe Crutchfield had been there from the beginning. He had contacted all the male church members to get them involved in the search and had stopped by with some encouraging words.

Hannah turned from the stove, sipped the coffee, and then put it down. She had not been able to eat much, just nibbling at her meals, but she had drunk too much coffee.

Her head came up at the sound of an approaching horse. As she moved to the door, Jenny stirred, as did Kat, both of them sleepy eyed. Hannah opened the door, and a man she had never seen before dismounted a strawberry stallion and pulled his hat off, saying, "I'm lookin' for the Winslow place."

"This is the Winslows'."

"Miss Missouri sent me over to tell y'all that she found your pa."

Hannah's hand flew to her mouth. She cried out and ran to the man. "Is he all right?"

"He busted his leg, but he's fine. I guess Miss Missouri didn't want to move him right now, but I can take you to him. My name is Henry Franks."

"We'll leave a note for Josh and Clint," Hannah said. "Can you tell them how to get there, Mr. Franks?"

Franks nodded. "You can tell 'em to go to Jesse Cannon's place. You know him?"

"Oh yes, we know Jesse."

"Well, he knows where Missouri Ann lives."

"Come on, we'll hitch up the wagon," Jenny cried out. "Are you sure he's all right?"

Franks smiled at her. "He's fine. When Missouri takes care of a man, he's all right."

★　★　★　★

Franks nodded ahead from astride his horse and said, "That's Missouri's place right there. Reckon you're anxious to find out about your pa."

"Yes, thank you so much, Mr. Franks," Hannah said.

They had made the trip quickly, and now as they pulled the wagon up in front of the log cabin, she saw a woman come out.

"Missouri," Franks said, "this here's Mr. Winslow's daughters come to see about him."

Hannah, Jenny, and Kat all jumped out of the wagon and approached the large woman who stood waiting for them. "I'm glad to see you," Missouri greeted them. "Your father knew you'd be worried about him."

"Is he all right?" Jenny asked quickly.

"He busted up his leg, but I set it. He'll be fine. Come along inside."

Lewis was sitting up, his back to the wall, his leg stretched out, when his children entered. They rushed over to him, hovering over him, all touching and embracing him together.

Missouri stood back and smiled. She was looking at the children carefully and thinking, *Fine-looking girls, all of them.*

Jenny finally said, "We're smothering him. Stand back and give him some air."

"Where were you, Daddy?" Kat said. She was so happy she could hardly speak, and she stood holding Lewis's hand tightly as if he would run away.

"Well, I fell in a gully, and if Miss Ramey here hadn't found me, it would have been pretty bad."

They all turned, and Kat looked at her with big eyes. "She saved your life?"

"She really did, and she set my leg too—as good as any doctor."

"I don't know how we can ever thank you, Miss Ramey," Jenny said as she extended her hand to the woman. When she took it, Jenny was amazed at the size and strength of it. She herself had to look up, for Missouri Ann Ramey was at least as tall as her father.

"Well, the good Lord does all things well." Missouri smiled. "It was all planned to be."

Lewis flinched, for he was sure that her next statement would be to announce their engagement. He intervened quickly.

"Where are my manners? Let me introduce my daughters to you."

As Lewis said their names, Missouri smiled and nodded at each of them. "You have beautiful children, Lewis." And then as naturally as anyone ever spoke, she said, "Since I'm gonna be your new ma, we'll have to get to know each other." The girls all stared at her with huge eyes and open mouths. "Well, I've been praying for a man, and God sent your daddy. But there's no hurry. While Lewis is healing up, we'll have plenty of time to get acquainted."

Lewis felt the shock that ran through his daughters and spoke up quickly. "Miss Missouri, I sure appreciate everything you've done for me, but I want you to understand that I'll never marry again. God may have said something to you, but He hasn't said anything to me."

Missouri was not at all perturbed by this. She smiled gently and said, "Oh, He will, Lewis. He just has to get you ready." Turning to the girls, she said, "I love babies. Mean to have at least two or three more." She shook her head and added thoughtfully, "I sure hope they look like Lewis. He does father some beautiful children."

CHAPTER NINETEEN

REVIVAL IN THE BARN

★　★　★　★

Dolly Cannon, at the age of eighty-one, had more energy than most young women a quarter of her age. She had heard Hannah mention how high the price of store-bought soap was, and on one Thursday morning in September she stopped by early and announced that this was soap-making day.

Hannah was delighted to see the elderly woman, for she had come to love the Cannons a great deal. The Winslows had rarely encountered such kind people. Jesse and Dolly had helped the Winslow family many a time when they were in need. As she and Hannah set up their soap-making equipment in the backyard, Dolly kept up a running commentary. "Y'all will have to make your own lye next year, but I brought plenty with me today. There ain't nothin' to it really. All you do is save your ashes from the fireplace in a barrel and let the rainwater drip down through it. Make a spigot at the bottom to let the lye drain out and collect it. I got plenty to do this batch of soap with today."

Hannah listened to Dolly explain as they poured the ingredients into a large black pot.

"We always burn hickory," Dolly went on. "It makes the best ashes."

After Hannah had been stirring for a while, following Dolly's instructions, the older woman said firmly, "The lye's all dissolved now, so we can add the grease. I always use breakfast bacon grease, but you can use most anything. Why, the other day a man offered me some mutton tallow, but I ain't never used nothin' but bacon grease myself."

Hannah leaned over the pot, fascinated. "It looks like chicken gravy, doesn't it?"

"Well, I never thought of it, but I reckon as how it do."

"Can you wash your clothes with this soap when it's done?"

"Oh yes, honey, shore you can! But you gotta keep it stirred up good. It gets thick like jelly."

Hannah stirred until her arm grew tired and she had to rest a moment. Meanwhile, Dolly disappeared inside the house, then came back out with a box in her hand. "I got some rose water to put in there. One of my grandchillens gave it to me as a gift, but I don't use no perfume. It'll go mighty good in this soap."

The two women talked and laughed, and Hannah thought that she'd never had such fun before.

When the mixture turned to a jellylike consistency, they spooned it out into flat pans. "Now we'll just leave this set until later this afternoon. When it's good and firm you can cut it into small squares and wrap it in this brown paper I brought." Dolly took a whiff of the soap. "My, oh my, but this is gonna be good soap," she said. "Your family'll love it."

Missouri Ann stopped by the house just as they were finishing. The three women enjoyed a pot of coffee together before Dolly left to go home. When they were alone, Missouri turned to Hannah and asked, "Why is it you ain't never been married, Hannah, a pretty woman like you?"

Surprised by the question, Hannah could not think of an answer. "I don't really know," she offered lamely.

"Well, I hate to see a good woman wasted."

Hannah blushed at her comment, and then Missouri grew very still and closed her eyes. "Is something wrong, Missouri?"

"The Lord's a-talkin' to me, honey. Be still."

Hannah blinked with surprise. Missouri walked closer to God than anybody she had ever known, and Hannah believed her claim that she heard directly from God. Finally Missouri's eyes opened, and she put them directly on Hannah.

"I'm gonna pray for you," she announced as she tucked her left hand behind Hannah's head and put her right hand on her forehead in a strong grasp. Whispered words started to spew out of the woman's mouth in a rapidfire stream that Hannah couldn't understand. And then in a loud voice, Missouri called out, "Oh, Lord, this woman is in bondage, and I'm gonna ask you to free her from every chain that binds her. Lord, take away those fears that have had her bound up for so many years. . . ."

Hannah had no choice but to listen, but she was shocked that Missouri would pray about the fears she had been entertaining for a long time. She rarely admitted this to herself, let alone anyone else. As the woman prayed over her, she realized that God was in that place. She began to tremble, and finally, when the prayer was over, Missouri looked deep into her eyes with a wisdom that Hannah instinctively recognized. For a moment the two remained silent, and then Missouri smiled and said gently, "Ain't no use for you to be afraid of men, honey. Men was made for women—and women was made for them. It's not good for you to be alone."

Hannah blinked in shock. How could this strange woman have seen so deep into her heart and known the secrets that she had let no one else discover? Wrenching herself away, she fled outside but knew that no matter how far she ran, she would not escape the secret that Missouri Ann had uncovered.

★ ★ ★ ★

Lewis tested his weight on his injured leg and found that the discomfort was now bearable. He had been relieved when Missouri had taken the splints off, and now he gave a sigh of relief. "Maybe I can get out of this house a bit now," he muttered. He started toward the door, but at that moment Missouri Ann came in smiling with a bulging flour sack in her hand. "Looky what I got here, Lewis."

"What is it?"

"Fresh homemade bread," she announced as she pulled a loaf from the sack. "Don't that smell like a piece of heaven?"

"It certainly does."

"And I brought the fixin's for a whole meal to go with it." She pulled over a chair and said, "Now, you sit down there and let me see about that leg of yours."

"It's all right."

Missouri Ann, however, simply put her hands on Lewis's shoulders so that he was forced to move backward. Lewis was five-ten and trimly built, and Missouri was one inch taller and solid. Lewis had never seen such strength in a woman before, and he resented it as she pushed him down into the chair as if he were a child. She knelt before him, pulled his pants leg up, and studied his calf. She kneaded the flesh so hard that he winced, and she looked up at him and laughed. "You're worse than a baby," she said, "but that leg's doin' fine." She stood up, and Lewis pulled his pants leg down and got to his feet.

At that moment Hannah came in, her expression troubled. Lewis started to ask what was wrong, but something prevented him. He did not understand this daughter of his and had spent considerable energy worrying about her life. He had been distressed at her hermitlike habits back in New York, and now that they had been thrown upon their own resources, he was amazed at how she'd emerged from the shell she had once built around herself. Now, however, he noticed that she avoided looking at Missouri, going straight to the kitchen to begin supper preparations.

Missouri said, "Hannah, I brought the fixin's for supper tonight. You just let me handle this kitchen."

"All right, Missouri."

Lewis said, "I'm going outside."

"You be keerful with that leg, Lewis. It won't be strong for a while yet."

"I'm not a child!" Lewis snapped and left the room.

Missouri went over to the kitchen and began pulling out the rest of the items from her flour sack. She spoke cheerfully of Lewis's recovery but soon noticed that Hannah was strangely quiet.

Turning to her, Missouri Ann said, "I hope it don't put you out none to have me for a ma, Hannah."

Hannah whirled about and stared at Missouri. "That hasn't happened yet."

"Oh, but it will. It's all writ down. God's got His plans for every one of us, daughter, and it's going to happen just like He says." She unwrapped some meat, dumped it into a pot, and went on, her voice completely confident. "Your daddy may squirm for a mite, but in the end God will run him to the ground." She reached out and touched Hannah's hair. "You've got such pretty hair. All of you are pretty young'uns. It'd be good to have children like you and Kat and Jenny, and I believe even Josh will come around. And then," she added, "I'll be havin' Lewis's babies after we get hitched."

Despite herself, Hannah found Missouri's confidence in this matter intriguing. "Don't you ever doubt God, Missouri?"

Missouri Ann Ramey turned and faced Hannah. "Doubt God? I reckon not! Ain't no profit in doubtin' the good Lord!"

★ ★ ★ ★

When suppertime arrived, the whole family gathered in the dining room. Josh, who had grown harder and harder for any of them to reach, was amused by Missouri's insistence that she was eventually going to marry Lewis. A devilish light gleamed in his eyes as he said, "Well, Ma, what have you got for supper tonight?"

Missouri turned and saw him grinning at her. She patted his cheek as she said, "Don't you be askin' questions, son. You just sit down and eat hearty."

Josh had meant for his comment to torment her, but she had obviously taken it as a compliment. He shook his head and took his seat.

Missouri had cooked the entire meal herself, and now she set the hot dishes out, including the fresh-baked bread.

"This looks delicious, Missouri," Jenny said. "What is it?"

"It's a surprise. We'll have the blessing first, Lewis, and then we can lay our ears back and fly right at it."

Lewis could not help grinning at Missouri's expression. If it were not for her insistence that he was destined by heaven to be her husband, he would have found her very good company indeed. Even though she was not educated, she had a quick mind and a witty streak in her. He had the feeling also that if she were properly dressed, she would be an attractive woman, but it was hard to tell since she usually clomped around in men's brogans and a pair of overalls. He bowed his head and asked the blessing, and as soon as he was finished, Missouri picked up the largest plate and took the dishcloth off of it. He looked down at the contents and said, "What is it?"

"Just eat up. You'll like it."

Everyone watched as Lewis spooned a very small portion of the main dish out and passed it on. When it got to Hannah, she took her share and stared at it, not sure what to make of it. Everyone else took a small portion, and Missouri insisted that once they'd tasted it, they'd be begging for more, but she wouldn't tell them what it was. Then they all loaded up their plates with what Missouri called "way out there grits." She would not explain why she called it that, but with butter and a little pepper it was delicious.

After eating the mystery dish, Lewis said grudgingly, "Well, that was good, Missouri. What was it?"

"Why, that was my specialty. Pig-tail casserole."

Lewis gulped and glanced around the table. "That was pig tails?"

"Oh yeah," Missouri said with a satisfied look on her face. "Nothin' better than pig tails if they're cooked right."

Josh burst out laughing. "Those were the best pig tails I ever ate in my life, Ma. How do you cook 'em?"

"That's for me to know and you to find out, son. Now, let's get on with it. I fixed some fried chicken with cream gravy too."

This dish proved to be more to everyone's liking, and after the main meal was consumed, Missouri brought a cake to the table. "I hope everybody likes this. It's my dessert specialty."

"What do you call it?"

"Pleasing Pappy Cake."

Kat had never heard of such a funny name for a cake. "Why do you call it that?"

"Because it's so good it pleases Pappy. Here, Lewis, you get the first slice."

Lewis took a piece of the cake, which was, indeed, light and fluffy and had a delicious icing. "Why, this is very good, Missouri! Maybe the best I've ever eaten. What's in the icing?"

"Oh, just some powdered sugar, butter, and a little dab of vanilla and a few glugs of milk."

"I love the way you give the exact measurements." Lewis grinned and winked across the table at Hannah, taking another large bite of cake and sipping his coffee.

"Somebody coming," Kat said, getting up and running to the door. "It's the preacher."

"Brother Crutchfield?" Lewis got up and joined her at the door, greeting the minister as he approached. "Just a bit late for supper, Brother Crutchfield, but there's plenty left. Come in."

Crutchfield stepped in, taking off his hat. He usually wore a pleased expression, but all of them could see clearly that tonight something was wrong.

The minister looked about and said, "Didn't mean to interrupt. Miss Jenny, could I see you privately a moment?"

Jenny rose at once from the table. "Why, certainly. We can just step outside."

"That would be fine. Pardon me, folks. We won't be long."

Puzzled, Jenny stepped outside and the two moved away from the house. She could not imagine what had happened. "Are the children all right?"

"Oh yes, they're fine. I left them with Mrs. Simmons."

"I thought they might be ill."

"No, nothing like that."

Jenny studied the man's face and saw that he was having difficulty speaking. "What is it, Devoe?" she asked, unconsciously using his first name. She often thought of him like that, but in public she always referred to him as Brother Crutchfield.

"I've got some bad news. There was a meeting of the church, and they've terminated me."

"Terminated you! What does that mean?"

Devoe shrugged his shoulders and a wry expression turned his mouth. "It means they fired me."

Instantly Jenny felt anger stirring within her. "Because of me?"

"I wouldn't put it that way. They're just some pretty narrow-minded people."

"Don't go," Jenny said. "You must stay."

"You don't understand how Baptist churches work, Jenny. Everything is decided by a vote, and the youngest member, even Kat, would have the same vote as the chairman of the board of deacons."

"When did this meeting take place?"

"It was a specially called meeting last night."

"Well, we're members of the church, and I didn't get a vote."

"I guess . . . there wasn't time to get to everybody."

Jenny's temper flared. "Why, it's terrible! Don't you see what's happened? Those deacons got everybody together who they knew would vote against you and didn't tell anyone else. It's like a crooked political thing."

"Don't say that, Jenny." Devoe put his hand on Jenny's shoulder. "They're good people, most of them, but—"

"I don't think they're so good. Come on, we'll have to tell my family what's happened."

"I'll just go on—"

"You won't go anywhere. Come in the house."

Startled by her aggressive behavior, Devoe followed Jenny into the house, where she announced angrily, "Those deacons have fired Brother Crutchfield, and I think it's awful!"

Lewis slammed the table with his fist. "Why, this is an insult to my daughter! They're hinting that something was going on between you two."

Devoe could not defend the action that had been taken, although he tried feebly. "I don't think most people feel like that, Mr. Winslow."

"Most people, my foot! They came sneaking around and called a meeting and got rid of you because they knew they couldn't do it any other way!" Lewis exclaimed.

Suddenly Missouri Ann lifted her hand and cried out loudly, "Hallelujah, praise God! To God be the glory forever."

Lewis, startled by her outburst, turned to stare at Missouri, who had risen to her feet and was walking around with her hand in the air. "Missouri, this seems like an odd time to be praising God."

Missouri's eyes were sparkling, and a pleased expression filled her face. "Why, it's what I've been prayin' for."

Crutchfield blurted, "You've been praying for me to be fired?"

"No, preacher, I've been prayin' for a church where God's Spirit is free, and as soon as I heard what had happened, the Lord spoke to me." She moved over to stand eye to eye with the preacher, who looked almost frail beside Missouri's sturdy form. She took his hands in hers. "We're gonna have a church where God's Spirit is free—and you're gonna be the preacher."

"What are you talking about, Missouri?"

"I'm talkin' about we're gonna have a church where the Spirit of God will have free course. You do the preachin', and I'll do the prayin' and the exhortin'. God's told me that He wants people in a church that won't go to a fancy one. He wants a church where the Lord Jesus Christ is uplifted and nothin' else, and where it don't matter what people wear or how much money they got. He wants a church where people will believe Him, and when they need a miracle, they'll know who to call on."

Everyone in the room was dumbfounded by Missouri's proclamation. She dropped Devoe's hand and moved around the room speaking in a voice that carried far beyond the dining room, giving vent to her innermost feelings with such joy that they could only stare at her. Ever the cynic, Josh muttered that Missouri's voice was loud enough to make one's hair fall out.

Finally Devoe said, "Wait a minute, Missouri. I've always wanted a church like that, but there's not one around here. There's no building."

Clint, who had been listening to all of this with astonishment, spoke up, surprising even himself. "Sure there is. There's the Pattersons' big barn standing empty. It could be made into a church."

Clarence Patterson was a well-to-do farmer. The previous year his house had burned down but the big barn was left standing. Patterson had moved to another farm he owned, but the barn was still standing empty.

"Why, shore," Missouri agreed. "Clarence is a good man. He'd probably even join the church. I bet he'd be glad to let us have that barn of his."

Devoe wasn't convinced. "But I don't have a place to live. I don't have anything to live on."

"Where's your faith, brother?" Missouri cried. "God feeds the sparrows. He can sure feed a skinny preacher and two ornery kids."

"You do have a place to live," Lewis said suddenly. He had not intended to speak up, but something about the situation had touched him. He had liked the man from the moment he had met him, feeling a compassion for him—a lone man with two children to raise. Now he said, "We've got this big old barn of a house, preacher. I reckon the garden's big enough to feed the three of you. So look on this as your home."

"That's generous of you, Lewis, but—" He could not speak

for a moment; then he looked at Missouri Ann. "I . . . I'll have to pray about it, Missouri."

"That's fine," Missouri cried out. "You start prayin', and while you're doin' that, the rest of us will get to work." She turned with purpose to Clint. "Clint, you and Josh go to the sawmill first thing tomorrow morning. Get some planks for pews. We'll need wood for a pulpit too, and I'll tell you what. I want a big mourners' bench 'cause we're gonna have lots of mourners." She turned to the others and said, "The rest of us are gonna get the word out. There's gonna be church in the barn on Sunday."

"But I haven't prayed yet," Crutchfield protested.

Missouri let out a loud whoop. "Praise God! Glory be to God and the Lamb forever. By the time you get all prayed up and you find out that what we're tellin' you is God's will, you'll have a church, Preacher!"

★   ★   ★   ★

When word got out that Devoe Crutchfield had been fired from the First Baptist Church of Summerdale, he was besieged by half of the membership, who were incensed at the way he'd been railroaded. Although many said they would form a new church with him as their pastor, Crutchfield begged them to stay in the Baptist church and work things out with the other members. He did not want to be party to splitting a church in half.

Many agreed to stay in the Baptist church, but they nonetheless threw themselves into the work of turning the empty barn into a church. Then there were others whom Missouri had rousted out from Dog Town, most of them no more religious than the dogs they owned in droves, yet they came with hammers and saws to help transform the barn. The owner of the sawmill, Jed Freely, a heathen if there ever was one, even gave a good price on the lumber—after considerable pressure from Missouri.

Miraculously the money was raised and the work done, and two Sundays after being fired from one church, Devoe Crutchfield stood up in his new pulpit for the first service of Bethel Church. The roomy barn was packed with people from all over the county who were curious about this pastor who was fired from his church. There was no piano or organ, but a choir loft had been built and was filled with enthusiastic singers.

Missouri was in her element. She surprised all the Winslows by wearing a dress, a rather presentable one at that, and Lewis was shocked to find that she appeared quite attractive and was not as big as he'd thought.

When Devoe got up to preach, he looked out over the congregation and had to swallow back the tightness in his throat. He bowed his head for a moment to pray for strength, and then looked up to see Jenny seated between his children, smiling up at him. Encouraged, he began confidently, "Miracles tell us that God is still on the throne. Look around you, my friends, for I'm here to tell you that today you're seeing a miracle!" Several *amens* resounded loudly, the most penetrating being the voice of Missouri Ann, who was sitting in the front row smiling at him and nodding.

"I know only one thing about this church," Devoe went on. "I want it to exalt the name of Jesus Christ. I want sinners to find Him as Savior as I have found Him, and as many of you have. And so this morning I'm going to preach a simple sermon. Before you leave here today I want you to know that all men are sinners, Jesus died for sinners, and all sinners can be saved through His blood."

As Jenny sat listening to the truths she had heard before, something felt different. The Spirit of God was moving powerfully, and as Devoe spoke of the death of Christ, she found herself weeping. Looking around, she found others weeping as well.

When Devoe gave the invitation, Jenny was amazed at the rush of people coming down the aisle to the front. The enormous mourners' bench filled up in moments, and Missouri Ann Ramey walked back and forth laying her hands on people, begging God to save them, hugging them, and crying with them. And still more came.

Josh had taken a seat off to one side. He had come out of curiosity, not expecting to witness anything like this. He hung his head, feeling angry and cynical, yet his affair with Dora and his bootlegging lay on him like a thousand-pound weight. While he knew he had not been perfect in his life in New York, he had never fallen to such depths as he was in now. He had been addicted to liquor for some time, and now he was addicted to

Dora as well. She was not a godly woman, driving him to drink more and engage in more and more immoral conduct. As he watched men and women kneeling and begging God for forgiveness, he had a strong impulse to join them. But he was too weak. He wrenched himself out of the pew and hurried outside, where he turned his head upward, as if seeking God in the heavens. But then he hung his head in shame and groaned, "No, God, I'm no good," before stumbling homeward on foot.

The service lasted long past the appointed hour, and when it finally ended, Missouri urged the pastor to have a baptism the next Sunday, to which Devoe gladly agreed. With a joyous smile, Missouri warned him, "Mind you, we'll have a bunch more saved next Sunday, so it's gonna take a lot of baptizin', Preacher."

After the crowd dispersed, Hannah stayed, unable to move from her place. She had been so moved by the service that she'd prayed until she felt weak. Now, sitting alone in the silence, she heard a voice behind her saying, "Preachin's over, Hannah."

Startled, she turned and got to her feet. Clint was walking down the aisle. "They sent me to look for you. Thought you got lost. We're about ready to go home. Everybody else has left."

"I just wanted to sit here and think about what happened here today."

Clint moved closer to her and shook his head in disbelief. "I never saw anything like it."

The two stood exchanging comments about the service, and finally Clint said, "Do you think Missouri's right?"

"You mean about marrying Father?"

"Yes. She's pretty sure about it."

"I don't think it'll ever happen. They're too different."

"You never know about things like that. I think they could find some happiness together if your dad could get over his reluctance to get married again."

"But they're so different. And Missouri isn't anything like our mother."

"There probably aren't many women around who could measure up to your mother." He gazed at the empty choir loft for a moment and then said, "Did you see Lee Foster talking to Jenny?"

Indeed, Hannah had noticed. She'd been surprised to see Foster there. He had come dressed to kill and had taken little part in the service, but afterward he had joined Jenny, and the two had left together.

Hannah said without thinking, "Are you jealous?"

"Jealous? Me? Of who?"

"Of Lee courting Jenny."

"Well, what makes you think I'd be jealous? He's pretty light-weight, but if she likes him, I guess it's all right." He looked at her closely. "What makes you ask a question like that?"

Hannah felt her face burning. "I . . . I thought you liked her."

"Well, of course I like her. She's a nice girl, but she's not for me."

Hannah felt foolish. "I thought maybe—"

Clint suddenly reached out and put his hands on her arms. She lifted her eyes, startled, as he said, "Hannah, you're a smart woman. Don't you know I have feelings for you?"

Hannah did not know what went through her at that moment. It was almost like a jolt of electricity. She had been so careful to keep her distance from men, but now she realized that this man had intrigued her ever since she met him. "No," she said, "I . . . I never thought that."

"Any other woman would have. I didn't think I was hiding it all that well, but now maybe it's time to tell you right out that I'm in love with you, Hannah."

His confession shocked Hannah into silence. When he pulled her close to kiss her, she felt a moment of panic, but then, feeling his lips on hers, she gave him what he asked for. She felt herself responding in a way she could not have thought possible, with a deep yearning she never knew existed. For so long she had avoided men, but she had watched this one, wondering at times about the complexities of his personality and wondering what drew her to him.

As for Clint, this moment was something new for him too. He had not asked her consent. In fact, he had taken her by surprise, much like the first time he had kissed her. Many women would have slapped him for his forwardness, yet here she was in his arms, giving herself to him willingly.

Suddenly he felt her pull away and saw her eyes fill with tears. "What's wrong, Hannah?"

"I can't marry . . . not anybody."

"Why not, Hannah?"

She said nothing, just pulled herself away and ran blindly toward the door, ignoring his voice as he called out after her.

PART FOUR

October 1930–January 1931

★ ★ ★

CHAPTER TWENTY

PEACE BY THE RIVER

★ ★ ★ ★

The sorghum that Clint had labored over all summer had grown into a waving amber field. For two days the entire family had harvested the crop, which had turned out to be more work than any of them had expected. Since leaving New York they had all been toughened and weathered by the southern sun. The labor required to simply keep the rudiments of a farm intact had overwhelmed them, but they had survived.

At first, harvesting the sorghum had been fun. They had gone out to the field with every available blade and knife, and Clint had showed them what to do.

"Chop it off close to the ground, then strip off the blades," he said as he demonstrated. "We'll save some of these heads for next year's seed. The rest we can feed to the chickens."

"Why, that's not hard!" Kat said. "Let me try it." She took her knife, which Clint had sharpened along with all the rest, and removed all the side leaves, then lopped off the bushy top and tossed it down. "Look, it's easy."

Clint grinned at her. "We'll see how easy it is by sundown."

As Clint had prophesied, the morning went well, but by afternoon, when the field was fairly well stripped, they were all aching from the labor. Hannah straightened up and placed her hand against her back. Arching her body, she said, "Clint, this sorghum better be good for all the work it's taking."

Clint glanced at her. She was wearing a simple blue dress, much faded, a pair of high-topped shoes, and a straw hat with her hair flowing out from under it. *It's a miracle how far she's come from being cooped up in one room.* Aloud he said, "Everybody's done well. Tomorrow we'll start making sorghum."

"Is it hard?"

"Just takes time like everything else. Why don't you quit and go on into the house, Hannah? We can finish up."

"No, I'll stay with it until we're finished." She looked at him and smiled. He was bronzed and lean and looked very fit. His teeth, as he smiled, were very white against his darkened skin, and she remembered how he had held her in the church and how she had fled from him. Since then, he had been standoffish for a while, but she could hardly blame him for trying to protect himself from being rejected again. She almost spoke of her regret at having behaved as she did, but what could she say? She turned quickly and walked away to resume harvesting the sorghum.

I don't know what's in her heart, Clint thought as he watched her go. *But it's got to come out of there somehow or other. She's too good a woman to waste.*

★   ★   ★   ★

Early the next morning, everyone gathered around the sorghum mill. It was a strange-looking affair built of heavy wooden timbers, which Clint identified as ironwood. "It lasts forever and it's tougher than iron." There were three rollers inside the works and one long wooden handle to which Clint had hitched Samson.

"Doesn't require any great skill," he said. "Giddyup, Samson."

The mule stepped forward and began walking in an endless circle. Clint picked up a few stalks of the stripped sorghum cane and shoved them into the press. The wheels inside gripped the cane, and soon a frothy juice began issuing from the side of the mill. It ran out a pipe into a burlap-covered barrel.

"This is all there is to this part," Clint said. "As soon as we collect all the juice, we'll start making up a batch of syrup."

Everyone took a turn at feeding the cane into the mill, and from time to time they stopped to empty the barrel into smaller vessels.

Several hours later Clint said, "Someone take over here, and we'll start making up a batch."

"I'll do it," Josh offered, shoving the cane into the press while Clint led the way over to the boiler. This was simply a furnace made out of stone cemented together, the crevice much in the shape of a bathtub. Clint started a fire underneath it, and as soon as it was blazing, he said, "Okay, grab the other end of that trough. Some people call it a boiler box." Lewis grasped the end of the metal box, which was approximately eight inches deep, four feet wide, and more than six feet long. They put the box over the furnace, and as it heated, Clint said, "Have you got that cloth, Jenny?"

"Right here, Clint. What do I do with it?"

"You and Kat stretch it out over the trough and let me pour this juice in there. We'll have to strain this several times."

As the two held the cloth, he poured the frothy juice into the filter, and they watched as it ran down into the trough.

"What are those plates in the middle for?" Lewis asked, pointing at three dividers that separated the box into four compartments.

"Well, the juice goes into this first compartment, then it boils awhile, and the pure stuff goes into the next compartment. As it passes through the different sections, the sediment gets left and the juice gets filtered out—purified, you might say."

They watched the bubbles rising from the bottom of the boiling juice. "When those bubbles get to be about two inches thick, it'll be done." Clint reached down in with a skimmer to remove the impurities.

As the molasses flowed out of a tube, they siphoned it off into jugs and bottles. They worked hard all day, until Clint finally called a halt to the operation. "We'll get the rest of it tomorrow," he said. "You've all done a good job."

"What do we do now?" Hannah asked.

"I'll clean out the boiler box here and bank the fires to be ready for tomorrow."

"What are we going to do with all this molasses?" Josh asked, looking at the odd-sized bottles and jugs.

"We'll eat a lot of it, and we'll try to sell the rest," Clint said. "I thought maybe we might work out a deal with the store to buy it from us—or maybe work out a swap for groceries."

"That would be good," Kat said. "Then we'd make some money."

Clint shooed them off, but it took him some time to clean the boiler box out. The residue was sticky, and he worked until dark. He went in just in time to clean up and eat supper, and after supper he walked outside and sat on the porch. He pulled out his harmonica and began playing his favorite tune, the song about the pilgrim.

The time passed quickly, and before long most of the family, exhausted from the hard work, went to bed. He sat on the porch steps playing softly and then turned as he heard footsteps. "Hello, Hannah. Come and sit by me."

Hannah sat down beside him on the steps and said, "What a pretty full moon."

"It sure is. Always liked full-moon times. It's almost like a spotlight in the sky."

Hannah was tired but restless. She sat there and listened to Clint as he went back to playing his harmonica. After listening for a while she said, "I love your playing, Clint."

He put the harmonica in his pocket and turned to face her. "I guess we've got to get something straight, Hannah."

Alarmed, Hannah turned to him. The moonlight made his features softer, but there was a look in his eyes that troubled her. "What do you mean?"

"I mean I've told you how I feel, and all you've said is 'I can't marry anyone.'" He took her hand and held it in both of his. "I think I deserve a better answer than that."

Hannah dropped her head. She was very much aware of the strength and the warmth of his hand. She was always aware of Clint's physical strength. She had tried more than once to share her heart with him, but she could not. There were too many obstacles.

"You can't just let a man lay his heart open to you and then tell him *nothing*, Hannah. If you don't love me, just say so. I'll understand that. I've been around enough to know that love isn't always divided out neatly into parts. Sometimes a man loves a woman and she doesn't love him. I understand that. So just say so if that's it."

"Clint . . ." Hannah tried to speak, and when she turned, he saw that her face was contorted, and she seemed close to tears. "I'm sorry! I can't tell you, Clint."

Clint exhaled audibly and then released her hand. He stood to his feet and took a deep breath. "All right, that's that, then."

"What do you mean?" she asked, alarmed.

"I mean I'm leaving. I can't stay around loving you with no hope of anything in return. A man needs a woman, and I haven't made any secret of that. So I'll be leaving."

Hannah was shocked at the tone of his voice. "Clint, wait!"

But he ignored her call and walked quickly across the yard. She called out again, but he did not even turn. She stood there waiting until he had disappeared into the night, and then she sat down shakily, put her face in her hands, and began to weep.

★　★　★　★

Overhead the moon was high, and Clint knew that it was well past midnight, perhaps even one or two o'clock. He walked for a long while beside the river, the moonlight illuminating the water in bright tongues of silver as it flowed over the rocky shallows by the bank. He finally sat down on a log and simply watched the river flow by. From far away came the bell-shaped tones of foxhounds pursuing their prey. Ordinarily Clint would have tried to guess what they were chasing, but tonight he paid no heed.

Finally he shuddered and looked up into the sky. The stars were bright, twinkling like tiny bits of fire, and he said angrily, "God, I don't know what you want!"

The sound of his voice startled him as it broke the silence, but he had fallen into a deep despair. He had known hard times, and as he looked back over his life, he realized that this was the hardest time of all. He thought he had found a home with the Winslows, and he thought he had found in Hannah Winslow a woman he could love and cherish. He had always yearned for love—although he would have been shocked to hear anyone say it that way.

As he stood up beside the river staring blankly into the night sky, he said bitterly, "God, this is my last chance—and I don't know what's wrong. I know she's a good woman, better than I am, but I need somebody—" He raised his voice then, "I need somebody, God, can't you see that? I know I sing about pilgrims, and I'm not even that, but I'm asking you to tell me what's wrong with me that I can't ever find a home or a woman."

The silence closed about Clint, and he stood there as if waiting for an answer. Then, to his immense surprise, he suddenly became aware of a presence. It was so real he almost looked around to see who was watching him, but he knew there was no one, at least no human eyes on him. He knew it was God's presence.

Clint had felt God's presence twice before in his life. Once when he was only a boy of twelve and he had gone to a camp meeting with his mother. He did not remember the sermon, but he remembered how, at some point, he'd become so aware that God was touching him that he began to cry. The moment had passed, and he had done nothing about it, but only two years ago this same feeling had come to him again. He had been walking down a road hitchhiking when unexpectedly he felt what he was feeling now—that God was there.

"What *is* it, God?" he whispered. "Please, just tell me. I need something!"

The river made a gentle shushing sound at his feet, and the stars glittered, coldly silent in the far reaches of space.

Without warning, the Scripture that Devoe Crutchfield had preached on the previous Sunday came to mind. *Christ Jesus came into the world to save sinners; of whom I am chief.* He remembered that the words were those of the apostle Paul, and then the words that he had heeded so little during the service began to grow within him. Memories came to him of things he had done over the years, some of which he had managed to forget or downplay, but now they paraded before his eyes and flooded his soul. Another verse the pastor had quoted on Sunday burned into his mind: *While we were yet sinners, Christ died for us.*

How long Clint stood there he never knew, for time had ceased to be a factor. He thought of his life, and he thought of Jesus Christ dying for him, and finally, from someplace deep within, he was conscious of words. *"I loved you enough to die on a cross to save you. Won't you love me?"*

Clint fell to his knees and began to cry out, "Oh, God, I'm a sinner, and there's no way I can ever be anything else unless you help me! I ask you, God, in the name of Jesus, to save me. That's all I know to do."

As soon as he prayed this prayer, Clint bowed his head to the ground and began to sob. He wept not because he was afraid, but because a strange peace and rest had come to him that he could not have described to anyone. The thought flashed through his mind, *I've been running all my life, but now I am a pilgrim on my way to a better place than this. . . .* And then he began to thank the Lord as joy flooded through him.

★　★　★　★

Missouri Ann had no official standing in Bethel Church, but she was, in some sense, the most powerful force there. The congregation was growing, and people were being converted at almost every service. Devoe Crutchfield was somewhat surprised when Missouri came to him after a service and said, "Preacher, it's time for another baptizin'."

It was like her words were carved in bronze. She was not asking him, he realized, but announcing what was going to happen. He smiled and said, "All right, we'll do it next Sunday. But it's November—people will freeze in the river."

"Don't you worry about that. We'll baptize 'em right here in the church."

"In what, sister?"

"In a horse trough. We'll heat up the water. They can bring a change of clothes."

★　★　★　★

The following Sunday, as Devoe looked at the people lined up for baptism, his heart swelled within him. Some were very young, but two of them were over eighty. He raised his voice and said, "God has given us a fruitful increase. We thank Him for it, and now we'll rejoice with these who have come to follow their

Lord in baptism." He stood outside of the tank, which came up as high as his waist. He gestured to Irma Jean Smith and took her hand as she mounted the steps that Clint had made for people to get into the tank. He noted that she had attached weights to the hem of her dress to keep it from floating up. He raised his hand, saying, "And now, in obedience to the command of our Lord and Savior Jesus Christ, I baptize you, my sister, in the name of the Father and of the Son and of the Holy Ghost." Supporting Irma's head while she held her nose, he lowered her backward, and she disappeared into the water. When she came up, Missouri's voice rang out, "Glory be to God and the Lamb forever! Alleluia! Amen!" Several others took up this praise, and each time he baptized an individual, the same rejoicing was heard. Devoe was not used to such enthusiastic baptisms. In the First Baptist Church, where Devoe had served for years, baptism had always been a quiet, solemn affair, as if everyone were afraid to speak, but here, Missouri Ann was a catalyst that would not be still.

Finally the last of the candidates was baptized, and Devoe began to say, "We give thanks that God has sent us these, and now I'll pronounce the benediction—"

"Just a minute, Preacher."

Every head turned, including Hannah's. She saw Clint, who had been standing over to one side, come forward. He had stayed in the barn since their conversation three days earlier, and her heart had ached for him. There was nothing she could say, however, but she had prayed that he would not leave. The thought of that had caused a riot in her heart that she had not anticipated.

"Yes, Clint?"

"I guess you've got one more."

"One more?" Crutchfield looked around. "Who have we missed?"

Clint flashed a smile, and Hannah saw a light in his eyes she had never seen. "You've got me, Preacher."

A murmuring went over the crowd, and Hannah felt her breath grow short. She clasped her hands together so hard that they ached as Clint spoke.

"When you preached last Sunday morning on how Christ Jesus died to save sinners, I didn't pay much attention. But three nights ago I was out at the river. I felt that my life had become pretty intolerable."

Hannah saw that Clint did not look at her, but she knew with a sudden stab of regret that she was the cause of this. She listened intently as he went on to tell of his experience. And then as he spoke of how he had called on God and asked Him to save him, she felt tears gathering in her eyes. Clint concluded, "And I did what I should have done a long time ago. I got on my knees and asked Jesus Christ to come into my life. He's my Savior now, Preacher, and I want to give testimony to that in baptism."

Wild applause broke out, and Hannah could not see for the tears. When she blinked them away, she saw Clint turn and look directly at her. She could not speak or move, but he smiled and nodded, then turned and said, "I'm ready, Preacher." He got into the tank fully dressed, and after Crutchfield baptized him, he came up out of the water, wiping his face. "May I follow you, Jesus, in everything I do."

Hannah broke out singing "What a Friend We Have in Jesus," and the entire congregation joined in.

After the song Hannah sat in her seat, her head bowed, and thanked God for Clint's salvation. "Whatever happens, I'm glad of this, Lord, and I know it's your doing," she whispered.

★ ★ ★ ★

She waited until Clint had changed into the extra clothes he had brought, and then she watched as a line of people went by to express their pleasure at his decision. Finally she approached him, feeling strangely weak. She held out her hand, and he took it, saying nothing, but his eyes were fixed on her.

"Clint, I can't tell you how happy I am."

"I knew you would be, Hannah. I would have come to you before, but I've been working some things out."

Hannah met his gaze and saw there a new softness and gentleness. "Well . . . will you be leaving now, Clint?"

Clint was still holding her hand. "You know that song we've sung so much, that pilgrim song?"

"Yes."

"Well, that's what I am. If the Lord says go, I'll go. If He says stay, I'll stay." Then he squeezed her hand and covered it with his other one. "But one thing I want you to know, Hannah Winslow. I've got to change a lot of things in my life, but I'll never change how I feel about you."

Hannah felt her throat thicken, and again she felt tears forming in her eyes. She blinked them away as quickly as she could, then removed her hand. She felt confused, but his words had warmed her. She knew that even if she never married this man, she would love him as long as she lived.

CHAPTER TWENTY-ONE

NOT A DEER IN THE WOODS

★ ★ ★ ★

Christmas had come—the second Christmas for the Winslows in Georgia. Now as Lewis put the string of threaded popcorn over the tree, he thought of how life had changed. New York, with all of its luxuries—the fine house, the clothes, the cars—all seemed to be a vague dream. Life now was getting the cow milked, making butter, putting in the garden, making sorghum, trying to keep enough cash on hand for the absolute necessities.

He sighed heavily, stepped down off the chair, and turned to Kat and Dallas, who were stringing red berries. "How are those strings coming?" Kat was always the bright spot in a generally dark picture, and she gave him a brilliant smile.

"Fine, Daddy. It's going to be a beautiful tree. Even better than last year."

"I ain't never had a Christmas tree," Dallas said, looking up. He closed one eye as he poked the needle through the berry, then looked up and smiled. "Christmas is nice, ain't it, Mr. Winslow?"

"Very nice, Dallas." Lewis had been amazed at how the boy, who had been eerily quiet when they had met him, had opened up. He knew Kat and the rest of the Winslow family were largely responsible for the change. Dallas and Kat had become best friends. They roamed the hills together, and Dallas had taught the girl the names of innumerable plants. He also had taken her hunting often enough that she had become quite proficient.

"Have you done that extra math work, Kat?"

"Oh, Daddy, I don't want to do that on Christmas Eve."

"You'll have to do it sometime. May as well get it over with so you can enjoy the rest of your vacation."

Kat sighed and shook her head. "I just don't like those word problems." Her math book was lying on the table, and she opened it. "These problems don't make any sense."

"What do you mean they don't make sense?"

"Well, just listen to this." Kat read off a long math problem having to do with the number of acres a farmer would have if he had so many acres of cotton, so many of corn, and so many of wheat and then sold off a different fraction of each of them. She flung the book aside. "Who could work that?"

"Why, that'd be two hundred twenty-six and three-quarters acres," Dallas said. He was stringing another bead, seemingly paying little heed.

Lewis stared at Dallas. "Have you worked that problem before, son?"

"No, sir, but she just read it out."

"He can do that, Daddy," Kat said with some pride. "Just give him two long sums to add together."

"How much is three hundred twenty-six and four hundred twenty-one?" Lewis said.

Without a moment's hesitation, Dallas answered, "Why, that's easy. Seven hundred and forty-seven."

"Give him four numbers like that, Daddy."

Lewis rattled off four three-digit numbers, and again, without hesitation, Dallas said, "One thousand, three hundred and twenty-three." He saw that the man was staring at him, and his brow wrinkled. "That's right, ain't it?"

"How should I know?" Lewis shrugged.

"It's right." Kat beamed. "He never misses."

Lewis was shocked. He had heard of such natural gifts but had never seen anyone demonstrate them. He said, "Let's talk about this a bit." He went over and picked up Kat's math book, and for the next twenty minutes he shot problem after problem at Dallas, who answered them all, seemingly without even computing.

"Isn't he smart?" Kat beamed.

"Certainly is. Son, you ought to be in school. You've got a gift there."

"No, sir! I tried to go to school once, but they just laughed at me."

"Well, they won't laugh at you now," Lewis said. "You must get some schooling."

Dallas flushed. "They'd jist laugh at me 'cause I ain't got no fittin' clothes, and they laugh at my grandma."

"I can't do much about your grandma, although I like her myself, but we can do something about the clothes, surely."

"I've been begging him to go to school, but he won't do it," Kat said.

"Well," Lewis said, "I'll talk to the principal. I think something can be arranged."

"Won't that be fun, Dallas? We can go to school together."

Dallas looked dubious. "I don't know about that," he mumbled.

"You've got to, Dallas. You've got to get an education." She reached out and tugged the boy's thin sleeve. "It'll be fun. You'll see."

★　★　★　★

Christmas was over, at least all except for taking down the tree. Lewis stood in the living room silently thinking about the day. He had not dreamed that he would have so enjoyed Christmas. He never had before back in New York. They no longer had expensive presents to exchange, but they shared a great meal together and were surprisingly happy. Missouri Ann had come and cooked the turkey, and Lewis thought about how often she had been in the house. The thought of Missouri troubled him, and he walked over to the window and stared out. The stars were almost obliterated by low clouds, and he felt that snow was in the air. But his mind was not on that. He thought again of how they had sung songs, Clint playing his harmonica and the rest of them joining in on the old hymns and Christmas carols. He had not missed how Hannah had lifted her eyes to Clint shyly when she thought no one was looking, and he muttered, "I wonder what that's all about." He still worried about Hannah, for life seemed to be passing her by.

As for Jenny, she had spent much of her time lately taking care of Crutchfield's two children, but Lewis thought she had a restless spirit. *She'll never be happy on this farm, but where can she go?* he wondered.

Then he thought of Josh. Josh had been strangely quiet for weeks now, even for months, and for a while at the Christmas celebration he had smiled and seemed like his old self, but then the mood had vanished, and he had sat silently throughout most of the evening.

Finally Lewis turned and walked upstairs, tired and already thinking about the work to do the following day. He went to his room and sat down to take off his shoes when a tiny knock came at his door. Surprised, he got up and opened it. "Why, Kat, what are you doing up?"

"I couldn't sleep."

"Well, do you want to come in?"

Kat looked disturbed. "I guess so, Daddy. I wanted to talk to you."

"Why, sure, honey. Here, sit down and talk all you please. I'm not sleepy." Lewis listened then as Kat began speaking of Dallas, and she asked him if he had been serious about getting the boy into school. Lewis had already decided to do what he could and tried to reassure her. "We'll do everything we can, honey, and I think it'll work out fine. I think he's a genius in math, and who knows what else is going on in that mind of his."

Lewis's words seemed to satisfy Kat as she sat cross-legged on his bed. Finally she looked up at him and said, "You know what, Daddy?"

"What?"

"I love Missouri Ann."

Lewis smiled. Kat did, indeed, care about her. Missouri Ann was teaching her to cook and do dozens of other tasks that had come with a lifetime of hard work. Lewis said, "I'm glad you do. She's a fine woman."

"Do you think you'll ever marry her?"

The question caught Lewis off guard. He flushed and ran his hands through his hair. "Oh, I don't know about that. I'm pretty old."

"Missouri Ann says you're not."

Lewis looked at his daughter. He hadn't considered Kat's feelings in the matter. "Would it trouble you if I married her?"

"No! I'd love to have another mother."

Lewis was shocked at the response. He had tried to put the woman's proclamation of marriage out of his mind. It seemed impossible to him that God would put the two of them together.

Kat leaned across the bed and put her arms around him. "I really would," she whispered, pressing her face against his. "I miss Mom, don't you?"

"Yes, honey, of course I do. It gets easier as the years go by, but I still think about her all the time."

"Me too. I wish she could've moved to Georgia with us."

"Perhaps it's better that she didn't have to go through these hard times with us."

"Maybe. But I still miss her."

Lewis hugged her, smelling the freshness of the homemade soap in her hair. He sat there quietly, stroking her hair and wondering what to do next.

★　★　★　★

Clint carried the rifle lightly and kept his eyes moving from point to point in the woods. He had come out seeking a deer and had wandered far from home. Deer had been scarce, and his luck had not been good for the past month, so the larder was lean. January had arrived, and Clint could not help wondering what 1931 would bring. In the few weeks he'd been a Christian, he had stayed up late at night reading the Scriptures and had spent a great deal of time with Devoe Crutchfield. He respected the preacher's knowledge of the Word of God. The last time the two had talked, he had said in despair, "I'll never learn the Bible like you know it."

"I've been at it a long time, Clint. You stay at it, and God will open things up to you. It's not how much you read the Bible, it's how open you are to the Spirit of God. Sometimes," Devoe added, "God will take one verse and it will mean more to you than anything you've ever known. More than a hundred chapters even."

Clint had taken comfort in this and had continued to study. He and Hannah spoke during the normal course of events, but he had said nothing more of his love for her, nor had she spoken of this to him. He saw that she was troubled and confused and had simply prayed that God would give her understanding. A peace had come to him about this matter, and he was now willing to wait for her for as long as it took. He had learned to bring things like this to God instead of carrying them himself, and now as he made his way through the woods, he felt a sense of joy at how Christ had changed his life.

He sat quietly and waited for a deer to show up at the creek, and when none came, he crossed the creek and headed toward the rising ground. Jesse Cannon had told him that the woods in this area were thick with deer, and indeed, he saw many signs of that. He noted not only the tracks but also where they had eaten away at the bark of the young saplings.

Finally he halted abruptly at a sound. His hand slipped to the trigger. Then he realized it was not animals he heard but human voices.

Must be other hunters, he thought. *I wouldn't want to be mistook for a deer*. He moved forward cautiously, and finally he caught a glimpse of movement ahead. He could not see through the thick woods until he had gone another thirty yards, and then he saw the outlines of a truck. A shock ran through him as he recognized the Winslow truck.

"Josh went out to haul somethin' for somebody in town," he muttered. "What's he doin' way out here in the middle of nowhere?"

Carefully he moved forward, and then he saw Josh with Dora Skinner. Alarm ran through Clint. Dora Skinner's bad reputation was no secret. Men talked freely of how immoral she was, and it disturbed Clint greatly to see Josh out with her. He started to head back the way he had come, and then he heard Dora say, "That's all of it, Josh. We made a good haul this time."

Clint took two steps forward and saw Josh pulling a piece of canvas over a cluster of bottles, and at once he knew the truth. *They're bootlegging whiskey!*

Clint did not hesitate. "Hello," he called, giving warning, and then walked out of the woods. He saw Dora turn to him, her eyes wide with alarm, but Josh simply stood still, his eyes fixed on Clint.

Clint stopped in front of the pair. "This won't do, Josh."

"It's none of your business, Clint," Josh snapped. Ashamed and angry at being caught, he burst out, "Just go on your way and leave us alone."

"I don't think I can do that. Have you thought about your family? If you get caught, it'll break their hearts."

"Like he said, that's none of your business, Clint," Dora put in.

"Yes, it is my business. I'm a part of the Winslow family, in a way. At least I care for them. Josh, what are you thinking of?"

Josh's mind was racing. As usual when he was on these runs with Dora, he had been drinking and could not think clearly. He had never known such shame, for he knew Clint Longstreet was right. "Look, just forget about this, Clint. I'll be okay."

"You'll be in the penitentiary is what you'll be," Clint said grimly. He would have said more, but suddenly his ears caught another sound. He whirled and peered down the old logging road that Josh and Dora had followed. "Somebody's coming," he said tersely.

"Revenuers!" Dora cried, turning to run. "Come on, Josh! Don't just stand there!"

In a drunken haze, Josh broke into a stumbling run and followed Dora. The two disappeared into the woods, leaving Clint there.

"Gotta get this truck out of here," he said. "They'll tie all the Winslows to this mess." He jumped into the truck, started the engine, and gunned it. The road was twisted and narrow, and he did not know where it would lead. Logging roads often just ended in the middle of a stand of large timber, where the loggers had cut back so far, then quit.

The truck lurched and careened over the uneven, broken ground. Clint saw first-growth timber ahead and knew that he was caught. He turned and headed into the woods, but he had not gone twenty feet when he ran into a six-inch-thick sapling that brought the truck to an abrupt halt.

Clint climbed out of the truck, knowing what he had to do. He turned and waited as the car, bumping and lurching, appeared. It stopped and two men got out with shotguns. One of them called out, "Put your hands in the air," and Clint did as he was directed. He had only one thought: *I've got to keep the Winslows out of this. They'll die if they find out what Josh has done.*

★ ★ ★ ★

Sheriff Beauchamp stared at Clint. The two government revenue men were seated at the table along with him. The interrogation had gone on for over an hour, and Clint had volunteered nothing. Finally Beauchamp said, "Look, Clint, you can't be in this alone. If you'll turn state's evidence, it'll be easier for you."

Clint had already settled this in his mind. "Just me, Sheriff, that's all."

The sheriff was bitterly disappointed. "I was there the day you were baptized," he said. "I guess that didn't mean anything, did it?"

Clint Longstreet had no answer. He dropped his head and thought of the hard things that were to come. He prayed, *Lord, help me keep my mouth shut. Please keep the Winslows from finding out what Josh has been doing.*

CHAPTER TWENTY-TWO

OUT OF THE PAST

★　★　★　★

"Why, good afternoon, Sheriff," Lewis said, smiling and opening the screen door. "Come in out of the cold."

Sheriff Beauchamp was wearing a green wool mackinaw and a broad-brimmed felt hat pulled down over his forehead. He pulled off his thick brown leather gloves as he entered, then stood hesitantly. When Lewis put out his hand, he took it but still said nothing.

"Come into the living room," Lewis said. "We've got a nice fire going in the fireplace."

At that moment Hannah stepped out of the kitchen and saw the officer. She smiled, for she liked the burly man very well. She came forward, wiping her hands on her apron. "I've just put some coffee on, Sheriff. You go sit down, and I'll bring you some."

"This isn't a social call, I'm afraid." Beauchamp pulled off his hat and turned it around by the brim. He had become quite fond of the Winslows, and now he looked ill at ease. "I'm afraid I've got some bad news."

Both Lewis and Hannah stared at him; then Lewis said, "Well, what is it? What's wrong?"

"It's Clint. He's in jail."

"In jail!" Hannah exclaimed, dismay washing across her face. "Whatever for?"

"It's pretty serious business, Miss Hannah. He was arrested for transporting illegal alcohol."

Lewis shook his head. "I don't believe it!"

"Well, we don't have much choice but to believe it, Lewis. Two federal officers caught him red-handed. He was in your truck out in the woods. They brought him in, and I had to hold him."

Lewis turned to Hannah and noted the shadows around her eyes and the corners of her mouth as she tried to conceal her shock. He waited for her to speak, but when she did not, he turned again to the sheriff. "What will happen now, Noel?"

"It's hard to say, but we have to face up to the fact that he's going to go to prison. I don't suppose you have any money for a lawyer?"

"No, we don't."

Beauchamp shrugged his beefy shoulders. "No one does these days."

"But what does he say?" Hannah burst out.

"That's the trouble. He won't say anything. I think he's shielding someone. We know he wasn't in this thing all by himself, but he won't talk about where the whiskey came from, and when we asked him if he was alone, he clammed up. That won't get him very far in a courtroom. They're crackin' down more on the moonshiners they catch in this county. Why don't you go talk to him, Lewis, or you, Hannah? After all, you're all the family he's got around here."

Lewis glanced at Hannah. "Yes, we should go, but one of us needs to stay here."

"I'll go, Father," Hannah said.

"That's fine. I'll take you in, Miss Hannah, and I'll see that you get back too." Beauchamp shook his head sadly. "I hate to think I've been fooled. I really thought Clint meant it when he said he was converted—but this looks pretty grim."

★　★　★　★

Josh paced like a caged animal, wondering what he and Dora should do next. They had fled through the woods until they had to stop to catch their breath. Dora said, "It's all right now, Josh.

They can't follow us through these thick woods."

Josh stared at her uncomprehendingly. He continued walking, with no idea where he was going, but Dora tugged at his sleeve, saying, "We'll have to go west if we're gonna hit the road, but we'd better not get on the highway because they'll be lookin' for somebody. They won't believe Clint was by himself." Dora plopped down on a big rock.

Josh didn't answer. He just paced back and forth, still unable to think clearly, although the shock of almost getting caught had definitely sobered him up.

Dora stood up and tugged on his sleeve. "C'mon. I'm ready to move on now. Let's head west."

Josh hardly felt the chill in the damp air. He followed her lead, marching on through the woods like a soldier who had been shot but chose to ignore his wound even as it drained away his strength.

They got to the point where they could see the road and began moving parallel to it while remaining a hundred yards away, out of sight. Cars passed from time to time, and they pulled back deeper into the woods.

Finally they reached a grove of pecan and hickory trees, and Dora said, "Let's slow down. I've got a stitch in my side." She leaned up against one of the trees, breathing heavily, her face pale. She watched as Josh paced again, then said, "We're going to make it now. We were lucky to get away."

Josh twirled and glared at her, his face twisted in a grimace of anger and fear. "Lucky!" he exclaimed. "I wouldn't call it that."

"They didn't catch us, did they?"

"Yeah, but they're bound to have caught Clint."

Dora did not answer. She knew Clint was very close to the Winslows, but he was not a family member. In her world family was everything, and outsiders had to look out for themselves. She had discovered, however, that Josh Winslow had odd ways of thinking. His ideas often took turns she would never have dreamed of. Overhead a red squirrel chattered angrily, then ran out along a branch and launched himself into space. He caught on a branch of a pecan tree, which sagged with him; then he scampered up it and disappeared. Silence fell back over the grove, broken only by the lowing of a cow in a distant pasture.

Josh pulled his cap off and ran his fingers through his hair, despair etched on his face. He stared at the cap as if it were a foreign thing, something he had never seen before. His hands trembled, and when he lifted his eyes, bitterness darkened them. "I never should have gotten into this!"

"You always knew there was a chance of getting caught," Dora said, glancing around nervously. "We'd better move on."

Josh, however, stood immobile, shut his eyes, and whispered, "I always knew I might get caught, but I didn't intend to get someone else involved—especially someone innocent. I should have known better. I must have been crazy to get into a thing like this!"

Dora came over and leaned against him, caressing his face with her fingers. Her answer to everything was physical. She whispered, "It'll be all right." She reached up to kiss him, but he shoved her away.

"All right? How's Clint going to be all right?"

"Well, it wasn't my fault!" she said angrily. She was not used to being rejected, and now she was angry. "What do you expect me to do?"

"I don't expect you to do anything, but I'm telling you this, Dora—it's all over right now."

"What do you mean? Between us?"

"Between us and between me and your family. I'll never touch another bottle of moonshine as long as I live."

Dora grew wary. She had fancied herself in love with Josh Winslow, but he was, after all, an outsider. She had always known deep down that he would never be a permanent part of her life. She was a woman, however, who took pleasure whenever it came and had learned to kiss joy as it flew by. Now her deep roots into the culture of the backwoods stirred, and her lips drew into a straight line. "All right, if that's the way you want it—but you'd better keep your mouth shut." Her eyes narrowed and glinted as she added, "Daddy will kill you if you talk. You know he will."

At that moment Josh realized how deeply he had fallen. He understood then that when a man sins, he does not sin only against himself or against the person he lays his hands on. He remembered a sermon he heard once on the verse that says "None of us liveth to himself, and no man dieth to himself," and now the meaning of that sank deep into his spirit. He said, "Good-bye, Dora," in a spare tone and then started walking toward the road, leaving her standing there.

Dora took two steps toward Josh, stretching her arms out toward him, and for one moment there was a tenderness on her hard features. She understood suddenly that she cared more for this man than she had realized, but now it was too late. She let her hands fall, and her features became set as she whirled around and plunged between the tall trees. She knew she would have to tell her family. But she also knew their vicious streak well, and she feared for Josh's life.

★   ★   ★   ★

Hannah had never been inside of a jail, and she was struck at once by the fetid odor—a mixture of urine, stale tobacco, and unwashed bodies—that overwhelmed her. She walked down the short corridor, noting that there were two cells on each side, all empty except for the last one on the right. She stopped as Sheriff Beauchamp inserted a key into the lock. It made a creaking, rusty sound until it clicked; then he pulled the door open. "I'll have to lock you in here, Miss Hannah."

"That's all right, Sheriff," she said, stepping inside. The cell seemed quite old, and she noted that the bunk bed was well rusted. It squeaked as Clint rose to his feet and watched her with a strange expression as Beauchamp's footsteps faded and the door at the end of the corridor clanged shut.

"Hello, Hannah."

"Clint—!" Hannah walked up to him and looked up into his eyes. "What happened, Clint?" she said, her voice unsteady.

Clint did not answer for so long that she thought perhaps he wasn't going to. Finally he stepped back against the brick wall. "I was arrested."

"I know that, but I'll never believe you did it."

"They caught me in possession of bootleg whiskey."

"I know that too, but what were you doing there? You're not telling me everything, Clint."

Clint Longstreet studied the woman in front of him. His love for Hannah had grown slowly, but now he realized how much of his heart she occupied. He had never known love before, and what he had experienced of it was insufficient. It was like a short blanket that didn't cover everything as it should, where your shoulders or legs had to protrude in the cold night. But this woman was *everything* to him. And now as he saw the hurt and dismay in her beautiful eyes, he felt a stab of pain, knowing that she was going to be hurt and there was nothing he could do about it. *But it would hurt her far more to find out about Josh*, he thought. *I'll just have to bear it.*

He crossed his arms over his chest and said, "There's nothing you can do for me, Hannah. Just turn and walk away. Forget you ever met me."

"I can't do that," Hannah said, her voice husky. "I . . . I haven't told you everything about myself, Clint, but I have come to care for you. And now I'm like a beggar that's put all my meager belongings in a safe place. My love is with you, Clint. I can't change that, and I don't want to." She moved forward and whispered, "Whatever happens, I'll be here for you."

Clint turned half away and shook his head. "Go back to your family, Hannah. I'm going down, and the only thing I can think of that's worse than going to prison would be to take you down with me."

Hannah stayed for ten minutes longer, but nothing she could say would shake Clint. Finally she turned away so that he could not see her face. She called out for the sheriff, and when he came and unlocked the door, she turned and whispered, "I meant what I said, Clint."

"Good-bye, Hannah."

Hannah followed the sheriff out of the cell area and into his office. "I don't believe he did it," she told him.

Sheriff Beauchamp had seen the hard side of life for many years. He had watched women stick with men who had gone to prison, and now a great sadness touched him, for he knew this woman's gentleness would not survive what was coming. "Come on, Miss Hannah. I'll take you home."

★ ★ ★ ★

The house seemed to be asleep. Certainly everyone had gone to bed long ago. Lewis had lain in his bed for what seemed like hours thinking about Clint. When he had told the rest of the family, they had received the disastrous news as he had expected. Josh had been pale and silent but said almost nothing. Kat had burst out weeping and crying, "It's not true! He didn't do it! He wouldn't do a thing like that!" Jenny had exchanged glances with Hannah and said, "We'll have to help him all we can."

In the glance between his daughters, Lewis had recognized that Hannah had strong feelings for the man who had been such a godsend to them. Lewis was very grateful that Clint had come into their lives when he did. For without his mechanical skills to get the truck in working condition and without his knowledge of farming, where would they all be?

Now as Lewis lay beneath the blankets in the silence of his room, he felt helpless. He had not realized how much his affection for Clint Longstreet had grown; he was almost like a second son to him. Lewis did not believe that Clint was involved in bootlegging. It was simply not in character with everything he knew of the man!

Finally he threw the covers back and pulled on his pants and then his heavy coat. He slipped into his shoes, thinking how different even this was. Back in New York he would have been wearing pajamas and then would have added a warm robe and fur-lined slippers. Now that was all like a vague dream.

Moving softly, he opened and shut the door carefully, then went downstairs. He stopped as he entered the living room, seeing that the fire was still going. Hannah was sitting on the floor in front of it, staring into the flickering amber flames as they danced and sent fiery sparks upward with a sharp staccato sound.

When Hannah turned to him, he walked over to her and said, "I couldn't sleep."

Hannah got to her feet and for a moment seemed about ready to flee. Lewis saw that her face was drawn and she had been crying. *Strange*, he thought. *She's been so sad all her life, yet I don't remember seeing her cry since she was a child.* He stepped closer to the fireplace and watched the flames dance. Hannah was silent, and he finally turned back to face her. "We'll stay with him, Hannah. We'll do all we can. I'll write to my brother, Aaron, and see if he can lend us the money for a lawyer. I hate to ask for help, but I know he wasn't hurt so badly in the crash, and if he can help, I'm sure he will."

Hannah fell against him, wracked with deep sobs. He held her in his arms, patting her shoulders gently and whispering words of comfort. When her grief was spent, she stayed still in his embrace, then stepped back and crossed her arms. "Father, I'm going to tell you something I've never told anybody."

Lewis blinked with surprise but said quietly, "Whatever it is, daughter, we'll be all right."

"You remember when Preston Banks was courting me?"

"Yes, of course."

"Everyone thought we were going to be married. You did, didn't you?"

"Yes, I did."

"Well, you didn't really know him, Father. I didn't know him either."

"What do you mean?"

"He came to the house one day when no one was there except me. I went upstairs to change while he waited, but then when I had pulled off my dress, he came in and . . . and he grabbed me. I tried to fight him off, but he was like a crazy man. He said since we were going to be married, it wouldn't matter if we went to bed together. But I wouldn't, and he began to beat me. But not in the face." Hannah's expression grew icy. "He knew better than that. He hit me over and over again, but I kept fighting him. Finally he hit me so hard I collapsed. I suppose that scared him. He had broken one of my ribs, although I didn't know it at the time. I just knew I couldn't breathe. He didn't even try to help me . . . he just glared at me and then left."

"He didn't—?" Lewis could not finish the sentence, but he saw the answer in her eyes.

"No. All he did was beat me terribly. I went around for weeks in terrible pain while my broken rib healed."

"We all remember you behaved so strangely. We thought you two had had a quarrel. Why didn't you tell me?"

"I don't know. I was so ashamed."

"Ashamed! But it wasn't your fault."

"But I was so in love with him, Father! He was everything to me, and after that happened, I just froze up every time a man came near me. I know it was foolish, but I couldn't help it. If I was so terribly wrong about Preston, how could I ever trust another man?"

Lewis pulled her close again and stroked her hair. "I think you should have told your mother and me. Things might have been different."

Hannah knew that her father was right. She had let her shame and anger at one man's cruelty embitter her whole life. There was no telling what might have been different if she had confided in her parents and allowed the wound to heal. Now as she leaned against her father, she whispered, "I'm going to have to tell Clint."

★ ★ ★ ★

Lewis had hitched up the wagon to the mules and now pulled it to a stop in front of Missouri Ann's house. He had not slept at all, and at daybreak he knew he had to talk to someone. As he stepped out of the wagon, Missouri came out of the house to greet him.

"Why, Lewis, I didn't expect to see—" Missouri broke off upon seeing his face. "Come into the house."

Lewis walked numbly beside her, and she insisted he sit down at the kitchen table while she fixed coffee. She poured two cupfuls and handed him the sugar bowl. She noted that his hands were not steady as he stirred the sugar into his coffee, but still she did not inquire.

"I've got to talk to somebody, Missouri. I don't have any right to dump my troubles on you, but you're all I've got."

"What is it, Lewis? Is it about Clint?"

"In a way it is. At least he's tied up with it. It's really Hannah I'm most worried about."

Missouri listened while Lewis explained the things Hannah had told him the previous night. He spoke in a tense, unsteady voice and finally said, "I feel like such a failure. I should have found out. We all knew something was wrong with her when she broke off with that man. I thought she had talked to her mother about it, and I suppose her mother thought she had talked to me.

But she never told anybody. I'd like to kill him! I probably will if I ever see him."

"No, you won't do that," she said firmly, putting her strong, well-shaped hands flat on the table. She knew Lewis Winslow loved his daughter deeply, and a great pity welled up in her as she saw the pain in his eyes. She'd had a hard life herself and in her deep wisdom knew it was the hard things that made a man or a woman what they were. She often said to those who were having a difficult time, "Raking is easy, but all you get is leaves. Digging is hard, but you might find diamonds." She found, however, that she could not speak like this to Lewis. "Some things you can fix, Lewis, but some things only God can fix, and I think this is one of them. We'll pray."

Lewis had known this would be the answer she would give. He bowed his head and put his hands on the table. He felt hers fall on top of them and found warmth and comfort in them. He could not pray aloud himself, and he was surprised when Missouri prayed in a soft and gentle voice. He had heard her pray in a voice that could make the heavens ring, but now there was such gentleness in her tones that just the sound of it comforted him.

After her final amen she said, "We're together in this, Lewis."

"Missouri," he said, "you're a comfort to me. I'd better be going back now. I don't want to leave Hannah alone."

Missouri walked with him out to the wagon, and when he climbed in, she looked up and said, "I won't be coming to your house much anymore, Lewis."

Lewis blinked with surprise. "Why? Have I hurt you?"

"No, it's not that. I think it's best."

Lewis felt a sinking sensation as he watched her turn and walk back into the house. Feeling empty and hurt, he slapped the reins and the mules stepped out. "What have I done?" he whispered.

CHAPTER TWENTY-THREE

THE RIGHT MAN TAKES
THE BLAME

★ ★ ★ ★

Hannah sat in the living room crocheting and listening to the radio, which had become a fixture in the Winslow home—the only real rival to the movies. Hannah couldn't help feeling that they were all spending too much time with it, and she almost got up to turn it off when she heard the new song "Life Is Just a Bowl of Cherries." *How ironic!* she thought. Seeing that the country was suffering one of the worst depressions of all time, the song seemed almost irreverent. Yet America had largely turned to entertainment to take its mind off of the bread lines and shantytowns that the poor and dispossessed had been forced into. President Hoover had not helped any when, in the first year of the decade, he declared that prosperity would return within two months. "What our country needs is a good big laugh," he said. "If someone gets off a good joke every ten days, I think our troubles would be over." Hannah shook her head, thinking about the country's woes and how Hoover's blind-eyed optimism had driven his presidency into ruin. She remembered seeing a hitchhiker recently with a sign that read, "Give me a lift or I'll vote for Hoover."

The radio continued with a softer tune, "Embraceable You," followed by one that always made her feel a little better, "On the

Sunny Side of the Street." Hannah looked up as Lewis entered the living room. "What would you like for dinner tonight, Father? We can have rabbit stew or fried rabbit or rabbit sandwiches. And whichever you choose, I'll serve it up with plenty of sorghum molasses."

Lewis sat down heavily and tried to smile. Indeed, he was not in good spirits. "Rabbit anything is fine, dear. Did you tell Clint what you told me?"

"Yes, I told him. And I also told him that I love him, and no matter what happens I'll wait for him."

"That's like you, Hannah," Lewis said gently. "You were always a faithful girl."

Hannah studied her father's face. He had always been a handsome man; he used to be a little overweight, but now he was down to a bare minimum. She remembered how careful he had been of his attire in New York, but now he wore overalls like most men in the South, at least out on the farms. His squarish face had always been unlined, but she noticed that his hair was turning grayer now. It gave her a little shock, for she had not thought of him as growing older. Now as she studied him, she saw that he was troubled. There was a shadow in his eyes, and it went straight to her heart. Things had been easier since she had told him of the cause of her withdrawal. Now, wanting to cheer him up, she said, "Father, I feel so much better now that I've told you what troubled me for so long. I don't know why I didn't talk to you before—and I know Mother would have listened. I suppose we hate to talk about the bad things."

Lewis shook his head. "Yes, we do. I've got some things in my own past I don't want to think about." He stroked his chin thoughtfully and looked at her with a wistful wisdom. He was starting to relax now, and his smile was a white streak against the bronzed tones of his face. "There was a man in our outfit who went up San Juan Hill with me. He lost a leg there. A few years after the war I heard he'd gone back. I never could figure out why a man would want to visit a battlefield where he'd been crippled."

Hannah said wistfully, "I guess all we can say is we see through a glass darkly."

"That's right—we understand so little of this life, but God gives us so much in this world to be thankful for. Given in good measure, pressed down, shaken together, and running over."

The two sat comfortably in the silence, and finally Hannah spoke again. "What's wrong, Father? You've been very troubled lately. Is it just what's happened to Clint?"

Lewis shifted in his seat. "No, I'm worried about that, of course, but I've been worried about something Missouri Ann said to me."

"What was that?"

"She said she wouldn't be coming to see us as much as has been her habit. I don't understand it. I asked her if I had offended her, and she said no."

"I can tell you what's wrong, Father."

Lewis lifted his head quickly. "Has she talked to you?"

"No, but it's easier for a woman to see than for a man," Hannah said slowly. She sat there trying to frame the words in a way that would not offend her father, the sunlight sliding across the auburn surface of her hair. "Missouri Ann is a woman, Father."

"I know that!"

"No you don't. You went into shock when she told you God had sent you to be her husband." Suddenly Hannah could not restrain a smile. She even laughed aloud softly and shook her head. "I guess we all did, but you most of all."

"I think that kind of thing would shock any man. I didn't know what to make of her. I still don't."

"She's had a hard life. I've talked to her a lot. Her husband wasn't a good man, not to her, anyway, and her children have never shown her any affection. Just think about how hard that would be. We all have each other, but Missouri hasn't had anyone except God. Of course, she doesn't complain, but I always see something in her eyes as she watches you. She keeps it covered up so you never see it, but she's lonely. And I think she's a wonderful woman."

"Well, so do I."

"Then why don't you let her know? Why, it's no wonder she's stopped coming over here, Father. She comes to cook and help with all the work—and you never treat her like a woman."

Lewis was silent as fleeting thoughts were reflected in his eyes. He started to speak once and then refrained. Finally he said, "Maybe you're right, but I can't just run up and tell her I admire her."

"Why not?"

"Well, I don't know . . . I just can't."

"Father, tell me one thing. Do you have any feelings at all for her—that go deeper than friendship?"

Lewis was startled at the question. He thought for a moment before answering, his voice tinged with wonder. "I . . . I guess I do."

"Then court her, Father. Ask her to go out. Take her to a restaurant for a meal. Take her to a movie. She needs some attention from a good man—and I think you need a woman's attention too. Mother wouldn't want you to go through the rest of your life without a companion."

Lewis got to his feet. "All right, I'll do it. She may think I'm crazy."

"No, she won't think that. Not if you do it right."

Lewis laughed. "Would you believe this scares me worse than going up San Juan Hill with the bullets whizzing around?"

Hannah got to her feet and came over. She put her arms behind his neck, pulled his head down, and kissed him. "How could she help but be in love with you?" she said quietly with a smile. "You're the handsomest and best man I know."

★ ★ ★ ★

Missouri met Hannah at the door with a smile. "Come in. I just been wishin' for company."

Hannah entered, saying, "You need to get a radio."

"I don't want one of those newfangled things. They got awful things on 'em."

Hannah removed her coat and hat and sat down at the table, where Missouri poured her a cup of hot sassafras tea. She started in talking about the foolish shows on the radio, but then finally she laughed and said, "But I do like that program 'The Shadow.' Guess that couldn't do much harm, now, could it?"

"No, I don't think there's any danger in 'The Shadow.' I must admit I did get caught up in the story when I was over to your house that time last summer!"

The two women sat talking for a time, and finally Hannah said, "Would you go into town with me?"

"Why, that'd be right nice. I'm out of sugar and several other things."

"I want you to buy some nice clothes, Missouri—a dress and some shoes and stockings. Even some nice underwear."

"What are you talking about, Hannah? I got plenty of clothes."

"I'm not talking about overalls. I'm talking about nice women's clothes, stylish clothes that'll make you look pretty."

Missouri had a good, full laugh, then shook her head. "Do I need to look pretty for the pigs? They don't mind the way I look."

"No, you're going to look pretty for your gentleman friend."

"What are you talking about, Hannah? I don't have no gentleman friend."

"You're going to have one, and I recommend him." Hannah reached over and took Missouri's hand. "Father's going to come courting you. He's going to ask you to go out with him, and I want you to look nice."

A silence fell across the room. Outside, the loud cries of the guinea hens filled the air, and Missouri's pet peacock lifted his raucous cry. She did not speak for so long that Hannah finally said, "There's nothing strange about it. He told me how much he liked you, and he was very upset when you told him you wouldn't be coming over anymore."

"I didn't want to be forward or to intrude where I weren't wanted. He was actin' like he had no interest in me."

"He was just confused and unsure of himself. Don't tell him I talked to you. Come on, we're going to town to buy you some nice clothes."

Missouri was bewildered. "I don't know if it's right or not, Hannah."

"Didn't you say that God sent him to be your husband?"

"That's what I said . . . but I've been wrong a few times. When Lewis didn't show no signs of wantin' me for a wife, I reckoned I didn't read what God was sayin' right."

"Well, this is a good way to find out. You two get together and go out a few times and go for walks, and you keep on praying, and God will tell you if it's right for you two."

"I'm so rough, and he's . . . he's such a fine gentleman! And I know how much he loved your mother."

"That's true, and he always will. But that doesn't mean he won't ever have room in his life for someone else. Come along, now. We're going to get you all fixed up. I hope you've got some money."

"Enough for some clothes, I guess." Missouri got up slowly, a smile on her lips. "I don't know much about bein' courted."

"Father said the same thing." Hannah smiled. "The two of you can learn together. Come on, now. Let's go spend all your money on frivolous attire."

★　★　★　★

After Hannah returned home from her shopping trip with Missouri, she went to Josh's room to talk to him. He was sitting in a cane-bottomed rocker simply staring out the window. "What are you doing in here all by yourself, Josh?" she asked, going over to stand beside him. She reached out and ruffled his hair. "You've become silent as a tomb lately. What's wrong with you?"

"Oh, nothing," Josh mumbled.

Hannah knew this was not the truth. Josh seemed sober at the moment, his face serious. She sat down on the bed and told him about her father's intention to court Missouri Ann and ended by saying, "I think it would be nice if they would get married. They're both so lonely."

"I'm surprised," Josh said. "Dad was so much in love with Mom."

"Of course he was, and she'll always be a part of him, but she's gone now and he needs somebody. We all do."

"What about you, sis?"

"I love Clint, and he loves me," she said simply. "If he goes to prison, I'll wait for him. I'm not as young as I'd like, but however long it takes, I'll be there for him when he gets out."

Josh stood, his jaw tense with determination. "Come on, Hannah, I've got something to tell you . . . to tell all the family."

"What is it, Josh?"

"I'll tell you all together. Come on, let's go find Dad. I want to get Jenny and Kat too. . . ."

★ ★ ★ ★

Sheriff Beauchamp looked up from the papers on his desk. He put down his pencil and leaned back in the chair. "Hello, Josh," he said. "Cold out, ain't it?"

Josh ignored this and stood directly in front of Sheriff Beauchamp's desk. He was tense, the sheriff could see, but when he spoke his voice was steady. "You've got the wrong man in jail, Sheriff."

"The wrong man? You mean Clint?"

"That's right."

"But he was caught with the whiskey. I know you like Clint, but—"

"I was the one who was moving the whiskey, Sheriff Beauchamp. Clint just blundered into the area when he was out deer hunting. He had nothing at all to do with it. I'll swear to that in court."

Noel Beauchamp motioned toward the chair. "Sit down, Josh, and tell me all about it."

Beauchamp listened as Josh told him the whole story, and finally he asked, "Who was in it with you, Josh?"

"I'm not telling that. Don't ask me to, Sheriff."

Beauchamp expelled his breath in disgust. "You didn't get into this on your own. Somebody helped you with it, and I've got a pretty good idea who it was."

"I'll never testify against anybody else, Sheriff, but Clint had nothing to do with it. What will it take to get him out?"

"Nothing," Beauchamp said, "but you'll have to stay. I'll get the charges against Clint dropped. Have you told your family about all this?"

"Yes."

Beauchamp saw that Josh would not speak further about it. "All right, if that's the way it is. I'm not going to go easy on you, Josh. You'll have to go to jail."

"I know that, Sheriff. I won't complain. I got myself into this. Now I'll have to pay for it."

★ ★ ★ ★

Dark had fallen, and Hannah was washing the dishes. The rest of the family was in the living room listening to "Sherlock Holmes" on the radio. They had all been shocked by Josh's confession. He had also told them, "There's no way you can help me, and I want you to go on with life. Do the things you've been doing. I'll have to go to prison, but when I get out, I'll come back."

Hannah had wept when she was alone, but she had kept her grief hidden from the others. She knew her father had been hit as hard by this as she, and Kat had taken it the worst of all. She had always loved Josh fiercely, and when he had left to go confess his crime to Sheriff Beauchamp, Kat had clung to him, begging him not to go.

"I've got to do it, Kat," Josh had said quietly. He'd hugged her, kissed her, and said, "You just keep praying for your wayward brother, and one day it'll be all right."

Hannah dried a dish and put it away mechanically. She heard the front door slam and could not imagine who it was, and then there were footsteps as she turned to see Clint standing in the doorway. His face was set, and he came straight to her.

"I'm sorry about Josh," he said.

Hannah fell into his arms. She held him tightly and felt him embrace her firmly. "You tried to save him, Clint, and we'll never forget that. None of us will."

As the two clung to each other, Clint said, "Perhaps this is no time to talk of personal things, but I don't want to put it off any longer. I want you to know that I'd like to marry you. I don't have anything. Probably never will have, but I need you more than any man ever needed any woman." He took her face in his hands and kissed her.

She savored his kiss; then when he lifted his head, she smiled at him. She felt very safe and secure, despite her worries over her brother. "We'll have each other, and we'll have to trust God for everything else."

CHAPTER TWENTY-FOUR

TO BE A WIFE

★ ★ ★ ★

Potter Flemming had served as mayor of Summerdale for ten years but had never felt as nervous as he did when preparing his client, Joshua Winslow, for the hearing that would determine his future. Flemming, a small man with scanty brown hair, was a fancy dresser, and now as he paced back and forth, he pulled at his tie nervously. "I've got to tell you, Josh, I have very little hope that we'll get anything good. I wish to heaven we had any judge except Pender!"

Strangely, Josh was much calmer than his lawyer. He was wearing a dark blue suit, a white shirt, and a maroon tie. It had been Flemming's idea to make him look as presentable as possible, but Josh had smiled faintly at the suggestion, saying, "I don't think the judge is going to pay much attention to what I've got on."

Now Flemming came to stand over Josh, who was seated with his hands clasped together on the table in the back room of the courthouse. It was an ancient building, filled with the damp smell of mold and decay. Josh was unaware of this, however, as he looked up at his lawyer. "Don't worry about it, Mr. Flemming. I know you've done all you can."

"If you'd only turn state's evidence, Joshua, I could get you a light sentence."

"I can't do that. We've been over it before."

Flemming snorted in disgust. "I still don't think you understand how serious these charges are. Why, you could get ten years or even twenty!"

"I'll have to take what he hands me, Mr. Flemming."

Flemming flung his hands out in a helpless gesture. "If it were any judge but O. C. Pender! They call him the hanging judge, you know. Of course, this isn't a hanging matter, but he hands out the stiffest sentence a law allows as often as not. I wish it were any other judge, Josh. He's going to put you away to the limit."

"You've done the best you can for me, Mr. Flemming, and I know we haven't been able to pay you yet, but Dad tells me he's borrowed some money from his brother."

"I'm not worried about my fee. I'm worried about you, Josh. You made a mistake, but I have the feeling you were drawn into it."

"I don't see it that way. Nobody put a gun to my head. I made a choice, and it was a bad one. Now I've got to pay for it."

"We all make bad choices."

"I suppose so, but some carry a stiffer penalty. This just happens to be one of them." Josh leaned forward, his eyes sad. "I know I'm going to prison, but that's not the worst thing. It's what I've done to my family. I'll never get over that."

"They love you, boy, and this won't make any difference as far as that's concerned. We'll try to appeal, but it won't do much good. Judge Pender hardly ever reverses his decisions."

★　★　★　★

Lewis pulled the wagon up in front of Missouri's place. He got out and went to the front door. Missouri opened it before he could knock and greeted him. "Come in, Lewis." She was wearing her customary working garb—overalls and heavy men's boots.

As Lewis entered she thought about the clothes she'd bought on the trip to town with Hannah but did not mention them. "Have you been to see Josh?" she asked as she led him into the living room. A fire was burning in the fireplace, and she sat down on the couch before it and waved him to sit beside her.

"Yes," he said. "It breaks my heart, Missouri."

"I know. He's got good stuff in him. He's made a terrible mistake, Lewis, but he's not the first young man to go wrong."

Lewis was terribly depressed. He had hardly slept for the last couple of days. "I'd rather go to jail myself than have Josh go."

"We always feel that way about our children. We'd like to suffer for them, but you know the saying—'Everybody has to eat his own peck of dirt.'"

"Well, this is a peck of dirt for me." He shifted uneasily on the couch and listened as she spoke quietly. He was thinking of the hearing that would come in a few hours, and now as she spoke of trusting God, he suddenly said, "You remind me of my wife, Deborah. She had such great faith. More than I had."

"You loved her very much, didn't you, Lewis?"

"Yes, I did. We had a good life together."

Lewis found himself comforted by Missouri's presence as they sat before the fire. He glanced at her from time to time, surprised by the depth of his feelings for her. She was not the elegant woman his wife had been, but Missouri had a heart of gold. He also thought with some embarrassment of his brief engagement to the wealthy Lucy Daimen. How quick she'd been to have nothing more to do with him when his money was gone! He looked again at Missouri, realizing more than ever how much he now valued this woman's godly character more than he judged her outer appearance. Finally he said, "We're all pretty well resigned to Josh's having to do some time in prison. It's discouraging."

"It is, but God will see you through it."

"I think tomorrow will be especially hard for me. I was wondering if you would be willing to help me through it."

Missouri gave him an odd look. "I'll do anything I can, Lewis, you know that."

"You're a fine woman, Missouri Ann!"

She smiled at the compliment, and her whole countenance lit up. Her smile turned to full-fledged laughter as she said, "I must have scared you half to death with all my talk about God sending you here and breaking your leg so you could be my husband. It's a wonder you didn't get up and run off, broken leg or not!"

Lewis found himself able to laugh with her, which struck him as odd, for he had not laughed much lately. Feeling at home with her by his side, he said, "Why don't we go out tomorrow night—get something to eat and take in a movie?"

"A movie! I've never been to a movie in my life."

"Well, it's just some foolish thing with the Marx Brothers."

"Who are they?"

Lewis was always slightly shocked at Missouri's lack of worldly knowledge. "Oh, they're just these funny fellows who do crazy things."

"I'm not sure the Lord would smile on that."

"Well, if you don't want to do that, we could just eat and then go for a drive maybe."

"Are you sure you want me to go, Lewis?"

"Yes, I am sure."

"All right. I'll do it."

Lewis stood up and said, "I'll come by in the morning and pick you up for the hearing—about eight-thirty. You may have to hold me up. I know it'll be hard on all of us."

She took both of his hands. "These things happen, Lewis. In the Bible, Joseph had to go to jail unjustly, but he was a better man for it, and he turned out all right. I've been praying for your son. He'll be all right. I just know it." She smiled, adding, "I'm hearing God tell me to ask Him for a miracle—and I'm doing it!"

★ ★ ★ ★

Judge O. C. Pender was a ponderous man. Instead of a judge's robe, he wore a severe black suit and a string tie. With his salt-and-pepper hair, he had a stern bulldog appearance. He was not a laughing man, and as Josh studied him, any hope that he'd had for mercy left.

Word of the hearing had gotten around, and the courtroom was packed. Josh saw his family sitting there, his father ramrod straight beside Hannah, Jenny holding her arm around Kat. His heart was grieved as he looked at them. *I've brought them down to the mud. It would have been better for them if I'd been shot.*

The judge skipped all the usual preliminaries and plunged right in. "We'll hear the case of the government against Joshua Winslow. Mr. Dean, are you ready?"

John Dean, the prosecutor, stood up, an average-looking man

whose political ambitions were well known in Summerdale. Anxious as always for a conviction, he addressed the bench. "Your Honor, this will be a very simple procedure. Ordinarily trials have more complexity, but this one will not take long."

"Suppose you just present your case, Mr. Dean, and let me decide how long it will be."

Dean was accustomed to the judge's sternness. "Of course, Your Honor. Well, here are the facts. At one-thirty on the afternoon of January 12 a man by the name of Clinton Longstreet was caught in possession of a truckload of bootleg whiskey in the woods not too far from town. He was apprehended by two government agents, both of whom have made their statements, which I will enter as Exhibits A and B. They could not appear in court, but I think the statements are clear enough."

The judge nodded. "I have read the statements. They are clear. Please continue."

"Several days later, the defendant, Joshua Winslow, confessed that he had actually been in possession of the truck and the alcohol and that the man in jail had been hunting for deer in the woods and had merely encountered Mr. Winslow just before the government agents appeared. While Mr. Winslow ran for the woods, the other man—a friend of the family—took responsibility in order to protect the defendant. The innocent man has now been released. We will urge the full penalty for Joshua Winslow. The state rests, Your Honor."

A murmur went around the courtroom. Everyone had known that it would be an open-and-shut case, but this set a record.

Judge Pender turned and put his eyes on the defendant but spoke to Potter Flemming. "Mr. Flemming, are you ready for the defense?"

"Yes, Your Honor."

Flemming rose and, for the next thirty minutes, made a valiant attempt at presenting the case for his client. He called several witnesses, but all they could say in truth was that Joshua Winslow did not seem like the type of young man who would do anything terribly wrong. His drinking was no secret, however, and he had not gotten involved in the life of the community as the rest of his family had done.

Finally Flemming said, "Your Honor, this is a difficult case, despite what the prosecuting attorney says. We have a young man here with half his life before him. We all know what prison can do to a man—turn him hard. He's made a mistake, and he has admitted it. He came forward voluntarily when he saw his friend wrongly arrested. That shows a good heart, and I would ask, Your Honor, to show consideration and mercy."

Flemming sat down as another murmur went over the courtroom.

The judge began to speak. "This case, to me, seems fairly simple, and—"

"Judge, could I be permitted to say just a word?"

Everyone turned to see who had spoken. Judge Pender stared at the woman in the ill-fitting brown dress who had stood up. Recognizing her, he said, "Mrs. Ramey, you have not been called as a witness."

"I don't know much about courts and trials, Your Honor, but I would like to say something if you would permit it." Missouri had told the family she wanted to sit near the back of the courtroom so she could more easily be in prayer throughout the trial.

"Are you appearing in favor of the defendant?"

"I want to say something about this young man on trial, yes."

Pender turned to Josh's lawyer. "Will you allow this woman as a friendly witness, Mr. Flemming?"

Flemming would have allowed anyone as a friendly witness. "Yes, of course, Your Honor. I would have called her myself, but I wasn't aware that she wanted to testify."

"Come forward, Mrs. Ramey." The judge waited until she had stepped to the witness stand and the bailiff had sworn her in. "What have you to say?"

"I haven't known Joshua Winslow long, but I know he comes from a good family. I know he's made a bad—a terrible—mistake, and I know he would probably get a lighter sentence if he agreed to identify the people who were with him in this business."

Pender said rather roughly, "Mrs. Ramey, the goodness of the defendant's family has nothing to do with his crime. You're right, he would get a lighter sentence if he were to identify the people with him, but he refuses to do so."

"Yes, sir, I know." Missouri Ann turned and faced the judge. "I can't say this man is innocent, but I wanted to say this, O. C. Before you sentence this man, I want to remind you of the time you stole a cow from me and my husband."

A shocked silence ensued, and the judge's face turned red. "That is not pertinent!"

"I think it is."

"I was only seventeen years old, and it was just a prank."

Missouri Ann said calmly, "But if my husband and I had pressed charges, as you certainly deserved, you would have gone to jail, wouldn't you?"

Pender had never had such a thing happen, and as he stared at the woman, he could do nothing but hem and haw. Finally he admitted grudgingly, "I suppose so."

"And if you had gone to jail, you wouldn't be a judge, I don't think. You did a wrong thing, but you'll remember that you had someone who cared about you and who didn't want your life ruined. 'Blessed are the merciful: for they shall obtain mercy.'"

With this final word Missouri stood up. She put her eyes on Pender, and the two remained with their gazes locked. No one had ever dared challenge O. C. Pender in his own courtroom, and most of the spectators fully expected him to find her in contempt. Pender, however, simply sat there while Missouri Ann turned and walked away.

Judge Pender sat still, his lips drawn together into a tight line. Potter Flemming leaned over and whispered, "She meant well, but she insulted the judge. He'll make it even worse."

"She did what she thought was right," Josh muttered.

Everyone was leaning forward waiting while Pender deliberated with himself. He kept his eyes on Missouri Ann Ramey as his mind went back to those days of his youth. Yes, he had stolen a cow, and despite the fact it was more of a prank than a theft, he could have been jailed for it. He had known men who had gone wrong with no more than a single misdeed. He remembered how frightened he had been as a mere boy and how his heart had cried out for help. He had not asked for help verbally from Missouri Ann or her husband, and he remembered how when they had refused to press charges, it had been like a mountain lifted off of him. He also remembered he had never really thanked the couple, being a thoughtless young man, and now as he studied her face, something touched his spirit.

"It is not an easy job being a judge," he started. "Those of us who do this work have to make decisions that often turn out to be wrong. I've never admitted this before publicly, but we all know that judges are subject to the same human frailties as all other men. I've always tried to be fair and just. They call me a hanging judge. They say I'm a hard man—and they're right. I have handed out stiffer sentences than other judges. I believe that people should bear the consequences of their actions."

A silence fell over the courtroom, and Hannah leaned forward. She glanced over at Missouri, whose eyes were closed and her lips moving, and Hannah knew she was praying for God's mercy.

The judge hesitated, then said, "This case is clear enough. We have a guilty man here. There's no question of that. The only question is what punishment shall be handed him. Some of you will be surprised at the sentence, but I will have to admit that Mrs. Ramey's words are true. I did commit a crime when I was a young man, and if Mrs. Ramey and her husband had brought charges, I would surely have been convicted and gone to jail. I don't know what would have happened after that, but mercifully, I was given a second chance."

Pender turned suddenly and said, "Will the defendant rise?" He waited until Josh stood alongside his lawyer, then pronounced his sentence. "Joshua Winslow, I find you guilty of transporting illegal alcohol, and I sentence you to two years in the penitentiary."

A gasp went over the courtroom, for that was the lightest possible sentence, but the surprises were not yet over. Pender continued, "I'm going to give you a second chance, young man. I suspend twenty-three months of that two years. You will serve one month, and I will be watching like a hawk, Joshua Winslow, when you get out! I trust you will not fail me, nor your family, nor this community."

Suddenly a shout went up from Missouri Ann, who had lifted her hands. "Praise God! Hallelujah!"

Lewis jumped up from his seat and headed straight to Josh. He put his arms around him and squeezed him with all his might, joined shortly by Jenny, Hannah, and Kat. It was Hannah who went first to the judge with tears in her eyes and said, "God bless you, Judge. I'll pray for you the rest of my life."

"Well, that young man had better go straight."

"He will, sir. I know he will."

Lewis stepped back to allow others to speak to Josh, mostly members of the church, and he found Missouri Ann. Taking her by the hand, he said, "Well, Missouri, it was a miracle. Thank God you were here."

Missouri shook her head. "It's all God's doing, Lewis."

After waiting for the people to clear away, the sheriff came to stand beside Josh. Beauchamp shook his head. "If you never see another miracle, Josh, you've seen one today. That's the first time I've ever known O. C. Pender to give out a sentence like that."

"God is good, isn't He?" Josh replied.

"You'll have to come along now so I can lock you up. You'll be taken to the state prison in a day or two, but one month— why, that's nothing!"

Josh said, "Could I say a word to the judge first?"

"I think that would be fitting." Beauchamp turned, and the judge, who had gotten down and was headed toward the back, stopped to put his eyes on Josh.

Josh Winslow put out his hand and said, "Judge, I can't say what I feel, but I promise you this. You won't be sorry. You won't be seeing me again in a courtroom."

Pender said gruffly, "See that I don't." A grin suddenly turned up the corners of his mouth. "I got quite a shock today, Winslow. I hadn't thought of that stolen cow in a lot of years. You'd better be glad that I did steal that cow—otherwise you'd be doing a lot of time!"

★ ★ ★ ★

As the crowd thinned out, Devoe Crutchfield, who had sat behind the family in the courtroom, approached Jenny, saying, "I'm so glad for you and your family, Jenny, and especially for Josh."

"It's wonderful, isn't it? Isn't Missouri great?"

"She is." He hesitated, then said, "Would you have time to go have an ice-cream soda with me and the kids?"

Jenny stared at the preacher. "I suppose so," she said. "I'm surprised you have money for that."

"I may have to work it out, but the kids want you to go." He hesitated. "And I do too."

"All right, I'll spend all your money on a banana split."

★ ★ ★ ★

Lewis pulled up in front of Missouri's house in the truck, got out, and brushed off the back of his trousers. He'd cleaned out the truck as well as he could, but it had seen a lot of hard service. He was wearing a dark gray suit and a shirt and tie, which felt strange. *Funny how a fellow can so quickly learn to get along without a tie,* he mused as he walked up to the house. He was surprised at how nervous he felt, and when he knocked on the door, he thought, *I remember when I called on my first young lady. I felt about like this. Here I am older than the hills and still getting goose bumps over going on a date.*

When the door opened, Missouri greeted him with her usual warm smile. "Come in, come in, Lewis."

Lewis opened the screen door and stepped inside. "I'm a little early—" He stopped abruptly, surprise washing over him at her appearance. He had seen Missouri in a dress only a few times, the same one—the ill-fitting brown homespun she had worn in the courtroom. Now, however, he could not speak. When he found his voice, he said, "You look beautiful, Missouri Ann!"

She was wearing a light green cotton dress with a V-shaped neckline. It was loose fitting, with a jacket of the same color, and belted around the waist with a thin black belt. The skirt had gathered side panels, and she wore silk stockings and black patent leather shoes that crossed over and buttoned on the side.

She flushed at Lewis's words of praise and then touched the sleeve of her garment. "I'm glad you like it," she said shyly.

"Your hair looks beautiful."

"First time I ever went to a beauty parlor." Missouri Ann laughed. "You know, of course, that Hannah did all this. Made me buy these clothes and get my hair fixed."

"You look wonderful. We'd better get something to put on the seat of that truck. It'll get your new dress dirty."

She reached up and touched her lips. "I'm even wearing makeup. First time in my life. Hannah helped with that too. I feel downright sinful, Lewis."

"You look like an angel. Come along. Let's go."

★ ★ ★ ★

"It's been such a good evening for me," Lewis said. "I don't think that movie's going to pollute your mind."

"It was silly but funny," Missouri Ann agreed. The two had stepped up on the porch, and she turned toward him. "I had the best time ever, Lewis."

"Missouri Ann, I'd like permission to court you."

Missouri whispered, "I think that would be nice."

"Are you really sure that God intends for us to get married?"

Missouri dropped her head for a moment. She did not speak for so long that Lewis thought he might have offended her, but finally she lifted her head and said quietly, "I'm not sure, Lewis. I've told you that I've made a mistake a time or two when I thought I heard from God and turned out I was wrong." She shook her head. "I'm not as sure about things as I once was."

Lewis laughed. "Now you really sound like a woman. Always keeping a man on pins and needles." He smiled slyly and said, "You know, I'm about to break a promise I made to my mother."

"What was that, Lewis? You shouldn't break a promise to your mother."

"Well, I'm going to anyway. I think she would forgive me if she were still living. It was a pretty serious promise."

Missouri Ann saw he was laughing at her. "I promised her I would never kiss a young woman on our first date." He waited for Missouri's reply, and when she said nothing, he put his arms around her and held her tightly. He kissed her gently and she returned the affection. After a few moments, he stepped back. "I can see this courtship's going to be interesting. Good night, Missouri Ann."

"Good night, Lewis. It was . . . it was good to be with you." Then she put her head back and laughed heartily. Putting her hand on his cheek, she said, "You see that you ask me again, you hear?"

"You'd better believe I will!"

★ ★ ★ ★

"Everything looks so dead," Hannah said, walking along the fields that bordered the house and past the brown, wilted garden.

Clint took her hand and said, "It'll be spring before long, and everything will be green and alive again."

Hannah turned to him and said, "I don't know how to be a wife, Clint. Other girls went through things I missed out on, so there's a lot I don't know."

"We'll just have to learn together." He reached out and took her hands and squeezed them. He looked into her eyes for a moment and then said, "I'll teach you how to be a good wife."

"How would you know?"

"Well, I've studied things like that," Clint laughed, putting his arms around her. "The best way to have a happy marriage is for the wife to wait on the husband hand and foot—and then give him all the loving he wants."

Hannah looked stunned but then realized he was smiling at her. She pulled his head down and whispered, "I can manage at least half of that!"

The World Is Spiraling Toward Destruction, and One Man Receives a Divine Mandate. . . .

Young Noah has found life good and whole-some . . . until he steps outside his village and discovers a world of temptation. Drawn by a beautiful woman yet repulsed by the pagan practices of her tribe's dark worship, his inner struggle keeps him in torment.

Noah strains to hear the voice of God—through the warnings of a prophet, through the kind teachings of his grandfather Methuselah, through the loving concern of his family, and ultimately through personal confrontation. The message he receives is terrifying. Will he find the courage to obey?

Opposition intensifies to the call he has received, and a precious medallion handed down from ancient times reminds him of who he is—a man with a . . .

Heart of a Lion
Book 1 in the LIONS OF JUDAH series
ISBN: 0-7642-2681-9

Dear reader,

Many years ago, someone suggested: "Gil, why don't you write a series of biblically based novels tracing one family from the Flood to the birth of Jesus?" At the time I was too busy to consider such a thing, but the seed fell into the ground. Six years later, the LIONS OF JUDAH came to me in a rush, each story idea falling into place with seemingly little effort on my part. Naturally each novel has to be hammered out with all the skill I possess, but the first novel, *Heart of a Lion*, seemed almost to write itself.

One goal of every good novelist is to give pleasure, to entertain. The other is to edify, to give the reader more than pleasure. The Scripture says, "He who prophesies speaks edification and exhortation and comfort." I am certainly no prophet, but I want every novel I write to accomplish these things.

Every story in the LIONS OF JUDAH series is intended to give pleasure, but I want readers to *learn* something too. I stick as closely as I can to accurate history. I also try to paint a reasonable picture of how ancient people lived from day to day. I hope to offer readers an overview of the Old Testament, fixing in their minds the general history of the times and putting the heroes of the faith in the spotlight. Not as a *substitute* for the Scripture. Far from it! Indeed, my hope is that readers will turn to the Bible as a result of reading these books.

I want these novels to exhort as well, to somehow give the reader a desire to become a more faithful servant of God. Most modern fiction does exactly the *opposite* of this—it urges the reader to indulge in the false values that have come to dominate our society. I spent many years teaching the so-called "great" novels at a Christian university. Many such novels stress the values of this world, not those of God. But I believe fine novels *can* dramatize godly values—without being "preachy."

Finally, great novels give comfort. I don't know how this works, but some books give me assurance and build my faith that dark times are not forever. God, of course, is the source of all comfort, but I know He uses poetry and fiction as well as people.

I pray that the LIONS OF JUDAH will give pleasure, enlightenment, motivation, and comfort to faithful readers.

Parents and teachers, here are books that will introduce young people in your charge to the most important history of all—how God brought the Messiah into the world to save us from our sins. I trust that the men and women of the Old Testament will come alive for readers young and old, so that they are not dim figures in a dusty history but dynamic bearers of the seed that would redeem the human race.

Sincerely,

Gilbert Morris